THE TEN THOUSAND THINGS

By the same author

PLAYS

*MacRune's Guevara*

*In the Heart of the British Museum*

*Shades of Heathcliff* and *Death of Captain Doughty*

*The British Empire, Part One*

NOVELS

*The Ragged End*

*After Zenda*

*A Book of Liszts*

CRITICISM

*Beckett the Playwright* (with John Fletcher)

*Graham Greene*

# THE TEN THOUSAND THINGS

A NOVEL

JOHN SPURLING

Duckworth Overlook

This paperback edition first published in 2015 by
Duckworth Overlook

LONDON:
Duckworth
30 Calvin Street
London E1 6NW
info@duckworth-publishers.co.uk
www.ducknet.co.uk
For bulk and special sales, please contact
sales@duckworth-publishers.co.uk
or write to us at the address above

NEW YORK:
141 Wooster Street
New York, NY 10012
www.overlookpress.com



A catalogue record for this book is available
from the British Library

*Book design and type formatting by Bernard Schleifer*

ISBN 978-0-7156-4956-5

Printed and bound in the UK

*For Gilbert*
*doughty defender of prisoners and alleged wrongdoers*

"Space and time are part of my mind. My mind contains space and time . . . The ten thousand things are condensed into the space, as it were, of a cubic centimetre, filling the mind. Flowing out of it, they fill the whole of time and space."

—LŪ ZHIU-YUAN (1138–91)

"The empire, long united, must divide, and long divided, must unite. Thus it has ever been."

—Attributed to LUO GUANZHONG:
*Three Kingdoms* (?14th century)

"The source of the Peach Blossom River is very near, but no one knows it."

—WANG MENG (1308–85)

# CONTENTS

# THE TEN THOUSAND THINGS

## From a Bookseller's Catalogue

*"THE TEN THOUSAND THINGS, translated from a manuscript rescued from the Hanlin Library fire by Dr Stephen Albert during the siege of the foreign legations in Peking." This refers to the 'Boxer' Rebellion of 1900 in what is now Beijing. Privately printed by the Kanhai Press (no place or date of publication). Bound in boards covered with red cloth, somewhat stained, scuffed, faded and foxed. Only known copy. Price on application.*

# 1. LANDSCAPE IN WINTER

The times are turning bad again. I have been arrested for going to see a private art collection. Can you believe it? An old man of nearly eighty, a retired magistrate, is put in prison on suspicion. Instead of sitting on a dais giving judgment, here I am sitting on a stone floor waiting to be judged. Of course I'm only on remand. No one has tried or condemned me yet for the crime I am supposed to have committed, but still I've been here for weeks—long enough almost to have got used to the stench of the bucket in the corner. The jailer—a friendly man—says that the prisons are so full of people arrested on suspicion that it will take months, if not years, to sort out who is guilty and who is not.

Guilty of what? Conspiracy. Five years ago the Prime Minister was executed for conspiracy and anyone who ever had anything to do with him is still under suspicion. What did I have to do with such an important person? I went with some friends to look at his art collection. A rare privilege, as I thought, which turned out to be a curse.

I must not think of it as such. At my age one should be wiser and calmer. A man of my age has seen everything, done everything that he is ever likely to see or do. If he does not understand life as he nears the end of it, he never will. I have spent my life looking intensely at the so-called "ten thousand things" that make up the world—man among them. I have constantly drawn them, thought and talked about them, drunk or sober, and they are not, in principle, difficult to understand.

Life turns out to be much simpler than one imagines to start with, when one is young and everything is new and confusing. It is just a matter of following one's nature, like a bird or a fish—in spite of such universal distractions as hunger, thirst, the urge to procreate, adversities and even disasters—always making, if one is a bird, for the thickest woods and if one is a fish for the deepest water.

Now suddenly, in my seventy-eighth year, chance, fate—whatever name one gives to something beyond one's own control—has thrown me into prison for the first time. A fresh experience, yes, but does it invalidate all my previous experience, does it falsify my understanding of life? Why should it? I have seen plenty of people sent to prison, I have sent some of them there myself. It is one of the things that happen to people, that men do to one another, for good reasons or bad, and not essentially different from being ill or injured in an accident or losing everything one has. If it cannot be avoided, it must be accepted and one must try as always to follow one's nature through it. This is the only wisdom I have acquired in a life lived through very troubled times and it would be folly, hysteria, and do no good at all to curse my luck. Better to bless my luck for bringing me to such an age without ever having been imprisoned before.

I can see the ironic side of it too: that I, for whom art has been my thickest woods and deepest water—the thing which sustained me through many difficulties, annoyances and sadnesses—should finally fall into a trap baited with art, like a fish or a bird caught by its own appetite.

Well, what can I do but continue to follow my nature and rely on art to lift me out of this hole? I shall revisit as much of my life as I can or care to remember, re-visualise it, re-imagine it. For although the principle of life is simple, its patterns of growth and survival and decay are complex. Every creature makes an individual pattern, human beings no less than fish or birds. But the clearest examples of this are plants, especially trees, whose patterns over time are, as it were, drawn on space. I shall try to see the pattern of my own life in the way I see a tree in a landscape and to look at myself as someone else. I shall be the scholar in the bottom corner of the painting who stands on a convenient crag and carries the viewer's eye away from himself and into the landscape. But in this case I shall also be one of the landscape's inhabitants. And so, as that person within the painting I shall experience time—life unfolding without knowledge of its future—but as this person on the crag, who has already passed through all that time, I shall experience it as a whole, as space, and perhaps perceive its pattern for the first time. Except, of course, for the relatively short time still to come when I shall have finished telling this story, viewing this landscape, when I shall turn away and go—where and how?

Rivers and mountains form the background to this story and from their perspective it is a straightforward one, except that in the eighty-fifth year of the Yuan Dynasty the Yellow River changed its course. This was a complication with important consequences for human beings, though perhaps it made no great difference to the Yellow River, which, seven years later, was re-channelled in its new course by an energetic Chancellor, a clever engineer, twenty thousand Mongol soldiers and a hundred and fifty thousand local peasants. That too had important consequences for the people of our Empire, but hardly for mountains, nor for the Yangzi River and the many smaller rivers to the south of it, where our story mostly happens, except that they had to carry away a lot of human blood and corpses. Rivers do that all the time during periods of bad government and make nothing of it.

Stories are about changes. Since mountains and rivers normally change only over many centuries or millennia, we can safely say that from their point of view—always excepting the unruly Yellow River—there was no story to tell about those two and a half centuries when the Empire was ruled partly or wholly by foreigners, or even during the final two and a half decades of anarchy and civil war when the Mongols were driven out and we recovered our freedom—or at least our independence. Yet those same mountains and rivers, whatever their own indifference, were both the setting for and the underlying cause of all the changes, since at bottom this is a simple story of landscape and its ownership.

We begin, then, in the eighty-fourth winter of Mongol occupation by taking ourselves south of the Yangzi River and letting our eyes slide down the flanks of a mountain. We notice a small stream, a clump of fir-trees, a single one-storey house with a thatched roof, a group of similar houses partly concealed by pines, a fishing-village away to the right and, immediately in front of us, a good-sized river, flowing swiftly but calmly over the rocky roots of the mountain. There are plenty of trees at this level: over there, on the far side of the river, is a wood of mountain-oaks with the occasional rowan, all bare of leaves, their branches lightly dusted with snow. Snow lies also on the turf-slopes above the river-bank and there are a few snowflakes in the air. If we raise our eyes again we can see the last grey wisps of the snow-cloud, but the sky above and around the mountain is blotted out by dense white vapour.

Lowering our eyes once more to the far bank of the river, we can pick out among the trees the figure of a man with a large red sack over his shoulder. He wears a peasant's wide-brimmed straw hat and grey-blue padded clothes and he is bent over, stooping to collect a fallen branch. He shakes the snow off it, breaks it into smaller pieces and drops them into his sack, then continues on his way to our left, disappearing behind trees, reappearing, stooping repeatedly, adding more sticks to his sack. On our side of the river, a fishing-boat is drawn into the bank and its owner, muffled and padded against the cold, crouches motionless in the bow, staring into the cloudy, rippled water. From the village in the distance there is the faint sound of a bell and a dog barking. Otherwise nothing moves or makes a sound, except for the river, a sudden scattering of disturbed crows and the man gathering firewood.

He is in sight of his home now, three or four thatched cabins on the far side of a little stream which flows out from under a covered balcony on the side of the house facing us and runs down into the river. He crosses a wooden foot-bridge, passes three tall pine-trees standing together on the lawn in front of the house, stoops for a last stick, which he keeps in his hand, and disappears round the side of the house.

His family name is Wang, a common name, but although we have seen him collecting firewood like a peasant, he is not a common man. On his mother's side he is descended from a famous general who rose to be Emperor and founded a long and successful dynasty. Wang even wears on the middle finger of his left hand a white jade ring, carved with dragons, which belonged to that fighting Emperor who two hundred years earlier healed and united the Empire after a previous period of civil war, chaos and foreign conquest.

Thirty-six years old, tall, usually slender and with a healthy complexion, Wang is at present pallid and overweight. He has spent too long in the city, poring over legal documents in an office, eating large meals and drinking too much with friends, taking too little exercise. Ever since he finished his education he has worked steadily and dutifully as a legal secretary in the local bureaucracy, earning enough for himself and his wife to live on, escaping from time to time in good weather to this country retreat under the Yellow Crane Mountain.

But what is he doing here in winter and why does a man of his age, ancestry and education not have a better job? Wang and his wife are at odds about this. He considers that he is kept down because the Mongol rulers favour their own people, whereas she points out that others in the family have become Governors of cities and suggests that if he showed sufficient ambition and drive or even simply made friends with the right people he would soon be promoted. Wang has responded angrily by resigning his post, leaving his wife in the city and coming to spend the winter alone in his country retreat. He is not, of course, quite alone. There are three local women cooking, cleaning and washing for him, there is a gardener-handyman and there is Deng, his young personal servant, who now meets him behind the house, takes his sack and is told to fetch tea.

The light is beginning to fade on this side of the mountain. Wang's studio, the covered balcony which we have already noticed built on slender wooden piles over the little stream, is still clearly visible, but we can only dimly see Wang as he enters and sits down at a large table facing the view of lawn and river-bank. He has already changed his padded clothes for a loose robe. Now, as he contemplates the drawing on the table in front of him, he transforms himself mentally from a pseudo-peasant back into the gentleman-artist that he really is.

Deng enters with the little tray of tea and sets it on a corner of the table, well away from the sheet of clean paper with the new drawing begun that morning. Wang scarcely notices. He is already eager to correct and continue the drawing, which shows the three pine-trees on his lawn, but wonders if the light is now too poor. However, the damp, dark texture of the bark excites him and, still staring at the trees, he feels for and picks up the inkstick with his right hand and finds the inkstone with his left. Deng, standing deferentially to his right, waiting to pour the tea for him but anxious not to disturb his master's concentration, sees him suddenly start and stiffen and glance at his left hand with horror. The Emperor's jade ring is missing.

❀

Now if anyone had still been watching from the far bank of the river he would have seen something quite alien to those calm, quiet landscapes made for contemplation and refreshment of the spirit. Out of the house in a flurry of haste and anxiety rushed Wang, Deng and the gardener, eyes down for every footprint, every mark in the thin surface of the snow. Past the pine-trees, across the lawn and over the footbridge they went. Wang even squatted down, put his head under the railing and peered into the stream in his desperation and the other two immediately imitated him, before all three got up and retraced Wang's steps back to where we first caught sight of him and beyond into further parts of the now dark wood. How to find a small circle of white jade on snowy ground in twilight? They returned at last to the house, abandoning the search until morning.

Wang hardly slept that night. He was full of regret and foreboding. Regret, because he knew that the ring was a little loose on his finger—his ancestor, the warrior-Emperor, no doubt had much larger hands—and occasionally slipped off when his hands were wet. He should have left it at home when he went out to collect firewood. Foreboding, because he felt that this loss was symbolic. Fate had given him the ring and now took it back. It was not that he thought of fate as a conscious being. It was merely the name for the secret balance in nature, for the way circumstances alter for good or bad according to forces and conditions beyond our knowledge or control. There might, for instance, be a succession of harsh winters and drought-ridden summers or of mild autumns and golden harvests, but the balance would be restored in time. His childhood had been privileged and fortunate and he was afraid he owed nature the balance.

The ring's previous owner had been his grandfather. He could not picture his grandfather's face, but he vividly remembered his hands, big, knotty, incredibly agile as he showed his little grandson how to rub a stick of ink on the inkstone and mix it with water, how to choose a brush suitable for dry or wet strokes, how to hold it and make the first bold mark on the clean paper. Miraculously, without hesitation, his grandfather's first mark became the back of a horse seen half from the rear, its right rump in the foreground, its great neck wrinkled as it twisted its head back to stare out of the paper. After that first line, Wang couldn't recall the many individual strokes which created the horse: his attention was focussed on his grandfather's left hand, holding down the paper, and the white jade ring at the base of the ring finger, looking as if it grew there, the flesh partly overlapping it. The ring, he believed then, was the source of the magic that conjured up the horse, and his belief was confirmed when the old magician paused momentarily to contemplate his work and say:

"Now you can see it's a horse, the principle of a horse. But which horse, which particular horse waiting to be mounted?"

And at that point he gave a little twist to the ring with his right thumb and forefinger and immediately laid his left hand down on the paper again, taking up more ink with the brush and finishing the drawing without another pause.

"Is the ring magic?" Wang asked, as his grandfather laid the brush on its rest and looked for approval.

"The ring? Of course. Do you think I could draw like that without it?" said his grandfather and then, seeing that he was being taken literally, laughed and added:

"But the funny thing is, you know, that I could draw like that *before* my father gave me the ring. So perhaps the magic is in my fingers and the ring helps to keep it there."

Wang must have looked bewildered. His grandfather stared at him for a moment, then suddenly took the little boy's right hand and held it in both of his.

"If there's magic in *your* fingers and you learn how to master it and bring it to the paper, you shall have this ring one day for your own."

So, from then on, he had the promise of the ring and often referred to it, even when he was some years older and began to understand that fingers can be taught to make magical drawings, but that magic rings are impossible except in stories.

"How soon can I have Grandfather's ring?" he would ask when his mother or grandmother praised one of his drawings with unusual enthusiasm.

His mother became irritated:

"Even if Grandfather decides to give it to you one day, you mustn't keep asking."

"But he promised."

"A gift must be given freely, not on demand."

"Besides," said his grandmother in a kinder voice, "he still needs it himself."

But Wang was not such an innocent by then as to think that, however well he drew, his grandfather would simply remove the ring one day and give it to him. He was just reminding them of his claim on it, being only too well aware that nearly every other member of the family was also an artist and afraid that the same promise had been made to them.

His fear seemed justified when his grandfather died and the ring still eluded him. His heart ached all through the week when the sealed coffin stood in the house, waiting for the funeral.

"Will it be buried with Grandfather?" he finally couldn't resist asking his mother in a whisper, as the cortege bearing the corpse and followed by a huge crowd of loudly mourning relatives, friends, servants and peasants left the house for the family tomb. His mother's grief immediately turned to anger:

"How dare you talk like that? Did you only love him for his ring? You don't deserve it. You're greedy and selfish."

Yes, he was; and humiliated too, to have exposed his greed and selfishness so crudely. At the same time he thought he did love Grandfather as much as his ring and that having the ring would somehow seal their relationship and keep it alive. Because by that time, when Wang was fourteen, his grandfather never scrupled to admit openly that although his wife, his brother, his son and his son's son—all of them his own pupils—were sensitive and skilled artists, none was as gifted as his daughter's son. Still, Wang never mentioned the ring again after that and tried to forget it himself, assuming it had gone into the grave, until three years later, when his grandmother was dying in her turn and Wang came to her bedside to say goodbye. Suddenly she said in her faint, distorted voice (half her still beautiful, clever face was twisted and rigid):

"Pillow . . ."

"What, Grandmother?"

"Yours at last, dear child!"

Glancing back at his tearful mother in case he had misunderstood, he received an almost imperceptible nod, then nervously put out his hand and felt about under the pillow, his eyes never ceasing to look into the nearest eye, the still living, glistening eye of his grandmother. And there it was, his fingers touched it and drew it out: the white jade ring carved with dragons which his grandmother had not been able to part with as long as she was alive, though she never wore it.

Turning constantly in his bed, Wang suddenly remembered that, after bringing the firewood home, he had washed his hands before changing his clothes. Had he still had the ring then? Did it slip off in the water? He got up and went to see, not troubling to light a lamp or to call Deng to light one for him, but feeling his way in the dark. The bowl had been emptied, of course, and there was no ring in the bottom of it. In the morning, first thing, they must search the ground where the dirty water had been thrown. He returned to bed, almost hopeful, almost forgiving himself his carelessness.

But he still found it difficult to sleep. He was reproaching himself now for not being a worthy recipient of the ring. We educated people make a great display of humility when we meet, trying to get the better of each other in unimportance. It is usually only a formality, of course, a polite mask for our feelings of superiority. All the same we are also peculiarly susceptible to genuine feelings of unworthiness, trained as we are from the earliest age to be conscientious as well as sensitive and clever, to defer to our elders and pay exaggerated respect to our ancestors. Half waking, half dozing, Wang began to imagine that it was his grandfather's spirit, rather than fate, which had slid the ring off his finger.

"I should never have given it to you in the first place," he seemed to hear the spirit say. "It's an Emperor's ring, not at all suitable for a small-time clerk. I should have given it to my own son, your uncle, the Governor of a city, who would have passed it on to his son, also an able administrator and likely to achieve high office."

"But you gave it to me for being an artist, Grandfather, and I have resigned from my despicable job precisely in order to concentrate on my art."

"Your uncle and cousin are both excellent artists. For people of our class, art is a recreation and a pleasurable adventure, but not a substitute for public duty. Besides, having failed in one direction, you will most likely fail in the other. The mistake was mine, I admit. Your gifts were great and you were a charming child, but I should have judged you by your character. Character makes the artist as much as it does the Governor."

There was no answering him. This grandfather, Lord Meng, was still young when the Mongols swept down into the southern part of the Empire and, like most others of his noble background and first-class education, at first turned his back on the conquerors and retired from public life. But Khan Khublai, the new Mongol Emperor, soon showed that he was a preserver more than a destroyer. He urgently invited our leading intellectuals to his court and persuaded many to take office again, Lord Meng among them. Under Khublai and his successors Wang's grandfather rose to become Governor of a province, Minister of State and Director of the Central Academy of Culture. On top of that he was recognised in his own lifetime and ever afterwards as a great artist and teacher of other artists. Khublai himself called him "one of the immortals" and an honorary Dukedom was bestowed on him after his death. Most titles in our Empire, as doubtless elsewhere, are acquired by nepotism, graft or violence, but a posthumous title is a true honour.

Anyone might feel unworthy to wear such a grandfather's ring, let alone if he lost it. Poor Wang! He began to wish he had never been born or at least not born to such an inheritance. And yet a question hangs over this "honour" and this inheritance, does it not? Given that of all the sins a properly educated gentleman may commit, disloyalty is among the worst, what is to be made of Lord Meng's conduct? It was not just that he served the foreign conquerors, but that he himself was descended from the founder of the native Song Dynasty, which the Mongols had overthrown. Perhaps a posthumous Dukedom does not seem such a very great honour when bestowed by barbarians on a man who has betrayed his own imperial ancestors?

No one, of course, disputes Lord Meng's abilities as an administrator or his genius as an artist, but wouldn't he have been a still better artist if his character had been less pliable? And although his art included landscapes, portraits and exquisite calligraphy, he specialised in painting horses. What could be better calculated to appeal to the taste of those galloping missiles, those weapons on horseback, the Mongols? As a matter of fact Lord Meng's eldest son, the Governor of Wuxing, was primarily a horse-painter too; so was *his* son.

But none of this was any help to Wang in his self-abasement. He would have angrily dismissed it as the envy and spite of more timid and small-minded people. Such people left the cities and went to live in isolated places partly because it was the correct thing to do, but partly also to avoid the Mongols' outrageous taxes. These well-born, well-educated dissidents occupied their enforced leisure by talking about art and literature and by writing and painting themselves. They copied and played variations on the styles of the most admired masters of the past, depicting the hills and forests, streams, mountains, fishermen, woodcutters and themselves and their friends in retreat, just as if the Song Dynasty still ruled. They despised those professional artists who stayed near the court to make a living out of their art and they thought it disgraceful to sell anything themselves. However, in many cases their means were slender and they did accept payment by one subterfuge or another: through a friend or relative or by giving a painting away in the front of the studio while finding a reciprocal gift in a back corner. Admirable and patriotic people!

How, Wang would have demanded, was his grandfather different? Not in his knowledge or practice of art, except that he surpassed all the rest. Not in giving his work away nor in retiring to his retreat in the hills whenever he could spare the time. Solely, then, in his incorrectly intimate relationship with the Mongol government. But it was precisely because of this, because of Lord Meng's influence and intercession with the government, that all those correct people avoided being harassed and could maintain their creative isolation. So, in Wang's view, his grandfather's brave decision to set aside the letter of traditional principles and serve Khan Khublai made him the best patriot of all.

Yes, of course, the Khan was a savage. He came from a wilderness where they live only in tents, while *his* grandfather, Jinghis, had been the most ruthless mass-slaughterer and destroyer of civilisations ever known on earth. Nevertheless, Wang would have argued, Khublai saw the point of civilisation, he desired to be civilised himself. And among those he looked to for guidance was Lord Meng. Should Meng have stayed away in the hills and left lesser, weaker, coarser, more trivial people to advise the new Emperor? Wasn't it the best principle in these circumstances to run the Empire *in our way*, so that as nearly as possible it made no difference how barbarous the ultimate rulers were?

As for painting horses to please Mongols, that sneer too Wang would have rejected, pointing out that we had horses long before Khublai seized the Empire. Horses were as important to us as to the Mongols, the difference being that we, not being primitive nomads, had other equally important possessions: temples, palaces, wine, silk, porcelain, sculpture, literature, painting, calligraphy, printed books, libraries, theatres, the examination system, the civil service, written laws, magistrates, trade, education, agriculture, gardens, canals, ships, bridges, baths, fountains, astronomy, philosophy, jewellery, jade.

In any case, must we believe that everything about the Yuan Dynasty was negative? Wang's grandfather didn't think so. "Everyone lives his life in this world according to his own times," was one of his sayings; and he even dared to point out that the Mongols, simply by not interfering, opened up new subjects to artists and freed their style from the rigidities imposed by the old Imperial Academy. And wasn't it Khublai who created our imperial post system, improving the roads and establishing decent inns at regular intervals, with relays of swift horses and messengers always in readiness? He also repaired and extended the Grand Canal, so that goods and passengers could travel quickly and easily half the length of the Empire: from the former Song Dynasty capital, Quinsai, south of the Yangzi River, to Khublai's new capital, Dadu in the far north.

Under this Mongol Emperor—why not admit it?—we were governed efficiently and not, on the whole, cruelly. Our civilisation was damaged but not destroyed. It's true that things began to go wrong under Khublai's successors, but how many dynasties thrive for more than a hundred years?

Wang's thoughts were still on his grandfather when the next day dawned and the search for the ring was resumed. It was not found either in the place where the bowl of water had been emptied or anywhere along the unlucky firewood-gatherer's route, though the snow had melted. The sky was overcast and the atmosphere heavy. Wang returned to his studio and sat down in front of the unfinished drawing. When Deng came in to say that the gardener had been searching the bed of the stream and still not found the ring, he was dismissed with an angry gesture as if the matter was of no further interest. Really Wang was angry with himself, as his mother had once been, for caring so much about a mere object and for showing others that he cared. Making ink on the inkstone and reminding himself yet again of his naked finger, picking up a brush and recalling his grandfather's left hand on the paper thirty years before, he ruined his drawing with distracted strokes.

He stood up and went to the window. It had begun to rain heavily and the irritation in the surface of the stream directly below, with the relentless beating on the roof above, matched and assuaged his own feelings. Often as a child he had stood like this watching downpours with mixed emotions of frustration and exhilaration in his grandfather's retreat in the Blue Bien Mountains. He remembered saying to his mother:

"They ought to be called 'Grey Rain Mountains'."

"Yes, but on a nice day they do look blue," she said.

"Not as blue as the sky," he said. "On a nice day they look black."

"They look blue from a distance," she said.

"But why 'Bien'?"

"Because a long time ago a man called Bien Ho found a wonderful piece of jade when he was walking in these mountains."

This explanation always troubled Wang. Surely the jade should have been called after the mountains (which must have already had a name even long ago), not after the man who found it? And didn't all mountains look blue from a distance?

That country retreat in the Blue Bien Mountains was a far larger place than this, a walled complex of many buildings, higher up and more remote. But although the carriages that brought visitors had to wind about the hills and cross five bridges over the same rushing stream to get there, it was not at all solitary in those days. The whole family was centred on Wang's illustrious grandparents. His grandmother, widely admired then and still famous now for her paintings of bamboo, had been Lord Meng's student and was several years younger than him. Children, grandchildren, cousins, in-laws, as well as friends and pupils assembled round these two masters and vied for their instruction and approval. The retreat was as much an academy as a summer holiday resort.

Wang remembered one summer especially, when, barely fifteen, he had fallen in love with a cousin of the same age from his grandmother's side of the family. Peony's grandfather had been a Mongol officer, who took part in the Mongols' unsuccessful campaign against the Annamese in the tropical south and was killed by the unhealthy climate. Her family was poor and particularly grateful for the good food and wine, the comfortable rooms and beautiful garden of Lord Meng's retreat, which they seldom visited because they lived much further north. Peony attended drawing lessons like all the children, but she was not very serious about her own art. When she saw what Wang could do, she told him that she felt like a mule trying to keep pace with a horse. That pleased him, since in everything else that went with being young—energy, high spirits, adventurousness, aptitude at climbing, playing football—she, brought up in the Mongol fashion without having her feet bound, was the horse and he the mule.

That year of Peony's visit there was a small group of older children who sat about talking and pretending to be adult; and there was another larger group of younger children who played and screeched through the garden and courtyards and were closely shadowed by their nurses. Wang and Peony were the only ones of their age and soon became inseparable. They must, Wang thought later, have looked quite comical together, she small, inclining to be plump, but very lithe and athletic, he much taller, gangling and clumsy.

The various families were lodged in separate thatched cabins round the courtyard dominated by the main, two-storey house with its tiled roof. Sometimes they would meet for communal meals in the house, sometimes they ate in their separate cabins, but the rest of the time, except for a few hours every day drawing and painting and occasional large expeditions into the hills, carefully planned and catered for in advance, was more or less free. Wang and Peony often walked and talked together in the garden, where he might be trying to draw one of the huge garden stones with epidendrum and young bamboo sprouting beside it—a favourite subject of his grandmother—but Peony would throw down her sketchbook and scramble up the rock, making faces at him to distract him.

One hot day she climbed the wall round the garden and beckoned him to join her. Clumsily, reluctantly, with a helping hand from her, he reached her side, when she immediately jumped down and ran into the fir-wood beyond.

"Try to catch me!" she called, leaning against a tree-trunk.

When he made the attempt, more for form's sake than imagining he could do so, she ran on, dodging round trees, laughing, leading him ever further and further until they emerged on a grassy knoll out of sight of the houses. Just below was the stream, deep and slow-moving at this point, with thick, dark fir-woods growing on either side.

Still half playing the game, she started down towards the stream. Wang called out that he couldn't catch her, never would, and begged her to stop.

"We've already come too far and I'm too hot," he said.

"It will be cool in there."

"But even hotter coming back up."

"Who cares? If we stay near the bank we can dip our hands and feet in the water whenever we feel too hot."

"The banks look too steep for that."

She smiled contemptuously at this feeble excuse and went on, Wang following. Actually it was almost too cold in the forest. The trees were very tall and there were only occasional splashes of sunlight down below. The place was full of huge black rocks in strange, complicated shapes, often with holes right through them. Wang had the sense that, just like the trees, they were alive and had grown that way organically, but of course over an infinitely longer time-span, so that as humans were to insects (of which there were too many) and trees to humans, the rocks were to the trees. She waited for him now and when he caught up with her, he told her what he had been thinking.

"And what to the rocks, then?"

"The earth itself, I suppose," he said.

"And what to the earth?"

"The sun and stars."

"Everything alive?"

"But growing at different speeds."

They came to a place where the stream fell suddenly down a long waterfall. Small birds darted away through the trees. She touched his hand.

"You left out the birds," she said, smiling, almost laughing, not at what she'd said, but at the sheer pleasure of the place.

Then they moved together, put their arms round one another and carefully, awkwardly, kissed for the first time; and after a while sat on a rock holding hands and staring at the waterfall below until the movement of the water seemed to make the banks move too. Wang pointed this out.

"Are we seeing them grow, then?"

"It's not really happening. It's a trick of the eyes."

That was how he felt too about the way they'd suddenly fallen in love. He remembered nothing more about the rest of that day, how they walked home—they must have walked, surely, not floated?—except the feeling of continuing unreality, of having entered a new time in which he saw everything with her eyes as well as his own, in which the effect of their sudden waterfall, as it were, transmitted itself to the whole of nature round them.

They secretly climbed the wall and went to the waterfall again another day, this time descending some way beside it, so that Wang could draw it and the rock on which they'd sat that first day. Peony became impatient after a while and wandered away to see if she could climb right to the bottom. The bank became precipitous and the undergrowth very dense and tangled over the rocks and Wang felt worried by her disappearance, but he wanted to finish his drawing and he knew it was useless to try to deter her from taking risks. Suddenly, from somewhere below, he heard her scream. Stuffing his drawing and his inkstone and brush into his bag—even in such an emergency making sure he didn't lose his work—he scrambled down in mounting panic, tearing himself on thorns and rocks, pouring sweat, heart and brain racing, limbs even more ungainly and uncontrollable than usual.

He found her at the bottom of an enormous boulder, her back against it, confronting a huge ape-like creature only a foot or so away from her. Wang shouted violently to distract the creature's attention and kept on scrambling down, but catching his foot in something slid and landed painfully on his bottom on the same small platform of earth as Peony and the ape.

"No harm, no harm," it said, shaking its head vigorously and approaching Wang with open hands. "I thought she would slip like you."

It was not, after all, an ape, but a short, heavy man of about forty, with wild black hair and beard, coarse features, eyes small and bloodshot, and dressed in torn, dirty clothes. From where Wang lay, sprawled on the ground, the man's feet in ancient, grimy sandals seemed particularly monstrous.

"You're both too young to be out alone in this dangerous place," he said. "What are you doing here?"

Perhaps he *had* only been trying to prevent her falling—the earth platform was directly above the waterfall and if she had slid down the boulder directly to the point where she was standing, could easily have plunged straight over. Still, she had screamed, she told Wang afterwards, because she thought he meant to attack her.

"I'm afraid you're being very naughty," the man said, perhaps deliberately using that childish word to assert his own seniority and respectability, insinuating too that if there was any sexual truancy involved, it was theirs. "Your parents would be horrified if they knew what you were playing at."

"I don't think so," Wang said, as coolly as he could, picking himself up with all his bruises and cuts beginning to hurt at once. "We've been here before and I only came to draw the waterfall."

"To draw it? Can you draw well?"

"Quite well," Wang said, modestly but firmly.

"Where is your drawing?"

Wang defiantly opened his bag and took out the drawing, now badly crumpled.

"Let's see!" holding out his hand, the wrist covered with black hair.

Reluctantly, Wang gave him the drawing. He glanced at it cursorily, the way one looks for politeness' sake but without expecting anything at a child's scribble, then looked again and going to the smoothest part of the boulder, laid the drawing against it and smoothed it out.

"Yes," he said, after examining it carefully, "you do draw well. You are an artist. So am I. The difference is that you are imitating some old master and I am original. Would you like to see my work?"

Wang looked at Peony. She had recovered from her fright, but evidently wanted to get rid of the man.

"We should go home now," Wang said.

"Yes, I daresay they will spank you both soundly," said the man. "But why not put it off a little? My home is only just there . . ." pointing down a narrow path leading to the platform. "You can see my work and then go home for your medicine. You will find my work a big surprise after the things you're used to copying."

Wang was not old enough to know how to refuse gracefully. In any case, the man's interest in his drawing had won him over.

"What do you think?" he asked Peony, in a tone that made it clear he'd already given in.

"Never ask a woman what she thinks!" said the man. "All she knows is that she thinks the opposite."

They both smiled weakly at this travesty of their relationship, humouring, as lovers do, the unaccountable sourness of old people.

"Come on!" the man said. "You won't regret it, I promise you."

They followed him down the path and soon came to a hut built into the rocks. It was small and weathered, with very old thatch on the roof, but its position directly over the deep pool at the foot of the waterfall was spectacular. From the little balcony in front, the fierce downpour of water diving into the pool looked like the rocks all round, except that it was filled with light and the light showed its movement in spite of its apparent stillness and solidity. Hand-in-hand, Peony and Wang stood gazing down, while the man was busy inside the hut.

Then he called them in. He had hung examples of his work round the walls. But the first thing they noticed was the floor, blotched all over with ink stains. The second thing was the smell of alcohol. The man had a flask open on a table in the corner and held a small cup in his hand. The paintings on the walls were large, wild and shocking. After a while Wang could recognise a mountain, a clump of bamboo, a tree of some sort. They had a certain crude life to them, but they looked as if they had been made with a stick instead of a brush, perhaps even with the man's thick fingers. The paper was of poor quality, there was no delicacy in the handling and a great many unnecessary marks. The man was standing back, studying their reactions, especially Wang's.

"You've never seen anything like it, have you?"

"No."

"Wouldn't you like to be able to paint like this?"

"Not really."

"You prefer those old dead painters?"

He refilled his cup from the flask in the corner and drank it down immediately.

"In a sort of way I like this too," said Wang.

He wasn't sure he did, but was afraid to offend the man.

"Can you see how it's done?"

"It must be done very quickly," Wang said, studying the marks more closely.

"It's done in a frenzy," said the man, smiling broadly and showing terribly decayed teeth.

He hung up another painting and Wang saw that it was meant to be the waterfall. It caught the savagery of the water, but none of its light or the complexity of its streams—Wang remembered thinking something of the sort, though he would not have formulated verbal criticisms at the time.

"This is Yang, the Active Principle," the man said. "You know all about the Passive and the Active Principles, Yin and Yang?"

"Yes," Wang said doubtfully, unsure whether he really did.

"Yes is the word," said the man loudly, refilling and immediately draining his cup. "You must say yes to life. You must always say yes, never no. You must give yourself to life—to both the Active and the Passive—and to the painting. Because you are an artist too, I am going to show you how it's done. You have been taking lessons with some good, careful, learned teacher, haven't you?"

"Yes."

"His grandfather . . ." Peony began, but Wang broke in and

stopped her, not wanting the man to know who they were, where they came from, afraid perhaps also that he might say something disparaging about an artist so far his superior.

"Yes," he said, "a very good teacher."

"I could see that," the man said, "but you ought to have more than one teacher and I will be your other."

He put down his cup, took a clean sheet of his coarse paper, held it up for a moment by its top corners, as if to demonstrate its virginity, and dropped it on the floor. Wang started forward to pick it up, afraid that the stained floor would spoil it, but the man waved him back.

"Let it lie, dear boy!"

He refilled his cup and drank it off again, then walked unsteadily round the room, staring maniacally all the time at the paper in the middle of the floor. Returning to his starting-point, he put down the wine-cup and mixed ink with a great deal of water in a larger cup.

"Stand clear!" he shouted, and the two children edged back towards the balcony.

Suddenly he rushed forward and tipped half the contents of his cup on to the paper. The ink made a pool at the centre with splodges all round and spatters as far as the edge and on to the floor itself.

"Ah, ah, good, very good!" he crowed, his smile even broader than before, his woeful teeth even more evident.

Then, shaking the sandals off his huge feet, he stepped straight into the middle of the ink and began to scuff it about with his toes. Stepping off the paper, he glanced quickly at the result, then circled round it, half bent over, and poured more doses from his cup with a circling motion of the arm, prodding and pulling at the wet ink with one or other of his big toes. It was a kind of dance, rhythmic, barbaric. Then, still in a tremendous hurry, he returned his empty ink cup to the table, seized a brush and, using the handle, manipulated the drying ink into smaller streaks and whorls, crouching close to the paper and darting all round it, looking even more like an ape. Finally he straightened up, went back to his table, poured and swallowed more wine, laid down the brush and suddenly sat on the floor, perhaps deliberately or perhaps because his legs had ceased to function.

"Pause for thought," he said, looking at Wang and Peony amiably, as they still stood astonished in the doorway. "Sometimes, you know, I even piss on it. But not today. Not in front of the lady."

He enunciated the words slowly and carefully and then became quite silent for a minute or two, his body relaxed, his eyes closed, dozing or meditating.

"Nowlesseewhatwegot!" The words all ran into each other as he staggered to his feet and approached the paper like a comedian in a play faced with something that might jump or bite.

"Ahahaha! Yeshyesh!"

He made large beckoning gestures, bowing and staggering as his bows and gestures caught him off balance. The children moved warily forward together, not holding hands, which would have seemed somehow undignified. Were they afraid of his ridicule or his disapproval? He was half child, half elder and they had no experience of how to respond to the irreconcilable mixture. They walked carefully round the paper, not knowing what to say. It looked a complete mess—no viewpoint much different from another—unreadable. And then suddenly Wang saw that it was like the pool below, at the point where the waterfall drove through the surface, spitting up spray, making a deep wound with wrinkled edges in the smooth skin of the pool, the buried energy forcing its way up again here and there in further disturbances round the centre.

"It's the pool," he whispered to Peony. "Don't you see?"

She shook her head. Without any depiction of the cause of the disturbance, the falling water, she couldn't decipher the effects.

"I want to go home now," she whispered back.

"It's very clever," Wang said to the man. "It's brilliant, but we must go."

The man sat smiling at them and didn't seem to mind. As they bowed politely and withdrew, he raised one arm in a lordly farewell greeting.

"Yin," he said. "You saw it? First Yang . . ." gesturing at the waterfall picture hanging on the wall, "then Yin receives Yang."

He rotated both arms vigorously in front of him to suggest the agitation of the pool he had depicted on the floor.

"It's really brilliant," Wang repeated.

"Come again, dear boy! Artist. Always welcome. Yes."

They did not go again, not even to the waterfall. The man had frightened Peony, but he had affected Wang deeply too, in a way he couldn't analyse or perhaps wasn't fully aware of then. Ever afterwards he still vividly remembered the episode and the exact look of the splash-painting and still felt he hadn't come to terms with it.

❁

Thinking back to those days of first love and hypnotic happiness, Wang went on staring at the stream below. Swollen by the rain, its opaque brown surface stretched out from beneath the balcony into long lines of force. Stanzas of melancholy poetry written over the centuries by people just like himself who had retreated into the hills to nurse their sadness or bitterness came into his mind and plunged him in self-pity. Yes, the significance of losing the ring was only too clear: he had abandoned his job in order to practise his art full-time, but he was no more fated or fitted to be an artist than an official. "Having failed in one direction, you will most likely fail in the other."

After a while Deng came softly in and put tea on the table. The small sound made Wang turn round. Deng was a handsome boy, about twenty years old, with a broad face and a charming smile. He smiled now.

"The gardener says, sir, that perhaps a bird took your ring."

"A bird?"

"Some birds are great thieves. When the rain stops, the gardener says he can send some boys from the village up the trees to search their nests."

"Not very likely, I'm afraid," said Wang. "But of course if the boys care to look and find it, there will be a reward."

Wang had no hope of either the boys or the birds, but he was touched by the servants' anxiety to help. He smiled to himself. He had come here to be alone, imagining that solitude was what he really needed. But he had never been alone in his life before and understood now that he was not the solitary type. He would stay here a while, work hard, fight off his corroding sadness, and then return to his wife and friends in the city. He drank tea and stood looking at his ruined drawing, then threw it away, laid out another sheet of paper, mixed ink and began to draw, firmly and swiftly, concentrating on the three pine-trees, their crusty bark, sturdy footing and the way they stood as a group, trunks apart, but branches close and sometimes touching, grown into sensitive relationships with one another.

# 2. ESCAPING THE WORLD

Wang had a cousin, Tao, who was a true solitary. Tao lived high in the mountains, half a day's climb even beyond the nearest monastery. In winter he was cut off completely and even in summer he often saw nobody for weeks at a time except his single bad-tempered servant. In the spring he sent Wang a brief letter:

> *I'm tired of reciting my poems to myself. I think they're good, but over-familiarity may be deceiving me. It's true that much of the authority of the classics comes from this sort of constant repetition, generation after generation. What is generally accepted and known by heart becomes impervious to criticism or even doubt, like wood that has been weathered. But are my poems worm-eaten in the first place? Please come and test them before summer is over!*

The first part of the journey could be made up-river by boat. Then the river entered—or rather debouched from—a series of rapids and it was necessary to go by land. The river-trip irritated Wang. It was hot weather and there were too many travellers. In some moods he could enjoy the raucous talk and noisy activity of peasants. But although he had a secluded place under an awning at the front of the boat, he was not at peace in his own mind and was therefore only further disturbed by the perpetual restlessness behind. Deng spent the voyage among the other travellers, but kept an anxious eye on his master in case he needed anything.

Since there was no wind to speak of—only a faint current of air caused by the boat's progress—the sail was useless and they were propelled by two men—naked except for their loin-cloths—running down the gunwales either side with long poles. Narrow meadows and gentle hills with occasional villages and farms bordered the river on one side, tree-clad slopes on the other, while in front the rising mist—it was still early morning—gradually uncovered the bases of distant mountains. The river itself was full of craft, large and small, travelling both ways.

There would have been much to interest a genre painter in the different types of boats and different examples of human oddity—weary, naïve or cunning faces, emaciated or swollen bodies, distorted or deformed limbs—and the curious bric-a-brac of ordinary living, but Wang felt more and more alienated from his fellow men. They had to struggle for their existence and were marked outwardly as well as inwardly by that struggle, he was not. Simply as an organism, he reckoned that he must already be at least ten years younger than his contemporaries among these people; while mentally—since they were no different from and had made no advance on their primitive ancestors—he was all the centuries of our civilisation more mature than them.

But although they might envy him his comfort, his relative affluence, his apparent leisure compared to their struggle for existence, they would feel no sympathy whatever for the way he made use of such assets. His perpetual feelings of insufficiency, his never resting thoughts, his unceasing assimilation, classification and digestion of what he saw and heard: all these would strike them as unnecessary and even mad. Yes, educated people are probably always on the edge of madness. Aren't they the self-conscious element in nature turned on itself? And doesn't that mirror reflecting the mirror begin to exclude nature and transform a man into a monster? By his intelligence and adaptability man rises above all other creatures. But take those qualities beyond a certain point and the man is no longer fit to live in any world except an artificial one of his own invention. A slip of the foot by one of those muscular pole-men running along the gunwales might pitch him into the river. A slip of Wang's mind might pitch him into incoherence, paralysis, lethal self-hatred. The boatman could be rescued from the river, but could the educated man from his inner abysses?

"Are you happy?" asked Deng suddenly, peering deferentially round the side of the awning.

What a question! What a noble question for a servant to ask his master, so unobtrusively, with such sincerity! But of course the word "happy" covers many meanings and his was, after all, quite mundane: did Wang require water, fruit, rice? Was he too hot?

"Thank you," said Wang. "And you?"

No, Deng was not happy. He had been trying to make up to a girl from one of the peasant families in the body of the boat and her parents had abused him and chased him off. Poor Deng lived uneasily between two worlds, his own and his master's, and had to be adept in the manners as well as the language of both. Perhaps it was this idea, perhaps it was the way the river far ahead seemed to vanish into the mountains that made Wang say:

"Do you know the old story of the Peach Blossom River, Deng?"

"No."

"How a fisherman, making his way up a small river in the spring, came to a forest of peach trees thick with blossom?"

"No, never heard of that."

"There were petals everywhere, with an overpowering scent. The fisherman was astonished. He'd never seen anything like it before. He paddled on and found himself at the end of the river—the beginning, I should say, the source. In front of him was a hill and in the hill a narrow opening, a little cave or tunnel, through which he could just see light. He beached his boat and entered the opening, which was so small that he had to go on hands and knees and was afraid he might get stuck. But after fifty yards or so he emerged into the open. It was a broad, sunlit valley, with fine buildings, roads, rice-fields, duck-ponds and fish-pools, mulberries, bamboos. He could hear cocks crowing and dogs barking and there were people sowing seed—it was spring, of course—and coming and going on the roads and paths, all of them, old or young, looking prosperous and happy, but oddly foreign."

"He was in some other country?"

"No, not exactly. But they were just as surprised by the way *he* looked. They took him to somebody's house, sat him down, gave him wine, caught, killed and cooked him a chicken and everyone clustered round to stare and ask him questions."

"Did they speak his language?"

"Yes, but in a strange way, which at first he had difficulty understanding. And their clothes were as strange as his were to them."

"Who were they?"

"They were people from many centuries earlier, from a time when the Empire was in chaos and there was no proper government. Bandits, warlords, foreign invaders were devastating the countryside. These people had run away from their own farms and villages and discovered this hidden valley. They settled there gratefully and never even attempted to go back. Nor had anyone ever found them until the arrival of this one fisherman, so of course they were very eager to know how the Empire was now, what dynasty was in power, whether people were happy."

"Were they immortals?"

"That depends who tells the story. In some versions they are immortal, but in others just the natural descendants of the original refugees. At any rate, immortal or not, they seem to have been perfectly ordinary people to look at and talk to, except that they were so unnaturally healthy and happy."

"Is it a true story?"

"We have only the word of the fisherman. After staying some days with them, he returned, you see, to our side of the hill, so as to say goodbye to his friends and relations and collect a few possessions before joining the people in the hidden valley."

"And he told people what he'd seen?"

"I'm afraid he did, though he'd been warned not to."

"The people in the valley didn't want to be invaded by all sorts of bad types."

"Certainly not. Nor even perhaps by better types, since I don't think it was a particularly large place and all the land was already occupied."

"But he did tell."

"Yes, he told the local magistrate. Who probably didn't believe him, but sent somebody back with him to check up."

"And did they . . . ?"

"No. Even though the fisherman had observed the route very carefully and was sure he knew exactly where the hill with the hole in it was, they never found it."

"Not even the part of the river with the peach trees?"

"Not even that."

Deng was silent for some time, digesting the story, staring far up the river to where it disappeared as if they might themselves hope to enter the Peach Blossom River.

"If they were not immortal," he said at last, "but real people, could they still be there?"

"The story was first told a thousand years ago. Somebody would surely have found them again in all that time?"

"But not come back. Or come back and not told. I wouldn't have told," Deng said, almost angrily.

"But whether you had or not, perhaps you still wouldn't have found it again. If the people were not immortal, if there was nothing magical about them, then there was no reason, was there, why the telling in itself should make any difference?"

"No," said Deng doubtfully, "but it was bad to tell."

"Was it really?" asked Wang subversively. "If he had not told, we shouldn't know the story and it's a good story. We should be poorer without it."

Deng sighed. Wang felt as if he had infected somebody else's thought with his own complications.

❁

They landed a little short of the gorge at a small market town. Behind it the cultivated hills turned suddenly into steep forests and then high mountains. It was late afternoon and the town was striped in sunlight and shadow as the sun declined beyond the mountain peaks. The main street was still busy with people buying and selling produce. There was an inn not far from where they came ashore and Wang sat down at one of the tables in front of it, while Deng inquired about a room for the night. Watching the rest of the passengers awkwardly crossing the gangplank with their unwieldy bundles of possessions and produce, their baskets, sticks, children, live chickens, rabbits, birds, pigs, Wang thought again of those legendary people beyond the Peach Blossom River.

Their happiness consisted in being settled and undisturbed. All human dreams of bliss in this world or the next are similar, yet the very desire for such a state and the search for it bring about the exact opposite. Travelling symbolises everything that makes human happiness elusive and illusory. Even peaceful travelling disturbs the balance of fate in one's disfavour, makes trouble, harassment and disaster many times more likely. But aggressive travelling—by bandits, predatory officials, invading armies—is the prime cause of human misery.

Wang's thoughts were interrupted by the appearance of a peddler. No doubt he had seen the boat arriving and, with the advantage of mobility over the stalls further down the street, hurried forward to be the first to tempt the travellers. He was a big man with a prominent belly and a huge, shapeless head like a soft boulder. He was raggedly bearded, his eyes were narrow and deep-set, his nose bulbous and his large mouth stretched into a permanent, professional smile. He carried a yoke over his shoulders, from which were suspended two great baskets, or better say skeletons of baskets. Circular shelves fitted to a central pole were crammed to bursting with pots, kettles, shoes, toys, brushes, fans, knives, cups, bowls, mirrors, flasks, scissors, salves—the longer items like rakes and brooms sticking out above and the less breakable ones hanging off the sides. Round his neck were strings of beads and medallions on leather thongs. Scarves, ribbons, aprons, and other small items of clothing fluttered from his waistband and even the red scarf tied round his head had women's decorative pins stuck into it, with children's paper windmills and a writing-brush tucked into the string that held it together.

He set his baskets carefully down in the dusty road, stepped out from under the yoke and with one hand began tinkling a set of cowbells round his neck, while vigorously shaking with the other hand a small drum with dangling clappers. He was a honey-pot to the travellers and especially to their children and seemed to sell something to almost everyone, though without making any noticeable inroads into his stock. Wang could not take his eyes off him and, busy as the man was with his sales as well as deftly recovering small things seized by the bare-bottomed infants foraging around his baskets, he glanced in Wang's direction several times. When his customers had moved on down the street, the peddler left his baskets and came nearer to Wang's table.

"And for you, sir?"

Wang smiled and murmured that he had all he wanted already.

"You are fortunate, sir."

"I suppose so. But I meant only material things."

"Perhaps I can supply other things too."

"Really? What sort of things do you mean?"

"That depends what *you* mean, sir."

"I don't think I mean anything in particular, except that no one can claim to be without any wants at all."

"Very true. Your honour is perhaps still looking for promotion? That I can't supply."

Wang laughed.

"No, I'm not at the moment an official of any kind."

"Who would care to be, these days?"

There was more meaning in his tone than in the words.

"Many people, surely?" said Wang. "Now that they've restored the official examinations again, there's apparently no shortage of candidates."

"But the foreigners pass more easily and get more places."

He leant against the post holding up the roof over this open part of the inn and the thatch above rustled slightly as the structure adjusted to his weight.

"Well," said Wang, "I'm too old to go in for examinations now. I think you are too."

"Oh, me!" the peddler said, scratching his belly and releasing a powerful smell from his weather-beaten, unwashed clothes, "I'm not a learned man, nor a wealthy one, but I prefer my masters to be my own people."

"I too," Wang said. "But I'm afraid that's one of the wants neither you nor I can satisfy."

The man looked at Wang in silence. His perpetual smile had disappeared. He seemed to be making a judgment.

"Time they gave us back our rivers and mountains," he said, quietly but distinctly.

Wang could not mistake the slogan. It was used by nationalists during a rebellion against foreign rule in the north a century earlier.

"I am only a retired and retiring intellectual," Wang said, "and I wouldn't know how to bring that about. But of course I wish it might be so."

He took some money out of the wallet on his belt.

"What sort of brush is that in your cap?"

"Wolf's hair," the peddler said, his salesman's smile returning.

"I'll take it."

"An inkstone too? A fine piece of Xixin stone."

"No, I have more than enough stones already. Are all your goods of such superior quality? Where do you get them?"

"Here and there, round and about. This brush . . ." he said, taking it from his cap and holding it out ceremoniously on his palm, "and the stone were sold to me by a scholar and gentleman like yourself, but less fortunate. He preferred, he told me, to sell his last, best things and then starve to death rather than make any compromise with the foreigners."

"Perhaps I *will* take the stone too. It seems wrong to part them if they have been used to working together in the hands of such a patriot."

The man reached inside his clothes and from some interior pocket withdrew the inkstone and a square of paper. Wang proffered more money, but the peddler brushed it aside, then carefully wrapped the stone in the paper and laid it on the table beside Wang.

At that moment Deng returned, wrinkling his nose in disgust at the man's stench and waving him and it away with angry gestures. The huge peddler looked down at him with amiable tolerance, then returned slowly to his baskets. He checked them cursorily to see that all their multifarious contents were secure, passed the yoke through them, bent a little beneath it and lifted it smoothly with his massive shoulders, then walked away along the street and out of sight.

"There is no free room, sir," said Deng, "but there is one free bed in a double room."

"Well, unless the other occupant is a thief, a murderer or a fighting drunk," Wang said, unwrapping the inkstone to see if it was genuine Xixin, "I will manage for one night."

"It's another gentleman," said Deng. "The problem is that he doesn't care to share."

"Then, of course, I won't trouble him. We must look elsewhere," said Wang, turning his attention from the stone, which was genuine but quite ordinary in design and colour, to the paper it was wrapped in.

"The innkeeper wants you to have the bed," said Deng, "and since he says there are no other decent beds in the town and the other gentleman refused to pay to keep the extra bed free, I think the matter is settled."

"Ah."

Wang was only half listening. The side of the paper that had been concealed was printed with characters:

> *The Empire is in great Confusion. Everything goes from bad to worse. Why was the beautiful city of Quinsai twice destroyed by Fire within a year? Why has the Yellow River changed its course, with floods and droughts and much suffering for the People? Heaven is warning the foreign rulers that they must give us back our Rivers and Mountains. Heaven is preparing the way for the Buddha of the Future. The Maitreya will descend to earth and be reborn and will bring us at last an Enlightened Ruler. Then Justice and Tranquillity will return.*

"Strange," Wang said. "Very strange!"

"I think the gentleman is quite poor," said Deng. "Or he may just be mean with his money."

"I was thinking of the peddler," Wang said. "Did you notice what he looked like?"

"I noticed how fat and greasy he was."

"Not unlike the Maitreya Buddha himself, didn't you think? I mean the popular images of him."

"The Buddha never smelt like that, did he?"

Wang re-read the paper and screwed it into a ball.

"No, I don't think he can have been the Buddha," he said. "Either he would have been more disguised or less. Suppose I were to meet this gentleman, Deng, and see how we felt about each other?"

"I offered him that, sir, but he said he didn't care to meet total strangers."

"I see. An impasse."

"And I said, sir, that if he slept in a double room and wouldn't pay for the other bed himself, he could hardly help meeting a total stranger."

"That was rude, Deng."

"I was annoyed, sir. You can't be as choosy as that, if you can't pay for the privilege."

"Did you tell him that?"

"No, but I think he understood. He said you could pay for the whole room and he would move out."

"Oh, dear! I couldn't drive him out like that."

"I told him I didn't think that was your way, sir. Nor the way of anyone descended from an important Emperor. And then he said that if you didn't object to strangers yourself and didn't intend to use the extra bed in your room, he would not object to sleeping in it."

"What, at my expense?"

"That seemed what he meant, but I couldn't quite believe my ears, so then I came to consult you."

"Ask him if he'll do me the favour of drinking wine with me!"

Deng hurried away before Wang remembered to give him the screwed-up paper, which he had intended him to drop in the kitchen fire. Wang put it in his wallet.

The man who soon came out to drink with him was tall and well-built, with a large, fleshy, egg-shaped face, neatly trimmed sideburns just turning the angle of the jaw, a small drooping moustache framing the full-lipped mouth, and an air of lazy superiority belied by an intense stare. He was a few years older than Wang and, from the moment he appeared, with Deng carrying the wine just behind him, gave the impression that he had taken the polite words of Wang's request at face value and was conferring a favour on him. They sat in complete silence for several minutes, drinking the wine and appraising one another. Deng refilled the cups.

"You've been here some time?" Wang said at last.

"No. I arrived today."

"From the mountains?"

"No. By water."

"I didn't see you on the passenger boat from downstream."

"I came in my own boat."

Wang showed surprise. A man who could afford his own boat could surely afford a double room.

"I live on it," said the man. "When I'm not staying with friends or permitting myself the luxury of an occasional night in a riverside inn."

"You mustn't let me turn you out," said Wang.

"You have."

"I'm extremely sorry. If there were any other room I could find . . ."

"It doesn't signify. I can sleep on my boat. I had intended to try the inn tonight, but it doesn't signify."

"But if there are two beds in the room . . . I would be perfectly content for you to occupy the other. I shall stay only one night."

"That's most generous of you and I accept."

Deng was standing behind him in the background and looked scandalised at the way Wang had walked into this easy trap. But Wang was fascinated by the man's steely self-esteem and thought the price worth paying in order to know him better.

"Do you travel much in your boat or are you usually tied up somewhere?"

"I travel most of the time. I cannot, as I said, always resist the comfort of sleeping in a proper bed and eating good meals in the company of friends, but the solitude of the river pleases me."

"How do you live?"

"I fish."

"You are a professional fisherman?"

"Certainly not."

There was an aggrieved silence, until Deng filled the cups again.

"I mean that I fish to eat," the man said. "I have very little to live on since I gave all my properties to my relations."

"For religious reasons?"

"For tax reasons. Why should I let those bloody Mongols screw me? I took to the water because it's the one place you can be almost certain of never meeting them. They gallop all over the earth, but they've never learnt to cope with boats."

"One doesn't see many in the mountains either," Wang said.

"Probably not. They're too lazy to walk, let alone climb. But I'm not partial to mountains myself, except at a distance. They crowd you in."

He shuddered a little, then finished his wine again.

"Perhaps I've offended you," he said. "You seem well off and you probably work for the bastards. Are you an official of some sort?"

"No. If I work at all, it's for my own satisfaction."

"In what sense?"

Wang touched the wolf's hair brush and the inkstone, still lying beside him on the table.

"A poet?"

"Sometimes," Wang said. "More often I draw rivers and especially mountains."

"Do you? I see."

He withdrew into silence again, staring mostly at the floor, but occasionally glancing sideways at Wang, while his left hand kept fiddling with his empty cup. Wang signalled to his servant to refill it, but his companion seemed not to notice and remained silent and self-absorbed.

"I bought this brush and stone just now from a peddler," Wang said. "But they're not the rubbish you'd expect."

"No," the other man said, "I see they're not. But what about your drawings?"

Wang laughed at the awkward way he put his question.

"Are you suggesting they might be rubbish?"

"How am I to know?"

Wang realised, with incredulity, that he *was* suggesting that. The blood rose into his face and he said angrily:

"Who are you to know one way or the other?"

Reaching out his hand suddenly, knocking over the cup and spilling its contents, but paying no attention to that, the man touched Wang's arm.

"Tomorrow," he said, "you shall see my stuff and judge for yourself."

The night was uneventful, except that, after a meal suggested and paid for by Wang, but not much appreciated by his guest, who picked over every piece of food before eating less than half of it, Wang was amused to notice how obsessively cleanly he was. Warm water was brought up from the kitchen to their room so that they could wash their feet, but the stranger insisted on a fresh jug to himself and proceeded to soap and rub himself limb by limb, section by section, from head to foot with fastidious care.

During the meal they had got to know one another better, not so much as people, but as connoisseurs of painting. Names, schools, epochs, critical opinions and theoretical *dicta* flew to and fro between them and gradually revealed—through their likes and dislikes, enthusiasms and coolnesses, interpretations and reinterpretations—first the main outlines and then the more detailed structures of their minds, like mountains emerging from mist.

Wang's new friend was called Ni. His houseboat was tied up all by itself at the far end of the town, out of the way of both the main passenger landing and the fishermen's moorings. The boat was much larger than Wang expected, but Ni explained that he sometimes travelled with his wife and children, whom he had left for some weeks at a friend's house so that the children could begin to be educated. Ni's squat little servant was still asleep, flung down like a dog in front of the door to the cabin. Ni startled him awake with his foot, then pointed in the direction of the distant inn. The man leaped ashore and ran clumsily but steadily until he was out of sight among the houses.

"Complete idiot," said Ni. "But he's good with the boat and doesn't chatter. Your cocky little fellow would drive me mad."

"I like Deng."

"Everyone to his own servant. Mine is deaf and dumb."

The work he showed Wang was all in the form of hanging scrolls about three feet high by one or two feet across. Seating Wang in the front part of the boat and lighting a stick of incense nearby, he brought them out one by one and hung them in turn from the top of a bamboo boat-hook which he then raised to lean against the cabin. The paintings flapped slightly in the early morning breeze like sails.

Wang, taking the scrolls at the bottom and pulling them gently towards himself so as to keep the images still while he surveyed them, didn't know what to say. They were shockingly austere, the ink dry and sparse, the brushstrokes tense and scratchy. There was more bare paper than drawing and they all looked very similar: at the bottom, a few dried-up trees growing out of a hump of rock; at the top, a low cluster of mountains; and between them empty space except for one or two small islands or outcrops of rock acting as steps to the viewer's eye. A few of the paintings included, in the foreground, a vestigial studio or hut, hardly more than a thatched roof on four corner-posts.

But Wang wasn't required to say anything. Ni simply put up a painting, allowed him sufficient time to make its acquaintance, then took it down and replaced it with another. The fourth or fifth he showed had an unusually low viewpoint, heavier rock-forms, juicier brush-strokes and—wonder of wonders—a single human figure in the hut.

"Quite a difference there!" Wang said.

"You prefer it to the others?"

"I don't know that I do, but it's easier to get into."

"It's the earliest thing I've kept—the last I did in that manner."

"You prefer to do without figures?"

"I don't know that I *prefer* to," said Ni. "It's just that I'm not convinced, when I'm alone, that there *is* anyone else."

"But in your paintings it seems that you choose to be alone."

"Well, yes, I prefer to be alone when I paint."

The sun was gaining strength now, the town coming to life and more and more boats passing on the river. The austerity of the paintings, the reduction of the earth's surface, with its colour, noise and movement to these few indications of mass and line in white space seemed to Wang all the more wilful and even arrogant. How dare the man take so little from such a teeming world?

Ni brought out three or four more paintings in the later manner, then stopped.

"Say what you think!" he said.

"Show me some more first!" Wang said, playing for time.

"That's it."

"I'm a bit dazed," Wang said. "I've never seen anything quite like them."

"Did you expect you would have done?"

"I came with an open mind."

"I imagine they have little in common with your own work."

"As little in common as our servants. Perhaps I could see them all again?"

"If you wish."

He replaced them one by one in reverse order. About halfway through Wang realised with surprise that he was enjoying himself and by the time he had seen them all a second time, found he had acquired a taste for this subtle abbreviation of the ten thousand things. It was indeed a kind of mathematics—a few simple symbols standing for great quantities.

"Once more?" he asked tentatively, not wishing to admit to his growing addiction.

"Time is going on," said Ni. "You told me you wanted to start early for the mountains. Your tiresome servant will scold you."

"We can go tomorrow," Wang said.

Time as well as space expanded and contracted in these paintings. Space and time narrowed to a viewpoint, hung still, then rushed dizzily out again. The process renewed itself endlessly from rocks to trees to ground to rocks to water to mountains and back to oneself, transformed into the eyes and mind of the artist. And now, when Ni put up his earliest scroll, with the thicker ink marks and the intrusive human figure, Wang felt almost contemptuous of its crudity. It was mere representation, not sufficiently distilled. It had too little of the alcohol of space and time that intoxicated him in the others.

Deng arrived to tell him that his bags were loaded and the mules kicking their heels, the deaf-mute arrived with Ni's bag from the inn, but Wang would have none of that. He went on re-viewing the paintings until the sun was high overhead. The bags were returned to the inn and the room was booked for a second night. By early evening Ni and Wang were seriously drunk, preventing themselves with difficulty from sliding together under the very same table where they had first met as mutually wary strangers twenty-four hours before.

"You liked my stuff, didn't you?" Ni asked at intervals.

"I did, I did," Wang replied as often.

"You never said so."

Wang had brought none of his own work on this journey and had nothing to show in return. He was glad of that since he did not feel he had reached the same pitch of maturity and would have been embarrassed to be seen still struggling by such a master. Ni was not, in any case, particularly curious about Wang's work. Why should he be? Those who have achieved the measure of their own minds tend to withdraw from the market-square where other artists are still exchanging ideas and filching solutions to difficulties. As for the lack of courtesy in such a lack of curiosity, Wang felt that Ni's sublimely severe paintings cancelled all his limitations as a man.

Nevertheless, when Wang left the town at first light, aiming to reach the monastery beyond in a single day, Ni rose to see him off, which, for a man so self-centred, who liked to sleep until at least an hour after dawn and besides had a thick head from the night before, was a mark of extraordinary esteem. He also tried to pay the inn's bill for both of them, explaining that he had at first taken Wang for an official and considered that, given the bribes and taxes he'd paid when he was trying to run his estate, every official owed him at least a night's lodging. When Wang refused any payment, Ni asked if he would accept one of his paintings on some other occasion when he was not in the middle of a journey.

"It would be worth more to me than the whole contents of my house," said Wang.

Ni noted the name of the village nearest to Wang's country retreat in case he should be passing that way. But although Wang longed to have the painting, he also hoped the visit might be postponed at least until he had achieved something fit to startle the visitor as much as Ni's work had startled him.

❁

Night began to fall as Wang and his servant left the lower hills and entered the gorge which led to the monastery. The gorge itself was already dark and the mules were even more nervous than their masters of the narrow uneven track carved out of the sheer rock. But the setting sun must still have been visible to those on the top or the far side of the mountains, the sky was still light and their eyes soon adjusted to the shadows. They could hear the river far below on their left and occasionally see its rapids flashing as the track turned a buttress. They had ridden most of the way to the hills, then rested for an hour or two at midday, then led the mules up the steeper slopes and ridden them again only on the downward or leveller parts. Now on this more or less level but precipitous final stage through the gorge, Deng led one mule in front with the baggage, while Wang rode behind.

They were all four, mules and men, exhausted when they rounded the last corner and saw the monastery before them. It was built on a rounded bluff at the junction of their gorge with another broader one turning northeast. Behind the monastery's bluff the mountains rose into sudden vertical fangs and the river descended almost beside it in two spectacular waterfalls. The monastery itself was built on two levels. On top of the bluff was the temple, crowned with its tower and partly concealed by a ring of spare, spiky trees. Nestling at the foot of the bluff and reaching to the river's edge were the living-quarters for novices and the visitors' pavilions, several built out over the water. A broad, flat, unrailed bridge of thin logs covered with matting laid on hefty wooden supports carried them over the river to this haven, where lanterns gleamed, a few other travellers already sat at small tables under the elegant, upcurved roofs of the pavilions, and the smell of their soup drifted across from the kitchen at the far side of the courtyard levelled from the rock.

But soup was all there was. Early next morning when he climbed the bluff so as to view the waterfalls, Wang was still hungry. Stopping to speak to a young novice sweeping the steps of the temple's lowest terrace, he learnt that the monastery had fallen on hard times. Travellers were fewer, even the wealthiest donors were being less generous and the whole district was suffering from a series of bad harvests and increased exactions by the government.

"I didn't realise things were so bad," Wang said. "The harvests in my own district have not been good, I know, but people are not actually in want."

"Where I come from, thousands are dying," said the novice.

He was a boy of about sixteen, tall, ungainly and emaciated, but evidently strong. His face was memorably ugly, almost grotesque, pitted with the old marks of smallpox, coarsened with outdoor living and lack of nourishment and structurally distorted by a huge, jutting jaw, as if a clumsy craftsman had assembled the part without considering the whole. Nevertheless, Wang was strangely impressed by him and couldn't quite tell why. His eyes were fiercely alive and he was obviously intelligent, but it was more his whole presence, his sense of himself, a sort of fearless dominance over his unpromising circumstances that caught the attention. He was perhaps better suited to be a bandit than a monk.

Wang felt that the novice was in some way impressed in his turn.

It might have been only that he had never talked before to someone from Wang's background, someone with such a different experience of life from his own. He offered to show Wang the temple precincts and when Wang said he had seen them on a previous visit and preferred to look at the waterfalls, the novice asked if he might come too. He had been told by his Chan master, he said, to practise meditation by staring for two hours at a brick wall, but had not found that helpful and wondered if something equally unchanging but in motion might suit him better.

They clambered down from the temple terrace and made their way over the slippery rock—it was raining slightly—to the edge of the chasm into which the higher of the two waterfalls dropped in a double stream from a height of some eighty feet. The enormous deep black pool which it formed debouched far below into the second, broader and shorter waterfall. Wang stood there a long time in silence, at first awed by the whole phenomenon and then gradually absorbed in noting and memorising its details. The novice—he was called Zhu—stood a little way back and moved about frequently. Eventually, when his restlessness became irritating, Wang suggested he return to the monastery if he had had enough of meditation.

"No," he said, "I want to talk to you."

They withdrew from the lip of the chasm and sat down on some boulders under a pair of starved trees. The rain had stopped, but the trees still dripped. It made little difference, since they were both already wet. Zhu wanted to be taken on as a servant. His life up to now had been even more appalling than could have been guessed from his appearance. Under the Mongols' system of clamping their conquered people into specific occupations, his grandparents and then his parents had been registered as goldpanners. But the local streams gradually yielded less and less ore and Zhu's parents could not meet their annual quota. In desperation they borrowed money and became tenant farmers, hoping to make enough profit to buy gold from the traders in the market. The traders, predictably, demanded exorbitant sums and, unable to meet their quota or pay their debt, the family fled to another province and found what work they could as casual farm-labourers. Then, this very summer, following the spring drought and an invasion of locusts, the whole district was devastated by plague. Zhu lost both his parents, two of his three brothers and both his sisters. Apart from himself, the youngest, the family was reduced to one married brother and a sister-in-law with a small child. Neither could take in Zhu, so he entered the monastery as a novice of the lowest sort, doing menial tasks.

Now, almost as if he had brought ill luck with him, the monastery itself was in trouble and could no longer support its novices. They would all have to go out to beg for food. Zhu hated the very idea of begging. He thought he would almost prefer to be dead and had accompanied Wang to the waterfall to consider that alternative. But seeing the way Wang contemplated the waterfall he had understood, he said, the mysterious sanctity of nature. For someone like him who had always seen nature as an unfriendly, cruel and even evil force, this was a most important revelation and he believed fate had brought them together so that Wang could reveal still more to him.

Wang was taken aback by what seemed to him a too elaborate, sanctimonious and insinuating explanation.

"You aren't afraid," he suggested ironically, "that the ill luck with which you infected the monastery might also infect me?"

"Are you afraid of that?" asked the novice earnestly.

"Not at all. I don't believe people carry ill luck in that way. But I must tell you that, although I liked you immediately and wish that I could help you, I am too poor to employ another servant and too loyal to my existing servants to dismiss any of them in your favour."

"I would not wish to take another person's job," Zhu said, looking very disappointed.

"No, I don't think you would. I also think, though I hardly know you and am relying only on instinct, that you are not the type to be a servant."

"My grandfather was a soldier," said Zhu. "He fought against the Mongols in the time of Khan Khublai."

"You may have inherited something of his strength and spirit. Perhaps soldiers will be needed again."

"Do you think so?"

"I can't really hope so. I dislike being ruled by foreigners, but when I consider all we would have to go through—far worse than we are already suffering—to drive them out, I think I prefer things as they are."

"For you it is only something in the mind."

"True," said Wang. "I live mostly in my mind. And it has its advantages. No one can invade your mind unless you allow him to. I have more or less driven the Mongols out of my mind, even if I cannot drive them out of my country."

"This is what my Chan master tells me. 'The Ten Thousand Things are only Mind.' But can the mind alter the world?"

"Not directly, of course. For me it only alters the way I respond to the world. But I think history teaches us that there are certain exceptional people who can even alter the world itself when they set their minds to it."

"What do you mean?"

"Suppose I set my mind to making a drawing of this waterfall, I may alter the way you and I see it, but not the thing itself. On the other hand, if I had come here long ago when this place was still entirely wild and set my mind to building a monastery on this rock, I should have altered the place to what everybody now sees. But if I had been Khan Khublai and set my mind to seizing the whole Empire, although I should not perhaps have made any difference to this particular place, I should have changed the world of everybody that sees it."

The boy was staring at him intently.

"Is it enough, then," he asked, "to set your mind on something to make it happen?"

"Certainly not where drawing is concerned," Wang said. "I sometimes wonder whether my whole life will be long enough to round up all my thoughts and discipline my hand to their service. But I am perhaps a poor example, being a cautious and often indecisive person. I also think that for those who determine to change the world itself, chance—or fate—plays a large part. I remember a painter I once met as a child who threw ink on his paper and then stirred it about until he had achieved something near to what he had in mind. To act on the world would be something like that, wouldn't it?"

The novice was staring at him now quite ferociously. Wang even wondered if he was a little mad and, feeling suddenly afraid of him, stood up.

"My servant will be waiting with the mules," he said. "We are going further into the mountains."

"But how could a beggar act on the world?" Zhu asked bitterly, also getting to his feet.

"I doubt if he easily could," Wang said, making his way back towards the temple, feeling stiff and chilled by his wet clothes. "All the same, he might have a better chance than a servant, at least a servant of mine."

"How?"

He was following Wang closely and his loud question, just behind Wang's head, sounded threatening.

"Because the beggar would be more *of* the world. Country servants of mine hardly ever go beyond my little retired property and the nearest village. Our town servants perhaps see more, but are very closely controlled by my wife and have little time of their own. But a beggar is free to go where he likes and sees every level of society. If he wanted to, I should think he could understand the world—at least the world of people—better than anybody, not excluding those who govern it. To make significant marks on paper one must first know one's materials and what can be done with them. I should think the same is true of the world."

Wang felt that his explanation was vague and unsatisfactory. Who was he, after all, to recommend the advantages of being a beggar? Zhu made no reply and they reached the temple's lowest terrace. Standing on the edge of the top step, Wang turned and faced the novice, so that he was forced to stand lower and could not dominate him with his height.

"I am sorry not to be able to employ you," Wang said. "But let me give you something to start you on your new life! Perhaps it will bring you luck."

He reached into his wallet for money, but in bringing it out dropped a screw of paper near his feet. Zhu retrieved it and handed it to him.

"That was a strange thing," Wang said. "The peddler who gave me that piece of paper looked like the Maitreya Buddha and it is a message about the Maitreya's promised return."

"It must have been the Maitreya," Zhu said, with complete conviction. "What does it say?"

"Read it for yourself!"

Wang smoothed it out a little and offered it to him. He seemed reluctant to take it.

"Can you read?" Wang asked.

"I am learning."

"Then keep the paper and practise reading it! It is all about changing the world."

He wrapped some money in the paper and put it in Zhu's hand. Zhu made a little token Buddhist bow with the palms of his hands flattened tightly together over the gift and Wang hurried away. He could no more have believed what this strange boy's fate would prove to be than that a magic cloud instead of a weary mule might carry him on to his destination.

❁

The track to Tao's hermitage wound steadily upwards, keeping to valleys where it could, crossing streams and sometimes ravines on narrow bridges, clinging to bastions of sheer rock on man-made platforms of timber, propped out perilously from the cliff beneath. But Wang was in no state to appreciate either nature's grandeur or man's ingenuity. The chill he had caught while observing the waterfall and talking to the novice was gaining control. He was shivering and feverish. Much of the way he was able to ride, but in some places had to dismount and stumble forward in a daze, holding tightly to his mule's bridle for support and trusting the animal to follow Deng and his without stopping or straying.

The track went on through the mountains and eventually down the far side, but Tao's house was situated a little above it, sheltered by a few wind-swept trees in a small upland valley. By the time they reached the turning off the track into this valley Wang was virtually unconscious. He remembered Deng struggling to get him up on to the mule again and Tao's look of dismay when he had run out to greet his guest and discovered what condition he was in, but he remembered nothing between or afterwards, for nearly two days and nights.

The fever passed after two days and on the third day Wang was able to leave his bed and sit with his cousin Tao on the veranda. Tao was younger than Wang, but his hair was white. He had caught a disease when he was still a boy that left him slightly damaged, with uneasy lungs and a staggering walk. He might as well get drunk, he often said, since as soon as he rose from his chair he looked as if he was. He was thin, but tall and well-made and if he had not caught the disease would no doubt have been unusually strong and athletic. As it was, even with his strange way of walking, he went up and down the hills like a goat.

He claimed that it was the disease which had made him a recluse, but it was chiefly the Mongols, for he had criticised them in his examinations, failed to get beyond the provincial level and abandoned any attempt to pursue an official career. This set him at odds with his own family, since his father and both his brothers held minor official posts, and he preferred to leave his father's home and isolate himself rather than be constantly quarrelling with those he still loved on account of those (the Mongols) for whom he had no love at all. He sometimes teased Wang about their grandfather's notorious disloyalty to the Song Dynasty and suggested that Wang himself should have known better than to take an official job.

But as a matter of fact, although they were already related, they owed their particular friendship to it. Tao's family had been trying to make a complaint about a property taken from them and Wang had privately advised them, from his lowly position as a legal secretary passing the papers on to superiors, that the case was hopeless. Tao's family had not paid much attention to Wang's opinion, but he was eventually proved right and in the meantime he and Tao met in teahouses and restaurants and discussed more interesting subjects. Their political differences only added piquancy to their relationship.

"I'm really delighted that you've stopped collaborating with the Mongols," said Tao.

"I'm afraid I've decided it was a mistake."

"Of course it was."

"I mean stopping," said Wang. "I'm not rich enough to keep my wife in Quinsai and my cottage in the mountains and I'm not morally strong enough to be a hermit like you and live on nothing."

"So it's just as I always suspected, nothing but a question of money. You don't even pretend, like our grandfather Lord Meng, that although you're openly working for the barbarians you're also secretly working for the good of our own people?"

"The work I do as a lowly official is of no importance to anyone. Quite different from what Lord Meng did."

"But what good would high officials be if they had no lowly ones to work for them?"

"All right. Then suppose the Song Dynasty was restored. Would you come out of your isolation and accept office?"

"No one would ask me," Tao replied. "I am not qualified."

"Of course you are, in every sense that matters," Wang said. "You'd make a first-rate magistrate."

"They wouldn't ask me."

"But suppose they did! Suppose I or some other friend particularly recommended you!"

"You! What would your recommendation be worth? You worked for the Mongols."

"But in principle," Wang said, exasperated, "in principle, you, an educated and clever man, should surely work for a government you approved of?"

"I would be useless to them. I have taught myself to gather firewood and make repairs to my house, my clothes and my boots; to watch the weather and walk safely through the mountains; to catch fish and rabbits; to write verses. I have lost the knack of sociability, forgotten the correct ways of eating, dressing and conversing, lost touch with all the normal activities of daily life. My only human contact—except for rare visits from friends like you—is with the village."

This village was on the far side of the mountains, roughly the same distance from Tao's cottage as the monastery, but the opposite way of the track. The owner of the village and the land around it was a friend of Tao, who, in return for food and wine, candles and oil, taught the landowner's sons. Tao was not widely known as a poet, but he had some reputation in the province and the village landowner was proud to consider him his *protégé*.

The two friends did not argue much on the first day of Wang's recovery. He was content to sit contemplating the view and frequently dozing in his chair. Towards evening, when a few clouds had appeared far down in the west and the sun was turning red, he accepted a cup of wine and asked Tao if he would recite one or two of his new poems.

"Only one or two? There are fifty or sixty."

"As many as you like," Wang said. "I have come all this way to hear them. But as you know, I prefer to take poems slowly and to hear the same one many times, until it begins to spread in my mind like a picture."

"These are mostly simple verses," Tao said. "I am not sure they will spread very far."

They were love poems, all concerned with his own feelings as a lonely and, as he pretended, elderly and crippled man who was maddened by occasional glimpses of his beloved, but could never reveal what he felt except to his brush and paper.

"Is this invention?" Wang asked, after he had heard a dozen or so.

"What do you mean?"

"This girl the poet adores—is she a figment of your imagination or does she really exist?"

"I think she exists."

"You *think* so?"

"I've seen her. Is that proof of her existence?"

"I should have thought so, for a pragmatic person like yourself. But are you really in love with her or is this a purely poetic passion, an artistic device?"

Tao declined to answer this question, but asked Wang to hear all the poems first.

"Are they all on the same subject?"

"I'm afraid so."

When he had finished, his voice by now distinctly hoarse, he said almost inaudibly:

"Unforgivable! I've kept you sitting here in the evening chill for nearly two hours on the first day of your convalescence. Are you asleep? Certainly cold as a stone."

"No," said Wang. "Neither. Since you've only recited each poem once, my impression of them is still very superficial, but they are extraordinarily powerful and memorable. You've never composed anything so direct, certainly nothing better, and I congratulate you on falling in love."

It was quite dark now, without a moon, and the only light came from the stars, Wang's brazier and a small candle-lantern at Tao's side which had been brought out by his servant after sunset.

"I still have to revise them," he said. "But I wanted your opinion before going any further. I couldn't be sure if they had any real value. Their simplicity—the way they almost wrote themselves—alarmed me. I was afraid I might have lost my judgment completely."

"But the girl?" Wang asked. "Where does she live? You mention a village, but you don't name the village any more than the girl?"

"I am trying to forget the girl."

"You write sixty passionate poems about her and you are trying to forget her?"

"My aim was to get her on to the paper and out of my head."

"You haven't succeeded."

"Not yet. A hundred poems may do the trick."

"You're joking."

But he was serious. His isolation and his low opinion of himself as a physical man—poor, white-haired, walking in such a comical way—made him determined that he must not even approach the girl. He preferred to reject himself on her behalf from the outset rather than risk rejection.

Tucking his sheaf of poems under one arm, he rose and helped Wang out of his chair. As they went indoors the candle in the lantern began to gutter. Wang quoted—as accurately as he could recall—one of his friend's new quatrains:

*Never open your heart like a flower!*
*How long do spring flowers last?*
*The flame of love lights my page,*
*Until my candle burns out.*

Feeling much stronger when he woke next morning, Wang suggested that they might walk to what Tao called "the secluded valley." Wang was always amused by this description, implying that the valley containing Tao's home was not secluded. But for Tao this huddle of three thatched cottages was the equivalent of a city.

"Noise, noise, all day and night!" he said to Wang on one occasion.

"Noise? Do you mean the wind?"

"No, my books. So many voices shouting each other down, urging me to take them out and read them again, trying to attract my exclusive attention. Books pretend to love one another, but they're really seething with jealousy. Every book would like to be the only one that was saved from a library that went up in flames."

Tao had spent most of the money that had ever come his way on books and many of them he knew by heart. Wang could hear him chanting aloud as he dressed or washed or paced about his study or the veranda. It was a city of ghostly scholars he inhabited, whose ideas and voices went on living through his. He visited the secluded valley, he said, to get away from them.

"Is that possible?"

"Once in that valley I never allow myself to quote a single line that has ever been written down."

So, followed by Deng and Pei with food and wine, the two friends walked over a low ridge to the secluded valley. It was similar to the valley where Tao's home was, but more cut off. The small stream running down the middle suddenly dropped over an escarpment of rock in a long slender waterfall, so that the valley was invisible and virtually inaccessible from the track below. In the centre of the valley, beside the stream, was a group of tumbled rocks, with two twisted pines rooted amongst them. The trunk of one pine grew out horizontally before thrusting upwards diagonally and it was on this natural bench that Wang and Tao sat down, side by side. Their servants brought them wine and fruit. Wang congratulated his friend again on his poems and asked him for the exact wording of one or two he half remembered. But this went against Tao's strict rule of keeping the valley free from old poems.

"Even your own poems are forbidden?" said Wang.

"Certainly, if they already exist. But I'm allowed to think of new ones."

"Well, if we can't discuss the poems as such, can we talk about their subject?"

Tao was reluctant, but Wang pressed him and after the servants had brought them rice with small dried fish and several more cups of wine, the truth came out. It was more or less what Wang had already guessed. The village mentioned in the poems was the one where Tao had got this wine and food, the girl was the landowner's daughter. It was not simply a question of whether he could face the humiliation of being rejected by her. He did not want to change his mode of life. To give the girl the slightest indication of what he felt about her would instantly destroy it. If she returned his love, he could not continue to live in his hermitage but would have to make his home "down below" among other people; while, if she rejected him, he would have to move anyway, because he relied on the village where she lived—or at least her father who owned it—to support his isolation.

"But this is madness," said Wang.

"It seems to me the only rational solution."

"To try to turn reality into unreality?"

"Don't we spend a large part of our lives doing that? Painting pictures and writing poems. It's what we specialise in."

Wang drank off his cup of wine and held it out for Deng to refill from the flask.

"This is a pleasant wine," he said. "A bit rough, but just what one wants out of doors. Suppose, though, it was raw alcohol! When you compose one of your poems you make a good wine out of raw emotion. But every time you go down to the village and see the girl, you drink raw emotion. It's not good for you."

"It *is* painful," Tao said. "But you agree that it makes good poems."

"It may give you a hundred good poems, but then what? A thousand more? I don't believe you can keep it up. You'll kill yourself. Look at this stream! What a small, gentle thing! But if you dammed it up, you'd very soon flood the valley."

"What do you advise?"

"You must try to marry her. If that proves impossible, you will have to move."

"Move either way. No, I prefer not to bring it to a head."

"But you *have* brought it to a head. Or rather, fate, dropping the girl in your way, has done it for you."

After their meal they slid down from the tree-trunk and rested their backs against it. Wang fell asleep in the warm afternoon sun and when he woke saw Tao throwing twigs into the stream.

"Those that get stuck," he said, "urge me to go on as I am. Those that are carried down out of sight are in favour of change."

"And what's the verdict?"

"Only two have got stuck. Ten or twelve have gone down the stream."

"Well, then!"

"But since I disbelieve in all forms of divination, indeed strongly disapprove of them, I think I must go on as I am."

"How do you think you can outwit fate when you can't even deceive yourself?"

Why was Wang so keen to make Tao press on with the business? No doubt he wanted to see the girl for himself; and don't we all take pleasure in stirring our friends into action and seeing them break their habits?

Soon afterwards they returned over the ridge to Tao's home.

"How would it be," said Tao, "if in return for your interference in the affair of my hundred poems, I were to ask you for a drawing of my house?"

"I thought you'd rejected my interference. But as a matter of fact I intended to draw your house anyway."

"And as a matter of fact I intend to go down to the village in a day or two."

"And what then?" asked Wang.

"Collect a few things we need . . . We'll see. But if your drawing turns out badly, we'll take that as an omen and not go any further with my hundred poems business."

"So you *do* believe in omens?"

"This girl is turning me into a moron."

❀

The next day was as fine and warm as the one before and the friends spent much of it basking amongst a circle of smooth boulders a few hundred yards below the cottage. They had drunk heavily the night before and it needed only a few cups of wine with their midday picnic to expunge all their anxieties and exalt their spirits. There was no ban on existing poetry in this valley and Tao was only too happy to recite his sequence of love-poems again at Wang's request:

*Dreaming of immortality in a thatched cottage,*
*I saw myself float westward over the mountains.*
*Turning from the world, I waved goodbye to you*
*Oblivious below, and to myself hunched at this window.*

This last stanza continued to echo in Wang's mind as he lay back against a warm rock and contemplated the cottage with its empty window.

"Why don't I draw that?" he said. "The poet hunched at his window, absent but present."

"Is that possible?" asked Tao. "Words, after all, are full of ambiguities and can go in different directions at the same time, but lines on paper always seem to me more single-minded. Of course I'm not much good at drawing and couldn't aspire beyond the simplest, most literal notation."

"I do aspire beyond it," said Wang. "In any case, there is no such thing as literal notation. The eye of the beholder and the style he chooses give meaning to even the simplest description."

Deng was told to bring out a table, some sheets of paper and drawing materials. Pei brought more wine. Wang mixed his ink, using his new Xixin inkstone, and picked up the wolf's hair brush.

"A patriot's brush and stone for a patriot's house," he said.

"But what if the painter is accustomed to work for the Mongols and therefore is *not* a patriot?" said Tao.

"Then we have already introduced a complication and gone beyond simple description, even before a line is drawn."

Pei refilled Wang's cup and he drank it down in a single gulp and put the cup out of the way on the ground with exaggerated care. Then, raising his eyes to the scene in front of him, he took a sudden decision and turned his paper so that the long sides were horizontal.

Drunkenness, before it passes into incoherence, is a state of extreme preoccupation with the present moment. Wang began to draw as if he had never existed anywhere else but there in front of his friend's cottage, as if every mark were the thing itself: the hard rock of the mountains, the brushy thatch of the cottage, the dense, low patches of moss or the more dispersed, anarchic clumps of grass, the light spiky foliage and the scaly bark of pines, the friable, shapeless lumps of earth, the insistently geometrical structure of the cottage at the centre of his view.

Clouds had begun to move swiftly across the sky, so that the sun was often briefly veiled. Wang became aware with peculiar intensity of the wayward independence of colours. There were no striking local colours here, no reds, yellows, blues added by the hand of man, no berries, butterflies or other bright things contributed by nature, but the colours were those of restless light. Light rather than space was the medium through which he grasped this present moment. But he had no colours with him and it seemed all the more necessary to emphasise the density of everything, the palpable textures of this place over which his eyes crawled like insects, exploring every bump and cranny.

Having completed the cottage and its immediate surroundings, he drew the small bunched shape of the poet at his window, arms resting in a circle on the table in front of him, head bowed over them as if he were sleeping. Then he immediately turned his attention to the left-hand side of his motif, where the ground fell suddenly away into space. He underlined and defined the space with a frieze of mountain peaks, softening and fading them into the distance at the same time as he dropped them towards the lower edge of the paper. The narrow band of sky visible above the cottage on the right became on the left an empty infinity of air, calling the eye away over the jagged horizon of mountains. Yet the solid foreground on the right, the four-square cottage and small human figure in its window pulled the eye back and constantly reasserted sober reality over the dream of escape.

When Wang looked at the drawing later in a more sober state, he was pleased with it, but also a little surprised. It seemed to represent a kind of *riposte* to Ni's work. Was that why he had turned the paper, because all the drawings Ni had shown him were done in the vertical format? Wasn't this horizontal drawing of Wang's a dialogue between his own vision of congested reality and Ni's austere minimalism, and wasn't the human figure of the dreaming poet firmly at the centre so as to counter directly Ni's provocative remark that the world was empty of people?

But Tao saw it purely as an illustration of his own poem. He professed almost to be able to see the poet's imaginary self floating in the great sea of empty space on the left and he took the drawing away to write the stanza that had inspired it in the top left-hand corner. He also added an encomium: "*Wang Meng has made his friend's bare patch of hillside an enchanted place and his humble cottage the home of a mountain god.*" Wang gave him the drawing and asked whether they would now be visiting the village.

"Is your health up to it? It's only a shopping expedition."

"Is that all?"

"Naturally I would value your opinion . . ." said Tao.

"Even if it disagreed with yours?"

"How could it?"

"Well, you are so cut off, as you said, from the human world that you have probably lost all judgment of people. This girl you think worthy of a hundred poems may in reality be nothing but a milkmaid."

# 3. RED-SCARF BANDITS

Leaving at dawn, they descended the western side of the mountain and reached the village by midday. It was sited among the foothills in a well-wooded valley with good soil and, like many such isolated places which had to rely on their own protection during the troubled times before the Mongols' conquest, was surrounded by a high earth wall, fortified with ramparts. The travellers were surprised to find the gates closed and barred.

"What's going on?" said Tao to the lookout posted in the small tower above the gates. "Are you expecting a siege?"

"They're talking about it now," said the lookout, a surly teenaged boy.

"Talking about what?"

"Opening the gates. Or not."

"Perhaps we should take this as an omen," said Wang, now suddenly feeling that he might have pushed his friend into a dubious course of action.

"No, we can't go back now," said Tao.

The servants Pei and Deng, standing behind Wang and Tao on their mules, grunted approvingly. They did not think it reasonable to go all the way up the mountain again without rest and refreshment.

"Don't be a bloody idiot!" said Pei in his loud, disagreeable voice to the boy. "Give a shout and let somebody else come and open the gates!"

The boy did shout, not very wholeheartedly, but the result was amazing. Half the villagers seemed to be on the scene immediately, either behind the gates or peering over the walls. When they were satisfied that their visitor was Tao, the gates were unbarred and the travellers admitted, to be greeted almost at once by the landowner and his two sons hurrying down the street from the manor-house at the centre of the village. All three were carrying swords and the villagers too were armed, a few with swords or bows, but most with sticks or pitchforks. The gates were closed and barred again behind the visitors.

"Are you really expecting an attack?" asked Tao.

"We have not made up our minds yet," said the landowner. "But you and your friend have come at just the right moment to give us advice."

He led them into the main hall of his house, where chairs were drawn up and the village council had evidently been in conclave at the moment they arrived. Tao and Wang were given the seats of honour on their host's right, two more chairs were brought for the displaced councillors, all sat down again and wine was served with a few small things to eat.

The landowner was an old man, white-haired, his face weather-beaten and deeply lined, with a wispy white beard under the chin. His movements were stiff, but he still seemed tough and resolute.

"The matter is this," he said. "If the gates remain shut, we can probably expect an attack, but if we open them, a celebration."

His two sons looked upset and even angry. The younger stared at the floor and kicked spasmodically at the dust with his toe, while the elder muttered:

"I wouldn't call it that."

"My sons want us to keep the gates closed and defend the village to the last," said the landowner. "But I am for opening them and receiving our guests according to the word I gave them."

"I begin to guess who your guests might be," said Tao.

"I'm sure you do," said the landowner. Then, seeing that Wang was looking at Tao for an explanation, added, "They are some people who settled last year on top of an outcrop not many miles away, where there are large caves."

Tao explained further:

"The country north of here," he said, "becomes very rugged and desolate. And since the main road northwards and eastwards skirts the foot of the mountains at that point and is visible both ways from the outcrop, it's always been a prime spot for bandits."

"These are not altogether bad people," said the landowner, "but mainly those who have lost homes and livelihood elsewhere and gathered together for protection. It's true that they rob travellers, but they've always been scrupulous in their dealings with us and other villages in the neighbourhood. What they require, they pay for."

"With the money taken from the travellers," said Tao.

"No doubt," said the landowner. "Nevertheless, who are these travellers? Foreigners, mainly—Arabs, Persians, Indians and, of course, Mongols. Not many these days are our own people. And even when they are, one might wonder how they came to be rich enough to be worth robbing, since most of us are reduced to poverty by taxes. The leader of these people on the outcrop is a pleasant and courteous person, almost a gentleman."

"Almost!" muttered the elder son.

"Speak up! Say what you want to say!" said his father. "This is a free discussion and I will not impose my will on anybody, even my sons. If the consensus is not to open the gates, so be it!"

"You say he's almost a gentleman," said his son, who looked absurdly like the father except that he was black-haired, clean-shaven, slimmer and stronger. "What you're trying to say is that he's almost *not* a robber. But that's exactly what he is."

"Literally speaking, yes," said the landowner. "If the times were normal, my view might be different. But the alternative to opening the gates may be at best many deaths and at worst the total destruction of the village."

"I don't think so," said his son. "I think if we show a little courage, these people will go away without much trouble. They may frighten travellers caught on the open road, but they are not a very formidable gang. If the magistrate cared to send out a couple of hundred soldiers he could drive them out of their caves and kill or capture most of them in a week."

"And then what would happen to our sister?" said the younger son. He was hardly more than a boy, smaller and less imposing than either his father or his brother, fidgeting constantly with barely repressed energy and emotion.

"Your sister?" asked Tao.

"We have not explained properly," said the landowner. "We are still tangled up in our own disagreements. The matter is this. The leader of these people has made an offer—a perfectly straightforward and honourable offer, without any suggestion of threats or violence—to marry my daughter. You have seen her, I think, from time to time?"

"I have seen her," said Tao.

"She's a fine girl, I think you'd agree?"

"Yes," said Tao.

"And in normal times would receive offers of marriage from prosperous people for miles around. But the times are not normal and are certain to get worse. Of course I would never agree to marry my daughter to a robber, if that were all he were, but he has only taken to robbery because, as I happen to believe, he is primarily a patriot."

"Almost a gentleman and primarily a patriot!" said the elder son with bitter contempt. "They can write that on the placard over the cart when they take him to be executed."

The matter was this, as the landowner kept saying—the phrase perhaps chosen to try to reduce such a horrible dilemma to rational, practical terms—that the robber-bridegroom and his party were expected in an hour or two for the betrothal ceremony and that everyone, including the landowner himself, dreaded the prospect. But the walls of the village were not in good repair, none of the villagers was a trained fighter, nor had they in living memory any experience of defending themselves. For nearly a century they had enjoyed the luxury of peace and depended on the order imposed on the country by its conquerors, although they had never accepted the conquerors' legitimacy.

In these illogical circumstances it was perhaps logical enough that the old man should want to pretend that those who now threatened the peace were patriots rather than criminals, especially since, if he defied them, he might lose not only his daughter, but his whole family and establishment, everything he possessed, including his own life. But his sons, more naively, if more honestly, thought that the crumbling village walls and their own fresh strength and spirit were enough to defend their sister's honour and that even if they weren't, it was better to lose everything in the attempt. The other villagers took no direct part in the debate, though they would probably decide the issue in the end by voting one way or the other. But no one so much as considered calling in government help against the bandits. There was, therefore, Wang thought, something oddly theoretical about the whole discussion. It was not at all a question of whether the walls were strong enough or the robbers could be successfully resisted, but whether robbery directed against the foreign conquerors and those who benefited from their rule could be considered an honourable or at least not wholly dishonourable profession.

At last, when the argument had rumbled back and forth on this theme for some time, the landowner turned to Tao.

"Will you give us the benefit of your advice?"

"What does your daughter herself want?" asked Tao.

"She will do whatever we think best."

"Has she met the prospective bridegroom?" asked Tao, still sounding as if he had no personal interest in the affair at all.

"She has seen him, but not spoken to him."

"How does she feel about living in a cave?"

"Oh, it is not quite as primitive as that!" said the landowner. "They began by sheltering in the caves, but when they were joined by more and more refugees, many of them skilled and hard-working people, they built houses and defences. It is quite a large and even comfortable settlement by now."

"Doesn't that make it more likely that the soldiers will be sent out to capture it?" suggested Tao. "A few robbers in caves are one thing, but a fortified base must threaten the magistrate's authority over the whole district."

"His authority is already diminished," said the landowner. "The town-prison was actually broken into and several prisoners freed by another group of bandits last month. The magistrate is very short of troops, since he had to send part of his regular force to the north to help cope with disturbances there."

"Are there any other women in the settlement?" asked Tao.

"Certainly. There are whole families."

"Highly respectable, you see!" said the elder son. "It's just that they live by stopping people on the road and taking their goods and money."

"Couldn't it be argued," said Tao, "that those who robbed us of our country a hundred years ago have been living like that ever since?"

"Precisely!" said the landowner.

Tao turned to Wang.

"What do you think?"

Then, before Wang could speak, Tao explained to the assembled company:

"My cousin is not only descended, as I am, from the first Emperor of our former Dynasty, but worked for a time as a government lawyer under the present Dynasty."

Hearing this, the whole village council seemed to sigh and bow in a kind of collective deference, as if they felt Wang's word alone would now decide the matter. But Wang was annoyed with Tao, both for trying to make him arbiter of the fate of the girl Tao was in love with and for the irony covertly underlying the description of Wang's past. For what the villagers took as a simple statement of his value as an adviser was, of course, also a mocking allusion to his disloyalty and therefore to his *un*suitability as an adviser.

"I was only briefly a legal secretary," Wang said sharply, "and I cannot see how my family connections are relevant at all. But I do believe that if this gentleman has already given his word to the leader of these people, the betrothal should go ahead. Unless the promise was obtained under duress or the girl is unwilling."

"My word was conditional on her agreement," said the landowner.

"Then let her say yes or no!" Wang said. "And if she says no, it may be that you will not have to fight at all—not at least if the man is as near being a gentleman as you say."

Everyone murmured approval, though the sons still looked doubtful.

"Speak up!" said their father.

"She is not able to decide for herself," said the elder son. "If either of us asks her, she says no. But if you ask her, yes."

"You have a mother?" Wang asked. "Perhaps *she* could ask her?"

"Mother just bursts into tears and then so does my sister."

"Suppose," said Wang almost without thinking, "my cousin were to ask her?"

Tao looked at Wang with horror and he smiled back disarmingly, feeling that he had repaid Tao for his own sly shaft. Yet had he really meant to—any more, perhaps, than Tao had really meant to mock Wang? It is hard to recognise even our own motives on the wing and if we try to clarify them in retrospect we are probably swayed by other motives—self-defence, anger, shame, pride—rather than the simple wish to know. Of all the complexities of the ten thousand things, the self-consciousness of man is ten thousand times the most complex.

"No, I don't think that would help," said Tao. "She would not see me as neutral."

Was he about to declare his own interest in her and thereby throw the whole debate into further confusion?

"As the friend of her father," Tao said, "often employed to teach his sons, she could only see me as seeking compliance with her father's wishes. It would be much better if my distinguished friend—being both a highly qualified man of the world, as I am not, and a complete stranger to the whole family—should ask her."

"I would not dream of doing so alone," Wang said quickly.

"Perhaps you would *both* talk to her?" suggested the landowner, looking puzzled by their disagreement.

The meeting was adjourned and the two visitors were conducted into the inner reception room. Their host left them there and went to speak to his wife and daughter. Tao and Wang looked at one another challengingly, each blaming the other for what had turned into a kind of duel with concealed weapons.

"Why couldn't you speak to her alone?" Wang asked. "Surely that would have been better than forcing her to make this impossible decision in front of a complete stranger?"

"How could I speak to her alone," Tao said, "when her attitude to me has not been as neutral as I led you to believe."

"You've told her what you feel about her, then?"

"No, not in words. But I suppose that looks and glances can say almost as much."

"So you think she feels the same for you?"

"I don't know about that. I'm very ignorant of women, as you know. But I suppose that like us they enjoy being admired—without necessarily wanting anything further. I myself did not know that I wanted anything further, beyond fuel for my poems. But the poems themselves, especially when I read them aloud to you and got your reaction, crystallised and perhaps even developed my feelings. This unwelcome offer of marriage may perhaps have done the same for her."

"I'm sorry," Wang said. "I have behaved insensitively and unkindly. What do you want me to say—or not to say—to her?"

"Nothing particular. It's too late. What can we do now but ask her whether she genuinely wants to marry this bandit?"

"And if she doesn't, the village will certainly be destroyed."

"I think so too," Tao said. "Bandits, I suppose, take care to arm themselves properly and to practise using their weapons. Whereas these villagers are armed like children and have never attacked anything more savage than a bale of hay or a stray dog."

"It's a pity their unexpected visitors today were not a couple of sergeant-instructors instead of scholars."

"Just as well," said Tao. "Even if we could have beaten off the bandits today, we would only have postponed the reckoning."

"So are you saying that she must be persuaded to agree to the marriage—whatever her own feelings—and yours?"

Tao made no reply and at that moment the girl came into the room. Without looking directly at either of them, she stood with her head bowed. Tao turned away and walked behind Wang, urging him with a gentle nudge of the elbow to conduct the interview.

The girl was young—probably no more than seventeen—tall, graceful and, Wang thought, well aware of her power to attract men. He himself immediately felt that if he had had the least notion of how to fight he would have fought for her. Her brothers' view of the affair seemed now entirely reasonable: better to lose everything, including one's own life, than tamely hand her over to a ruffian.

"Your father has asked us . . ." Wang said.

"I know," she said, without raising her eyes.

"I do not think," Wang said, "that you have to consider the wishes of anyone but yourself. How could you, in any case, when your father wants one thing, your brothers another and the villagers do not seem able or willing to say what they want? It will not be your fault if the village has to fight these people. If you choose to marry their leader and offend your brothers, that will not be your fault either. The choice which fate has offered you looks heavy and difficult, but in reality, for you, it is light and easy. Do you want to exchange promises with this man or don't you?"

She raised her head and looked at him for the first time. Her dark brown eyes were large and lustrous, the whites slightly bloodshot—perhaps from weeping with her mother. Her face was strikingly handsome, though not conventionally beautiful: an active, intelligent face, longer than it was broad, with fine skin drawn tightly over the bones of cheek and jaw and a generously curved mouth. She was certainly no milkmaid.

"I have hardly seen the man," she said.

"No, but that is often so with betrothals. In this case what he looks like is perhaps less important than his circumstances."

"I do not want to marry *any* bandit," she said.

"No, I see. Then the matter is settled. There will be no betrothal."

She looked surprised.

"I didn't say that."

"But the man is certainly a bandit," Wang said. "No one disagrees about that, even if, as your father believes, his kind of robbery can be justified."

"I would not like to marry a bandit who was just a robber," she said.

"You mean that if he was primarily a patriot . . . ?"

"Yes."

Wang looked at Tao, but he refused to look back.

"So it's not a question of not knowing your own opinion, but of not knowing whether to believe your father or your brothers?"

"Yes."

The more Wang looked at her, the more attractive he found her. Her voice was low and deferential, but determined.

"May I ask you," Wang said, "whether, if this man had not appeared, you would have preferred somebody else?"

"I don't know what you mean."

"Somebody who was not a bandit at all, but perhaps a landowner like your father or even . . ." Wang laughed to suggest he was only joking, "a scholar and poet like my cousin Tao?"

A pause here.

"It would depend, wouldn't it?" she said.

"Depend on what?"

"What sort of person he was."

"But there's been no such person up to now?"

She was silent again. Out of the corner of his eye Wang could see that Tao was watching her closely. But she did not even glance at him and spoke quite casually:

"No, not really."

"What do you think about living in a bandit-lair?"

"A bandit-lair?" She smiled with the faintest trace of mockery in her tone. "I don't know. But they have good horses."

"Stolen, I suppose," said Tao.

"From the Mongols," she said. "I wouldn't mind stealing horses from Mongols. They always take the best horses and leave us the rest. I'd like to ride one of those horses stolen from the Mongols. A white one."

She stopped, seeing that they were both astonished.

"You noticed the bandits' horses then," said Wang, "even if you hardly noticed their leader?"

"I saw him in the distance. He was a good rider."

"Are you a good rider yourself?"

"Yes. Especially if I had a good horse."

Wang looked at Tao again. The girl of his poems had not been at all like this, but a purely passive creature, animated only by his one-way passion.

"I had no idea . . ." said Tao, bemused, speaking partly to Wang, partly to her. He was smiling, almost as though he was more relieved than put out to discover that the real girl and the girl of his poems were such separate beings.

"I have no more questions," Wang said, turning to Tao in case he wished to seize this last opportunity to compete with his glamorous rival.

"Tell me," Tao said to her, still smiling, taking one of his limping steps towards her as if to emphasise his own deficiencies, "if they give you a good horse, will you be robbing travellers yourself?"

She met his eyes and smiled, then immediately lowered her eyes and became demure again. Wang got the impression, he told Tao later, that if his friend had written less poems and spoken to her before the bandit made his appearance, his life might have been altogether different.

"No doubt," Tao replied on that later occasion. "But I would have to have been a different person. It's an illusion to think that a choice is open to us, unless we are open to that choice."

❀

The gates were duly unbarred. The villagers seemed happy enough and put away their inadequate weapons. The girl's brothers accepted her verdict glumly, but without complaint.

"If she wanted to marry a bandit," said the elder brother, "she could have done a lot better than that one."

"And if she just wanted a white horse," said the younger, "*we* could have stolen it for her."

Towards evening the bandit-chief and about thirty of his men rode up the valley and stopped on a little knoll a few hundred yards from the village, sending a messenger forward to see if they were still expected.

"They must have thought the gates *would* be closed against them," said Tao.

"But they must also have had hopes of a better outcome," Wang said, as the messenger returned to beckon them on and they all suddenly lit lanterns before cantering forward in the dusk.

Indeed, when they passed through the gate and slowed to a trot down the village street, they could be seen to have come in all their finery: new leather boots, belts studded with gold plaques, robes and trousers embroidered and brocaded, and, on their heads, red scarves to which fresh flowers had been attached.

"Their most recent victims must have been a haberdasher, a bootmaker and a florist," said Tao.

But they were well armed too, with swords and axes, bows and crossbows, pikes and daggers, though some of them also carried musical instruments slung across their backs. Their leader, thickly bearded in the old military style of the Song Dynasty and dressed all in blood-red edged in gold, with a gold silk belt, high-heeled boots and the red scarf they all wore, had a flower stuck behind his ear and sat his dappled grey horse like a true hero from romance. But when he jumped down at the entrance to the courtyard in front of the manor house, where the landowner, flanked by his two sons, was waiting for him, he looked less impressive. His legs were short and bandy and his face—what could be seen of it through the beard—was narrow and thin-lipped, with small close-set eyes and a wary expression. He looked, Wang whispered to Tao, more like an ex-court messenger or prison-warder than a gentleman.

Tables were laid out in the courtyard as well as inside the hall and coloured lanterns were hung in the trees and from poles. The visitors mingled easily with the villagers and as the wine flowed, some of the latter began to sport the former's red scarves. Evidently the girl's decision had also resolved the knotty problem of whether these men were to be regarded as bandits or patriots. The red scarf had symbolised violence with a political agenda—violence justified by oppression—since long before the Mongols' conquest. There was no shortage of food or drink, while the bandits and villagers took it in turns to sing and play exuberant music. As Tao said, both parties had been equally prepared for siege or celebration.

Tao himself seemed jovial and relaxed, but every so often an expression of distaste crossed his face as the coarse voice of the bandit-chief—sitting on the landowner's right—proposed another toast to friendship, love, the mountains and rivers, the north, the south, good people everywhere . . .

"He ought to toast the roads and rich travellers," said Tao.

The people in the courtyard were now beginning to shout and fall about and even the superior people in the hall were losing their dignity.

The landowner led his daughter discreetly away into the inner part of the house.

❁

Returning the next day up the track towards Tao's house, Wang asked him if he thought the marriage would really happen.

"I have my doubts," he said. "No date has been fixed. I wonder if the old man is not counting on fate to annul the betrothal."

"Meaning?"

"That is a very small-time robber, I should say. If he is not caught and sliced up by the authorities, he will probably be driven out by a bigger bandit or murdered by some of his own gang."

"The girl is certainly much too good for him," Wang said.

"Yes, as her brothers, who knew her much better than I did, recognised."

"Will you finish your hundred poems?"

He shrugged, still following his previous thought.

"But perhaps she *will* marry him. It wasn't just the horse, it was what it symbolised. She liked the idea of being a bandit herself, didn't she?"

# 4. A GARDEN OF FORKING PATHS

I am enjoying this attempt to see myself from outside as another person and indeed I am almost another person now that I have been a prisoner for so many months. The Wang that went freely wherever he cared to is only a memory now and my cell begins almost to seem part of myself, an almost private place (except for the jailer and regular visits from my friends), where one is never disturbed except at set times and then only for the body's minimal requirements—food twice a day, and washing myself and emptying my bucket once a day. It is how a monk lives, how the Emperor might have lived if he had not become Emperor. What a strange irony!

❁

Wang was living in Quinsai again, serving as a prosecutor in the northern sub-prefect's court, when he received an unexpected invitation. Brought to Wang's house by special messenger, this invitation much excited his wife, who thought that since it came from a high official in the Branch Secretariat it must promise promotion. Bunjan Chöl was President of the Board of Observances, in charge of cultural, religious and social affairs for the whole Yangzi River region. He came originally from a distant part of Central Asia conquered by the Mongols in the time of Khan Jinghis and had a reputation for being able and cultivated.

These foreigners imported by the Mongols as administrators were often very well-educated and sometimes admired our civilisation so much that they came to believe they alone were capable of appreciating it properly, seeing us as a crushed people who had lost the energy of our ancestors and were unworthy of our inheritance.

Chöl loved our poetry and theatre and was a keen collector of paintings and antiques, jade and porcelain, but his taste was not always as good as he thought. Many of his friends were Asian commercial people with conventional or frankly vulgar tastes, while more discriminating native friends who might have improved his understanding were unwilling—out of politeness or deference to his important position—to correct him. So, since he was never contradicted, he had come to believe that his judgment was impeccable.

But why should a grandee like Chöl extend an invitation to such a humble official as Wang, whom he had not even heard of? It was because Chöl had recently been introduced to an artist known as Old Huang—revered by all those who knew his work, then or afterwards, as a great master—and wished to celebrate the completion of Huang's latest and probably last work by displaying it to a select group of connoisseurs. Huang had been permitted to invite a few friends of his own and Wang was one of them.

When he explained to his wife that he was only going to see a friend's painting and that she must not expect him to return with even a single grade of promotion, her excitement turned to anger. Other people, she said, would be able to take advantage of such an opportunity and if he failed to secure at least a sub-prefecture, he might as well go back to his shack under the Yellow Crane Mountain. Wang often longed to do so, but he had run through his savings and, with prices rising alarmingly due to the Mongols' latest issue of devalued paper currency, it was impossible to keep himself and his wife, their servants and their town-house without a regular income. He understood very well that from his wife's point of view their life was altogether too modest and cramped, but he also knew that he could never give his whole heart or even half of it to promotion. It was a great pity, he thought, that women of her class, unless they were artists or matriarchs like his grandmother—who was both—had so little scope for their own powerful energies that they were reduced to terrorising their servants, playing backgammon with each other and savaging their husbands.

The house occupied by the President of the Board of Observances was in the hill district called Ten Thousand Pines, on the south side of the city, not far from the old Imperial Palace of the Song Dynasty. This district had escaped the serious fires that had twice devastated Quinsai during the previous decade and the villas and gardens here were still as luxurious and beautiful as they had been under the Song. Set amongst tall trees and behind high walls, they were mostly invisible from the road and from each other, but one could catch glimpses of them in the distance from the lake, towards which their best rooms and terraces faced. They had always belonged to high officials and it must be admitted that, even if the present owners were mostly alien, at least they cared for and preserved what was not rightfully theirs.

Once admitted through the outer gate, Wang found himself in a broad straight avenue flanked by plum trees with deep crimson leaves and lanterns painted rust-red and gold, hanging from thin black posts. However, the sun being still high over the lake, the lanterns were not yet lit. The avenue led directly to a short flight of steps in front of the open front door, where the host awaited his guests and, considering the difference in their status, greeted Wang with admirable courtesy. Bunjan Chöl had taken the trouble to find out Wang's relationship to Lord Meng Zhao and, although it was only on the female side, was clearly glad of any excuse to feel honoured by this undistinguished guest's arrival.

"I have a little drawing by your grandfather," he said. "Bamboos and rocks, very small and unassuming, but graceful. Nothing from your grandfather's hand can be considered wholly insignificant."

Chöl wore an orchid in his cap, was expensively scented and spoke with a strong Turkic accent. He was short and bulky, with a face so smooth and cared for that he could almost have been a eunuch. But he was well known to be very fond of actresses, preferring those that were intelligent and well read as well as beautiful.

Servants led Wang into the main reception room, where he found the eighty-two-year-old guest of honour seated, with a young pupil of about twenty, Chen, who had escorted him here, standing nearby. Also present were a bearded Bokharan merchant—a fellow-countryman of Chöl's—and Huang's two closest friends, an elderly painter and a Daoist abbot. Servants brought round cups of wine and a few small titbits to eat. The room was large and full of light, with a terrace in front and a magnificent view of the lake and the mountains encircling it on the far side. Several paintings hung on the walls, a large antique bronze pot stood in one corner and on a small black lacquer table were a cream-coloured porcelain vase and a white stoneware bowl with an olive-tinted glaze, both from the Tang period. Behind Huang's chair was a yellowish screen painted with bamboos and cranes, while at one end of a long and otherwise empty table in front of him lay a long sandalwood box. Rolled up inside it was the painting whose completion they had come to celebrate.

"Is our host proposing to buy it?" asked Wang.

"He would like to," said Huang, "but unfortunately I've already inscribed it to my friend over there."

He indicated the abbot.

"Unfortunately?" said Wang.

"Master Huang can barely afford to eat," said his pupil Chen, "so it might have been better if he'd taken some money for the painting."

"I did not mean unfortunately for myself," said Huang, "but for our host. The fact is that I was so pleased to finish after three years tinkering, that I thought I would get it off my hands at once before I was tempted to make any more alterations. Besides, the abbot was very kind and hospitable to me. Besides, what does a man as old as I am want with money?"

"You could repair the leaks in your roof and the gaps in your walls," said Chen.

"They don't bother me," said Huang.

"But they must be bad for your health."

"I feel very well. Perhaps they are good for my health."

Certainly, with his bright eyes and still well-fleshed, well-coloured face, Huang looked healthy, though he suffered from severe pains in his joints which he might have avoided by living in a warmer, drier place.

The party was joined now by their host with the two remaining guests, both important officials recently arrived from the capital. When introductions had been made and more food and wine brought, Chöl began to show off some of his treasures—as appetisers, he said, for the great feast that awaited them when Living in the Mountains of Pure Happiness was unrolled. In a second reception room as large as the first, with a more south facing but equally magnificent view, Wang was shown his grandfather's small drawing and found himself discussing it with one of the officials from the capital. He was an elderly but still handsome and robust military administrator who, as a young member of the Imperial Bodyguard, had met Lord Meng.

"I particularly remember his smile," said the General. "It must have been only a year or two before his death, but he seemed so young and optimistic, as if his life was only just beginning. This drawing has the same freshness and cheerfulness, don't you think?"

Wang was not used to military men who had opinions about pictures and replied vaguely that he thought it was a quality one could find in all his grandfather's work.

"That may be so. But do you think such an attitude would be possible today, even in a man as energetic and gifted as your grandfather?"

"You mean that the times have changed?" suggested Wang cautiously.

"Don't you think so?"

"I'm sure they have, but . . ."

"But . . . ?" pursued the General.

"I was going to say that they have probably changed less here than in other places where one hears there have been . . . disturbances."

Wang was not at all happy with the political turn to this conversation and tried to divert his companion's attention to a pair of large porcelain vases, lavishly decorated in the new technique of underglaze blue with scenes of lovers in a garden from a famous play. On one of them, the lovers were shyly meeting in secret for the first time; on the other, the scholar-hero was addressing a mournful farewell to his beloved before leaving for the capital. There he would sit the examinations, take the top place and be rewarded with spectacular promotion before returning to claim her in marriage. How different, Wang thought, from his own home life!

"They were probably made in the factory just down the road, at the bottom of Phoenix Hill," he said to his companion, forbearing to add that he thought them over-decorated and obviously designed to appeal to the flashy taste of foreigners.

The General gave them hardly a glance.

"Don't be afraid to say what you think!" he said, taking Wang by the arm and leading him out on to the terrace, where the other guests were already admiring the view and identifying the various monasteries that could be seen nestling amongst the hills across the lake. "I'm anxious to know where people like you stand. People, I mean, of good birth and education who have found it possible to be loyal to this Dynasty. How would you react if the disturbances spread? Where do you think your interests lie?"

"All our interests lie in stability," said Wang. "But what does it matter? We are not allowed weapons and have had no training with them. We could neither take part in disturbances nor help to suppress them."

"I understand that. But suppose weapons and training were to be made available to you! On whose behalf would you and others of your class be likely to use them?"

"I doubt if we would join the bandits," said Wang. "And those of us who have shown our loyalty to this Dynasty by working for it would probably think it wrong to switch allegiance."

"Probably?"

"It is a disputed point whether the same loyalty is owed to a foreign Dynasty as to a native one."

"And your own view?"

"What was good enough for my grandfather should be good enough for me."

The General laughed.

"Your grandfather was indeed famously loyal to this Dynasty."

He paused as if about to point out that Lord Meng was also a notorious example of *dis*loyalty to a former Dynasty, then went on quickly:

"In any case, I suppose your value as a supporter of the government depends on your standing with the people in general."

"Of course."

"Do they trust your judgment? Would they follow your lead?"

"It's hard to say. Our 'standing,' as you call it, has been eroded. We have been and still are treated as underlings by the government and to that extent the people have ceased to respect us."

Wang immediately regretted the note of bitterness that had come into his words and his voice. He preferred always to speak as if his rank were what it should have been, rather than reveal that he felt humiliated. The General merely grunted and turned away, losing interest in someone who did not even claim to be respected.

The other guests had now left the terrace and were descending the steps to the garden, where more servants attended them with cups of wine. Chöl was waiting for Wang and his companion and accompanied them down the steps. He spoke to the General:

"Did you see anything of the great river project as you came south?"

"Certainly. Sections of the Canal are still being dredged. We had to travel overland for some distance. But the project is on schedule.

The new dikes were already visible and the work goes on without stopping from dawn to dusk. The whole valley is a city of tents and temporary shelters."

"Dangerous," said Chöl.

"I don't think so. The engineer knows exactly what he is doing. The river will not find it easy to misbehave again, not for many generations."

"I was not thinking of the river but the workmen."

"They too are under strict control."

"We have heard otherwise. That agitators are stirring up disaffection and the soldiers are failing to contain the unrest."

"That is exaggerated. There are certainly criminal elements in the work force, but we saw no signs of serious unrest. The officials we spoke to were confident of maintaining discipline and completing the project."

The General sounded annoyed. It was clear to Wang that the disagreement between him and Chöl went beyond the river project, which was itself only one aspect of the government's new policy of centralisation. Chöl no doubt owed his appointment to the previous Chancellor, who had favoured regionalisation, while the General was probably a supporter of the new Chancellor, Toghto.

This Toghto was a man of exceptional vigour even by Mongol standards. Seeing the Empire falling into decay and confusion, he was impatient of partial solutions patched up by people with limited local powers. It was he who had initiated the ambitious attempt to confine the Yellow River to its new course, treating a mighty force of nature with the same resolute authority as he treated his rivals and critics in the government. His principal aim was to improve conditions for the millions of peasants affected by drought and disease and do away with the causes of revolt. At the same time, by dredging and repairing the Grand Canal, he would reopen the Empire's main passage of communication between north and south. Then, even if the peasants remained obstreperous, it would be easy to overcome any resistance with swift and overwhelming military force. But, as so often with such audacious remedies, there were other consequences which Toghto did not take account of, or chose to ignore. The enormous cost of controlling the river would lead to further devaluation of the currency and worse hardship for the poor, while the temporary recruitment of so many myriads of strong men with nothing to lose was only storing up manpower for the Dynasty's enemies.

Chöl's garden was a landscape in miniature. Ponds of various shapes and sizes simulated lakes, small streams seemed rivers and heaps of rugged stones, set about with dwarf trees, resembled mountains. The ground was uneven, piled into hills or scooped out into valleys, traversed by forking paths which now and again crossed the streams or led across a pond to an island over little arched bridges with scarlet rails. The guests, as they followed the meanderings of the paths or stood on the bridges staring down at gold and silver fish gliding among lotus plants, looked weirdly out of scale, like giants at large in a human world. Wang stopped to contemplate an island, on which, nestling among dwarf pines, was a miniature pagoda faced in blue tiles, aping the real pagoda not far away on Thunder Point, at the southern end of Quinsai's real lake.

He decided that he did not much like this garden, any more than he had liked the two vases decorated with theatrical scenes. You could not but admire the skill and ingenuity which had created them. But by their very nature, as purely mimetic, closed worlds, they denied you any share in the act of their creation. This, he considered, was the crucial difference from a master's painting, where you stepped instantly, as through an open window frame, into the still vital feelings of the creator for his creation, just as if he had invited you into the very house of his spirit.

Wang was impatient to go inside and see what he was sure, from repute and his own knowledge of Old Huang, must be something extraordinary. But the other guests were still ambling about, exclaiming at new surprises, wasting the precious daylight. Wang looked anxiously at the sun, trying to calculate whether they had as much as two hours left. He began to feel trapped and irritable and to blame his host's vanity and lack of taste for detaining them with a mere curiosity. Not that the garden had been created by Chöl, who had probably only spent money and time on resuscitating and improving it. Such gardens were not uncommon during the former Dynasty and owed nothing to foreigners, but foreigners always particularly liked them. It seemed to Wang at this moment that the garden was not simply a charming little replica of their native landscape, but a stark image of its alien possession, as the conquerors' functionaries strolled with amused arrogance amongst these shrunken rivers and mountains and cast gigantic shadows over them. Then he smiled at his own hypocrisy. He was one of their functionaries too and had more or less told the General that he would remain loyal whatever happened. Was that true? He regretted that it probably was.

The guests had now all coalesced into a single group and were moving slowly back towards the house, following their host, who was walking beside Old Huang with his stick. Wang hastened to join them and found himself next to the second official from the capital, a Yugur from the much-feared Inspectorate Department. He was a generation or more younger than the General, but probably no less important and he did not look youthful since his face had been badly damaged by a blow or an accident and was puckered up on one side around a sightless eye. He was elegantly dressed in the finest purple silk and to emulate the flower in his host's cap he had stuck a willow-leaf in his own.

"Outstanding garden!" he said to Wang. "Do you know anything about this old fellow who's done the painting? Seen one of these landscape paintings, seen them all, in my opinion."

Wang could think of nothing to say to that, but the next moment Huang stopped and they all halted around him in front of a dark-brown "mountain crag" down which ran a long thin pipe of water as if it were a hundred-foot waterfall. On top of the crag, basking in a patch of sunlight, was a large butterfly, cinnamon-coloured, with orange and black speckles.

"Wonderful!" said the Yugur. "You even have eagles perching on your mountains."

Everyone laughed politely.

"Remind me, Abbot," said Chöl, "of that Daoist saying about the butterfly!"

"You're thinking of Master Juang's dream?"

"Surely."

"And that when he woke up he asked, 'Am I Jo Juang who dreamed I was a butterfly or am I a butterfly dreaming I am Jo Juang?'"

"Perfect! And isn't that the essence of Daoism?"

"Certainly a helpful image," said the abbot guardedly.

"I don't find it so," said Old Huang. "To me it suggests the weakness of Daoism. Not so much of Daoism itself as of those who make use of it to excuse their own weakness. During my long life I have been an official—a very lowly and unsuccessful one by comparison with the present company—and I have also taught the rudiments of Buddhism, Daoism and Confucianism in my School of the Three Doctrines in Pingjiang. All of which has given me ample opportunity to observe in myself as well as in my pupils a strong desire to escape reality. But I now believe that the true purpose of every religion and every philosophy should be to confront reality rather than encourage people to avoid it. This saying of Master Juang's proposes the opposite. Conjuring up a poetic simile, Juang entices us away into a world of fantasy, a world in which nothing has any more weight than a butterfly. We are permitted to behave, he insinuates, and to evaluate behaviour just as we please. We do not have to decide between right and wrong, between truth and falsehood, because, according to this foolish saying, nobody can tell the difference between dream and reality."

"Then you are against all religions that speak of another world?" asked Chöl.

"No, he is not," said the abbot, when Huang made no reply. "He is a truly religious man. It is just that he is against—if he will allow me to speak for him—any interpretation of religion which makes light of the reality of this world while we are part of it."

The abbot, Wang thought, was trying to claim Huang for Daoism, while excluding its rival Buddhism. But Huang himself, having said as much as he wanted to, remained silent, staring at the butterfly, which was slowly raising and lowering its wings as if to applaud his wisdom and assert its own reality.

"But you are a painter," said the Yugur official. "Are paintings not fantasies just as much as dreams?"

Huang seemed not to hear. His old friend Zao answered for him.

"Of course they are fantasies, but they don't pretend otherwise. When we draw a mountain we don't expect you to take it for the original and be uncertain which is real and which is fantasy."

"Master Huang is not really talking about fantasy and reality at all," said young Chen. "Everybody can tell the difference between them. He's just saying that morality, the distinction between right and wrong, belongs to reality and cannot be evaded. It's really very simple."

Chen was gesturing and jumping about so much that he alarmed the butterfly, which suddenly flew away.

"That butterfly is a sensible creature," said the Yugur, "not at all concerned with morality."

"Oh, but it is," said Chen. "Its morality is built into it. It can only behave in the right way for a butterfly. Unlike us, it meets no forking paths."

"Old Huang should have left that child at home or taught him not to push himself forward so much," muttered the Yugur to Wang, loud enough to be heard by everyone.

"Perhaps Old Huang should have left himself at home," said Huang quietly, touching Chen's arm to stop him making any retort of his own.

"Let us go in now!" said Chöl and led them towards the house.

❁

But even when they were all gathered in the room where Huang's painting lay rolled in its sandalwood box on the table, they still had to wait while the servants brought more food and wine. Wang examined the paintings hung on the walls, but none was of much consequence. The best was a landscape by Mo Sheng, a pretty, sweetly-coloured fantasy. Its trees and hills were so toy-like and artificial that it could have been worked up from a sketch made in Chöl's garden. Behind Wang, as he stared with increasing dissatisfaction at this painting, he heard the Bokharan merchant complaining loudly to the General about his trading difficulties.

"How am I to price my goods when they may take a month to arrive and the value of money falls every week? Worse than that, the goods will probably never arrive at all. This coast is infested with pirates. You can't send things overland because the Canal is blocked and you can't put them on a ship because it will be boarded and ransacked. I don't know how things are in the North, but down here we're all being ruined."

"The Canal should be operating again early next year," said the General. "I can also assure you that as soon as he has tamed this disorderly river, the Chancellor will turn his fiercest attention to human disorder, by sea and land."

"Too late for me," said the merchant. "I'd do better to fix up a deal with the pirates."

The General, who was a Mongol, suddenly lost his temper.

"You people have reaped such profits over so many years," he said, "that you've forgotten to whom you owe them. Who brought you here in the first place, who gave you special privileges and sank precious government money into your selfish enterprises? How did you come to be so stinking rich? You'd like to fix up a deal with pirates? I should think you'd understand each other bloody well!"

Wang took another drink from a servant and glanced over his shoulder. The General, his face red and eyes bulging, was standing right up against the merchant and looked as if he meant to bite off his nose or at least push him out of the room. Thoroughly intimidated, the merchant stepped back and made gestures of regret. At that moment Chöl clapped his hands.

"Master Huang's masterpiece!" he said; and very reverently, with practised care, lifted the painting from its box and placed it on the table ready to be unrolled.

As he did so, summoned no doubt by the hand-clap, five girls with musical instruments entered the room and, passing between the red-faced General and the white-faced merchant, went to stand in an arched alcove. Then, as Chöl unrolled the outer brocade flap, laid it under the box to hold it flat, and came to the title sheet with its bold and beautiful characters announcing *Living in the Mountains of Pure Happiness*, the girls began to play a popular tune on lute and guitar, accompanied by clappers and drums. Wang looked with horror at Old Huang, where he sat in his original chair some way back from the table, facing Chöl. Had he known that this had been planned? Could he conceivably approve? Music before or afterwards, by all means! But a musical accompaniment to the viewing of his work, as if it were an entertainment in a theatre? There was a faint movement on Huang's face, but it was more like a smile than a grimace and as Chöl looked up at him from behind the table with an anxious expression, it became distinctly a smile. Huang had evidently not known what was prepared, but he did not mean to spoil the occasion for someone, however barbarous, who had only tried to do him all possible honour.

As the singer launched into an old ballad about an immortal bringing gifts to a princess, Chöl unrolled the first five feet or so of Huang's painting and carefully laid a heavy stave of carved ivory against the still rolled part to hold it back. Then he rose and invited his most important guests—the two officials from the capital and the merchant—to occupy the three seats behind the table, while Wang, Chen and Huang's elderly painter friend were ushered in to stand behind the chairs. Chöl stood at one end of the table, the abbot at the other. They already knew the painting from beginning to end of its eighteen-foot length.

All the viewers gasped and exclaimed as they saw what lay in front of them. Even the one-eyed Yugur seemed impressed.

"Now that *is* a landscape," he said.

"Without a doubt it confronts reality," said the General, smiling genially at Old Huang.

Wang felt congestion in his chest and his eyes filled with tears. He had seen many fine paintings, many that moved him to admiration and love, but none to compare with this. It was alive with detail: islands, houses, individual rocks, reeds, many varieties of trees and a few tiny human figures crossing a bridge, carrying firewood through a copse, fishing from the back of a boat. But these wonderfully characterised small things could not stop your eye sweeping up and down and along the enormous panorama of land and water. All the details were absorbed into the complex rhythms of mass and space, the heavy folds and swelling sides of the foreground hills pressing inward or outward against the slower march of the mountains behind, your gaze passing over and into them as if it were the eye of an eagle in flight. The abbot was right: Old Huang was truly religious. Viewing his painting, one became, with the artist, a Daoist visionary making the "Journey into the Distance," travelling through and out of oneself as the imagination soared past this landscape of pure happiness.

Huang had used wet brushes and then dry. The ink was sometimes so diluted as to be little more than a grey stain, sometimes thick and black. The brush strokes were relaxed and even rough, altered and added to—as Huang had said—with cheerful disregard for professional perfection, but conveying his exuberant delight in the medium itself and what it could conjure up: scratchy textures and bald slopes or dense covers of foliage and deep fissures; always finding the specific nature of the motif but never losing the harmonious flow of the whole. There were changes and improvisations, but no fudged or wasted space. The landscape seemed to heave and settle, to contort itself into tight, irregular coils or slowly and majestically open out and expand. It was as if the ten thousand things were recreating themselves in dabs and patches of ink before your eyes.

Wang felt enormous pride, not only in the old man who sat so calmly facing him, but also in what he represented, the thousand-year tradition whose latest master he had become. Wang was almost grateful now for the annoyances that had preceded the viewing—he even forgave the brash musical accompaniment. What had they done but increase his sense of the strength and purpose of a work which so easily erased all taint of the second-rate? How could he be irritated by a toy garden, a toy vase, a toy painting, when the world also contained this? What did it matter if the Mongols thought they owned the rivers and mountains, when Old Huang truly possessed them and gave them back in this coded, spiritual form to their real owners?

"Another section?" asked Chöl at last, looking at Huang for permission.

Huang smiled.

"I'm afraid it's too long a journey," he said. "But perhaps another mile or two would not exhaust your guests."

The next section was unrolled to further murmurs of delight, but Huang refused the unanimous demand for a third.

"All journeys are better ended when you still feel the energy to go on," he said.

"But are we not to see the rest at all?" asked the Yugur.

"It is just more mountains," said Huang. "more trees, more river—a lot more river—and two or three more fishermen. You can easily imagine the rest."

"I daresay I can," said the Yugur, "but if one goes to a play one likes to see the whole performance."

"Quite true!" said young Chen contemptuously. "If one goes to a play."

The Yugur stirred angrily in his seat and was about to reply, when the General broke in abruptly.

"Let it go!" he said. "It's not their custom to show the whole thing at one sitting, even when it's a damned sight shorter than this one. Odd, perhaps, but part of the ritual."

The girls had come to the end of a song just as he said this and there was an awkward silence. The General's words had finally disrupted the remote reality of Huang's painting and replaced it with the immediate reality of where and who they were. The Mongol, the Yugur and the rich Bokharan stood up from their seats and moved round the table to join their host in congratulating the capricious old artist. His own countrymen stood deferentially aside for them and the singing-girls struck up a lively tune.

❀

When Wang returned after nightfall to his house, he was astonished to find his friend Tao there. They had not seen each other since Wang's visit to Tao's cottage in the mountains at least seven years before.

"I wrote to warn you," said Tao, "but your wife says you never received my letter."

Wang's wife had forgotten her anger over his wasted opportunity for promotion in her sympathy with Tao. She explained that he had been forced to leave his home because the village on which he depended had been destroyed.

"By the bandits?" asked Wang. "Did the landowner refuse, after all, to let his daughter marry that robber?"

"On the contrary," said Tao. "It was because they *were* married that the village was destroyed. The magistrate accused the village of giving support to the bandits and sent soldiers to arrest the landowner. The villagers barred their gates and tried to defend their walls, the bandits came to their aid, but the soldiers were too many and too well armed. The landowner, his two sons and his son-in-law, the robber-chief, were all killed and the whole place set alight."

"And the daughter?"

"I don't know. When I went down there some days later and discovered what had happened, there were only a few villagers still about, trying to salvage what they could and rebuild their homes. Most had gone to other villages where they had relatives. The ones that remained were still shocked and not very articulate. They thought the girl had escaped—at any rate no one had seen her body."

"Perhaps she was captured?"

"One of the villagers said that since she was the only one of her family left alive she had no doubt ridden away as so as to be able to take revenge. That might have been wishful thinking."

"Let's hope she had her white horse and was as good a rider as she claimed," said Wang.

He tried not to think of what would have been done to her if she had been captured, but he also knew very well that if he had been the magistrate of that town, even more nervous of his superiors than of the bandits, he could not have done otherwise than have her savagely beaten and beheaded.

Tao himself had packed up his possessions and walked with his servant Pei to Wang's retreat under the Yellow Crane Mountain. Wang's servant Deng received them there and directed them on to Quinsai.

"I filled your study with my books, I'm afraid," said Tao, "and your excellent Deng promised to take care of them. I shall have to go home to my father, near Pingjiang. He'll be pleased to see me, but he's old and poor and can't provide for me. I shall try to find work as a teacher. My father told me I was a fool to go and live in the mountains. Now he'll be able to tell me so every day."

"You can stay here as long as you like," said Wang. "Or if you prefer, you can be reunited with your library in my house under the Yellow Crane Mountain. I seldom go there these days."

"Nothing I would like better," said Tao. "But those dead authors have no needs, except protection against damp and insects. What would I live on?"

"Well, you must stay here," said Wang's wife.

Tao enjoyed the unfamiliar sights of the city for a week or two. During the first part of the day he walked about the streets, beside the canals and through the parks by himself. He had tried going out with Pei, but his servant was so irritated by the dense crowds and became so easily involved in altercations with passers-by that Tao was afraid he would end up fighting and being arrested. In the late afternoon and evening, after Wang had finished work at the sub-prefecture, he and Tao would meet and talk together in a tea-house or visit Wang's friends.

At the house where Old Huang was still staying before going back to his draughty cottage in the southern mountains, they were able to pore over Huang's painting and see the second half that had not been shown to Chöl's guests. This part was emptier and more austere than the first part. The mountains behind became lower, the river widened, the foreground opened and flattened into a bank of rock, almost treeless. Finally, the ground at the front heaved up into a great cone of rock, the land ended, the river predominated and the distant mountains narrowed and pointed into vacancy, as if the earth one stood on, the water and the horizon were all swallowed up together by featureless, timeless space. Huang, who could be so silent and withdrawn and was reputed to sit alone for days at a time staring at the same cliff-face or the same eddy in a river, would also sometimes talk volubly about how he painted and how the masters he admired had worked. Tao became fascinated by what he said and asked if he might take notes.

"No need to give yourself that trouble," said Huang. "I'm only repeating what has already been written down."

"By whom?" asked Tao.

"By me. My cottage and my friend the abbot's rooms in his monastery are full of my notes on these subjects and I'm too old now to say anything new."

"You should make them into a book and publish it."

"Perhaps. But it would need a lot of work and I think I'm finally tired of working."

"After finishing this painting, that's not surprising."

"No, that wasn't work. Work entails effort and anxiety. But I didn't tire myself over this and I never let it worry me. I just went to it when I felt like it, filled it in as I pleased, left it and came back to it. It was more like copying what was already there or answering questions asked by someone else."

The eventual outcome of this conversation was that Tao did not go back to living with his father and enduring his reproaches. Instead, he accompanied Old Huang to the Daoist monastery where most of his notes were kept and made a book out of them, which later became very influential.

"Did fate destroy that village," he asked Wang long afterwards, "and kill my good friend the landowner and his two sons only so that I should preserve the thoughts of Old Huang, which might otherwise have been lost?"

"Nothing about the workings of fate surprises me," replied Wang, "when I think of that piece of paper given me by the peddler, which I meant to throw away but passed on instead to a novice at your local monastery who could not read."

But this conversation happened many years in the future and we only mention it now because we shall have no more to say of Old Huang, who died three or four years after completing his eighteen-foot masterpiece, *Living in the Mountains of Pure Happiness.*

# 5. RETURN TO THE YELLOW CRANE MOUNTAIN

Wang's mother died about this time. She and Wang's father lived a hundred miles north of Quinsai, in a region which remained even under the Mongols the heart of literary and artistic life in the Empire. Wang's parents were leading figures in this world, she as the daughter of the famous Lord Meng and sister of a high official (who was also a distinguished painter), he as a well-known poet and collector of paintings and antiques. Wang's mother had been ailing for some years, but although her death had been expected, he felt her loss deeply and was grateful for the rule that prescribed three years' official leave for mourning a parent. After the funeral he and his wife stayed for some months with his father, then sold the house in Quinsai and moved to the country retreat under the Yellow Crane Mountain. Wang's wife did not care for the country, but he persuaded her that it would be not only cheaper but safer.

The news from the North was increasingly disturbing. The Yellow River project had been completed and the Grand Canal restored to use, but the army of labourers assembled for the work did not go quietly back to their homes. Not many of them had homes—or at least farms that could support their families—worth going back to. A few thousands were re-employed on the Chancellor's next great public project: nothing less than to transform the northern plain into what it had never been before, a rice-growing area for the capital, Dadu. This was Toghto's riposte to the pirates along the coast, whose activities had by now seriously affected the capital's food supplies from the south. The rice was to be grown on state farms and huge works of irrigation were embarked on, though, as things turned out, never completed. But the project was not only more ambitious than the taming of the Yellow River, it was even more expensive. To cover the deficit, more paper currency was issued and, already devalued, now became completely worthless. Traders would only accept the old strings of coins, but the labourers had been paid in paper.

What were they to live on? As gangs of displaced farmers turned bandits and preyed on the villages, more and more people saw that their only hope of survival was to join the bandits; as the gangs swelled and became more desperate, they began to threaten the smaller towns; and as the local magistrates struggled to resist them and were frequently defeated, their native soldiers went over to the bandits. Gaining weapons, expertise and confidence, the bandits soon attacked larger towns, acquiring yet more weapons, winning over yet more soldiers. Soon the whole valley south of the Yellow River was out of Mongol control and the gangs of bandits began to coalesce into real armies, with fortified towns instead of rocky crags or marshlands as their bases and professional military men as their leaders and instructors.

But what made this growing insurrection so particularly dangerous to the authorities was its religious colour. It was not only villages and towns which were overrun and plundered, but also monasteries. The peaceable lives of monks were disrupted as much as those of farmers and townspeople. And some of these monks, as angry and intimidating as disturbed hornets, transformed what had started as merely social and material agitation into a spiritual campaign with wild beliefs in the imminent rebirth of the Maitreya Buddha and the inauguration of a new world order. Maitreya Societies, preparing for the Buddha's return from Heaven, had existed for centuries and fomented rebellions even under the native Tang and Song dynasties. Their beliefs perfectly suited times of bad government and hardship, since it was supposed that this Buddha was only waiting for humanity to descend into the lowest depths of evil and misery in order to reappear, restore the true teachings of the original Buddha, save mankind from its wicked folly and bring peace and happiness under an enlightened Emperor. The Mongols at the height of their power had briefly tolerated Maitreya Societies, but then banned them completely, with the inevitable result that they grew all the stronger for meeting in secret, mostly at night.

In popular superstition the Maitreya himself was a figure of fun, a comic vagrant known as "the Laughing Buddha," with a perpetual smile on his face, an enormous bare belly and a sack containing every sort of object, useful and useless, given him by well-wishers. When asked how old this sack was and what it contained, he was supposed to reply that it was as old as space and contained all that space contains. But, pressed into service by ex-monks as a means of stirring up rebellion, the Maitreya was nothing to laugh about. His red-scarfed devotees declared that they were the advance-guard of the "Emperor of Light," but their ruthless pillage and slaughter were if anything worse than those of ordinary bandits.

In the aftermath of the Yellow River project the Red Scarves burst into the open and, with their millenarian Maitreya doctrine, gave purpose and coherence to all the disparate gangs of bandits in this central area of the Empire. There were soon two main rebel armies. The Southern Red Scarves chose an enormous, cheerful peddler—the embodiment of "the Laughing Buddha"—as their figurehead, captured a large city and made it the capital of a new Red Scarf Dynasty, with the peddler as Emperor; while the Northern Red Scarves took another city and proclaimed their leader a descendant of the Song Dynasty and his young son "the Prince of Radiance."

All this was deeply alarming to officials throughout the Empire, many of whose relatives, friends and acquaintances in the affected areas lost their property and even their lives. Urgent measures were taken—soldiers and supplies mobilised, local militias recruited and special

Defence Commissioners appointed in all regions—but there was a general feeling among the official classes that, although they were not sorry to see their Mongol overlords dismayed, very evil times lay ahead for everyone. They could not comfort themselves, as the peasants did, by believing that a saviour from Heaven would miraculously bring light out of darkness.

Mourning his mother amongst all this general alarm, Wang felt particularly disorientated. The thought of never seeing again this person of whom he had once been part, who had then been part of him, made it seem as if his whole childhood and his own identity as a child, created and sustained by her love for him, had been suddenly excised. After that, a great sense of loneliness and exposure came over him. Few now of the older generation of his family were left and, having no children of his own, it was as if he were mounting a single steep path to the summit of some mountain, with no prospect of turning back or aside or indeed making any further choices. His life was set now on that straight, stony course from middle-age to old age to death and he wondered how he had ever been able to imagine himself surrounded with possibilities. Of course, he realised, that was a delusion of childhood and youth when, not knowing yourself, you saw yourself reflected in all the varied people around you and mistook their multiplicity for your own. The only remedy, surely, was Old Huang's, to fling yourself out amongst the ten thousand things and by contemplating and drawing nature to lose sight and memory of your own inadequacies and regrets.

Wang's wife, however, sensitive to his grief over his mother and gloom about himself, treated him with special affection and gentleness and, as usually happens when one partner changes attitude like this, he responded in the same way. So these few months of peace and quiet under the Yellow Crane Mountain were among the happiest of their lives together. Wang's wife also, after a few days of treating Deng as high-handedly as she was accustomed to treat her town-servants, began to be as fond of him as Wang was. Deng was now married to the daughter of a fisherman from the nearest village and the couple, living in the servants' quarters behind Wang's cottage, had kept the whole place as clean and dry and well-repaired during Wang's long absence as if it had been their own.

The high point of this short interval of happiness, before the troubles of the outside world reached the Yellow Crane Mountain and swept over the Wangs like the edge of a hurricane, was a surprise visit from Ni. He arrived in his boat at the fishing-village, sent a note by the hand of his deaf-and-dumb boatman to the Wangs and after hasty preparation of the guest-room—both Wang and Deng remembered Ni's obsession with cleanliness—was fetched from the village in a hired carriage. He brought good news from the outside world to replace the dubious rumours that passed for news in Wang's country retreat. Toghto, the high-handed Chancellor, far from being alarmed and discouraged by the spread of rebellion, had left Dadu and led a powerful army southwards to reconquer the valley of the Yellow River. Town after town had been retaken, the supposed descendant of the Song captured and executed—though his young son escaped—and both groups of Red Scarves forced on to the defensive. The Maitreya's followers, it seemed, had once again misled the people and promised a false dawn.

Ni brought a roll of his paintings with him and had not forgotten his promise to give one to Wang.

"These are all new," he said, before hanging them up one by one in the main room of Wang's cottage. "So it may be that you'll like them less than the old ones and prefer to be released from my promise."

But Wang did not find them essentially different from nor in any way inferior to those he had seen eight years before. They were just as austere and they concentrated as before on the basic elements: a few trees in the foreground, mountains in the background and mainly empty space between. The variations were few and subtle and would probably have escaped the eye of a casual viewer. Wang was mesmerised by them all over again and at last chose one with only three trees in the foreground, very low mountains at the back and not even a shelter to suggest the presence of humanity, because, he said, it contained the least and demanded the most of both artist and viewer, as well as being as far as possible from anything he might hope to achieve himself.

Ni stayed a week or two. He would perhaps have stayed longer, but he and Wang's wife were uneasy with one another. Not appreciating his work, she was impatient with his domestic eccentricities, his need to have incense burning near him (though he brought his own supply with him) and to be constantly washing, his habit of dusting every chair before sitting on it, his fussiness over food and the way it was served. She could never understand why he had abandoned the rich estate he inherited. One warm evening after supper, as they sat outside on the lawn staring at the darkening river, Ni talked about his earlier life.

"My father died when I was only three years old," he said. "Then, when I was still young, my elder half-brother and my stepmother, both of whom I loved dearly and depended on, died too. I was left to look after my own mother and the estate. It was too much for me. My nerves went to pieces."

All the same, it had taken him many years to make up his mind to abandon what he saw as a sacred duty: the upkeep and improvement of his inheritance.

"I still dream," he said, "of those gardens and pavilions. There were three pavilions I brought almost to perfection. The one I usually entertained my friends in was a tower three storeys high, with windows all round. From two sides one had different views of the lake and from the others of the gardens and the distant hills. The entrance was through a courtyard paved with white tiles and filled with pots of multi-coloured flowers. What a nightmare, though, keeping those white tiles pristine! Dust, rain, earth seeping out of the tubs, footprints, slugs and snails, wet leaves! The courtyard had to be washed two or three times a day and I was always picking up fallen petals. Inside, there were more plants in pots—miniature firs, cassia-trees, bamboo, epidendrum, chrysanthemums—and exquisite pale green carpets: an indoor paradise. But imagine what the feet of my guests did to those carpets! Of course they took off their shoes and changed into slippers, but it was never satisfactory. I introduced more slippers, then more, until they were changing every few yards. Hundreds of pairs of slippers I had eventually."

Wang's wife stared at him open-mouthed.

"One likes floors to be clean, of course," she said, "but surely that was going too far?"

"I kept my books in that pavilion," he said sternly, "and my collection of musical instruments. One could not make any concessions to the inward march of dirt. My antiques were in another pavilion—jades, wine-jars, bronze pots, paintings, calligraphy. The problem there was mostly outside, the paulownia trees and the ornamental rocks. Those wonderful emerald green leaves gave me no pleasure under a layer of dust and the rocks were dirt-traps. The leaves had to be washed and the rocks scrubbed regularly. I hardly ever admitted guests to the third pavilion, 'The Cave of the Snow Crane,' where the carpets were white and the tables covered with Emerald Cloud paper."

"I can see that it must have been a worry to you," said Wang's wife, "but how could you bear to give it up?"

"I never would have done, if it had not been for the taxes. I had to trail round from official to official trying to mitigate their outrageous demands, flattering their self-importance, humiliating myself with long waits in vile surroundings. At last I realised that I was spending more time and energy trying to preserve my enjoyment of the place than I was in actually enjoying it, and that even when I had achieved some temporary respite, my mind was so disturbed that I couldn't enjoy it at all. There is a point beyond which it is impossible for a single person to keep up the standards of civilisation when the rest of the world is bent on destroying them. One's health suffers, one falls into depression and melancholy. Better to take to a boat, I decided, and abandon dry land to the barbarians."

Ni always spoke with complete sincerity and seriousness, but Wang could never be quite sure he was not joking and looked for a smile or a glance that would undercut his apparently absurd perfectionism. Yet Ni, if he was playing a part, never for a moment let his mask slip. He really did consider, it seemed, that perfection and purity were all that mattered. So, if he was driven out of his fortress of civilisation, he must retreat and retrench rather than surrender his principles, until at last perhaps he himself, his own body and mind, would be the only remaining redoubt. Some years later he was to give extraordinary proof that this was indeed so.

Wang's wife, meanwhile, still failed to understand the real peculiarity of Ni's character: that it was not luxury in itself he enjoyed or aimed for, but the perfection of luxury—an abstract ideal. She saw no reason, therefore, why the mere demands of tax officials should have made him give away an estate which still produced an income and could support Ni's relatives in comparative affluence.

The time had now come for Wang to show his own paintings to Ni. None had been visible when Ni arrived, since Wang's study was still filled with Tao's books and the other rooms contained a few paintings and precious objects which had belonged to Wang's mother. Ni had looked about eagerly, not only as a once avid collector, but also because he was hoping to see some example of his host's work and assess his quality. When, after a few days walking by the river and up into the lower hills, Wang asked Ni if he would care to spend tomorrow on a more artificial, indoor excursion, Ni asked suspiciously:

"Whose?"

"My own."

"I was beginning to wonder, you know, whether you still went in for that. People told me you did, but no one seemed to have seen anything for many years."

Wang smiled. He was pleased with his own work and felt that even if Ni disliked it, he would not much care. He had been powerfully influenced by his encounter with Old Huang's masterpiece. Its freedom and fluidity, its bold enthusiasm appealed to everything in Wang's mind which was fenced in and pressed down by his conventional and careful approach to ordinary life. He had never had doubts of himself as a technician, but his very skill had inclined him to be unadventurous, content to adopt a style and play with it. Now, inspired by Old Huang's example, he had begun to let feeling rather than good taste or technical accuracy guide his hand.

The first painting he showed Ni, however, dated from long before. It was the one he had made of Tao's hermitage, *Dreaming of Immortality in a Thatched Cottage*, which Tao had deposited with his books in Wang's study. Wang unrolled it and laid it out on his table. Ni, sitting bolt upright and completely motionless in an armchair, stared at it in silence, without even a flicker of expression. But when, after some while, Wang was about to replace it with his next painting, Ni raised one finger.

"Give me time!" he said.

At last he leaned forward to read Tao's poem and inscription.

"Very bold!" he said. "Empty against full. The balance is precarious, but it holds. A bit showy, though, flaunting your skill at both emptiness and fullness and at reconciling the two."

"It was done some time ago," said Wang, "and I was quite drunk and shameless."

He replaced it with another horizontal composition, a view of the house they were in, with himself sitting in the study over the stream, the other buildings concealed by the three pine-trees on the lawn in front. Immediately behind the house was a rampart of two humped hills with higher, sharper ones beyond dissolving into misty distance. A tumble of broken rocks, sprouting undergrowth and small saplings, curved round the left foreground, while the zig-zag stream, passing under a small tree and crossed by the little bridge, echoed this framing device on the right.

"How you love this place!" said Ni. "How safe and protected you feel here! Even the hills are like a woman's breasts."

"It's the shape they are," said Wang defensively.

"No doubt. But although I've been here several days, that hadn't occurred to me until you showed me this painting."

The next painting was in a vertical format, long and narrow, and Wang hung it up instead of laying it on the table. He had been doubtful about showing it to Ni at all, because its low, distant mountains in the background and its middle ground of a broad sheet of water broken by a single island so blatantly reproduced Ni's own formula. In the foreground, however, instead of a few bare trees on a knoll and an empty shelter, there was an inhabited cottage surrounded with trees, whose branches formed a dense network veiling much of the emptiness behind. Ni's eyes swivelled to meet Wang's.

"Are you trying to domesticate me?"

"I think it was the other way round. I wanted to venture out from my own closely packed environment into your vertiginous space."

"I'm flattered that a painter of such skill should borrow from one with no skill at all. I understand how angry you must have been when we first met and I doubted your powers."

Wang was silent, surprised again by this strange man's generosity, flowing like the sap in a pine behind the abrasive outward surface. He hung up several more recent vertical paintings which were further developments of his dialogue between fullness and emptiness. The emptiness became gradually more and more beleaguered. The distant mountains grew higher and craggier; the space in the middle ground was fragmented and scattered, so that the eye, setting out, as it were, from its home in the foreground—where a scholar, as often as not, sat writing in his study—picked its way from clearing to clearing in a winding upward progress, impeded by rocks and trees, to a grassy slope, a pool below a waterfall, a broad stretch of river, or a field where a man was ploughing. But when the eye reached the top of the painting the high crags which had dominated its ascent seemed to draw aside like curtains to offer a final clear passage to the sky.

Glancing slyly sideways to assess his audience's reaction, Wang saw that Ni was now lying back in his chair, his eyelids lowered, as if asleep.

"Enough?" asked Wang softly.

"Enough is a weak word," said Ni. "Has there been anything like this for four hundred years? Since the great Tang masters?"

But when Wang asked if he would care to take one away with him, he shook his head.

"I no longer keep anything precious," he said.

"As a favour to me, then," said Wang. "And after all they have no market value."

"Well, I will take this one of your own house," said Ni. "It is less ambitious than the later ones, but it will remind me of where I first saw the others and of how snug you are here."

"How primitive too, I'm afraid, and close to the earth and insufficiently clean."

"Yes, look at the way you draw attention to soil and weeds and grimy rocks in this painting! Look at that old plank bridge, the weather-beaten straw on your study roof, the piles driven down into the river mud! Everywhere signs of the struggle for survival against encroaching chaos!"

Now, surely, Ni was laughing at himself, though he still kept a straight face.

"You won't be able to bear the sight of it," said Wang.

"Oh, you misunderstand me. What I require for myself is not what I require for other people. I'm not an ideologue, you know. The world is infinitely various. I am one variation and you are another. But what most distresses me about your work is not its content, but its art. Your extraordinary control of the ink. Look at the needles on those pine-branches! Look at the knots in their trunks! I could not begin to imitate them. No, I shall not be able to bear the sight of it too often in case I feel I have to give up painting trees altogether. And then what should I use to occupy the foreground?"

When Ni finally stepped on board his boat, which his boatman had moored to the bank of the river just below the front of the house, and raised his arm once in a princely farewell greeting, Wang felt sad and empty. But Deng and his wife looked at each other with relief, while Wang's wife sighed and said:

"It would be easier to entertain the Emperor."

# 6. REACHING THE BEND IN THE RIVER

Deng's wife was pregnant with their first child and Wang was amused and touched to see how his own wife began to take a close interest in the coming birth, almost as if the Dengs were her children, or at least her relatives, rather than servants. But when Wang proposed one day to make sketches a few miles down river and wished to take Deng with him to carry his food and materials, he was less amused to be told by his wife that he must go alone. Deng's wife, she said, was not feeling well and her husband should be at least within call. Wang thought this ridiculous—one might treat servants with kindness, but one shouldn't allow their needs to interfere with one's own—and Deng himself thought the same, but Wang's wife was adamant. If Wang did not care to carry his own things, let him go another day or take the gardener.

"The gardener would be quite unsuitable," Wang said coldly. "He would be fidgeting and talking all the time."

"Just tell him to shut up!"

"That's not how I treat servants."

"How do you treat servants, then?"

"I don't ask them to carry out tasks for which they have no capacity or training."

"Well, you can use this opportunity to train the gardener."

"Why should I? I want to concentrate on the motif. I already have a servant trained to accompany me for this purpose."

"And if something happened to Deng?"

"I suppose I would have to train someone else. But it would certainly not be the gardener."

"I'm only asking you to manage without Deng for this one day."

Their quarrel, which hardly amounted to a quarrel but was more, Wang felt, a bare-faced attempt by his wife to increase her own power over Deng, ended with this admission on her part that no precedent was being created and that therefore no ground had been gained or lost. Wang changed his plan and, instead of walking, arranged to go by boat to the site he had chosen. Deng's fisherman father-in-law would take him there in the morning and return to collect him towards evening.

It was a fine early summer day, the air constantly freshened by a light breeze along the river. It was too hot to be out in the full sun, but Wang established himself under a small grove of trees near the water's edge and concentrated for some hours on sketching a sheer cliff of rock that rose directly above him and whose top bulged out like the head of some monstrous creature. The more he studied and drew it, the more he came to think of it as something living. The fissures in its surface became the wrinkles in an armoured hide, the head took on the features of a huge monkey-devil. After some hours he ate the cooked rice and fruit he had brought, drank some wine and lay down at the foot of the rock for his customary siesta.

The creature he had seen in the rock haunted his dreams. At first it seemed to be the ape-like "original" painter from long ago in the Blue Bien Mountains, who was sneering at him for his artistic timidity.

"Let go, boy, let go!" it said. "Be yourself! Enough of these finicky little lines and dots! Throw the ink on your paper and splash about!"

"But that would not be myself," Wang protested. "I am not that sort of person, not that sort of painter. Besides, I have only brought a small quantity of ink."

"Painting is easy," said the creature. "The difficult part is to be yourself."

"No, that's not it," said Wang. "The difficult part is to see the ten thousand things clearly without always getting caught in my own tricks for drawing them."

"And now what are you seeing?"

The monkey-features suddenly looked like his own face, anxious, tired, blurred, as if reflected in running water. He half woke, confused about his own identity. Surely the ugly face he had seen was not his own, but an old man's, the splash-painter's?

However, when he returned to dreaming, the thing was no longer a man, but definitely a rock. He seemed to be trying to find a tunnel through and under the rock. Deng was with him, their boat was drawn up nearby on the shore, and he, Wang, kept exclaiming, "It's here, just here, this cleft, I remember!," only to find that the cleft led nowhere. Deng kept saying "I wouldn't have told," not angrily, but mildly, reproachfully, looking at Wang as if he had lost all faith in him and could never believe anything he said again.

"But it was only you I told," Wang said, "and you always go everywhere with me. If I find my way back to that lost country beyond the Peach River, I wouldn't think of going there without you, would I?"

Deng shook his head and smiled.

"You'll never find it," he said.

These were the fragments of the dream that Wang remembered when he woke up fully, his head aching, though he was never quite sure, in the light of what was to happen soon afterwards, that he had not embroidered the last part of the dream with hindsight. Going to the edge of the river he bathed his face with water and then returned to his drawing. But, after a few hours, as the sun began to go down and the fissures in the rock grew darker and deeper, he could hardly be certain that he was not still dreaming. The face on the rock's bulging top seemed to become more and more pronounced and its expression more unpleasant. Wang shivered, as much with fear as cold, and wished Deng's father-in-law would turn up to take him home. He had told him to come as the sun went behind the mountains and surely it already had. Even the far side of the river was in shadow.

When it was too dark to draw, Wang packed up his things. Why hadn't the fisherman come? He was probably absorbed in his daily task, half asleep in his boat somewhere, forgetful of everything but the surface of the water and the sliding shadow under it that might betray his last, best catch of the day. Pacing to and fro for half an hour or so, Wang finally lost patience, slung his bag over his shoulder and began to walk home. Irritated at first by his boatman's fecklessness and then rehearsing to himself the recriminations with which he would greet his wife, the ultimate cause of this inconvenience, he began gradually to change mood. The movement and exercise of his whole body after a day in which all his energy had been narrowly focussed into his eyes and fingers relaxed his mind as well as his muscles, drove away his irritation and erased the cutting phrases he had been preparing for his wife.

After passing through a belt of trees beside the river, he had to follow a path over a rocky outcrop. It was steep and rough underfoot, but lighter than under the trees. Wang breathed in the fresh, cool air, aromatic with pine-resin and herbs, looked up at the first bright star of the evening and saw the three-quarter moon appearing behind hills in the south. He thought that it was really as if he had found his way up the Peach Blossom River and through the hill. For, even if the fortunate people who lived in that lost place were immortal, they were still human and must be subject to many of the usual kinds of adversity—family and social disagreement, bad seasons for their crops, pests and diseases—and above all the fear of being discovered and invaded by people from outside. Except for bad government and the threat of death—and, after all, they were perhaps not even immortal—their world was scarcely different from his own. Perhaps that was the true meaning of the story. It was not a myth of paradise but a reminder that in normal times and for all but the most wretched people, paradise is not so hard to find.

Following the path down to the river-bank again and, as the moon rose higher, stopping to contemplate its reflection in the water, his mind was infused with a sense of well-being; but tinged with melancholy. Why should that be? he wondered. Was it the effect of his encounter with that sinister rock and the way it entered his dreams? Or the knowledge of his own separation from nature, however he might try to lose himself in its intricacies? No, it was surely that the moment he thought about it consciously, he became aware that this sense of well-being was inevitably transitory and abnormal. Yet such awareness in turn actually sharpened his pleasure at this moment when he was standing by a moonlit river in paradise. That barely perceived dark edge gave his happiness body, as a line on paper gives body to a space. Paradise could not be defined without its shadow, immanent loss; nor loss without the memory of the tunnel at the end of the Peach Blossom River and the hope of one day discovering it.

The real river passed round a series of bends from here on, making the journey longer than the direct walk through the hills above, though for a walker the effort of going up and down probably cancelled out any advantage, even in daylight. Wang chose to continue beside the river, partly because it was easier to find his way without thinking about it, partly because in his present mood he was in no hurry to get home. When at last he rounded the last bend, he hardly realised he had done so, because he was not immediately aware of the village in front of him. Then, as he came nearer to it and saw the shapes of huts and the outlines of boats and masts beside the jetty, he wondered why he had not noticed them sooner. But, as he reached the near end of the village he suddenly understood why. All his sense of well-being vanished instantly. There were no lights burning anywhere. The place was absolutely silent and seemed to be deserted.

Wang walked down the village street trying to peer through the windows. It was too dark inside to see if people were there or not. He felt that they were, that they saw him but gave no sign, that for some dreadful reason they wanted their presence to seem like absence. Even the dogs were silent. If they were still there with their owners, they must have been muzzled. He caught the faint sound of something—perhaps chickens—scuffling about in a shed. He reached the hut belonging to Deng's father-in-law and knocked on the door. There was no answer. He knocked again more loudly, then called the fisherman's name. In the absolute stillness, except for the faint rippling of the river, his knocking and his voice must have been heard by the whole village, but there was no response at all. Either the village was empty or its inhabitants were all holding their breath at the same time. He did not call again, but walked on to the far end of the village and, as he left it, heard—or imagined he heard—a faint rustling, sighing, a collective intake of breath.

If only time could hold its breath! This narrative, imitating time but less inexorable, can do so for a moment, disinclined to follow Wang, as with tight heart and sharp foreboding he went with long, hurrying steps, almost running, round the river-bend separating the village from his home. Why should I go on with my story? Why not stop here on the bend as all my feelings urge me? Don't we all fear pain, detest cruelty, prefer beauty to ugliness, peace to confusion and contemplation to action? But perhaps not when telling or listening to stories. Perhaps then we are glad to escape from our too retiring selves; or to enhance the beauty and peace of our own lives by contemplating the ugliness and confusion of others'; or to dilute our own pain by being reminded that it is universal.

In any case, having reached this bend in the river, I can spare my feelings only at the cost of abandoning that world and time and returning to my own, which are hardly less distressing. I heard today from my jailer that still more people have been arrested for their supposed connection with the Prime Minister's conspiracy. My trial will be further delayed and I may have to share my small cell with others.

As Wang entered the wood where he often gathered firewood and had once lost the white jade ring, it was the smell that greeted him first, the bitter smell of smoke and damp, charred embers, of a fire doused with water. Insects seemed to be settling on his hair, face and shoulders, but when he brushed them distractedly away, more of them immediately settled and he realised they were floating ashes, some still glowing like fireflies. As he came out of the trees and reached the little bridge over the stream, he saw that his house was strangely altered. His studio had gone. Jagged pieces of its blackened floor hung down from the undamaged piles towards the stream below. Standing on the bridge, he felt numbed and sick. Ashes continued to float around him and stick to his hair and clothes: were they all that was left of his sketches and paintings, of his books, of Tao's library?

There were lights in the house and the sound of voices. But Wang continued to stand where he was, slowly coming to terms with the catastrophe, telling himself that such things happened and there was nothing to do but bear them. He remembered how Tao had once said jokingly that every book wanted to be the only one that survived a fire and he began to hope that Deng and the gardener might have contrived to save something. Then he walked firmly across the lawn to the house and saw, only as he mounted the steps to the veranda in front of it, that his main room was full of people, strangers, rough men wearing red scarves on their heads, sitting on the chairs and the floor eating and drinking, with weapons beside them.

It was too late to step back out of sight. The two men nearest him were springing to their feet. At the same time, as he half turned with the idea of running away, he was aware of someone immediately behind him, at the foot of the steps, a sentry, no doubt, who had been concealed by the pine trees and had allowed Wang to cross the lawn so as to cut off his retreat. Terrified now, but not knowing what else to do, he stepped over the threshold as the sentry came up the steps at his back and the two men inside confronted him.

"Wang Meng, is it?" said one of them, a small man of about forty with a narrow, weaselly face and prominent ears.

Wang nodded, looking away from him and round the score or so men in the room, in case there was one he knew or who seemed more sympathetic than the rest. They were all staring at him with the same intensity, not so much hostile as appraising. He did not feel like a man who had walked into his own house, but as if he had stumbled into a cave occupied by dangerous creatures—a nest of snakes, say—all suddenly alert and waiting for his next move.

"Pity about your house!" said the second of the two men immediately in front of him, young and sturdily built, one hand resting on the hilt of the sword protruding from his belt, his legs apart, his round face expressionless.

"Where is my wife?" asked Wang.

"It was a terrible burn-up," said the man with satisfaction, "but you can thank us for saving most of it."

"Is my wife here?" asked Wang.

"You can thank us that the whole place wasn't destroyed," said the round-faced man, coming closer to Wang.

"Thank you, then. But where is my wife?"

The conversation seemed to Wang ridiculously low-key in the circumstances, but wanting to conceal his fear of what they might do to him, trying to retain his own presence of mind, he continued to speak to this armed bandit as if he were an ordinary stranger, as if nothing very disturbing had happened.

"It was an accident, but you can see we saved the rest of the house."

"Yes. Thank you," said Wang.

"It was all that paper that made the thing flare up so quickly."

"Your wife's out at the back," said the smaller, older man. "With the Chief and the other woman."

"Can I see her?"

"Nobody's stopping you."

"No," said Wang, realising suddenly that against all his expectations no one had so far even laid a hand on him. "I'll go and find her, then."

He looked cautiously for the easiest passage through the crowded room, with its fifteen or twenty faces staring at him.

"You can come with me," said the man behind, who sounded less like a peasant than the others. "Best go round the outside."

"Yes, of course," said Wang, turning at once to descend the steps, glad to escape all those eyes and uncertain intentions.

The sentry—at least a head taller than Wang—walked beside him without saying anything more. The yard at the back was as full of horses, tethered in groups to the posts supporting the houses, as the main room had been of their riders. There were lights in Deng's house on the far side of the yard, but the kitchen was dark. The horses stirred and stamped as Wang and his companion passed through them.

Wang had never been inside Deng's house and he stopped punctiliously at the top of the steps in the open doorway. Deng's wife was lying on a low bed, his own wife was sitting beside her, holding her hand, while another person, dressed like a man but with a woman's face, stood at the foot of the bed watching them. There was a lantern on a low table beside the bed and another on the floor near the stranger.

"I've brought the owner," said the sentry, standing slightly behind Wang and speaking over his head.

Wang's wife and the stranger looked sharply towards the doorway, but Deng's wife was evidently asleep. Wang's wife put her finger to her lips. The stranger picked up the lantern from the floor and crossed the small room with long strides.

"Outside!" she said in a low voice, as she brushed past Wang and his companion and stepped down into the yard.

Wang went a little further into the room.

"Are you all right?" he asked his wife.

She nodded and again put her finger to her lips, then, as Deng's wife stirred a little in her sleep, made urgent signs to Wang to go outside. He found the strange woman waiting for him in the middle of the yard, while the sentry was making his way back to the front of the house.

"She may lose her child. She has been in great distress and has only just fallen asleep. I'm afraid this must be a shock for you, Mr. Wang. The fire was not intentional. We are very sorry."

"What happened?"

"It was a lamp that fell over. All those books. All that paper. Your servant did what he could, but very little was saved, I'm afraid."

"Where is Deng?"

"It was not his fault."

"I'm sure it wasn't. No one could be more careful and responsible than Deng."

"It wasn't our fault either. It was a misunderstanding."

As the woman spoke, though he could not see her properly in the darkness of the yard, with the lantern in her hand enhancing the shadows over her upper body and face, Wang began to feel that she was somehow familiar. He was struggling to recall where he could have met her before and only half attending to what she said.

"Who are those people in my house?"

"Those are my people."

"But surely they're bandits?"

"The Mongols call us that," she said. "But you should not."

Irritated by her reproving tone, Wang momentarily lost control of his stifled emotions.

"If I come home to find my house full of uninvited strangers with weapons and my work and my books destroyed, I don't know what else I can call them."

"We did not come to burn your work. I told you, that was an accident. Your servant stepped back suddenly and knocked over the lamp. That was the cause of the fire."

"Where is Deng?"

"You want to see him?"

"Yes, of course."

She turned and walked towards the dark kitchen, then stopped on the threshold of the small hut next to it, also in darkness. It was a storehouse for oil, tools, water-jars and firewood. Without going in, she raised her lantern so that Wang could see inside. On the floor near the door was a pile of empty sacks.

"Deng?" he called uncertainly into the shadows beyond the lamplight and, getting no reply, said, "Are you sure he's in here?"

"He's dead," the woman said. "I thought you knew that. Your wife told us to put him here."

Wang stood for a while without moving, his mouth open, as this second shock, worse by far than the one that had hit him when he saw the ruined studio, passed violently through his mind and made his whole body stiffen. Then he stumbled up the steps into the hut and knelt down beside the pile of sacks.

"Deng! Deng!" he said, not as if he hoped to get an answer, but simply to say something, to release some part of his anguish.

The woman followed him inside and stood nearby holding the lantern. Wang pulled away some of the sacks and saw Deng's barely recognisable face, red and raw, the head hairless, the mouth twisted in agony, the eyeballs seeming to press against their closed, lashless lids. The body, when he lifted more sacks, was braised red, turning black and yellow in places, glistening with a newly-formed skin. Wang felt as if he himself were scalded with horror and grief. His mind could hardly accept what his eyes told him. He stood up and walked jerkily to and fro, then flung himself down again beside the body.

"He was trying to save your books," said the woman, "when the burning thatch suddenly collapsed on top of him. It was some minutes before we could pull him out. His clothes were all on fire and he was screaming with pain. What could we do?"

Wang said nothing, but got to his feet again and paced up and down, groaning aloud. After a while he knelt down and put his head on the floor close to his servant's.

"Deng! Deng!" he said, as if reproaching him for being dead and causing his master such sorrow.

There was dried blood on the corpse's chest and Wang saw that it came from a deep gash over the heart.

"What's that?" he asked accusingly. "You lied. He didn't die in the fire. You killed him."

"There was nothing else to do," she said. "He was suffering so much."

She sat down on the other side of the corpse, while Wang rocked to and fro in silence.

"I loved him very much," he said at last. "More than I knew. This is worse than any death I've ever experienced."

She and her followers, she told him, had arrived just as the light was failing and Deng, carrying a lamp, had said his master was away. Not being sure he was telling the truth, they pushed past him into the house, whereupon he rushed towards the studio and, placing his lamp on the floor, held out both arms and blocked the entrance. When somebody drew a sword and threatened to cut him down, Deng stepped back instinctively, caught his foot in the lamp and started the fire. After that, while the rest of them found buckets and jars and began to throw water from the stream on the blaze, Deng had been inside trying to rescue the books and drawings, until suddenly the roof fell in and he was trapped under it. After pulling him out and finding that he was too badly burned to be saved, they had been able to prevent the fire reaching the rest of the house.

They had kept the news of Deng's death from his wife, telling her only that he was hurt. Wang's wife had been afraid that if she knew the truth, Deng's wife might lose her baby as well as her husband.

"I know who you are now," Wang said, "though you've changed so much since I last saw you. You are the daughter of that landowner, Tao's friend, and you married the bandit-chief. We attended your betrothal ceremony."

"Yes, of course," she said.

"You have suffered terrible losses yourself."

"Yes."

"I was very sorry to hear about it from Tao."

So far his eyes had remained dry, but now tears welled out of them as he remembered that and all the other occasions when he had taken Deng's presence for granted.

The landowner's daughter left the storehouse and went to join her followers in the house, but Wang stayed for some time longer beside the body of his too loyal servant, before covering it again with the sacks and going to join his wife and share the vigil over Deng's widow and her unborn child.

In the morning Wang himself went to the village to tell the people that they had nothing to fear from the bandits. It was Deng's father-in-law, fishing from his boat on the far side of the river and, as twilight fell, about to cast off and go down the river to fetch Wang, who had seen the mounted bandits descend on the house. When the studio suddenly burst into flames, he hastened to warn the village. Some of the villagers had immediately fled and spent the night hiding in the hills; others, including Deng's father-in-law, had stayed in their huts, hoping that if they kept quiet and showed no lights, the bandits would remain unaware of them and move on somewhere else.

The fisherman seemed to have forgotten in his panic that he had undertaken to fetch Wang and that, in any case, Wang too might have been glad to be warned that his house had been set on fire by marauders. Wang did not reproach him. He felt that the man's thoughtlessness and lack of imagination only underlined the extraordinary difference between Deng's sensitive character and the coarse background he came from. Born in another village, Deng had lost both parents while still a child and been brought up by his grandparents in this village. The grandfather had been Wang's steward and brought Deng into Wang's service as a houseboy; and Deng had been so quick to learn and so reliable that, young as he was when his grandfather died, he had been judged the best person to take the old man's place.

Wang had by now spoken at some length to the landowner's daughter and could reassure the villagers that these were not ordinary robbers. They had not come to prey upon this or any other village and, although they required food, they could pay for it. He also told them how the fire had started by accident and how Deng had been caught under the blazing roof.

Deng's grandmother was still alive and Wang visited her hut to tell her the sad news. However, she was very decrepit, deaf as well as blind, and he was not sure that she understood. Deng had been well liked in the village, but no one there, it seemed to Wang, felt as deeply wounded as he did by Deng's loss. The general reaction was mainly one of relief that the bandits intended no harm to the village. Deng's father-in-law took Wang home in his boat and the mother-in-law came too, to help care for the widow and try to ensure the safe birth of her child. The fisherman promised to arrange the funeral as soon as possible so that Wang could take part in it.

After his long conversation with the landowner's daughter, Wang had agreed, though he did not mention this to anyone except his wife, to go away with the bandits. For they had come to this distant place precisely to find either him or Tao. After the destruction of her village, the landowner's daughter had, as Tao guessed, ridden away with a few of her husband's followers, determined to survive and take revenge on the magistrate who had ordered the attack. Riding her white horse and always wearing a white scarf on her head as a sign of mourning, she had immediately taken command of the remaining bandits and become a far more daring and successful leader than her husband had been.

As the whole country on that side of the mountains dissolved into anarchy and the authorities retreated into their fortified cities, she had recruited more and more followers. Several times she had defeated the companies of soldiers sent out against her, enlisted many of those who were captured into her own ranks and become known throughout the district as "The White Tigress." But although the magistrate was not strong enough to defeat her, nor was she strong enough to capture the town and take her revenge. She had hoped, as the rebellion swelled out from the valley of the Yellow River, to join forces with the main army of the Southern Red Scarves and make use of their numbers and military resources for her own purpose, which was also in a general way theirs. But the resurgence of the Mongol forces under Toghto had put that out of the question for the moment.

She believed fervently that in the long run she and all the other bandit-patriots would succeed in driving out the Mongols, but she was too fiercely single-minded about her first duty of personal revenge to be willing to wait any longer. She seldom slept, she said, without dreaming of her father's and brothers' angry ghosts. To capture the town by force would require an army with siege-engines. Failing that, one could only hope to enter it by some trick. But what trick? Her followers were certainly strong enough and brave enough for any enterprise, but unfortunately they were not clever enough to devise stratagems. Some of them were ex-soldiers who could half remember stratagems they had been told about or even taken part in. But what use were they? Stratagems depended on every detail being exact and they had to fit the particular circumstances. The real problem was, she said, that neither she nor any of her followers was properly educated and trained to think. At last, almost in despair, after dreaming again about her angry father and brothers and this time her husband too, she had recalled the betrothal ceremony so many years ago and the two highly educated people who had attended it, the only such people she had ever met. She had heard that, after the destruction of her village, Tao had left his home in the mountains and gone to Wang's house under the Yellow Crane Mountain. So she had set out at once with a party of her followers to recruit one or both of them to her cause.

In the immediate aftermath of his shock over Deng's death, Wang listened to her explanation with his usual sense of being pursued by an unlucky fate. If he had not visited Tao at that particular time, if Tao had not fallen in love with the girl and written all those poems, if they had not insisted on entering the village when they found it barred, if they had advised the landowner to reject the bandit-chief as his son-in-law, if they had never spoken to the girl, if Tao had taken refuge with some other friend and given the responsibility for protecting his library to some other servant . . . Deng would still be alive. Wang also blamed his wife for keeping Deng at home on that one unlucky day and himself for giving way to his wife.

His mind already a morass of emotions, Wang could not help being flattered and stimulated by the admiring attention this young, beautiful and strong-willed woman was paying him. She had come several hundred miles through unknown and hostile territory to find him. He did not imagine for a moment that he could really be of any help to her. The idea that a scholar, educated in the literary and philosophical classics and with some experience of administration in the sub-prefect's court, would necessarily be qualified to devise a stratagem for entering a town and killing its magistrate, seemed to him ludicrously naive. So naive, indeed, that he did not even bother to point out that he was himself a state official—though on compassionate leave—and could hardly take part in the murder of another official without completely reversing the direction of his life and becoming an outlaw. He agreed to accompany the White Tigress back to her lair and to consider the problem of how she could accomplish her revenge partly because he felt it would distract him from his sadness, partly because he did not know what else to do with himself—most of his work was gone with his servant—but chiefly because she looked steadily into his eyes and asked him to.

He did not tell his wife that he was leaving voluntarily, but made it appear that he had no alternative, that if he did not go the bandits would complete their destruction of the house and its inhabitants. He promised to return as soon as he could and urged her meanwhile, if Deng's child was born alive, to do all she could to support the mother and see that the child had the best possible upbringing.

"How long do you expect to be away?" she asked, taken aback by this long-term injunction.

"A month or two."

"Then we can talk about all that when you return."

"Of course. But in case of the worst . . ."

He knew very well that she would be as anxious for the child's welfare as he was—she had been almost equally shocked by Deng's death—but he wanted, without actually saying so, to make it clear that if he should never return, he considered that Deng's child had a claim on his estate.

The geomancer discovered an auspicious day for the funeral later that week. Deng was buried in the cemetery on the hill behind the village, next to his grandfather. Wang added to the usual paper images of food and money which were meant to accompany a dead person into the next world a small drawing of the Peach Blossom River, with the trees covered in flowers, the fisherman paddling his boat and the entrance to the tunnel through the mountain just visible at the source of the river. Wang's wife admired the drawing so much that she was reluctant to allow it to be burned with the other images, but Wang, though he did not believe in another world, was adamant.

"I made it for him," he said. "It is no doubt quite useless to him. He will never know or care again whether the Peach Blossom River exists or not. But suppose that I'm wrong! Suppose there is some truth behind the superstition! How could I live with the thought that he gave his life for my drawings and Tao's books, but that I would not give him one small drawing as his passport to paradise?"

"You are too full of contradictions," said Wang's wife. "Perhaps they're not so much contradictions as concealments. You pretend to be rational, but you are really superstitious. You pretend to be mature and clear-headed, but you are riding off like an irresponsible boy with the White Tigress. You pretend you are being forced to, but I can easily see that you want to go. You pretend you only want to live quietly and master your art, but you will have no chance of doing either with this gang of bandits. You will probably end up being executed for treason when you have pretended all your life that the most sensible and patriotic thing to do is to be loyal to this government."

Wang made no reply. He was not sure himself whether these were contradictions or concealments or perhaps something else again: uncertainties, flaws, rifts in his own being deeper than his conscious mind was able to penetrate but which, as a would-be rational person, he tried to throw bridges over.

The funeral was attended by the bandits as well as all the people from the village. Even Deng's grandmother was carried up the hill in a litter, though she still did not seem clear that it was her own grandson who was being buried. She probably assumed that since Wang was paying all the costs it was some relative of his. But Deng's widow was not there. Her child—a boy—had been born the night before and the funeral banquet, for which everyone returned to Wang's house, became more a celebration of this new Deng than a mourning of the old.

The next day, mounted on a steady horse which had been brought specially to carry him or Tao, Wang rode away behind the White Tigress. Skirting the Yellow Crane Mountain, they headed north-westwards towards the next range of mountains and Tao's old home.

# 7. THE WHITE TIGRESS

At first there was no sign of the devastation which was gradually spreading outwards like a bloodstain from the centre of the Empire. But when the White Tigress and her party reached the mountain monastery where Wang had stopped on the way to his friend Tao, they found it looted and partly destroyed. Most of the lesser buildings had been burned and the temple stripped of its ornaments. The few monks still occupying the place for lack of any other refuge could not say whether it was government soldiers or rebels who had done the damage. Almost certainly, in such a remote place, it was rebels, but the monks were shivering with terror in the face of this fresh incursion by red-scarfed marauders and were no doubt afraid to say anything that might annoy them.

Remembering the strange-looking novice he had encountered there on his last visit, Wang looked about for him, but the surviving monks were all elderly. He asked one of the oldest, whose face and right leg were bandaged with bloody rags, but who seemed more willing to talk than the rest, if he knew anything of a novice called Zhu.

"He was a boy with a strikingly ugly face," added Wang, "and I think he was sent out to beg."

"Yes," said the monk, "but he came back after a year or two. He was one of those who wanted to defend the monastery by force. He thought the Maitreya Buddha would protect us."

Wang smiled politely, looking at the ruined temple, with its door missing and a gaping hole in the roof.

"But who can say? What does protection mean?" asked the monk, peering round with his single eye. "A temple is only a building and can be rebuilt. I have lost my eye and my foot, but at least I did not spoil my chance of a better life by killing anyone."

"And Zhu?" asked Wang.

"He probably killed several. He was very strong and determined."

"And was killed himself?"

"Who knows? He was hiding with us in a cave under the cliff for some days. But he disappeared as soon as the attackers had gone. There was nothing left to eat here and he had an appetite as unbridled as his face. He told me he'd decided to join the bandits himself, though I tried to convince him that it could not be what the Maitreya wanted of him."

The monk suddenly remembered that he was talking to somebody who was in the company of bandits.

"But who can say? Bandits may also be good people in bad times."

❀

As they descended the far side of the mountains, the party stopped at the cemetery near the White Tigress's former village, so that she could pay respects to her murdered family and promise that vengeance would not now be long delayed. Wang attended the ceremony with a grim face and clenched hands. It is gloomy enough to concentrate one's thoughts on the dead, but he stood here in addition as the supposed bringer of relief to their ghosts.

He had enjoyed the freedom of riding through the mountains and the unfamiliar pleasure of being accepted as an honoured member of a community with a clear purpose to fulfil, even if that purpose was ultimately murder. While they rode through wild scenery in warm sunshine or clattered occasionally into frightened villages to find food and lodging for themselves and their horses—for which they paid in silver—the adventure was exhilarating. Nor could Wang pretend that he did not feel rejuvenated by the constant attention and flattering respect shown him by the White Tigress. She was always closely escorted by the second-in-command of the party, Li Yen, the sturdy young man with a round face who had originally told Wang about the fire in his study and who was perhaps her second husband or at least chosen lover. But she took the opportunity of being in Wang's company to explore intellectual capacities which must have lain dormant up to now. Li may have enjoyed her most intimate favours by night, but by day Wang had the full benefit of her ears, her voice and her large, alert eyes and he had little doubt that for her this was the more stimulating experience of the two.

He told her much about the history of the Empire, of which she knew only that the Mongols were foreigners with no right to rule who had seized it by force from the Song Dynasty in the time of her grandparents. But of the dynasties before the Song and the many previous periods when the Empire had been disputed and fragmented she knew nothing. She was quite unaware that there had often been uprisings before, when people calling themselves "Red Eyebrows" or "Yellow Scarves" or even "Red Scarves" as at present had rebelled against bad governments, usually making things even worse.

"You mean," she said, "that this time it will be no different?"

"The difference this time is that the rulers are foreign."

"Which never happened before?"

"Never to the Empire as a whole."

She had no notion of the Empire's size, that it contained sixty or seventy million inhabitants and that, even on the good roads made by the Mongols, it took ninety-six days to ride from Yunnan in the far south-west to the capital Dadu in the north-east.

"Have you been to Dadu?" she asked.

"Yes, but Dadu is a new city, built by the Mongols, not to be compared to Quinsai, where the last Song Emperors lived."

"Why not to be compared?"

"Dadu is large, but plain and dull, with a bad climate and gloomy people. Quinsai is warm and full of light—the sun flashing off the lake by day, and at night coloured lanterns everywhere, reflected in the canals that criss-cross the city. Hundreds of streets and alleys, innumerable shops, restaurants, inns and tea-houses, the main streets teeming with people and with carts and carriages and porters carrying sedan chairs. The canals are full of traffic too: barges loaded with cargo and smaller boats carrying passengers. And on the lake to the west of the city are fishing-boats and pleasure-cruisers and islands with banqueting-houses where people go for their marriage feasts. Everything you can imagine and much you can't is for sale in the shops and market-places. Bells are ringing from the monasteries on the hills to the south and west. The markets and pleasure-parks are full of entertainers: acrobats, jugglers, singers and storytellers, actors and actresses in the theatres. And all this life and noise hardly stops, day or night. Quinsai is near the sea and huge ocean-going ships put into port at the mouth of the river from all over the world. Those foreign sailors and traders walk about with wide eyes and tell us that Quinsai is by far the biggest, most civilised, most wonderful city they have ever seen, anywhere on earth."

"Then why did you leave it?"

"I don't really like cities," he said.

When she laughed, as she did now, it was not just her face that shook but her whole body, beginning with the shoulders and right down to the legs, so that her horse thought she was signalling for more speed and would have galloped away with her if she hadn't quickly shortened the reins.

In amongst the history of the Empire he inserted poems and passages from plays and the stories of remarkable men, scholars, philosophers, generals, emperors. She liked best, of course, the story of Wu Ze-tien, supposed reincarnation of the Maitreya Buddha and the only woman Emperor ever to reign in China. She had been a Buddhist nun and the concubine of two successive Emperors of the Tang Dynasty and, when the second died, seized power from the legitimate heir and executed hundreds of the noblemen who had monopolised the Empire's administration.

"That was her important contribution to our history," Wang said, "taking power away from the landed aristocracy and giving it to those with intelligence and learning. It was not she who invented the competitive examinations for recruiting administrators, but it was she who made examinations the systematic basis for all future governments until the Mongols abolished them."

"Was she the best Emperor in our history?"

"She is generally considered a monster. She allowed her relations and favourites and the Buddhist monasteries to grow extremely rich, but most other people, especially farmers and peasants, were fined and taxed into poverty. So, after twelve years as Emperor, at the age of eighty-two, she was forced to abdicate."

"You think women are not fit to be Emperors?"

"Few people are fit to be Emperors. There have been far more bad male Emperors than good ones, so how can we judge women's fitness from a sample of one?"

The White Tigress was thoughtful for a while, though she continued to scan the hills around them and to turn in her saddle from time to time, checking that all was well with the column behind them.

"I should not care to be Emperor," she said at last. "I am too ignorant."

"Emperors rely on their ministers. Ministers rely on their civil servants, who have access to all the written and stored knowledge of the centuries."

"So they can only do what has been done before?"

"They can be guided by what has been done before."

"Or misguided?"

"Usually it is a matter of fitting fresh circumstances to similar but never identical ones from the past and the advisers very often disagree among themselves."

"And the Emperor decides between them?"

"A strong one decides, a weak one dithers until it is too late. It's not nearly so important for an Emperor to be learned as to be intelligent, shrewd and decisive."

"But I suppose," she said, "that no one from the lowest class has ever been Emperor?"

"There was a farmer, a small landowner like your father, called Liu Bang, who lost his land through debt or some other misfortune and had to take a very humble job guarding convicts. I forget whether on this occasion they were working in the fields or whether he was escorting them into exile. At any rate, some of them escaped and Liu Bang, knowing he would be executed, ran away himself and became a bandit. The Empire, which had only recently been unified for the first time in our history, was beginning to fall apart again with the death of the First Emperor, and after many years and much fighting and anarchy this Liu Bang, the ex-farmer, ex-prison guard, ex-bandit, became Emperor. The dynasty he founded, the Han, lasted four hundred years."

"When did this happen?"

"Liu Bang became Emperor about fifteen hundred years ago."

"Our lives are very small and short," said the White Tigress, "and history makes them seem smaller and shorter. No, I wouldn't care to be Emperor. Let me just perform my duty to my father's and brothers' ghosts and I shall be content."

Wang had doubts about the duty of vengeance and he did not believe in ghosts. They were ideas which seemed to him to belong to more primitive times, useful to storytellers and playwrights, but hardly worth discussing in real life. But then he had never lived in the country except as a recreation and had never until now mixed with country people. Most of these bandits were really just villagers who had lost their houses and strips of land. Their ideas had come down to them with little modification by word of mouth through innumerable generations for perhaps a thousand years. The White Tigress was at first astonished that they could even be questioned.

"I have never seen a ghost myself," said Wang.

"If your father and mother and brothers had been murdered, you would have done," she said.

"I'm sure I would have dreamed about them, as you have. Does that mean they are real ghosts?"

"What else can they be?"

"Things in your mind. Things very important to you, of course, but with no existence outside your mind."

"I've seen them standing in front of me, or walking towards me."

"By day? Or only at night?"

"At night. That's when ghosts walk."

"So you were dreaming and dreamed you were awake. That's very common."

"But everybody sees ghosts," she said. "Why do you want to make out that they don't?"

Their horses were passing at this moment along a narrow defile bordered with fallen rocks, and Wang took advantage of being forced to drop back into single file to ponder this question. For a villager, the world teamed with spirits. It was almost his definition of life, that every one of the ten thousand things had an invisible, indestructible spirit within its visible, vulnerable body. Why, then, was he, Wang, so certain that they did not, that life was purely physical, endlessly reproducing itself after its kind, but blindly and mechanically? When the track widened he rode up beside her again.

"Even if there are ghosts," he said, "they are feeble, unimportant things, dying leftovers from life, not the thing itself. When we bury the dead, we burn paper tokens of real things. But the ghosts are like disintegrating paper themselves. We, the living, and all the living things around us, are the only reality. When we pay respect to ghosts it is only paying respect to our own feelings about what they once were and meant to us, and acknowledging that we too will one day disappear from the world."

"You are wrong," she said. "If you were right, I would be able to control my feelings, as I control this horse. But my feelings control me.

I am the horse which is being ridden by my angry brothers and my father towards this vengeance."

And as if to prove the point she suddenly galloped forward away from him and even after she had slowed down again and allowed the column to catch up with her, avoided all further conversation with him that day.

Now, in the cemetery, Wang was only too well aware that if she was her ancestors' horse, he was hers and that although he had contrived to keep reality at bay during the journey, it was close upon him now.

❀

That same evening they reached the outcrop where the bandits had made their fortified settlement around the original caves. Several hundred people—men, women and children—welcomed them at the gates of the stockade. Their safe return and the accomplishment of their mission to acquire a strategist were celebrated that night in the communal hall with huge quantities of food and drink, as if victory were already achieved. Sitting in the place of honour at the right hand of the White Tigress, Wang shut out all thought of tomorrow and drank himself unconscious.

He woke up sometime after noon the next day and found himself in the small house that had been set aside for his use and to which they must have carried him the night before. A servant, who had been sitting quietly in the corner of the room, immediately brought him tea and told him that the White Tigress was waiting to speak to him. Wang asked to be left alone a few hours more to meditate and, returning to his bed, tried to recall any stratagems for the capture of towns which he had ever heard or read about.

There was, of course, the most famous one, the occasion during the wars of the Three Kingdoms when Kongming, the brilliant strategist of the Kingdom of Shu, found himself trapped in the town of Xicheng. The enemy General was advancing swiftly at the head of a hundred and fifty thousand troops, while Kongming had only some two thousand in the town with him and no reinforcements anywhere near. Instead of attempting to defend the town, Kongming opened all four gates and, as the enemy came in sight, sat on a tower overlooking the nearest gate, burning incense and coolly playing the zither, while soldiers disguised as ordinary citizens swept the open gateways with brooms. The enemy General, being himself a cunning strategist, knowing Kongming's fearsome reputation and certain that this was a characteristically colourful ploy to lure him into the town, led his army away.

Wang's problem was that this was a stratagem for defending a town, not taking it, and that he could not now remember a single alternative. If only Tao had still been living at his house in the hills, within a day's journey! His library, especially strong in history, would surely have contained innumerable alternatives. The horrible memory of its destruction and of Deng's with it came over him again and he lay writhing with regret for the past, until the consciousness of his own present predicament as a strategist without a stratagem drove out one misery with a greater. He coaxed his unruly mind back on to the only path he could discern. What would Kongming have done if the situation were reversed, with the superior enemy *inside* the town? Wouldn't he have given the impression that he was *not* going to attack? But in order to convey such an impression he would first have had to threaten an attack and how would he have done that with an obviously inferior force?

Many hours later, as it began to grow dark, Wang called the servant and told him that he would see the White Tigress, but that she must come to him in the morning and come alone. He did not want to expose his still incomplete idea to the criticism of a whole roomful of bandits and besides he had remembered that when the King of Shu wished to enlist Kongming on his side, it was the King who went to the scholar, not the other way round. Wang would not go so far as to keep the White Tigress waiting several days, as Kongming had the King, but he was beginning to understand that actions are not necessarily simpler than words nor manipulating other people than putting significant marks on paper.

He slept well that night, after he had eaten a frugal meal of fruit, rice and wine brought him by the servant. He had sat for a while observing the sky, glad to note that the colours at sunset had been predominantly yellow, promising bad weather, that there were already clouds over the mountains, and that the moon was waning. He dreamed —no doubt because they had been so much in his thoughts—of the White Tigress's father and brothers. At first they looked angry, flourishing their swords as they had when Wang first saw them coming down the village street to greet him and Tao on the day of the White Tigress's betrothal to the bandit-chief. But although he knew that they were dead, Wang was not at all afraid of them. Indeed, it seemed that he had deliberately summoned them, for he welcomed them warmly and urged them to sit on his bed, all three in a row. It is always strange in dreams how one seems to be plunged into the action as a participant, unaware of exactly how things reached this point or of how they will turn out, while actually being their source. It is only the same as storytelling, of course, except that the dreamer's participation seems deeper and more inexorable; and this must be because, unlike the conscious storyteller, he is altogether cut off from the real world. Blind storytellers, they say, are the best. Unless the White Tigress's view is the correct one: that dreams are not created by the sleeper's own mind but enter it from another, hidden world.

"The matter is . . ." said the old man, very agitated.

"The matter is," said Wang, "that I have thought of a plan and need your help to carry it out."

"We are too few," said the elder son. "You want an army."

"One dead man is worth a thousand living," said Wang.

Did they mind him calling them dead? he remembered thinking. But apparently they did not.

"*Ten* thousand," said the old man. "Even ten thousand would be nothing to one dead man."

"Still too few," said the younger son, staring at his feet.

"Aren't you forgetting Fen?" asked Wang, referring to the bandit-chief who had been the White Tigress's husband. "Isn't he dead too? Can't he be found?"

"Fen is never in our company," said the old man, "but never far away."

"Forty thousand might be enough," said the younger son, still looking at his feet.

After that Wang found himself dreaming of the White Tigress, as she had been when he first saw her, young and shy, not meeting his eyes. But then she did meet his eyes, and held them, as she so often had on their journey, and the dream became deliciously erotic, until Wang began to wake up and, consciously trying to continue the encounter, knew that he had floated back into the real world and lost his chance of satisfaction.

❀

The White Tigress did not come to see Wang alone, as he had asked. The ever-present Li Yen was with her. He did not enter the house, however, but remained on the step outside. The White Tigress, sitting down on the middle of Wang's bed, while he drew up a stool to face her, was uncharacteristically embarrassed.

"I'm sorry," she said. "He insisted on coming."

"What is he afraid of?"

"He is very jealous."

"Is he your second husband?"

"He would like to be."

"What are his chances?"

"My first husband's spirit is not yet at rest."

"Then he must be hoping that I will remove that obstacle for him."

"Yes, of course."

"Then he should treat me with less suspicion."

"He is doing the best he can. You can be sure that if he did not believe you were necessary to us, he would already have cut your throat."

"Ah."

Wang tried to appear unconcerned, but he felt the blood drain from his face and there was a blockage in his throat which prevented him speaking immediately.

"He thinks I have fallen in love with you," she said. "I told him that it was your knowledge I wanted, not yourself."

"Good!" said Wang indistinctly through the phlegm in his throat.

"He replied that he was sure *you* had fallen in love with me and that was why you asked me to come and see you alone."

"Did he think I would try to overpower you?" asked Wang, smiling as he recovered his speech.

"He said you would refuse to reveal your stratagem until I made love to you."

"A strategist himself, then."

"Was that your plan?"

She had looked directly at him all the while, sitting on the middle of the low bed with a straight back and her long trousered legs, half bent at the knees, stretched out together in front of her, her small feet in military boots set evenly on the floor. He could not tell whether she was inviting or accusing him. She seemed quite relaxed and simply seeking further information from him, as she had throughout their journey, yet he himself felt a powerful urge to continue his dream where it had broken off, take her in his arms and make love to her. Was this urge all on his side? Even if it was not, he could hardly forget that Li Yen was just outside on the step, no doubt with his ears pricked and one hand on his sword-hilt.

"It was not my plan," he said. "But I almost wish it had been."

She smiled, but he still could not tell what she really felt, whether relief or disappointment or indifference.

"Then he had nothing to fear," she said. "And you had nothing to fear from him. Now tell me your stratagem for taking the town, or at least killing the magistrate!"

"Yes," he said. "But since Li is such a clever fellow I would like him to hear it too."

He went outside and invited Li to join them. Li did not conceal his feelings. A huge smile broke across his round face and springing up he bowed deeply to Wang in thanks and respect. Wang called his servant to find another stool and when it was brought, seated himself and Li either side and equidistant from the White Tigress and each other, forming a perfect triangle.

Wang's stratagem pleased both his hearers, not least because it was simple in principle but elaborate in detail. They were confident that they would have the patience required to make it succeed, since, as Li said, they had exercised their patience for so long already that it had become a habit and almost a skill. And if it did succeed, the White Tigress added, it would surely go down in history.

❀

The weather had already changed in their favour: clouds covered the sky and a little rain was falling. Soon after their meeting another lucky thing happened. Spies living in the town kept them constantly informed of what was happening there and the latest news was that military reinforcements were expected from the north, presumably intended for use against the bandits. Wang at first took this to be bad news, but Li and the White Tigress thought otherwise. It was unlikely these days, considering how much more serious the fighting was in the north and east, that the authorities would be able to spare Mongol soldiers for a small, out-of-the-way town with a minor bandit problem. And if not, if they only sent native soldiers on foot, it would be easy to ambush and trap them as they followed the main road round the foot of the mountains.

Wang did not witness, let alone take part in the ambush. He was now the bandits' most valuable asset and remained inside the stockade with the women and children and a few sentries, while virtually the whole male population of the settlement—several hundred—rode out to set the ambush.

When they returned their numbers had almost doubled, for the soldiers, as soon as they found themselves under serious attack, made little attempt to fight, but threw down their arms with such alacrity that scarcely any were even wounded. Their Mongol captain and two of his lieutenants—the only ones who were mounted—had galloped away towards the town, leaving the bandits with a rich haul. The magistrate had clearly been intending to launch an attack on the settlement, for the column of soldiers was accompanied by artillery, five cannons for firing stone balls and a large quantity of gunpowder and rockets. The artillery specialist captured with them was Chinese—a muscular, heavily bearded man called Ling Zhen—and not at all sorry to change sides.

Welcomed warmly to the bandits' victory feast—at which a large consignment of wine intended for the magistrate's personal use flowed freely—Ling Zhen was seated, as the next most honoured guest, beside Wang, who questioned him about the capacities of his weapons.

"The cannons will not kill many people," said Ling Zhen. "But they make a great noise and it is very confusing and dispiriting to the enemy to have large chunks of stone falling about their heads. Everybody fighting in a battle is already on the edge of his nerves and the use of cannons can push soldiers over the edge and incline them to run away. As for the rockets, they are really nothing but frighteners, though if you shoot them into a town you have a good chance of hitting thatched roofs and starting a fire."

"But couldn't the cannons be used to knock down the gates or breach the walls of a town?" asked Wang.

"They are not much use against gates, but they can certainly damage walls, especially those that are made of brick. It takes time to make a breach, however, and you could only do it in the course of a long siege. You couldn't hope to make a sudden assault that way."

Wang liked the man immediately, but although he would have been glad to have his expert opinion on the feasibility of the stratagem, thought it unwise at this stage to give anything away to a person whose new loyalty had not yet been tested. So when he had learnt what the artillery could do and how many times it could be used before the gunpowder and rockets ran out, he dropped the subject and asked Ling Zhen for news of the rebellions elsewhere.

"The Red Scarf movement has split in two," he replied, "but neither the Northern nor the Southern group is doing well at present. And the more the Mongols succeed in confining them to small areas and shutting them up in towns, the more the rebel leaders, all seeing themselves as tigers when they are mostly rats, quarrel with each other. Rats in a bag."

"So you think the Mongols will succeed in crushing them?"

"The government forces are also very disorganised and of course it is all a question of loyalty."

"Loyalty to whom?"

"Precisely. Many of the less important officials at the local level are Chinese. Their instincts and training tell them to suppress bandits, but if the central government looks weak and the bandits begin to look like Chinese armies, then their loyalties become uncertain."

"Which way do *you* think it will go?"

"It is very nicely balanced at present, not only in general, but in every particular encounter. The government's most dangerous enemies now are not the Red Scarf movements, but two independent warlords. Fang Kuo-chen is a pirate whose ships, working from small offshore islands, control most of the southern coast and have almost completely cut off the grain supplies to the north."

"But surely they can go by the Grand Canal?"

"No, because a crucial stretch of the Canal, just north of the Yangzi River, is controlled by the other independent warlord, a former salt-smuggler called Zhang."

"So between Zhang and Fang the capital must be very short of grain. What are they going to do about it?"

"The government's only solution so far has been to try to get one or other of these enemies on their side by offering them official appointments and monopolies. Fang has accepted their offers several times and then reneged, while Zhang receives their embassies, delays and cogitates for a while, and then cuts off the ambassadors' heads."

"It must be hard to find new ambassadors," Wang said.

"I should think so. Perhaps they choose people already under sentence of death."

Wang smiled, but thought to himself that anyone engaged in this absurd game of fighting for some nebulous advantage—all those present, in fact, including himself—was under the same sentence.

"But if that is the government's only solution, to try to placate these bandits and pirates," he said, "it must be near collapse."

The artillery officer was amused.

"Excuse me," he said, "but you sound more like a government supporter than an honoured guest in a bandit camp."

"We live in strange times," Wang said, lowering his voice, "and I never thought to find myself where I am now."

"You are here against your will?"

"My will is not quite clear to me. Events decided for me. As they did for you, I suppose."

"I must admit that I intended to change sides at the first opportunity," said Ling Zhen. "We have been a military family for many generations. My grandfather fought for the Song Dynasty against the Mongols. What was he to do when the Song was defeated and the whole Empire united under the Yuan Dynasty? He must either take his family into the mountains and starve or continue to be a soldier under the new dynasty. The Mongols do not allow anyone to change his traditional occupation. So my father was a soldier too and so now am I. But if the Yuan Dynasty can no longer control the Empire, why should I continue to fight for foreigners? It is typical of their attitude that, although we knew we would be passing a bandit stronghold and might be ambushed, our Mongol captain was not in the least worried. 'They are led by a woman,' he said, 'and cannot be very well organised. Besides, if they come out and attack us, it will save us the trouble of going to fetch them out later.' But I thought to myself that if they were led by a woman they must be unusual bandits and so it proved. Their ambush was impeccably prepared and carried out, so that when we thought they were about to attack from the front, they suddenly attacked from behind, and as we turned to counter that attack, the main thrust came after all neither from the back nor the front, but from a wood on the left. Either this is a clever woman who leads them or she has a clever adviser."

"She is a clever woman," said Wang, "and she learns fast."

It seemed to him that the ambush described by Ling Zhen already owed something to the ideas he had discussed with her and Li.

"But I was surprised," said Ling Zhen, "that they allowed the captain to escape so easily. They shot a few arrows after him, but they were all on horseback and never even attempted to ride him down."

"I daresay they were glad to let him carry the bad news to the town," said Wang. "It will unsettle the soldiers there and dismay the magistrate."

"I am glad I changed sides," said Ling Zhen.

❀

The weather had turned wet and the nights were dark. But although conditions were now suitable for carrying out Wang's stratagem, the White Tigress was a cautious commander and not willing to attempt anything until the captured soldiers had been individually assessed and, so far as possible, assimilated into the bandit force.

They were divided into groups and the groups placed with different sections of the bandits. The best of those that could ride were picked out to take part in the initial phases of the stratagem. But most were to be kept back for the present as guards and foragers and their loyalty, discipline and value to the bandits carefully observed. Several who seemed unsatisfactory for one reason or another were immediately turned out of the camp, to go wherever they pleased. But the White Tigress warned the rest that if they chose to stay and proved unsatisfactory in the days ahead they would not be released but beheaded. This threat immediately weeded out several more. All the recruits were treated roughly, kept short of sleep and fiercely disciplined, as much to test their response as to turn them from lazy, disaffected soldiers into reliable fighting men.

Two or three were indeed beheaded and Wang could not help comparing this White Tigress, savage and inexorable in her role as a bandit-chieftain, with the pale, ghostly image of her he had received from Tao's love poems. Yet he still admired the poems, many of which he knew by heart. Although they were not true to the White Tigress, they were true to Tao's feelings, formed around a fantasy of his own creation, just as a painter often prefers, like Ni, to invent his own landscape rather than merely copy a real one.

These thoughts were rudely scattered a moment later as he heard the shouts of derision and triumph from the crowd watching the beheadings a few hundred yards away. He had angered the White Tigress by refusing to attend, but he knew her well enough by now not to be too alarmed for his own safety. When she was angry she was most feminine, flushing deeply, her voice higher, her fists clenched, her breasts shaking. But she never acted from her feminine side, only from her masculine side, showing no outward emotion, her voice deep and steady, her mind already made up, her course calculated in advance. It was just as if her actions really were directed by her father's and brothers' spirits or as if she became them on those occasions. Or rather, Wang preferred to think, she shared their male characteristics whenever male characteristics were called for. Yin and Yang, surely, were present in everyone of whichever sex and it was only the way that tasks were normally apportioned between the sexes that made men appear more often governed by Yang and women by Yin. At any rate, he judged that she would do him no harm just because she was angry with him, but only if she decided that he was no longer of any use to her.

A few nights after the beheadings a party of about seventy bandits, led by Li and accompanied by Ling Zhen, rode down the hill and across the plain to the town. Lighting lamps, shouting and beating drums to draw attention to themselves, they rode right round the town, before launching an attack on the east gate. It was only the semblance of an attack. They shot arrows at the guards on the towers and sent a few rockets over the walls to cause fires and rouse the inhabitants, but before dawn, when the whole town was in turmoil and before anyone inside could see how few the attackers really were, they rode back to the bandit camp.

"Attacks" of this sort were repeated night after night, each time at a different gate, for ten days. But whereas the attackers worked on a rota system, so that everyone had several days and nights of rest to make up for a single sleepless night, the town's garrison and most of its inhabitants were disturbed every night, since they could never be sure at which gate the next attack would come or whether this time it might not be a more serious attempt to force an entrance.

The magistrate, in particular, as the White Tigress learnt from her spies inside the town, was being worn down by these incessant night alarms. As middle-ranking officials tend to be, he was an anxious and irritable man at the best of times and the moment he heard the shouts and the drums beating round the walls, he would be out of bed and rushing about overseeing the defences, marshalling the fire-fighters and angrily lashing with his tongue and whip all those who failed to do exactly what he ordered or who simply got in his way.

On the eleventh night drums were beaten and rockets fired from outside the north gate and as the weary garrison, driven on by the now almost maniacal magistrate, rushed to that side of the town, a second "attack" was directed at the south gate. On the twelfth night, which was somewhat too clear for the bandits' purposes, no attack was made at all, but on the thirteenth night three gates were "attacked" in swift succession, and on the fourteenth, all four. On the sixteenth, when, as the White Tigress had discovered from her spies, the magistrate intended to strike back by opening whichever gate was first attacked, sallying out and engaging in open battle, there was no attack. On the seventeenth, when the garrison was again mustered for a sally, the bandits again stayed away. On the eighteenth, nineteenth and twentieth nights drums were beaten close to the walls throughout the hours of darkness, but when on the twentieth a half-hearted sally was made by a small number of exasperated defenders, they heard hooves galloping away but found no enemy.

Early on the twenty-first day roughly written papers appeared on the public notice-boards in different districts of the town. The magistrate had the papers swiftly removed, but not before their message had been read and spread about among the inhabitants: "Walls are no Barrier to the Vengeance of the Dead." This was no part of Wang's original plan, but a sudden inspiration born of his sense of fellow-feeling with the unfortunate magistrate, whose shoes he himself might have been wearing if he had done as his wife wanted and worked more assiduously for promotion. Remembering how, in his own perturbed state of mind when he first arrived in the bandit camp, he had dreamed of the spirits of the White Tigress's father and brothers, Wang felt sure that for the mind of the man he took the magistrate to be—that's to say a version of himself, rational, well-educated, self-sufficient, but also suggestible, nervous and secretly emotional—such a message, on top of twenty sleepless nights in a position of isolated responsibility, would act like the last firm blow with the flat of one's hand to the trunk of a tree already almost severed with an axe.

So it proved. The bandits heard that the magistrate was not seen outside his compound all day and that all scheduled court business had been cancelled until further notice. The question confronting Wang now, as he conferred the next day with the White Tigress and her chief officers, was whether the moment had arrived for their final strike or whether it would be better to continue the softening-up process for another ten days or so. This was what Wang had originally envisaged, though he conceded that if they encountered a spell of clear weather the moon would soon be too full for their small numbers to be concealed. Li Yen was impatient to strike.

"The magistrate is sick," he said, "the garrison exhausted, the people frightened and also tired out. What more can we achieve by waiting?"

"Perhaps the magistrate will die of his own accord," said Wang, "and save us any further trouble."

He spoke lightly, but the White Tigress took him seriously. Up to now she had been inclined towards caution, the more so since Wang himself seemed to be and the remarkable success of his stratagem so far had caused her to treat him more and more as an infallible authority.

"He must not die before I can kill him," she said.

"Must you do it with your own hand?" asked Wang.

"Absolutely."

It was agreed then that unless reports reached them that the magistrate was up and about again, the bandits would make one more false attack, but that their real attack would be mounted the following night.

Accordingly, drummers and a few rockets kept the town awake that night, while early the next morning, as soon as the town gates were opened, ten bandits joined the usual crowd of farmers and other suppliers going in to market. The ten included Li Yen and the White Tigress disguised as elderly peasants with a cart full of vegetables. The guards at the gates were by now so tired and careless that they scarcely glanced at the people going in and out. Once inside the town the bandits dispersed to the houses of friends and relations and remained there resting through the day.

Before night fell the whole bandit force left their camp and began descending to the plain. Including many of the soldiers captured in the ambush, it numbered some five hundred. There was a strong wind, driving black quilts of cloud across the sky, but the stars and the young moon were often visible and most of the bandits and their horses had by now made their way so often along the road to the town on much darker nights that they could travel briskly and easily. Nor did it matter now if their enemies could see them, since they were no longer a few pretending to be many.

But they did not ride faster than a trot. This time they were taking not only all the remaining rockets but also ten carts containing the five cannons and a large quantity of stone balls. The commander of this force was the White Tigress's senior military adviser, a former sergeant-instructor called Kuo Chong, who had once been part of the town's garrison but was severely disciplined—flogged and reduced to the ranks—by the magistrate for drunkenness. Kuo Chong was not an habitual drunkard, but on this occasion had quarrelled with his wife, whom he suspected of being unfaithful, had spent the night drinking and failed to appear for duty the next day. As soon as he recovered from his flogging he deserted to the bandits. He was a tall, hard, unsmiling man of about fifty, no less eager to take his revenge on the magistrate than the White Tigress was, though his bitterness extended, as hers did not, to the whole town, scene of his humiliation as both husband and soldier. The artillery expert, Ling Zhen, was also, of course, a key member of this small avenging army, and at his side rode Wang.

Wang had no particular part to play in the final attack and had assumed that he would remain in the camp while it was carried out. But after the conference the day before, when he had returned to his house and lain down on his bed for an afternoon sleep, he suddenly opened his eyes to see the White Tigress standing over him.

"I came to thank you," she said.

"It may be too soon," Wang said, struggling up on to one elbow.

"You've done what you promised," she said, sitting on the bed near his feet. "The rest depends on me."

"But suppose the attack miscarries and my stratagem therefore proves a failure?"

"Well, then, it would be difficult to thank you, so it is best done now."

"You will be cutting off my head, I imagine."

"What a waste that would be!" she said. "All that knowledge and cleverness lost at a single blow!"

"I'm sure the magistrate's head is better stocked than mine, since he holds an important post and is no doubt older. Nonetheless, you intend to deprive him of it."

She was silent for a while, staring out of the open doors in front of the house.

"Human life is very easily made," she said at last, "and very easily destroyed. It has no value in itself. I can kill a man with no more anxiety than I can kill a chicken. But when this magistrate's soldiers killed my family, they destroyed bodies, faces, hands and heads full of thoughts and memories that were of value to me, though not to the magistrate. It is his turn now to lose everything that is valuable to him—his wife, his children, his servants, the knowledge in his head and his own life. If he did not, how could I claim to value what he took from me? And I am the only one left alive to give that value to lives that are otherwise forgotten and valueless. Even if his head contained all the wisdom and knowledge in the world, which could never be replaced, I would cut it off."

Wang understood the force of her desire for vengeance as much through his eyes as his ears. He was mesmerised by its physical effect on her. Her face was still in profile and she was leaning slightly forward, the muscles of her neck and jaw and of her shoulders and arms neither strained nor wholly relaxed. She was like an athlete poised for some difficult feat but entirely confident of performing it, indeed she was like the tigress they called her, balanced on the point of springing. She was life itself, he saw, life intent on its own survival by killing, beautiful, savage, tenacious, predatory, vulnerable, tender, ephemeral, evanescent, already changing posture, already turning her head to look at him and breaking the image. He sighed to himself, wanting to have the moment back, thinking that all the knowledge and experience he had so far acquired were the mere borders to this single, central revelation of the value of life to itself.

Hearing him sigh and catching his distracted look, she perhaps misinterpreted his feelings. He had no desire to touch her. But she touched him. She reached out and put her hand on top of his, where it lay resting on his thigh.

"I liked you," she said, "the very first time you spoke to me in my father's house, so calmly and sympathetically in the middle of such a crisis. Besides, your tall, elegant appearance and your courteous manner quite overwhelmed me. I had never seen such a good-looking man, like the hero of a story. Then, when you cried so little for your burnt studio and so much for the death of your servant, I saw that in spite of your education and your imperial ancestors you had more love than pride in your heart. And I have grown to like you still more. You have a soft, clear voice, like good running water, your eyes are always busy and feeding all around you, like bees in a meadow, your fingers are as agile as a goat's legs and as sensitive as a dog's nose, and your mind is more richly stored with words and stories and knowledge of the ten thousand things than the greatest merchants' caravan we ever robbed of silver and silk."

Wang lowered his eyes and bowed his head as if deliberately offering her the back of his neck.

"You will not cut off my head, then, whatever happens?"

"I suppose that whatever happens you will want to go home?"

"I have hardly thought of that," Wang said, with complete honesty and some surprise.

"You haven't?" She too was surprised. "I thought you never stopped thinking and must have considered that."

"No, really not."

"Will you stay with us, then?"

"For what purpose? I'm not qualified, nor, to tell the truth, very pleased to be a bandit."

"We are only small bandits," she said. "But with you to guide us we could be more. We could make our own kingdom, like Zhang in the east."

"You've decided, after all, to be Emperor?"

"No, not Emperor, but why not a small king? With your help."

He laughed.

"Why do you laugh? You think I'm ridiculous?"

"A small king is somewhat ridiculous. But not you."

"I want you to stay," she said.

He had no doubt now that she was offering herself, with or without the small kingdom.

"What does Li Yen want?" he asked.

"I'm not afraid of him."

"Am I to abandon my former life?"

"Why not?"

So the choice confronted him. In a sense he had already made it when he willingly left his home in the company of bandits. But he had done that in a state of turmoil and unhappiness, when nothing seemed very real to him, least of all this woman from his friend Tao's dreams. But even after he had come to know her in reality he had made his own dream out of her and now that dream seemed to be absorbing reality.

"Do you never do anything by instinct?" she asked, impatient at his silence.

But she misunderstood him. His instinct told him to throw off the whole dream, to wake up, go home and resume being the person he recognised. Instinctively, he rejected a closer relationship with someone so much stronger and wilder than himself, a relationship which she would certainly control.

Instinctively, he believed in the loyalties implicit in marriage. His own marriage was of the customary kind, no sort of love-match, but a family contract made with a friend's younger sister. Nonetheless he and his wife had treated each other from the start respectfully and considerately. Wang's wife might complain of his lack of interest in official promotion, which after all affected her own life directly, but she knew very well how gifted he was as a painter and appreciated, if she did not share, his intellectual passions. After the miscarriage of their first child and the loss of any prospect of another, they had grown at first closer, then more distant, and their relationship had continued to fluctuate between warm and cool, like the weather in a mild climate, without ever becoming distinctly hot or cold. Wang might ignore his wife or respond intemperately when she was intemperate with him, but he never deliberately hurt her. That would have hurt his own self-esteem as a sensitive person.

Human instincts are instilled by blood and training and what was his former life but the outwardly visible skin of that inward pattern, as a pine-tree's bark identifies the pine-tree within? The desire to put his seed in a woman was also an instinct, of course, a still more basic one, common to most of the ten thousand things in their various ways. But the desire to make love to the White Tigress was more like an appetite for some rare dish or wine, or, come to that, for consuming with his eyes and entering with his mind the secret country of a master's painting. Except that those appetites could be satisfied and left behind in an hour or a day. The invitation to satisfy this appetite was extremely tempting, but the thought of its long-lasting and unforeseeable consequences was daunting. A quiet, orderly, law-abiding, decently-married scholar might as well choose to rebel against the government and be an outlaw as become this woman's lover. And in this case he was asked to do both.

"Well," she said angrily, withdrawing her hand, "you are free to go whenever you wish."

"I would like to see the outcome of the stratagem," he said. "To be present, I mean. And I have overcome my instincts. I will stay."

## 8. THE CANNONS ROAR

Kuo Chong deployed the main bandit army in front of the town's eastern gate. It was a measure of how weary and demoralised the garrison had become by now that the arrival of this large force on a comparatively clear night aroused hardly any reaction in the guards on the towers. Some thirty bandits, meanwhile, made their way round to the western gate, where they beat drums and fired three rockets. This was both to distract attention from the real point of attack and to signal to the ten bandits inside the town that the action was beginning.

Wang had himself devised the plan—or at least its main components—and had come to see it carried out, but, of course, neither he nor anyone else could see very much. In the first place it was night and in the second place the action was so dispersed that it would be only in retrospect in the mind that any clear view could be had.

The attack on the east gate began as soon as the third rocket was fired to the west. Volleys of arrows assailed the guards on the towers and walls and, while they were ducking down and taking cover, five of the bandits who had been lurking all day inside the town darted out and killed the two gatekeepers, then drew the bolts and opened the gate.

As they did so and as the sleepy soldiers from the guard-house near the gate were rushing out to defend it, the five cannons roared and balls of stone hurtled through the opening, knocking down several soldiers, scattering the rest. The cannons roared again and behind this second storm of stone galloped the whole bandit cavalry, passing through the half-open gateway three abreast, cutting down those guards who were still trying to close the gate. Then, as another volley of arrows struck the towers, detachments of the invading horsemen leapt off their mounts and rushed up the stairs to kill or capture the soldiers cowering there. The rest of the horsemen, led by Kuo Chong, made straight for the magistrate's compound at the town centre.

Wang, holding his hands over his ears, could dimly see all this from his place at Ling Zhen's side behind the cannons. After the horsemen had passed out of sight, seventy or so bandits on foot—mostly the former soldiers who had surrendered in the ambush a month earlier—moved forward to finish off any guards who were still alive and had not fled, and to make sure that the gate stayed open for the horsemen's return. The cannons remained pointing at the opening in case of a counter-attack, but after the tense hours of preparation, the night march and the violent excitement of the attack, lasting perhaps no more than ten minutes or the passing of one long cloud across the moon, there was nothing now for Wang and Ling Zhen and the remaining hundred bandits in reserve to see, nothing to do but wait. Shivering, pacing quickly up and down to get warm, his ears still buzzing, his nose and throat filled with the bitter smell and taste of gunpowder, Wang was aware that Ling was congratulating him, though he could not make out a word he said.

"So far, so good," he shouted back, outwardly modest and cautious even in these dramatic circumstances, but inwardly exhilarated by the way his ideas had been transformed so successfully into reality.

Over and over again in his mind's eye he repeated the spectacle of the gate opening with seemingly ceremonial slowness (though it could only have taken seconds), the fearful roar of the cannons and, in the silence that followed, the drumming of the horses' hooves on the earth and the clattering on the flagstones as they passed through the gateway and disappeared into the dark street beyond. He understood now what he had never understood before—always considered a kind of madness or stupidity—why people should want to be soldiers, risking their precious lives for causes in which their own stake was minimal. It was because they had no thought of risking their lives, but were intent only on the action itself. How glad he was at this moment to have overcome his own safety-seeking instinct and dared to launch himself on to this swiftly-flowing river of fate in the company of so many brave, reckless men! It was not so much that he had overcome his fear of taking the wrong course or even of dying, as that he was freed altogether from such considerations and was drunk with the wine of action, though his head seemed clearer than usual—all its usual contradictions and irrelevancies swept away like dirt and cobwebs. He wished only that he had not agreed to stay behind with Ling and the reserves, but had insisted on riding with Kuo Chong into the town. Waiting now seemed far the harder part.

"Why are they taking so long?" he said to Ling, not expecting or getting any answer except a lift of the shoulders.

Ling was warming his hands on the barrel of one of the cannons, but, like all the men grouped behind the cannons, eagerly watching the town and listening for any sound of distant fighting.

Not that there would necessarily be much fighting. Wang's plan had been for the White Tigress and the main force of bandits to break into the magistrate's compound and then, their work of slaughter accomplished, ride back out of the open gate. But the White Tigress had been afraid something might go wrong, that it would take too long to force the gate open and that the magistrate might be given time to escape in the darkness and take refuge somewhere else in the town. This was why she and Li Yen had gone secretly into the town the previous morning, so that as soon as the third rocket was fired from the west and the attack began from the east, she—with Li and their three companions—would enter the magistrate's compound and take her revenge. According to this modified version of Wang's plan, the main bandit force under Kuo Chong was still to make straight for the compound, but only to ensure that, if the White Tigress had failed to enter the compound or was herself in difficulties, the magistrate did not escape.

But in case this plan too went wrong and Kuo Chong with his three hundred horsemen was too long delayed, while the White Tigress, having killed the magistrate, was beset with an overwhelming number of the garrison, Li Yen introduced a further modification. He and the White Tigress and their comrades would not wait for the arrival of the main force, but as soon as they had finished with the magistrate go straight to the south gate, kill the guards, open the gate and leave the town. Outside that gate they would be met by the group of bandits who had beaten the drums and fired the rockets at the west gate and would then ride back with them—five spare horses being provided for the purpose—to join the reserves and the returning main force outside the east gate where the cannons were.

Wang had objected to this plan that it was too complicated. Furthermore, he said, if it was designed to allow for the failure of the weakest link in the whole plan, namely the opening of the east gate from within, it introduced a second equally weak link, namely the opening of the *south* gate from within. Indeed, this second weak link was likely to be even weaker than the first, since whereas the five bandits charged with opening the east gate would have the advantages of freshness and of being already concealed near the gate so as to achieve surprise, the White Tigress and her party would have expended much of their energy in the magistrate's compound, would then have to run through the streets and would surely be spotted by the guards on the south gate before reaching it. Li Yen countered that after the false attack on the west gate and the real attack to the east, only a few guards would be left at the south gate and they would certainly not expect to be attacked from within. He suggested, however, that if the five bandits who had the job of opening the east gate succeeded, they should immediately make their way to the south gate and be ready to assist the White Tigress and her companions there as soon as they appeared.

Everyone now agreed that the plan was being encumbered with too many "ifs" and the discussion ended with a compromise: the White

Tigress and Li Yen and their three companions would wait for Kuo Chong and his three hundred horsemen at the magistrate's compound, unless something went wrong and they were in too much danger. In that case, they would adopt Li Yen's plan, go to the south gate and force their own way out. Unfortunately, everyone was so confused by the various modifications and their partial cancellation that no one remembered to tell the leader of the false attack on the west gate about riding with five spare horses round to the south gate in case the White Tigress and her party broke out there.

As he waited and thought about all the arrangements and whether they might be working or not, this point occurred to Wang for the first time. No doubt, he thought, Li Yen or the White Tigress or Kuo Chong had given the correct instructions to the group outside the west gate, but suppose they hadn't? Of course, in the best case, the White Tigress would not have to force her way out of the south gate at all, but in the worst case? Then there might be no one to meet her and she would have to make her way round to the east gate on foot and might easily be ridden down by pursuing soldiers. He explained his anxiety to Ling Zhen and added:

"Obviously you must stay here with the cannons, but I am quite redundant. Shall I go and see?"

"That's surely unnecessary," said Ling Zhen. "The attack went through so quickly and conclusively that the horsemen must have reached the magistrate's compound almost before the White Tigress and Li Yen had done their work there. I'm sure they'll have no need to go to the south gate."

Wang, however, was by now determined to go. His short-lived exhilaration had given way to his normal state of anxiety and, with no previous experience of warfare, he had not developed the professional soldier's tolerance of the long intervals of dreary waiting inseparable from most kinds of military action. So, untethering his horse, mounting and waving cheerily to Ling, he set off southwards at a trot. Not being a very adept horseman—how could he possibly have imagined himself galloping into the town in Kuo Chong's cavalry charge?—he did not try to make his horse go faster. The ground was even, the horse sure-footed and the town not particularly large, so that even making a circuit at a safe distance—beyond the flight of an arrow from the walls—with very little light from the sky, it was not a long or difficult journey.

As he went, his head constantly turning towards the town, his ears cocked, he thought he could hear some noise that was neither the wind nor the creaking of his saddle. He pulled up the horse and sat listening. Yes, it must be the distant sound of fighting, or at least shouting. Did that mean that the garrison was resisting? Could the magistrate be still alive and in command, regaining control of the town? Perhaps they had all underestimated the magistrate. Perhaps he had seen through Wang's long-drawn-out stratagem from the start and made careful and clever plans of his own to counter the real attack when it came.

Riding on, Wang began to make out the towers of the south gate jutting above the walls. He could not tell whether they were manned or not at this distance and did not care to go any closer. He could now hear the noise more distinctly and it certainly seemed to be fighting. Drawing level with the gate, he peered about in the darkness for the group of bandits from the west gate who should already be waiting somewhere in this area, then rode slowly round in widening circles, but at last had to admit that there was no one. What was he to do now? Ride on to the west gate and bring them here as quickly as possible? Surely it would be too late? Besides, if no one had given them instructions to ride round to the south gate, they had probably already gone to the east gate to rejoin the rest of the bandit army. What Wang should have done in the first place was to bring with him a party of reserves, with spare horses, but he had been too impatient and had not wanted the trouble of persuading Ling Zhen, who was in command of the reserves, into letting him do so.

While he hesitated, the noise grew louder. It seemed to come from just the other side of the gate. Dismounting and leading his horse carefully towards the gate—he had some idea of sheltering behind the animal if the guards noticed him and started loosing their crossbows—he could now see dark figures moving about in the towers. Since there was no sign of anyone having seen him, their activity must be concentrated on what was happening the other side of the walls, inside the town.

And then the gate began to open, slowly, clumsily, just as the east gate had opened earlier that night. But this gate opened only a little, only the width of a human body. The noise of the battle beyond suddenly swelled, until the gate was immediately closed again. Three figures had emerged, however, and after a moment's pause, began running towards Wang, all three close together, as if linked in some way. Alarmed, hoping they might be his friends, but afraid they could be enemies, Wang tried to mount his horse too hastily. The horse was startled, moved away, and Wang fell on the ground. When he got up he could see no sign of the three figures and, nervously peering about for them in the darkness, edged backwards towards the horse.

"Bring the horses here! Quickly! Quickly!"

It was Li Yen's voice.

"There's only this horse, my horse," said Wang, and, seeing Li now sitting on the ground only a few yards away, added: "Is the White Tigress with you?"

"Where are the others?"

"I'm afraid the instructions were never given. There's nobody here but me."

"Disaster!" said Li.

He was holding the White Tigress in his arms, her head on his lap, an arrow sticking out of her neck below the left ear. The other man was kneeling nearby, he too wounded with an arrow, but only in the upper arm.

"Shouldn't the arrow be removed?" Wang asked, dropping to the ground beside them, horrified, sickened, meaning nothing practical by his words, but rather that the event itself should be removed from reality.

"No, I don't think so," said Li. "Certainly not here."

Stumbling and knocking into each other, their hands slippery with the White Tigress's blood, they got her up on to Wang's horse, having removed the saddle, laying her head on the horse's rump, her feet against its neck, holding her in place as gently as they could, and walked slowly, all too slowly, towards the east gate.

❀

To begin with, everything had gone well with the White Tigress's part of the plan. When night came, she and Li Yen and their three companions made their way from their separate hiding-places in the town to a previously arranged meeting-place in a street behind the magistrate's compound. As soon as they saw the third rocket from the west—only one rocket would have signalled the cancellation of the attack, in case that had been necessary for some unforeseen reason—they climbed the compound wall and dropped into the magistrate's garden. The sentry on duty there was dozing in a corner and took no notice at all of the rockets—after all, he had seen so many in the previous three weeks. They were able to seize him and cut his throat with hardly a sound.

The magistrate's own private access to his garden was from the back of the house by way of a small terrace with steps, but the door there was likely to be well secured. The five bandits, therefore, crept through the garden to a side-door leading to the kitchen and servants' quarters, from which the sentry would have reached his post. The White Tigress paused to tie her white scarf on her head, then, hearing the distant roar of the cannons at the east gate, Li Yen tried this side-door and found it unlocked.

The kitchen was deserted, but there were sounds of people waking and calling out in alarm as they too heard the cannons. Quickly crossing the kitchen and leaving it by a door that led into a small yard with a covered way, the bandits posted one man to prevent anyone coming after them, while the remaining four broke the lock of the door leading into the magistrate's own quarters and rushed in.

There were four small sleeping rooms there, two either side of the central room, which was the magistrate's office and inner council-chamber as well as his private living-room. It contained about a dozen chairs, one or two low tables, chests holding the records of the court and the town administration and, in an alcove in the corner, a large porcelain vase containing autumn twigs in front of a hanging scroll. Li Yen, who gave all these details to Wang, could only say that he thought the vase was decorated in green and red and that the scroll showed a peaceful view of mountains and rivers.

A large door led from this back half of the building into the public court-room at the front. Li and one man quickly took up position in front of this door, while the other man guarded the side door they had just come through. All this had been carefully rehearsed beforehand, since the magistrate's compound was constructed to a standard design and in any case their spies had passed them a rough plan of it.

Disturbed first by the double salvo of cannons and now thoroughly awakened by the sound of their servants' door being broken open, the various members of the magistrate's family were emerging from the side rooms. Several were holding candle-lamps, so that the spectacle reminded Li, with the leaping shadows and the wild appearance of these people just woken, in their night clothes, with quilts or coats round their shoulders, their hair loose, of a ghost scene he had once seen performed by travelling entertainers in this very town. On this occasion, however, it was not the audience but the "ghosts" who, seeing the White Tigress confronting them with the white scarf on her head and her drawn sword, screamed and shrank away in terror.

The last to emerge from his bed was the magistrate himself. He was, said Li, very obviously sick, shaking and sweating even before he set eyes on the White Tigress. As he did so, they could all hear a tremendous hubbub from outside in the streets. Kuo Chong's cavalry charge had met determined resistance from the garrison housed in the main military barrack beside the magistrate's compound and quickly mustering in front of it.

During her unexpected visit to Wang's house the previous evening, the White Tigress had asked him what she should say to the magistrate before killing him. Wang was dismayed.

"It's not a play," he said, "and I am not a playwright. Even if I were, I should not wish to compose a text for a real death."

"You don't think he deserves death?"

"He may or may not deserve it," said Wang, "but I know that you are determined to kill him and I'm not trying to stop you. Indeed, I've done everything I could to help you. But this is not . . ."

He stopped, not sure what he meant to say.

"Not what?"

"Not dignified," he said.

She looked at him with astonishment.

"What are you saying? Not dignified for me to say your words? Or for the magistrate to hear them? Or for you to compose them?"

"It would be better to say whatever comes into your head at the time," he said, still not sure himself what he had meant by "dignified."

"I know what it is," she said, flushing and her voice rising. "You think this is some kind of peasant business, a peasant who wants to kill an official. You don't mind helping the peasant achieve her purpose from a distance, but you don't want even your words to go near the deed itself. Because really you sympathise with this official murderer, who belongs to your own class."

"I sympathise with him, yes," said Wang. "How can I help imagining myself in his position, putting down rebellion, as I would be bound to do if I were him, and perhaps killing many innocent people in the process—not, of course, with my own hands, but by my orders? This is only natural, bred and educated as I am. And it is only natural for you, sorrowing for your family and your husband, to want revenge and to take it. I cannot easily resolve this contradiction in my own mind."

"It would not be a contradiction if you lived in your heart instead of your mind," she said. "Your heart should tell you whether I am more important to you than this magistrate you have never seen and also whether the magistrate's power and laws are really worth the respect you give them. You say he was 'putting down rebellion.' What rebellion? Was *he* not in rebellion against his own people? You say he killed 'innocent people.' No, my family was not innocent. We rejected his authority. We have lived in these mountains out of all memory. Why should we accept the power and laws of foreigners and of outsiders such as this magistrate who prefer to serve foreigners rather than their own people? You yourself are descended from the great Song Emperor. How can you sympathise with those who are so disloyal to his dynasty?"

"You are right, of course," said Wang, "though I do not think it is a question of heart and mind. It was my mind that directed me in both those ways, to follow you and to drive out the foreigners. But my mind also tells me that peace is better than war, good government than no government, laws than private vengeance, mercy than execution. My mind tells me now that I could never slice off this man's head with my own hands, therefore that it cannot compose words to justify such an act without hypocrisy."

The White Tigress looked at him with contempt.

"You had better go home to your wife and your books," she said.

"My books are all burnt."

"You are not one of us and never can be."

She stood up and walked out of the house without a backward glance.

It can be imagined how badly Wang felt after this argument, though he still rejected her facile distinction between heart and mind. It was not so much that she was right about where his loyalty should lie, as that she was right about his own character. She had twisted him this way and that, as one tries to break a still living twig. First she had encouraged him to go against his own nature and make the reckless decision to remain with her and the bandits, now she had forced him to acknowledge that his nature could not be changed so easily, if at all. It was only too clear that if he kept to his decision and stayed with her, this kind of scene would recur. The desire he felt for her and her desire—or at least admiration—for him would be constantly punctuated by these lacerating disagreements.

He therefore revised his decision. He would stay to see the final phase of the stratagem carried out and then, if it was successful and while she was still pleased with him, he would ask to go home. Let their parting be on this high note, but let him have no further illusions that it could be anything but a parting!

His mind now settled and calm, Wang immediately—without asking himself why he should now feel able to do what he had just so categorically refused—set it to work composing an epitaph for the magistrate. When he was satisfied, he took out the brush and inkstone and paper he had brought in his small leather travelling-bag and wrote down what he had composed, using the elegant, aristocratic running-script—clear, vibrant and quite thickly inked—which he had first learnt from his famous grandfather.

What would Lord Meng, scion of the Song Dynasty but loyal supporter of the Yuan, have felt if he could have seen his grandson using the script for this purpose? Wang did not pause to ask himself that either, but called his servant and told him to take the paper to the White Tigress. He was not altogether sure that she could read, but he perhaps secretly hoped that she might come back to his house, either to have him read it to her or at least to thank him for it and signify that their quarrel was forgotten.

The servant returned to say that he had delivered the piece of paper, but had no message. The White Tigress did not come back. She was probably too busy preparing to enter the town as soon as it grew light. Wang did not see her again until he found her lying in Li Yen's arms in front of the south gate, with the arrow in her neck.

He had actually composed three epitaphs, specifying that they were intended for three different eventualities. The first was to be used if she killed the magistrate during a fight, the second if she killed him as he was running away, the third if she killed him after he begged for mercy. The first was "You fought in an unjust cause," the second, "You cannot escape justice," but the third turned out to be the appropriate one, since the moment the magistrate saw the White Tigress with her white scarf and drawn sword and her dark eyes glowing with triumphant hatred, he fell on his knees and banged his head on the floor in front of her and asked for mercy.

"And then did she say anything?" asked Wang.

"Only five words," said Li Yen. "'The dead have no mercy.'"

"And immediately killed him?"

"Almost immediately. He tried to roll aside and the first blow went deep into his shoulder. The second blow struck the side of his face. The third blow severed his head."

As soon as the magistrate's head rolled on the floor and as his watching family screamed and ran about in panic, the White Tigress with Li Yen and the other two bandits pursued and killed them all: his wife, his mother, a nearly-grown-up daughter and three young sons. Two guards who had been in the outer hall and must have heard the pandemonium inside, even against the noise of battle from the street, opened the door, but turned and fled when they saw what was happening. One was caught and killed, the other got away into the street.

When every possible hiding-place had been searched and every member of the magistrate's family slaughtered, Li Yen told the White Tigress that it was time to leave the compound. They had no idea who was winning the battle they could hear outside and they might find themselves trapped if the soldiers got the better of the bandits. But she was inexorable. Her vengeance was not yet satisfied. Returning to the kitchen and servants' quarters, where the man posted at the door had already killed an old man who had poked his head out, the five bandits killed every servant they could find: cooks, kitchen-maids, a gardener, two small children and a groom. One or two had no doubt already escaped through the garden door, but the White Tigress—or the vengeful spirits that possessed her—was now at last content and did not insist on searching the garden.

She and her four companions climbed the wall and returned to the street, hurriedly conferring there about what they should do next. Deciding that they would be better not to join the melee at the front of the compound, since in the darkness they might easily kill or be killed by their own side, they made for the south gate through back streets. Unfortunately, they missed their way at one point and emerged too soon into the main street leading from the centre to the gate. Here they encountered a squadron of soldiers—fifteen or twenty—led by a Mongol officer, perhaps the very man who had escaped from the bandits' ambush a month earlier. He was evidently bringing up reinforcements to the battle at the town centre from the guard-house at the south gate.

The five bandits immediately ducked back into the side street and, pursued by some of the soldiers, ran the way they had come until they reached the turning they had previously missed. Most of the town's population must have been wide awake by now, but all their doors were fast shut. The bandits kept running, conscious of innumerable eyes watching from the spy-holes in the window-shutters, until they had shaken off their pursuers and were once more approaching the south gate, this time from the side. The whole area seemed to be empty, suspiciously so, with no guards visible at the gate or in the towers.

"They are lying in wait for us," Li Yen whispered.

"It can't be helped if they are," said the White Tigress. "That's the way we must go."

"At least take off your white scarf!" said Li Yen. "It makes you too obvious a target."

Her scarf by now was hardly white. Adjusting it several times with her blood-stained hands, she had blotched and speckled it red. But she refused to remove it.

"Let them kill me if they can!" she said. "I have done what I came to do."

Then, without another word, she ran straight for the gate. The others ran after her.

"And, of course, it was a trap," said Li. "The Mongol officer must have turned his soldiers back and ordered everyone around the gate to hide. As soon as we broke cover, arrows flew down from the towers and soldiers appeared everywhere, from the guard-house, from the shadows beside the gate, on the towers, from the side-streets. The Mongol himself intercepted the White Tigress as she reached the gate, while soldiers closed up behind us. But she showed no sign of being tired or hesitant. She still seemed to be possessed with the strength and fury of several men. Perhaps the Mongol meant to capture rather than kill her—if so, he miscalculated. He should have fought for his life or hers. Their swords clashed two or three times and then she stabbed him through the belly. The soldiers behind us, discouraged by their officer's fall, drew back a little, while the guards at the gate ran out of her way."

Li quickly drew back the bolts, but now the soldiers surged forward again and, as Li struggled to pull open the gate, almost crushed the bandits against it. Two were cut down as they tried to drive the soldiers off. There was now hardly the space to wield a sword and in a moment the three remaining bandits would have been overwhelmed and captured. But in that moment—which Wang had witnessed from outside—Li got the gate open sufficiently for himself, the White Tigress and their remaining comrade to slip through. The gate, with the weight of soldiers pressing on it from the other side, immediately closed behind them.

But, as they paused and looked about for the rescue party, they forgot that, whereas the inner side of the door was set under the wall, the outer side was flush with it and the towers so constructed that they jutted out directly over the gate. That brief pause was all the soldiers on the towers needed to sight their crossbows and, as the three bandits, catching sight of Wang's horse silhouetted against the sky, began to run towards it, five or seven arrows flew, missing Li Yen, but finding their companion's arm and the White Tigress's neck.

By the time Wang and his companions reached the cannons in front of the east gate, the battle inside the town was over. No one, not even the former sergeant-instructor, Kuo Chong, had expected it to be so ferocious. He had warned the bandits that the garrison's general was an experienced and careful commander, but the hope had been that after so many weeks of false attacks, even this man would be caught off guard. It seemed, on the contrary, that he had not only kept his best men under constant discipline but had even made use of the strain they were all under to tighten their standards of readiness and obedience. At any rate, his soldiers were already running out of their barrack and forming lines of defence as Kuo Chong and his horsemen charged up the street from the east gate. Foot-soldiers, of course, have little chance against cavalry in the open, but the confined space here cancelled much of the horsemen's advantage. So long as the general was directing his troops, the bandits could make no headway towards the magistrate's compound and were sometimes in danger of being driven back.

Marking down the general, who was organising and energising his forces from the steps at the entrance to the compound, Kuo Chong made repeated attempts to fight his way through to him, which were repeatedly baulked. Indeed the bandit commander, always at the front of the attack as his chief enemy was always at the rear of the defence, must have seemed far the likelier of the two to be killed, except that his fierce determination, exceptional skill as a horseman and swordsman, and the long spiked club which he continually whirled with his left hand gradually cleared a larger and larger space around him. At last, when this space was sufficient, he—with ten or twelve of his nearest companions, inspired by his obdurate fury—charged straight at the solid ranks of soldiers still between him and the general. The soldiers' nerve failed, they tumbled and leapt sideways like grasshoppers scattering in front of someone running through long grass. Too late the general jumped off the steps and tried to escape along the base of the compound wall. Kuo Chong swerved after him, leaned right out of his saddle and with a slanting blow of his sword cut the general in two, from neck to hip.

That was the end of the soldiers' resistance. They ran away down the streets or surrendered.

Kuo Chong dismounted, entered the court-room, where the dead guard lay in front of the judgment dais, and then the inner room, littered with corpses and splashed with blood. Beyond that he found the old man dead by the kitchen door, the shambles in the servants' quarters and the dead guard in the garden, and concluded that, since there had been no sign of the White Tigress or her companions during the battle, they must have decided to make for the south gate. He sent horsemen there immediately and a messenger to Ling Zhen outside the east gate to check whether she had already returned.

Kuo Chong's messenger arrived only a few minutes after Wang and Li with the wounded White Tigress. She was now lying on the ground, the arrow still jutting out of her neck, while one of the reserves with some medical knowledge examined her. She was unconscious but still breathing. Li Yen sent the messenger back to tell Kuo Chong the bad news and urge him to send the best doctor he could find in the town as soon as possible. Li gave no other instructions, but assumed that Kuo Chong would now gather all his horsemen and those who had stayed to keep the east gate open and leave the town. There had never been any plan to capture and hold it. The Mongols might not make great efforts to avenge the death of a native magistrate, but they surely would to recapture a town and it would have been too easy, the bandits reckoned, for them to do so.

Kuo Chong wasted no time in finding the doctor, who had been a near neighbour of his before his disgrace, but he did not return himself. The news of what had happened to the White Tigress, whom he adored, seems to have pitched this strong, self-disciplined man, excited by his victory, into a fit of mad anger. No doubt his long-brooded hatred of the town that had disgraced him was part of it too. He assembled all his remaining horsemen—eighty or so had died in the street battle—and instead of leading them away, ordered them to sack the town, looting what they wanted, killing anyone they cared to, setting the houses on fire.

"Even if every man, woman and child dies," he told them, "even if the whole town burns to the ground and nothing remains but ash and smoke, this will be too little punishment for what they have done to the White Tigress."

❀

The doctor was examining the White Tigress, with Wang and Li Yen standing miserably nearby, knowing—though they could not quite admit it—that there was no hope of saving her, when they suddenly heard uproar and crackling from the town and saw that it was in flames.

"What are they doing?" the doctor cried out, abandoning his examination and getting to his feet. "My wife and children are there, my brother and his family, my sister, my mother . . ."

"Can you save the White Tigress?" asked Li Yen.

"Can you save my relatives?" said the doctor.

"What can we do?" asked Li. "We had no intention of harming the town. This must be an accident or a misunderstanding."

The doctor began running towards the east gate. He was a small, stout, middle-aged man, not very fit. Li quickly overtook him and seized him by the hair.

"You will die here and now," said Li, "I will kill you myself, unless you save her. But if you do, I will go into the town with you myself and search for your relatives."

"She will die very soon unless the arrow is drawn out," said the doctor. "But I cannot draw out the arrow because its barb is deep in her flesh. One would have to cut the barb out of her flesh with a knife, but the knife would kill her. There is nothing to be done for her. But perhaps there is still something to be done to save my family. Please let me go!"

Li dropped the man to the ground, but still stood over him and seemed about to draw his sword. Wang went forward and put his hand on Li's shoulder.

"I'm sure he's told the truth," he said. "He would save her if he could. Let him go!"

Li said nothing, but went and knelt beside the White Tigress. Wang called the horseman who had brought the doctor and told him to carry the doctor quickly back into the town, to find Kuo Chong if possible and say that the doctor should be given all possible help to save his family. Then, as the man rode away with the doctor behind him, Wang too went and knelt beside the White Tigress.

The doctor had opened her jacket and shirt in order to examine the wound. Blood covered her white skin and ran down between her breasts. Her eyes were closed and she hardly seemed to be breathing. Li was lying right up against her now, his head touching hers, clasping her right arm as if he meant to go with her into another world. The artillery officer, Ling Zhen, squatted at her feet, his head between his hands, his face full of anguish. All around, not packed close but grouped irregularly with intervals between them, like a forest of young trees filtering the light from the burning town, stood all those who had been waiting in reserve, quite silent and hardly moving. Wang leaned over and kissed her forehead, just below the edge of the stained white scarf. As he did so, the lines from Tao's hundred poems which he had once quoted in such different circumstances came into his head and he spoke them aloud, slowly and distinctly so that everyone there could hear:

*Never open your heart like a flower!*
*How long do spring flowers last?*
*The flame of love lights my page,*
*Until my candle burns out.*

As he finished, he thought that her mouth moved as if meaning to smile, but it was probably only the flickering light or her last gasp of breath. She had avenged her dead father and brothers and was dead.

# 9. THE ROSE-TREE ROTS

When anything ceases to grow, it begins to decay. There is no point of rest. Upwards or downwards, outwards or inwards, change is perpetual. This is as true of empires and dynasties as of all the ten thousand things. Khan Khublai conquered the Empire once ruled by the Han, Tang and Song Dynasties and founded the Yuan. He reigned for thirty-four years and had ten successors, few of whom reigned more than a few years, most of whom were murdered or replaced in internecine quarrels, until the last of them, Toghon Temür, came to the throne as a boy of thirteen and reigned for thirty-five years.

His first Chancellor, Bayan, saw that the Dynasty had been decaying ever since the death of its founder and wanted to apply the remedy a gardener applies to rose-trees, cutting right back to the ground. The new boy Emperor was given the same reign-name as Khublai and the calendar was restarted from the beginning of the Dynasty. But these were not real remedies so much as superstitious invocations, and although by a strange chance Toghon reigned for almost the same length of time as his great ancestor, it was all in reverse: piece by piece he lost everything Khublai had won.

After seven years Chancellor Bayan was ousted and exiled by his own nephew and protégé, Toghto—tall, well-educated and an expert bowman—who became Chancellor in his place. Toghto was determined to reconquer and bring under central control everything that had been lost to regional interests, religious fanatics and bandits and it seemed for a time that his strength and energy—he was only twenty-six when he seized power—would revive the Yuan. He did everything on a scale to match the size of the Empire and its emergencies.

First he tamed the Yellow River, whose sudden change of course had brought floods and droughts, followed by plague and rebellion. Then, when the supply of food to the capital was disrupted by Fang's pirates along the coast and Zhang's bandits astride the Grand Canal, Toghto initiated a huge scheme to grow rice in the Yellow River valley, where it had never been cultivated before. Finally, advancing southwards at the head of a very large army, he set about crushing all the rebels, beginning with Zhang.

Closely besieged in a small town and defeated every time he tried to break out, Zhang was on the point of surrender when a message arrived for Toghto from the Emperor. The Chancellor was to relinquish his office and his military command and go into exile. This was the work of Toghto's enemies in the capital, but unfortunately for the Emperor and the Dynasty, Toghto was too loyal to disobey. He abandoned the siege, went meekly into exile and was poisoned a year later.

Zhang at once grew far stronger than before, as did all the other rebels Toghto had intended to suppress. The Empire became divided into numerous fiefdoms, some still obedient to the Dynasty, others intent on its destruction, while in the capital, Dadu, and the Emperor's own palace, family squabbles and political factions continued to eat away the heart of the government. The rose-tree was now fatally diseased, the Dynasty doomed. That was evident to everyone when, only five years after the fall of Chancellor Toghto, an army of Red Scarf rebels captured and burnt Khan Khublai's original capital, Xandu.

Wang had never been to Xandu, but his grandfather, Lord Meng, once had, and Wang received a garbled version of that visit from his mother. The city was built by Khan Khublai in empty lands close to the northern frontier and, like its founder, had a double identity, reflecting both the nomadic barbarism of the Mongols just across the border and the sedentary civilisation to the south. Xandu was a square within a square within a square. The innermost square, containing the marble Imperial Palace and other palaces and government buildings, was walled with brick; while the square surrounding it, where most of the inhabitants lived in houses made of mud or wood, was surrounded by a high earth wall. There was nothing outlandish about this design. It was modelled on older Imperial cities and used again, in rectangular form, for Khublai's second and larger capital city, Dadu, built some fifteen years afterwards.

The peculiarly Mongol element of Xandu lay in the outermost square, enclosing the other two in its south-east corner. This was a huge hunting-park of meadows, streams and woods, where deer, white mares and cows roamed freely. After Dadu was built, ten days' journey to the south-east, the Mongol rulers used Xandu, which was much higher and cooler, as their summer residence, taking the most important members of their court and government with them. Yet, for the Mongols themselves, Xandu was much more than a summer resort. It was here that Khublai, who took so much trouble to understand and make use of the customs, beliefs and culture of the complex Empire he had conquered, kept in touch with his simple, nomadic origins. Here he hunted on horseback, which had always been a kind of military training for the Mongols, and here he performed the sacred rituals of his own people.

At the end of every summer, before leaving Xandu, he took part with four shamans in the ceremony of sacrificing a horse and sheep and scattering the milk from specially-bred mares so as to invoke the spirits of his ancestors and ensure good fortune for the coming winter. His successors followed his example. In Dadu they were chiefly Chinese Emperors, but in Xandu, Mongol Khans. When the Red Scarves destroyed Xandu, it was as if they were cutting the Mongols' tap-root.

These Red Scarves came from the northern branch of the movement, based in the valley of the Yellow River. They had already captured Kaifeng, the ancient capital of the Song, and proclaimed the restoration of the Song Dynasty. Their figurehead was a boy claiming to be the tenth-generation descendant of a Song Emperor and known as "The Young Prince of Radiance," since he was also supposed to be the forerunner of the Maitreya Buddha, who would soon come to cleanse the world of evil. But Heaven, it seemed, did not want the Song Dynasty restored. These people were driven on by religious and patriotic zeal, but soon driven back by lack of organisation and consolidation, losing all their gains, including Kaifeng.

To Wang, now back with his wife in his house under the Yellow Crane Mountain, the news of all this was merely a distant northern echo of the struggles for territory and mastery, the tides of advance and retreat between the Mongols and their enemies and amongst those enemies themselves, which affected his own region south of the Yangzi River.

After his unexpected escape from Toghto, the ex-salt-smuggler Zhang expanded southwards, crossed the Yangzi and seized the beautiful city of Pingjiang with all its hinterland, including Wuxing, where Lord Meng's home had been and where most of his family, including Wang, were born. The Mongol government, having allowed Zhang to become so powerful—he had now awarded himself the title of Prince of Wu—could only hope to enlist him on their side. They were reluctant to trust him because of his habit of refusing their overtures and executing their ambassadors, but what was the alternative? He was still astride the Grand Canal disrupting their food supplies and they needed him as a bulwark against the Red Scarves. So they sent a further embassy, offering him legitimacy as ruler of all the territory he had taken and the official title of Imperial Marshal. This time he accepted and the ambassadors kept their heads.

But meanwhile another warlord—previously a Red Scarf bandit, now commanding his own independent army—had also crossed the Yangzi, captured the important city of Nanjing on its south bank and become a serious rival to Zhang. By the time the news of the burning of Xandu reached Wang, this new warlord's generals had advanced still further and occupied much of the territory to the south of the Yellow Crane Mountain.

This new warlord, called Zhu, was from the humblest background—his peasant family, it was said, had all died of plague and he himself had been a mendicant monk—and was scarcely educated. But he now came south in person, set up his headquarters in a town called Wuzhou and sent invitations to all the scholars in the region—it was full of them—to come and dine with him. If they accepted, as many did, he questioned them closely and, when he liked their answers, urged them to join him in Nanjing as advisers and administrators. This seemed less like the behaviour of an ignorant and arrogant bandit than of a wise ruler. Several of Wang's friends and acquaintances made reference to the lowly origins of the first Emperor of the Han Dynasty and remarked that it might be sensible to be on Zhu's side from the outset.

Wang himself, after his experience with the White Tigress, wanted no more military adventures, but the warlord's name and reputed background intrigued him. Surely it wasn't possible that this was the boy with the huge ugly face who had once begged to be his servant? The months went by, however, and no invitation came. Wang's wife began to be afraid that he would not be invited at all.

"He's probably leaving the unimportant officials until last," said Wang.

"You should write him a letter," said his wife.

"Saying what? 'You wanted to be my servant, now let me be yours!'"

"Just bring yourself to his attention and say you think you may have met him once before."

"He will not care to be reminded of that. Or else he'll have forgotten all about it and think I'm trying to impose myself on him."

"You can tell him that you already have experience as a military adviser to people wearing red scarves and that the stratagem you devised for them was brilliantly successful."

"Except that their leader was killed. Not a happy precedent, don't you think?"

He could speak flippantly now, six years later and especially to his wife, about the death of the White Tigress, but he thought of her often with both longing and horror. He longed to be in her company again, but could not forget the horrible outcome of her revenge: her savage massacre of the magistrate and his whole household, her own dreadful death, the destruction of the town and hundreds of its inhabitants, and finally the violence that broke out—almost as if a horde of evil spirits had been released—among the bandits themselves.

As soon as they had buried the White Tigress and as they turned away from her grave in the family cemetery, Kuo Chong angrily blamed Li Yen for failing to protect her, whereupon Li accused the former sergeant-instructor of taking his own personal revenge on the town, which Li said would have appalled the White Tigress if she had lived and would disturb her spirit. Supporters of both men quickly formed battle lines and took their weapons in their hands. Ling Zhen, the artillery officer, bravely intervened to try to make peace between them, but the supporters of Kuo Chong were more numerous and extremely belligerent, no doubt because they were the ones who had taken part in the atrocity.

The upshot was that both Li and Ling Zhen, with many others, were killed almost on the grave of the White Tigress. After this, though Kuo Chong expressed his sorrow at what had happened, Wang and most of Li Yen's surviving supporters made haste to leave the encampment.

In the six years since that time Wang had lived a very quiet life, not returning to his official post in Quinsai even when his three years' compassionate leave for the death of his mother was over. There were many other people living in the hills around them now, avoiding the expense and danger of life in Quinsai during these troubled times, and Wang's wife had plenty of female company. Indeed, she admitted that it was more fashionable these days to be out of town than in it. Besides, she was very happy to see Wang again and he her.

He told her most of what had happened to him in the company of the White Tigress, but not his mad idea of staying with her if the stratagem succeeded. He and his wife often still spoke to each other with their old asperity, but it concealed a new relationship of warmth and trust which had begun before he went away. After his safe return, which neither of them had dared count on, it was as if they recognised, without ever saying so, that from now on they would always prefer to meet the world's shocks together. Also, it must be added, they were both now well into middle age and had a better understanding of their own as well as each other's limitations.

She had had his studio rebuilt while he was away and although at first he could hardly bear to go in there for fear of his thoughts, but preferred to be always active, walking, gathering wood as he used to, visiting friends, she gradually persuaded him to begin painting again. So many of their friends admired his talent, she said, that to paint something specially for them would be a good way to repay their kindness to her during his absence. He found, then, of course, as soon as he reluctantly set to work, that there was no better escape from unpleasant thoughts about himself or regrets for the past than to make peaceful scenes of rivers and mountains, with scholars enjoying summer days in their houses among the trees.

There was something false about it, of course, as the Empire disintegrated round them, armies drove each other to and fro, people died in their thousands and towns were sacked. But there was also something true, for the mountains and rivers continued to stand and flow, the seasons to change and the scholars very frequently to enjoy summer days in their houses. Also, what gave Wang consolation to paint gave others pleasure to own and contemplate. Perhaps he painted friends less as they were than as they wished to think of themselves, relaxed in idyllic settings, but there was nothing false about that in itself. If he had made their settings look threatening and themselves full of anxiety, would that have been any more true? Both were true so far as they went, both false when set against each other. At any rate, in his present state of mind, he preferred what he privately called "Peach Blossom River paintings."

The invitation from Zhu came at the beginning of summer. The journey to the warlord's temporary headquarters at Wuzhou took three days. Wang rode a donkey, while his new servant, Kong, walked behind with the travelling-bags slung on a pole over his shoulder. The days were gone when Wang could afford to keep more than one donkey or mule. They stopped the nights at inns.

Kong was a very different sort of person from Deng, older, coarser and lazier, somewhat greedy and overweight, less intelligent, but more worldly-wise. He came from the city not the country and had been recommended by one of the friends of Wang's wife. His previous master, an elderly doctor in Quinsai, had recently died. At first Wang was irritated by Kong, who had virtually run the doctor's life for him and did not much care to be instructed. Kong could see no point in standing for hours staring at trees and rocks and making sketches of them. He would have understood it better if Wang had ever sold his paintings, but to work without financial profit seemed to him foolish and self-indulgent. On the other hand, he always did what Wang told him to—if somewhat slowly and with a disagreeable grimace—and gradually learnt not to fidget, cough and spit during the hours they spent in front of nature. Many times, comparing him unfavourably to Deng, Wang made up his mind to get rid of Kong, but then relented, reflecting that, after all, he did not want a servant who reminded him too closely of Deng, and that in a way he liked Kong's lack of comprehension. It put Wang on his mettle, spurred him to see in nature what his companion refused to see, made the whole enterprise more serious to him because he wanted to convince Kong to take it more seriously. It is probably impossible to teach materialistic people the value of spiritual things—and the other way round—but Wang felt challenged to try.

The country they passed through—foothills with orchards and a river-valley with rice-fields—had not been fought over, so there were no signs of disturbance. Indeed, the roads were probably safer than usual, since the small groups of robbers one might have met in more peaceful times had mostly now become soldiers in Zhu's army, which was particularly well-disciplined and strictly forbidden to do any harm to the civilian population. The town itself was carefully guarded and Wang had to show his letter of invitation at the gate. He was then conducted to an inn specially requisitioned for the warlord's visitors and told to present himself at the magistrate's compound at sunset.

The weather had already turned very hot and it was a sunset of flaming red. Soldiers were camped in the magistrate's outer hall. Wang and five fellow-scholars—none of whom he knew—showed their invitations, were searched for weapons and then led through to the inner hall, where Zhu was already seated with two of his generals and his chief adviser, Li Shan-chang, formerly a tutor in a country landlord's household. All rose courteously to receive and seat their guests, who were placed on either side of Zhu, while the generals and Li Shan-chang took the lower places.

The moment he saw his host, Wang recognised him as the novice from the monastery with whom he had watched the waterfalls and to whom he had given the peddler's piece of paper with some money wrapped inside it. He saw no answering recognition in Zhu, however, and was glad of that, for this man, though he had the novice's unforgettably clumsy face, was in every other way a new person. Fourteen years of beggary, banditry, warfare and gathering ambition, as he discovered how easily he could dominate other people, had transformed him from a sixteen-year-old orphan into a thirty-year-old prince.

Wang had been partly alarmed by him at their first meeting, now he was not so much alarmed as astonished. He had never known anybody of this kind. Of course there had been people he fervently admired, such as his grandfather or Old Huang the painter of *The Mountains of Pure Happiness*, or was impressed by, such as Ni, or whose energy and charisma could lift him up and sweep him away, as the White Tigress had, though in her case it was hard to distinguish her qualities of leadership from her sexual attractiveness. Zhu, however, emanated power and presence even when, as now, he sat quite still and merely questioned and listened.

The hall was not particularly well lit—this prince cared little for ostentation. He was unusually tall when he stood up, but did not appear so when seated. The lamps left him mostly in shadow, but it was almost as if he were the main source of light. As food was served and Zhu questioned the scholars round him about the meaning of Confucius' ancient precepts, how they had been interpreted and modified down the centuries and how they might best be translated into practical measures of government, Wang, seated three places down to Zhu's left, could hardly take his eyes off the questioner. None of the other guests showed much quality of mind. They were lowly officials like himself, two quite young, the others middle-aged, but all ponderous and conventional in manner, showing off their knowledge of the classic texts like students at an examination, obsequiously shifting their opinions if they thought Zhu disagreed, but unable to avoid a tone of patronising pedantry towards someone who smilingly admitted his own lack of education.

"I first learnt to read," said Zhu, "by puzzling out a crumpled message about the return of the Maitreya Buddha."

For a moment Wang wondered if this was aimed directly at him. But it seemed not.

"I was given it by a passing scholar," Zhu said. "I never heard his name and I've forgotten what he looked like, except that he wore the usual scholar's clothes. But he made me feel ashamed."

Wang immediately decided that he would not own up to having made this man ashamed.

After some time Zhu paused in his questioning, clearly tired of listening to these people's answers, similar versions of which he must have heard over and over again during the previous months.

Suddenly Li Shang-chang, the warlord's adviser, said:

"You have not spoken at all, Wang Meng, and you have not eaten much either. Perhaps you are unwell?"

"No, I am perfectly well," said Wang. "I always eat lightly and I have nothing to add to my colleagues' answers."

"What is your view of the burning of Xandu?" asked Li Shan-chang.

This was not at all the sort of general theoretical question that Zhu had been asking and Wang was not sure what its purpose was, or if it had a purpose. But he knew that Zhu had begun his career as a bandit with the northern Red Scarves, the very group that had destroyed Khublai's summer capital, so he assumed that the correct response was approval. He preferred, however, after all the dull speeches made by his fellow-guests, to say what he really thought.

"It seemed to me to be wanton destruction. Surely Xandu had no strategic value?"

"Don't you think it was symbolically important?"

Li Shan-chang's manner was authoritarian and although Wang would not have minded being examined by Zhu, whose relaxed manner made his personality seem all the more imposing, he saw no reason to show particular respect towards this inflated village schoolmaster.

"Symbolically of what?"

"It was built by Khublai in the days of Mongol power. Now, like Mongol power, it is gone."

"We did not choose to have Khublai as our Emperor," said Wang. "All the same, he was not a bad ruler, was he? He built these two new cities—Xandu and Dadu—in the northern part of the Empire, where such cities didn't exist before. If a robber took my house and put a valuable thing inside it and later by some chance I got my house back, would I destroy the valuable thing? Symbolically or otherwise?"

"I suppose, then," said Li Shan-chang, displeased with this reply, "that like your famous grandfather, Zhao Meng-fu, you are still loyal to the Yuan?"

Hearing the name of his grandfather, Wang's fellow-guests looked at him with new respect, mingled with some apprehension that their own loyalties too might be questioned.

"My grandfather's times were different from ours," said Wang. "There has been no second Khublai, even if the present Emperor does bear the same reign-name. I have served the Yuan myself—surely most of us here have—but not for the last few years. I am not at all certain where my loyalty lies now, or where it ought to lie."

There was an uncomfortable silence. Several of Wang's fellow-guests were clearly thinking hard about how they would deal with this delicate subject. The silence was broken by Zhu.

"If you gave your loyalty to me, what would you expect in return?"

"Peace and good government," said Wang. "Isn't that all anyone asks of a ruler? Unfortunately, history tells us that it is very difficult and very rare for any ruler to provide it."

"How would you advise me to try?" asked Zhu.

"I don't think I could. My experience has been too subordinate and too limited. I'm afraid I have become addicted to retirement and to staring at mountains and waterfalls."

Why did "waterfalls" slip out, instead of the more usual "rivers?" No doubt because he still associated Zhu with the waterfalls they had once stared at together. The word immediately stirred Zhu's memory.

"I remember your voice," he said. "Perhaps also, now I look more carefully, your face."

Wang said nothing. He had already aroused the adviser's hostility and had no wish to antagonise his much more formidable master. Before the pause could become embarrassing, Zhu turned away from Wang and asked a few more trivial questions of the other guests, then, as the meal ended, thanked them all for making the journey to see him and rose to show them politely out. But instead of bowing formally to Wang as he did to the others, he touched his sleeve.

"Stay a little, please!" he said, a command more than a request.

When the doors had been closed behind the departing guests,

Zhu dismissed the two generals and Li Shan-chang with a nod and invited Wang to sit down again beside him.

"You are the one who gave me the piece of paper, aren't you?" he said. And when Wang, considering what to say, still made no reply, added: "I was too anxious and confused then, I suppose, to register your face, but your voice gave you away. No doubt that was why you kept silent?"

"No," said Wang, "I had no idea you would recognise me. I am sorry you've done so. I am sorry I made you feel ashamed."

"You should know," said Zhu sternly, "that you also made me sit through a great many tedious lectures from very boring people."

"*I* made you?"

"Not all have been boring, of course. But I could have narrowed my search for good administrators mostly to those from the higher grades, if I had not also been searching for you."

Wang shifted uncomfortably on his chair. Was he to be punished for once making this disturbing man ashamed?

"How was I to find you without sifting through all the chaff, since I knew nothing about you except that you were a scholar? It was Li Shan-chang's idea to recruit advisers by inviting them to dinner, but it was mine to ask all and sundry in the hope of catching you."

He smiled with great satisfaction, appearing suddenly younger and more like the peasant he had been.

"Well, you have caught me," said Wang, contemplating his hands in his lap and thinking but not saying "and now you are playing with me." "I repeat that I'm sorry."

He looked up, met Zhu's eyes and looked away.

"Yes, you are the very one and I have got you at last," said Zhu, sounding now as if he had trapped a criminal and meant to treat him appropriately.

Wang bowed his head again.

"I have learnt something about the world and its harshness and treachery," said Zhu. "You told me I would if I became a beggar. I have learnt a great deal about fighting, strategy and ruthlessness. But I am still very ignorant of other equally important things. For example, should one or should one not burn Xandu? You made a great impression on me when I was very low and almost without hope and there is still something about you that interests me. I'm not sure exactly what it is, but I would like you to come to Nanjing to teach me all you know. Then I shall not only be less ignorant, but may discover why you seem so ordinary that I couldn't remember your face and so out of the ordinary that I went to all this trouble to find you again."

❁

"You refused to go to Nanjing?"

Kong was outraged when he heard the outcome of Wang's interview with the warlord. They had already left the town of Wuzhou well behind. The sky was cloudless, the day not yet as hot as it would be and a light breeze stippled the glittering surface of the river beside them. When two geese flew across to land on the water just in front of him, Wang felt as if he were part of a "blue-and-green" landscape by his grandfather's teacher, Chien Xuan.

Chien, an official under the Song Dynasty at the time of the Mongol conquest, refused to serve Khan Khublai and spent the rest of his life in retirement. He blamed the Song, however, for bringing about its own defeat through carelessness and decadence, and painted his landscapes in an archaic "blue-and-green" style going back many centuries to the court-painters of the Tang Dynasty. His aim was not to imitate them exactly, but only to bring them to mind in an obviously simplified manner, as if to say that the glory of the Empire in those distant times was now beyond recall. Wang's grandfather also painted in a naive, antique manner and, in case anyone should misunderstand what he was doing, wrote on one of them: "the most precious quality in a painting is not the style but the true spirit of antiquity." This was how he asserted his inward resistance to Khublai's government, even while outwardly serving it. Today Wang admitted to himself that Chien's was the better solution: not so much for political reasons as because of the sense of masterful freedom it must have given him.

"You refused to go to Nanjing?" Kong hurried forward to walk abreast of him.

Yes, yes, he had. And now he was free and this was why, as his donkey ambled along the road home, his eyes saw the ordinary sights of the river, geese, clumps of reeds and willow-trees, but his mind entered a charming blue-and-green landscape in Chien's style. His pleasure was such that he wanted to laugh at Kong's harshly repeated question. Instead, he said gravely:

"Not in so many words."

"This Zhu is a very powerful man," said Kong.

"Yes."

"And he asked you to be his teacher, and you refused?"

"I said I had nothing to teach him."

"As good as refusing."

"More polite," said Wang.

Kong could not help spitting, though on the far side from Wang, who could not help smiling.

"That's a very big and important city," said Kong reproachfully.

Wang smiled again, still congratulating himself on his own escape, knowing how much Kong would prefer to be going to Nanjing than back to the Yellow Crane Mountain.

"So why did you refuse?"

"I am not a Confucian," said Wang quietly, silencing Kong less by his cryptic words than by urging his donkey a little ahead so as to re-establish their master-servant relationship.

His answer encapsulated what he had said to Zhu as they sat together alone in the inner hall of the magistrate's compound, with Zhu's army all around them.

"I am deeply grateful for your interest in me," said Wang, "and flattered you should remember so much about our conversation so long ago in front of the waterfalls. But as far as advice or administration go,

I am just as ordinary as I look. There is nothing I could teach you in Nanjing which I cannot tell you now."

"What can you tell me now?" said Zhu.

Taken aback, Wang cleared his throat and, gathering his thoughts, stared for several moments at a moth fluttering round the nearest lantern.

"There are three ways," he said at last, "by which a very ordinary person like me can improve himself—or at least partly rise above insignificance. Through religion, through public service, or through study and reflection on the natural world."

"You mean 'The Three Doctrines'—Buddhism, Confucianism and Daoism?"

"More or less, though each doctrine has many variants which, like colours, shade across into one another. I prefer to avoid those terms and think of three paths which sometimes fork out of one another and often meet again. The first path, religion, I leave aside. I cannot believe in gods or supernatural beings of any kind, nor that souls are reborn either in this world or another—as Pure Land Buddhists believe. All this seems to me fantasy and wishful thinking."

Zhu was annoyed. He was, after all, a former Buddhist novice and still nominally attached to the Red Scarf movement which believed in the imminent return of the Maitreya.

"The Buddha lived on earth and taught disciples. Are you saying that all his teaching and the teaching of his disciples was worthless?"

"Not at all. Only that I myself have never set foot on that path. It is the other two paths—public service and the contemplation of nature—that I have followed, taking this fork or that as I came to them, but always, I must admit, finding the third more to my taste."

"Easier and pleasanter, I suppose," said Zhu scornfully, "to contemplate waterfalls than to work for a better society."

"For me, yes. But surely not for you? I remember you finding such passive contemplation, whether of walls or waterfalls, hard and distasteful. And everything you've done since then suggests you are a master of action."

"I was not offered the luxury of choosing one path or another. My circumstances pushed me down the path I am following."

"Did they? When I first met you, it was far more likely that you would follow the first path and become a monk. Were any of the other monks in that monastery pushed down the path towards becoming bandits?"

Zhu frowned and his large jaw seemed to thrust out ominously.

"Even if they were," said Wang quickly, "I have not heard that any of them proved to be leaders of armies or that they captured cities."

Zhu relaxed and smiled.

"My grandfather on my mother's side was a soldier who fought against the Mongols," he said.

"I remember now you told me so."

"He filled my head with stories of adventures and heroes. He could also look into the future and foretold a bright destiny for me."

"So, you see, you were well prepared to be pushed down that path. *My* grandfather on my mother's side divided his life between activity and passivity, between serving the state and contemplating waterfalls."

"What are you really saying, Wang Meng? That because your grandfather served Khan Khublai and you too have served the Mongols, you cannot take part in driving them out?"

Wang was tempted for a moment to tell Zhu that he had already taken some part in doing so, but he curbed his tongue. He had no desire to be asked to devise any further stratagems.

"There are resemblances in both of us to our respective grandfathers. But the resemblances are not exact and the differences are to your advantage, not mine. Your grandfather was a soldier, but you are the leader of an army. My grandfather was one of Khublai's principal ministers, but I am a lowly official."

"You lack ambition."

"I lack that ambition."

"You said you would be loyal to any ruler who provided peace and good government."

"Must loyalty be given only from an official's chair? Could one not be loyal while contemplating a waterfall?"

"What use would that be?"

"There was a man of my grandfather's generation, a scholar called Liu, a very distinguished teacher. Important officials often came to him for advice, though he was not always willing to give it, or even to receive them. When Khublai conquered the Empire, he sent for this man, intending to offer him a high post in the Confucian Academy. Liu refused. He was asked again, he refused again—several times, but always politely, with suitable excuses about his own poor health and the illness and death of his mother. Finally, Khublai told his officials to leave the man alone, remarking that he had heard that in ancient times there were 'servants who could not be summoned.'"

"Meaning?"

"Khublai was referring to a saying of Meng Tzu, the great disciple of Confucius. Meng Tzu wrote that a prince who is going to do great deeds will certainly have 'servants he cannot summon.' Why? Because no prince is worth serving who does not honour people of virtue and allow them to acquire virtue in the way best suited to them."

"Khublai had read the works of Meng Tzu?"

"I hardly think so. This precedent was probably found for him by one of his Chinese advisers. But he took notice of it and acted upon it. My grandfather, you see, did not serve a complete barbarian."

"And if I learn from Khublai, I will show myself less of a barbarian? Is that what you mean?"

Talking to Zhu, Wang felt, was like sitting in a cage with a lion or tiger, which every so often bared its fangs and flexed its claws. The best thing in such a case, he had always heard, was to maintain eye contact and not to retreat.

"Barbarian or not, Khublai was certainly a great prince."

"Yes, but are you a scholar in the same class as this Liu?"

"Not at all. I would never dare claim to be a servant who could not be summoned. I am suggesting only that you might allow some virtue to the contemplation of waterfalls."

"I wonder what its 'virtue' is. Are people who claim 'virtue' in such detachment from the world deceiving others or themselves? Are they charlatans or fools?"

Zhu stood up abruptly and walked to the far side of the hall and back, stopping behind Wang's seat.

"It seems to me," he said, speaking from his great height directly above Wang's head, "that if it leads anywhere at all, your so-called third path is only a primitive version of the first one. You want to put nature where *we* put the Buddha."

The emphasis on "we" was threatening, as if to remind Wang that this warlord did not fight only for himself, but in a religious cause which swept aside unbelievers.

"Indeed, there are temples and priests of Daoism," said Wang, trying to put his thoughts in order, inhibited by the figure he could sense but not see towering over him. "And there have been periods of strife and competition between this Daoist religion and Buddhism. It is also true that in the distant past our primitive ancestors imagined gods and spirits in mountains, trees and rivers, much as the Mongols still do today. Neither of these kinds of nature-worship is what I mean."

"Explain!"

"You spoke of detachment from the world. You mean, from human society. But human society is only one enclave within the world and the universe and perhaps not as important a part of it as it seems to us, nor in any way detachable from it. The universe is huge and awe-inspiring in its complexity, but it is most foolish to worship it, considering that, although there are many forms of life and forces of nature which are superior to us physically, there are plainly none with our mental and spiritual powers. You might expect nature, if it had the capacity, to worship us. But that would be foolish too, since we ourselves are also *part* of nature. Not only physically, but intellectually. We *think* as we have been formed to think by nature. We observe and classify and enumerate from within nature, according to its own materials, its rules, its capacities. What we cannot understand, what seems mysterious, does not belong to some other order of being—spirits or gods—but to the same all-embracing, all-interwoven universe as ourselves. It is mysterious only because we have so far failed to observe and think about it closely or cleverly enough."

Zhu sniffed, as if unconvinced, but said nothing.

"Gunpowder, for example," said Wang, recalling his conversations with the artillery expert Ling Zhen. "What could be more mysterious or more terrifyingly god-like? But it is just a mixture of three ordinary elements from the earth: saltpeter, sulphur and charcoal."

Zhu abruptly sat down again opposite Wang.

"Is that what people think about when they contemplate waterfalls?" asked Zhu, his eyes glittering with excitement. "Inventions and improvements? I can see some virtue in that. What I want are explosions as big as earthquakes, cannons that knock down whole city-walls instead of single bricks."

"I am neither a chemist nor an engineer," said Wang unhappily, wishing he had thought of another example. "That is not quite what I meant. Since we keep mentioning waterfalls, take water itself: softer than fur, stronger than rocks, yielding but insistent, always finding its way down or round or through every barrier, to the lowest level, but constantly renewing itself and giving life to all living things . . ."

Zhu had ceased looking at him. His eyes had wandered to a corner of the room where two mice were crouched, waiting for the humans to move away so that they could dart out and carry off the scraps of food on the floor.

"We should be like water," said Wang, "finding our own level, accepting our own nature and our part in nature, as we observe and contemplate the ten thousand things and move amongst them, gaining knowledge of ourselves as we gain more knowledge of them, penetrating the mystery of the ordinary. This is what the philosopher Zhuang Zhou called 'riding on the normality of the universe.'"

Zhu stood up and stretched.

"This is all you have to tell me? That we should be like water?"

"This is all."

"You prefer to wait and see whose army is strongest and which is the winning side?"

"I was not thinking of that. But can I doubt, considering how far you've come on that path, that it will lead you farther still?"

Zhu looked closely at him, as if gauging his sincerity, then nodded slowly.

"I believe the future is bright," he said and, going to the door, opened it and showed Wang into the outer hall, where the soldiers sprang to attention.

"If I ask you again," said Zhu sternly, "I shall expect you to come."

Wang bowed.

"You admitted, didn't you?" Zhu added, "That you're not in the top class of those who cannot be summoned."

His pock-marked cheeks creased and his boyish smile appeared for a moment, then he bowed briskly, withdrew into the inner room and left Wang to be conducted out of the building by a soldier.

❀

Why had Wang accepted the invitation in the first place, if he did not wish to be summoned? Out of curiosity, certainly, to see if the warlord really was the former Buddhist novice; also perhaps to please his wife and show their neighbours that he was not an altogether negligible official; also because, in these difficult times, it could do no harm and might even save one's life to be acquainted with one of the new men of power; finally because he did not really expect to be summoned and certainly not to have to make up his mind about whether to go to Nanjing there and then. Indeed, he might still have been open to persuasion, if he had not listened in silence for so long to his colleagues' attempts to ingratiate themselves with Zhu.

No doubt because of the painful experiences he had been through—the deaths of so many people close to him, the violence of the attack on the town and its terrible aftermath—he felt uncomfortable with the conventional pieties of the society he had grown up into. Not that he questioned the original idea on which they were based, the central Confucian doctrine that human society was composed of five cardinal relationships—ruler to subject, father to son, elder brother to younger brother, husband to wife, and friend to friend—and should reflect the moral order of the universe through mutual respect and social justice.

Confucius himself had lived in a wretched period of small warring states, long before there was a united Empire, and never saw his ideas put into practice. His disciple Meng Tzu, believing that all men were essentially good and would love each other if they first learnt to love their parents, taught that the ruler must surround himself with humane officials, who would themselves be fathers to their people. But Meng Tzu lived in even worse times of disunity than Confucius. Once the Empire came into being, however, their ideas proved so valuable and workable as a basis for strong and legitimate government that, however often the Empire broke apart again, the Confucian way of thinking—the basis of all education, all promotion, all administrative arrangements—survived, becoming more and more entrenched and taken for granted.

Was there, after all, any better way to govern than this, which assumed that the proper way to treat people was the way you wished to be treated yourself? The only alternatives were anarchy or arbitrary rule by autocrats and their favourites—often concubines or palace eunuchs—with no sense of justice or duty to anyone but themselves. Why, then, did Wang feel such a lowering of the spirit as he listened to his colleagues? Was it because they were reciting lessons instead of articulating their own convictions, covertly seeking personal advantage rather than a truly just society? Or because Confucius' and Meng Tzu's benevolent ideas had been transformed by sterner minds into a rigid system of rituals, laws and penalties. Human ideas flow like water and, properly channelled, can give life like water. But constricted too long in the same channel, fed into ornamental ponds without renewal or cleansing, they become blocked and stagnant. On the other hand, shouldn't he have felt comforted and hopeful that a peasant boy with a powerful army should be seeking the advice of educated men and listening carefully to their answers?

The day was now very hot and they stopped at a small inn for rest and refreshment. Kong ordered pork and rice dishes for both of them and Wang, regretting his earlier display of superiority, invited him to sit at his table.

"I hope this is not one of those fearful places one hears about where they serve human flesh instead of pork," Wang said lightly, noting the roughness of the tables and benches and the absence of other customers.

"I looked inside the kitchen," said Kong. "It was definitely a pig they had hanging up and I saw them take slices off it."

"I was joking," said Wang.

"No, it is not a joke. Such inns exist in lonely places. My former master, the doctor, told me of one where they gave the travellers drugged wine, then dragged them into the kitchen and robbed and murdered them. Then their flesh was served up to the next travellers."

Wang was silent. He had completely lost his appetite.

"When the innkeeper brings the wine," said Kong, "I'll make him taste it himself before he serves us. But I don't think the man's a robber."

"How can you tell?"

"I am good at judging people," said Kong. "I learnt it from the doctor. He always looked at his patients with great care before treating them. At their hands and feet and ears as well as their faces. How they moved and spoke, whether they were nervous or over-confident, 'what their eyes said,' as he put it, and 'what their words did not say.'"

"What a pity that it was I, not you, who was asked to go to Nanjing!" said Wang. "Zhu could have made good use of your skills, whereas they are wasted in our country retreat, where everyone already knows everyone else and strangers are rare."

The innkeeper was quite willing to drink from his wine-jug and seemed not surprised to be asked. When he had returned to the kitchen, Kong pronounced him harmless.

"How do you know?"

"You can see from the deep lines on his face, the roughness of his skin, his big hands, and the stooped way he walks that he does a lot of work in the fields. An innkeeper who lived by robbing his guests would have no need to work out of doors. Besides, he took more than a sip of the wine and smiled with real pleasure, as if it tasted good."

Wang sniffed the cup of wine that Kong had poured out for him, but Kong immediately emptied his and poured himself another.

"Are you waiting to see if I fall on the floor?" he said. "No need to worry! I learnt a lot about the smell of drugs and poisons when I was with the doctor. This is good wine—no, not all that good, but the best you could expect in a poor little roadside place like this."

Wang drank his wine, but ate no more than a few mouthfuls of the pork when it arrived. Kong was only too glad to finish all the dishes.

"Are you going to tell me now why you refused to go to Nanjing?" he said finally, licking his fingers, wiping his mouth with his sleeve and pushing the empty dishes away.

Wang looked at his large, flushed, sweating face, wondering, as he so often did, how it was that of all the ten thousand things, man alone seemed capable of making himself gross and ugly. Did other creatures ever feel the same distaste for each other? Perhaps so. But now he felt less distaste than affection. He was glad of Kong's company and not even offended by his table manners.

"There are other things I prefer to do," he replied.

"Drawing rocks and trees?"

"Yes."

"You do it well," said Kong.

"I want to do it better."

"But for a gentleman like you, from an Imperial family, highly educated, it's only a leisure occupation, isn't it? You're filling in time until this Zhu or someone else makes you an offer you can't refuse."

"No," said Wang, "it's not really as simple as that."

Having tried to explain himself to Zhu, he did not feel like trying again to Kong. If he had said he wanted to enter some Buddhist or Daoist monastery as a monk, both of them would have thought they understood him, without really doing so. They would have assumed, in other words, that he was more intent on another world, anxious about his soul and perhaps his death, rather than his body and his life. But according to their ideas, there was no third path. You could turn away from this life into religion, or you could live this life as what your fate made you: peasant, farmer, fisherman, bandit, soldier, merchant, craftsman/artist, doctor, teacher, administrator. And if you were from the scholar-gentleman class, you might amuse yourself in periods of voluntary or enforced retirement from your official duties with civilised pursuits such as painting, composing, calligraphy, collecting. He had done that himself and almost everyone he knew was the same. Of course, under the Mongols, those who refused to serve the Dynasty had, so far as their means allowed them, devoted themselves almost entirely to civilised pursuits, but seldom thought of them as more than adjuncts to the normal practical lives they would have been leading in better circumstances.

Wang had spoken in loosely Daoist terms to Zhu and put forward or at least compromised on the somewhat crude notion that his "third path" merely led to contemplating waterfalls and studying the mysteries of nature. No, it was not that, it was far less practical and intellectually respectable. Nothing would come of it that was of any use to anyone—beyond himself and a few friends who might take pleasure in the results.

To draw and colour, to do nothing but look at the natural world and draw and colour his own feelings about himself and it—neither as a religious exercise nor as a gentleman's leisure occupation—this was the third path he wanted to follow. Everything that was "Confucian" in him argued against it and ridiculed it. He could not even be certain that such a third path existed—he would probably have to clear the ground and mark it out as he went along. But that, of course, would be his subject: discovering with his brush, beyond the limited scope of Confucian social normality, the normality of the universe.

Kong had some difficulty in shouldering the baggage when they left the inn.

"Nothing wrong with the wine," he said, when Wang gave him a worried look, "and it was certainly pork. Mind you, I've heard that 'two-legged mutton' is delicious. The doctor told me there used to be a restaurant in Quinsai—run by people from the north—where they served it regularly. All the different sorts—old women, old men, young girls, children—had their own special names on the menu."

"What kind of names?"

"'Little sweet wingless ducklings' or 'autumn-ripe bell-wethers.'"

"You're making it up, Kong."

"No. There's something of everything in a big city, that's what I like about it—and especially all the people."

"Some of them on the menu."

The sun was lower now, but it was not much cooler as they left the river behind and began to climb. Wang was glad he had eaten and drunk so little. Kong, suffering badly from indigestion and too much wine, had an unpleasant journey to their stopping-place for the night, ate nothing when they got there and was still unwell when he came to wake Wang soon after dawn the next morning.

"The pork must have been hanging too long," he said in a weak voice. "What a mistake to eat in a place with no customers!"

Wang put off continuing the journey that day, so that Kong could rest and recover, and himself went out sketching in the neighbourhood. He was still delighted with his new-found sense of freedom. In reality, of course, he had been just as free before, but somehow the refusal of Zhu's request for his services seemed to mark an important turning-point, a definitive fork in his path. On the other hand, he reflected wrily, to declare himself not a Confucian was in itself a thoroughly Confucian thing to do, a recognition that his freedom could only be experienced in isolation, beyond the boundaries of that powerful area of social obligation.

Sitting on the bank of a small stream, watching the way most of the water flowed swiftly past him, but a little at the edge found its way into an indentation at his feet and remained there almost motionless, he smiled at the way his mind immediately gave this perfectly straightforward, natural phenomenon a symbolic dimension, as though the water, like him, were choosing not to be active. Was it ever possible to look at anything in nature except through one's own feelings? In fact, a little further down, where the indentation in the bank ended, the quiet water seeped invisibly back into the rushing stream, so that it was only taking a slower route to the same goal—or rather, not so much taking it as being taken to it by the momentum of its own nature and circumstances, which a human being might grandly call "fate."

I have had to break off this narrative for the last week, because, as the jailor warned me, another innocent victim of the Emperor's purges was put into my cell. I assume he was innocent, he certainly thought so himself. His crime was to be a distant relation of the fallen Prime Minister. He was very young, hardly more than a boy and quite terrified. His terror could only be assuaged by talking and so we talked day and night. He intended to become a monk and I remarked jokingly that our present circumstances might be considered good preparation for the life ahead of him.

He misunderstood me. He was quite sure he was going to be killed—as apparently most of Hu's family had already been—and he thought I meant life in another world. He asked me about that and I had to explain that I had no belief in any other world. That was perhaps selfish and cruel of me, but it did not matter. He was quite sure I was wrong because the best and most holy people always removed themselves as far as possible from this world in order to prepare for the other. He was only so frightened, he said, because he had not been given time to prepare. I said that if another world existed, his certainty about it would surely admit him to it and that his youth and innocence would excuse him for not being sufficiently prepared.

He was taken out of our cell early this morning and has not returned. The jailer, when he brought my meal this evening, would not say in so many words what has happened to the boy, but when I asked if he was still in the prison, the jailer shook his head and looked grim. He has grown-up sons of his own and is a kind man and I think he would have smiled if the boy had been released.

Since then I have been thinking about this great need we all have to believe in another world, something for which we have no evidence at all. Just because we can reason and imagine—because we are nature conscious of itself and even so cannot control ourselves or it—we look about desperately for something that can. We want to appeal beyond unconscious nature to some far-sighted, self-conscious, benevolent superior. Let the Emperor, then, the so-called "Son of Heaven," deputise for Heaven! Indeed, he does control us to some small degree. We gratefully accept his limited power and prostrate ourselves in front of him. But his power is only our own feeble power piled up in a heap and handed over to one of ourselves.

We look beyond Heaven's deputy, then, to the sky itself. Absurd, childish, irrational! Even when it fails to answer our prayers, does nothing whatever for us, we want to convince ourselves that something or someone is there, open to pleas, ready to be influenced in our favour, capable of working miracles and interfering with the mindless mechanics of nature. We demand a mighty and mysterious, reasoning, organising beneficent version of ourselves. And failing that, almost preferable to nothing at all would be the opposite: a vicious, cruel, greedy, irrational, irresistible force bent on our destruction, a heavenly horseback Mongol. What we find so appallingly incomprehensible is our own insignificance, whether in triumph or disaster: the fact that nothing that happens to us matters at all to anyone but ourselves and a few close friends and relatives.

Our noisy celebrations, our solemn festivals! How pathetic it is to read about ancient Emperors whose tombs were filled with women and horses in a last desperate attempt to prove their significance! Nature would have continued its course regardless if they had taken every living person into their tombs with them. If they had turned the whole surface of the earth into a burial-mound, the sun would have continued to shine, the rain to fall and the weeds to sprout. The Mongols in their desolate lands make sacrifices to mountains, rivers and trees, understanding nature's power over us, but failing with primitive infantility to understand that its power is quite random and unconscious. Only a few people—those who think and look about them—seem easily able to understand and accept the straightforward truth: all nature, including ourselves, including the sky, is one; our fate is all one too, nothing so grand as a destiny, but a mere tangle of circumstances; and there is no other self-conscious entity in heaven or earth except us.

❁

Fate, as it happened, soon carried Wang out of his quiet retreat under the Yellow Crane Mountain. Kong, still a little shaky the next morning, as he saddled the donkey and shouldered the baggage for the rest of the journey home, would have been encouraged to know that before long he would again be living in a large and prosperous city, though not Nanjing.

# 10. MOVING HOME

Wang's father owned a modest but profitable estate near Wuxing and contrived to evade the Mongol government's punitive taxes. It was a matter of one's contacts, of course. The much richer but less well-connected Ni Zan, for instance, had been driven by greedy and hostile officials to give his estate away to relatives and take to a wandering life on the waterways in his houseboat. Wang's father, having married Lord Meng's daughter, whose brother was also a high government official, could count on better treatment.

The region he lived in, the Yangzi River delta, was perhaps the most beautiful and fertile in the whole Empire, a low-lying landscape of rivers and lakes and picturesque conical hills, whose centre was Lake Tai, some thirty miles long and twenty-five miles across, shaped like a moon three-quarters full. The town of Wuxing itself, where Lord Meng and his family lived and Wang had been born, was full of civilised people and amenities, while a day or two's journey away, on the far side of Lake Tai, was the city of Pingjiang, famous for its gardens and antique-markets, its literary gatherings and book-publishing.

Wang's father, who collected books, paintings, calligraphy and antiques and was an accomplished poet, knew everybody of note throughout the region and, although he was not rich enough to be one of the leading hosts and patrons, often entertained guests at his villa overlooking Lake Tai, with distant views of the West Mountain on an island near the lake's centre and the East Mountain on a peninsula opposite.

He was a quietly-spoken but autocratic and sharp-tongued man, respected by his servants and those who worked on his estate, but not much liked. He demanded efficiency and exactitude and did not spare anyone's feelings in getting them. On the other hand, he was fair and even forgiving if he thought an excuse for failure was genuine, and probably most people would prefer to have to work hard on a well-run estate than to be laxly-disciplined on one which is going to ruin. He was proud of his son's talent for drawing, but thought him lazy and self-indulgent and openly disapproved of his poor standing as an official and preference for retirement under the Yellow Crane Mountain. Nor could he understand why, if Wang had no taste for public administration, he had no desire either to inherit his father's estate.

"I suppose you're afraid it will be too much work?"

"No," said Wang. "I'm afraid I don't know enough about rice or silk-worms or estate-management."

"All that can be easily learnt if you're prepared to work."

"It doesn't interest me enough."

"I wonder what does interest you."

Wang was silent. His father knew perfectly well what interested him, but did not consider it a full-time occupation for anyone but an old man. Growing old himself now—he was over seventy—and much saddened by his wife's death, Wang's father was, therefore, thinking of selling his estate and moving into Wuxing, when the area suddenly became a battle-ground for rebels and government troops.

These troops were ferocious Miao tribesmen imported from the mountains on the southern borders, led by a Mongol general, but more like an angry swarm of killer-bees than a conventional army. Wang's father, taking refuge within the walls of Wuxing, was lucky to escape with only partial damage to his rice-fields and farm-buildings. The swarm was soon driven off and eventually eliminated, squeezed between the southward advance of Zhang's army to the east and Zhu's to the west. Zhang now seized control of most of the region round the lake, including Wuxing and Pingjiang, and, as we have already mentioned, was recognised as its Imperial authority by the Mongols in return for restoring the supply of rice to the north. For most of the officials and landowners in the area, including Wang's father, this seemed the best possible outcome.

Zhang, a large, loud, sensual man with an angry temper, had been, with the help of his three younger brothers, a bold and ruthless leader, but he had had enough of fighting for the present and his ambitions seemed to be temporarily satisfied. It was not so long, after all, since he had been a salt-smuggler wanted for arson and murder. Now he was living in a Buddhist temple—converted into a palace—in his new "capital," Pingjiang, lording it over an especially prosperous part of the Empire and enjoying all the pleasures life has to offer. It was only a question of protecting his territory from his nearest rival, Zhu, and perhaps extending it southwards to Quinsai, which he had already tried and failed to capture from the Mongols, whenever the time was ripe.

Zhang was happy to leave military matters now to his two surviving brothers and other generals. The youngest brother had been the best strategist and most uncompromising commander in his army and if he had still been alive, would probably have galvanised Zhang into a more active policy. But this brother was captured in a battle with Zhu's troops and, rather than give any advantage to the enemy, starved himself to death in prison. In the event, nothing could have been more disadvantageous to his elder brother's cause than his own removal.

For the present, however, Zhang settled down happily to a princely life and, for a decade, the region flourished under his rule. The rice harvests were good and only a small percentage ever actually found its way to the Mongols in Dadu. The boats carrying much of the salt for the Empire from the marshes on the coast had to pass through this former boatman's territory and contributed richly to his treasury. The leading citizens gratefully repaired their damaged estates and resumed their cultural pursuits. Ordinary farmers and labourers were less pleased with Zhang's regime, since they were heavily taxed and forced to work on various public building and engineering projects, but most of those who had been administrators under the Mongols retained their posts under Zhang. He was content to make use of their experience and they, without any fear of disloyalty, to serve him, who was now officially designated "Imperial Marshal."

In these circumstances, Wang's father decided to move to Pingjiang rather than Wuxing, which was only a few miles from the Blue Bien Mountains to the north-west, where Zhu's territory began. Wuxing was strongly garrisoned and fortified and still full of highly civilised people, not least the senior surviving members of Lord Meng's family and the military man in change of this south-western district, General Pan. In fact, it was General Pan who bought Wang's father's estate. But for an old man, in troubled times, a town so near the border, however well defended, however civilised, could not give the same peace of mind as Zhang's relaxed, luxurious capital.

It was clearly Wang's duty, once his father had made this decision, not only to help him move—no small matter with all his valuable possessions—but to remain there with him and make a home for him in these new surroundings. Wang and his wife, therefore, sold the retreat under the Yellow Crane Mountain, left a little money to provide for Deng's widow and son, who were staying to serve under the new owner, and, accompanied by the jubilant Kong, made their way first to Wuxing and then, in a procession of carts and carriages, to Pingjiang.

Once settled there, in a good-sized house in a city which seemed suddenly relieved of all anxieties and intent only on the pleasure and civility it was famed for, everyone in Wang's family felt happy and relaxed. Wang's father grumbled still about the loss of his estate and his son's failure to take it on, but Pingjiang was full of his friends and his sharp comments became milder by the day. Kong and Wang's wife also soon had friends all over the city. Wang, however, to begin with, hardly stirred beyond his new studio. He was painting a large hanging scroll, a valediction to the life he had promised himself and been baulked of.

Far from being a gloomy work, it turned out to be humorous, even ironic. The subject he chose was suggested to him by the move they had just made. It was based on the story of the Daoist Ge Hong who, in the long-ago time of the Six Dynasties—a thousand years before—had given up his official career and settled on a mountain to study herbs and alchemy and discover the secret of immortality.

The painting was called *Ge Hong Moving Home* and showed the philosopher standing on a bridge in the foreground, beside a magic Daoist deer, which was waiting to lead him upwards; while, just below, his wife and small son, riding an ox led by a servant, were approaching the same bridge round a great bluff of rock. Beyond the bridge, a sheer waterfall dropped into the stream and the mountain rose in tight twists to the very top of the scroll. Just below its summit, clear, bright and idyllic at the top of the path, was perched the philosopher's new home, which might indeed just as well be the home of an immortal, as Ge Hong was reputed to have become.

Although it was not usual these days for scholar-artists to use any colour—that was left to professional craftsmen—Wang could not resist tinting red the thickets that clung to the rocks, suggesting the autumnal season of their move, but also alluding to the Daoist association of cinnabar with the elixir of immortality. Wang gave the painting to his father, wishing him immortality in his new home in the city, though his father, enchanted with it, immediately understood its double meaning.

"We have lived apart so long," he said, "that I had no idea you could do anything like this."

His eyes filled with tears as he looked at it.

"The twisted tree-trunk against dense foliage at bottom right," he said at last, "and the rocky shore it stands on remind me of an old masterpiece by Fan Kuan which was once in your grandfather's collection."

"Yes," said Wang, "I did think of that. To my eyes, Fan Kuan was the greatest master of all and I never can get him quite out of my head. But I also remembered what he said about copying: that he found himself learning from a man, but it would be better to learn from the things themselves."

"And added," said Wang's father, "that it was best of all to learn from his own heart. I think you have done so here. I think you have given me Fan Kuan as well as your own feelings both about him and about the mountains you turned your back on for my sake. I am full of shame to think that I wanted to make Fan Kuan's true successor the manager of my wretched little estate."

After this, as his father's friends came to the house, saw the painting and spread word of it about, Wang was swept up into a succession of parties, expeditions and visits to country villas. His father seldom went much beyond the city and its suburbs, but Wang travelled all over the region and soon found not only that his paintings were much appreciated in these sophisticated circles, but that he had no difficulty in painting them under other people's roofs. Indeed, the more his work was appreciated, the bolder and more fluent it became, and he admitted to himself that fate had been kind in sending him to Pingjiang.

He had, after all, spent many years studying nature closely and improving his powers of composition and drawing. To have continued doing so in isolation might have had the same effect as too much study on candidates for examination: clogging the mind with detail, inducing anxiety and timidity in the expression of ideas. He might have supposed that in this broad, open landscape his preoccupation with the vertical and the sense of density, enclosure and upward movement would have proved unsuitable, forcing him to change his style and format. But, on the contrary, it was as if the open landscape made his feelings all the stronger, and for the most part he still preferred—as Ni did, who had lived in this region all his life—the format of the vertical hanging scroll to the long horizontal hand-scroll of the kind Old Huang had used for *Dwelling in the Mountains of Pure Happiness.*

One day, at a birthday-party in one of the city's private gardens, Wang re-encountered Old Huang's spirited pupil, Chen, who, at the viewing of *The Mountains of Pure Happiness* had so much annoyed the one-eyed Yugur official. Chen, now about thirty, was working as an aide-de-camp to General Pan in Wuxing, but he often visited Pingjiang carrying confidential messages between the General and the warlord Zhang. Chen's father had died, but his mother lived on a small estate just outside the city, cared for by Chen's elder brother, who made that his excuse for a life of almost complete retirement and refused all offers of public office. The Chen brothers' temperaments—the elder quiet and withdrawn, the younger sociable and bursting with energy—seemed almost laughably complementary and their relationship was a little like that between Wang and his cousin Tao: they disagreed adamantly about most things and especially about serving the Yuan Dynasty, but were very attached to each other. The younger Chen was delighted to meet Wang again, took him to visit his mother and brother, with whom Wang immediately felt at home, and arranged for him to be invited to a five-day gathering at the famous Jade Mountain Villa.

The owner of this large and beautiful estate on the shore of a smaller lake east of Lake Tai was Ku Ying, a very rich man of about Wang's age. He had retired from an official post several years ago and devoted himself to running the estate and encouraging poets and painters. Eight or ten guests at a time were accommodated in their own rooms, gathering in the large Thatched Hall to read and compose poems, play music or make paintings. The Thatched Hall, built out on piles over the edge of the lake, its large veranda lit at night with lanterns whose reflections in the water below gave the whole place a magical aura, was suitable for all weathers. But in particular weather conditions the guests would be invited into the smaller, two-storey Cloud Hall, from whose upper floor one could see the top of Jade Mountain wreathed in clouds; or the even smaller Lotus Pavilion, overlooking an inlet dotted with the flowers that gave it its name; or the Jade Hall, furnished only with a few choice ornaments made of the precious stone and a jade-green carpet; or the Peacock Pavilion, decorated with wall-paintings of the stately birds, several of which, in the flesh, paraded and displayed their tails on the lawn in front, or lay on the brick wall enclosing it, or perched in the trees hanging over the wall.

In spring, if the day was very warm, as it often was in this subtropical region, everyone would go out into the garden and sit in the shade of a thirty-foot paulownia tree, the dusky blue of its long, trumpet-shaped flowers set off by the paler hue of the stand of blue-tinted bamboo growing near it. Pretty servant-girls and pages brought food and drink, burned incense and played flutes. If the weather allowed, there would be boat-trips, when the guests, liberally plied with wine, would take their brushes and inkstones and paint landscapes or calligraphy while the scenery shifted slowly around them to the sound of a zither or a flute, and the water lapped softly underneath. As darkness fell, the boat headed briskly home to the freshly-lit lanterns outlining the whole fairy-tale cluster of halls and pavilions.

Everything was of the very best and the guests themselves, the leading poets, painters, scholars, collectors and connoisseurs of the region, with any distinguished people who happened to be visiting from elsewhere in the Empire, were of the same quality. Here, in the midst of very troubled times, when nothing could be relied on not to change suddenly and irrevocably for the worse at any moment, Jade Mountain Villa defiantly reasserted the value of the civilised arts, perhaps for the last time. Wang liked this aspect of the place, the high standard it set itself and maintained, but, grateful as he was for his host's hospitality, did not much like the man himself. Ku's love of beautiful things, whether made by nature or man or both in combination, was genuine enough and his desire to share them with others, without counting the cost, unquestionably generous and admirable, but his personal vanity intruded too much. He was always at the centre of everything, always imposing his small, sturdy person and fussily domineering personality on every scene. His halls and pavilions, his flowers, his wine, his food, his scrolls and ornaments, his lovely girls and pages, his choice guests all served one paramount purpose: to frame and glorify Ku Ying, owner and creator of Jade Mountain Villa now and in the light of history, past and future. The informality and equality that were inseparable from the true pleasure of shared occasions were absent. Wang felt sourly—wishing he didn't feel so—that everything would indeed be perfect, as Ku wished it to be, if only Ku himself were absent. Of course, as Chen—shocked at Wang's attitude—pointed out, this was nonsensical.

"Would any of it be like this, if not for Ku? Isn't the perfection his, since he sees to every detail?"

"But in being seen to see to it, in fingering it so obsessively, he tarnishes perfection. Every time one feels spontaneous pleasure, one glances up and there's Ku, waiting to be congratulated—and the pleasure's gone."

Nor did Wang like the competitive creativity required of Jade Mountain Villa's guests. He had no objection to composing a poem or painting a picture in company, especially when wine flowed as freely as it did here. But a system of forfeits was imposed, whereby anyone who failed to compose or paint in the time allotted, on the theme or rhyme or first line chosen by Ku, was made to drink two cups of wine. Wang had no difficulty himself in composing some doggerel that fitted the rules, but it seemed to him a childish, facile and, for those who had no easy knack of this kind, humiliating exercise.

On the second day of his visit, Wang avoided the gathering under the paulownia and, sitting alone in his guest-room, referring to sketches he had made the day before, painted a hanging scroll of the guests seated round the lawn—figures with faces too small to be recognised, not particular portraits. Beside them a stream ran down into the lake and behind rose Jade Mountain, the path to its top appearing and disappearing behind clumps of trees and bulwarks of rock. The figures were conventionally drawn and not particularly lively, but the mountain, liberally flecked with dark spots of ink and its structure brought out with curling strokes from the side of the brush, was the real subject of the picture. When Chen came to look for him towards evening, he was loudly enthusiastic—he had been drinking all day.

"We thought you must be unwell and now look at this!"

Wang, still working on the top of the mountain, didn't at first raise his eyes from the paper.

"What a lot of people on that lawn!" said another voice. "Or is it a troop of gibbons down from Yellow Crane Mountain?"

Startled, Wang looked up and saw Ni, who had been expected at the gathering but failed to arrive the first day. Rising quickly, Wang joyfully greeted his friend and was shocked to see that he had suffered from an accident. One eye was bruised black and swollen and raw flesh showed along his cheekbones. When Wang took him by the arm, he winced.

"Did your carriage turn over?"

"No, but my boat nearly did."

"What happened?"

"I had a brush with one of the smugglers."

"How do you mean?"

"Zhang's next brother—nasty piece of work!"

"He attacked you?"

"Not in person. He sat by, while two of his boatmen beat me with their oars."

"Where was this?"

"On Lake Tai. Pure misfortune. Our boats happened to be passing through the same channel beside an island. I saw it was him and made haste to steer behind some reeds and keep my head down. But apparently he caught the smell of the incense I always like to have burning near me to keep off mosquitoes and disguise the pungent smells of mud and boatmen. So he immediately guessed it was me. I suppose I was lucky in one way. His hulks wanted to finish me off and drop me overboard, but younger brother Zhang was uncharacteristically merciful."

"He admires your paintings," said Chen.

"Well, yes, it seems he does. That was why he was so angry with me. He wanted one for himself."

"And you refused?" said Wang.

"He sent some underling with a length of silk and requested—demanded, I should say—a painting on it."

"And didn't like what you did?"

"Didn't get it. People can't treat me like a tailor. I don't paint to order. In any case, I prefer paper to silk."

"So you sent it back?"

"No. I was angry. I tore it up."

Wang began to laugh, then Ni laughed too, flinching and bending forward as the laughter hurt his bruised ribs, but continuing to shake without making any sound. Then Chen, at first nervous of offending either of these elder men, both of whom he greatly admired, joined in, and the three of them went out together arm-in-arm and, still laughing, stood on a lawn near the Thatched Hall. The rest of the guests, who had been composing competitive poems, came out on to the veranda and looked down at them with astonishment.

"So it was an ill wind that blew us together," said Ni.

"Or at least carried the smell of your incense," said Wang.

"What did you say when he recognised you?" asked Chen.

"What could I say? One doesn't tear up a large length of expensive silk into quite small pieces and drop them on the ground by mistake."

"You are lucky to be alive," said Wang.

"At the time I was hoping soon to be dead. It was a very severe beating. The smuggler was waiting for me to cry for mercy. I didn't give him that satisfaction."

"You still said nothing."

"I made no sound at all."

"Not even of pain?"

"No sound at all. That would have been vulgar."

The sun was going down on the far side of the lake. The moon, very large and low, was already visible behind Jade Mountain. All three of them were quite silent now, as Ku Ying, flanked by servants with trays of small things to eat and cups of wine, came towards them from Thatched Hall. Wang thought that never in his life had he felt so sure that the good and gentle side of life was stronger and more permanent than the bad. He apologised profusely to Ku for missing the day's events and, before he left three days later, finished the painting, called it Brilliant Gathering at Jade Mountain Villa, and gave it, with a fulsomely grateful inscription, to his vain but essentially good and gentle host.

❁

Ni's favourite lady in Pingjiang was an actress called Sai, famous for her singing and dancing. She was as passionate about cleanliness as Ni himself and her stage name was appropriately "Heavenly Scent." Young Chen wondered privately to Wang whether Ni and Sai ever actually managed to get into bed together, since the slightest speck of dust anywhere in the room would surely have sent them both into paroxysms.

"And just imagine," he said, "if either of them began to sweat as they made love! They'd have to break off and both have another wash. No, I think they just sit together and contemplate one another, enjoying each other's scents and soaps and indulging in pure cleanliness together."

One day in autumn, a year or two after their re-encounter at the Jade Mountain Villa, Ni took Wang to visit Sai. She lived in a fine house reserved for the very best ladies near Zhang's palace, the former Buddhist temple and monastery—not all monks are as careless of transient pleasures as they profess to be. The walled courtyard in front, as Ni and Wang entered from the street, was full of sweet-smelling flowers in raised beds and pots, and a servant was brushing up fallen leaves and petals.

"Flowers!" said Ni wearily, "So irresistible, so fragile, so unbearably messy!"

Inside, they were greeted by the old woman who ran the house and conducted to a terrace overlooking one of Pingjiang's many canals. She left them there, seated in the shade of a willow which screened the terrace from people passing over a wooden bridge just beyond, while she went to call Sai and make tea.

Sai appeared soon afterwards, a very slim, almost white-skinned woman, dressed in turquoise silk with a jade-green shawl. Her face, Wang thought, was too long and thin to be beautiful, but it was her body that caught one's attention. She walked as if she were about to dance or even fly, hardly seeming to touch the floor with her tiny jade-green slippers. Ni took out his handkerchief and dusted her chair before she sat down, then introduced Wang to her as the grandson of Lord Meng.

"Are you serving the Prince of Wu?" she asked.

"The Prince of Wu!" said Ni scornfully. "She means the smuggler."

Zhang's ambitions had recently flared up again. In the spring he had sent an army to attack the Northern Red Scarves—the followers of "The Young Prince of Radiance"—who had sacked Xandu and subsequently been driven back into a city north of the Yangzi River. Zhang's attack had not been entirely successful. "The Young Prince of Radiance" was rescued by his nominal adherent, the ex-Red-Scarf-bandit Zhu, but Zhang at least gained a large swathe of territory.

Now, in the autumn, Zhang had broken with the government again, stopping all supplies of rice to the north and again proclaiming himself Prince of Wu, while General Pan lunged southwards and captured Quinsai. All this expansion was made possible by the fact that Zhu, whose territory bordered Zhang's immediately to the west, was currently locked in a deadly struggle with a third warlord, Chen Yu-liang, whose Southern Red Scarf army held the territory on Zhu's other flank, further up river to the west.

Zhang's renunciation of his allegiance to the government, however, made things difficult for many of his officials, who during his period of tranquillity and legitimacy had been able to think of themselves as still serving the Yuan Dynasty. Now they had to decide where their loyalty really lay—with the Prince of Wu in Pingjiang or the Emperor in Dadu, who had lost half his Empire.

"I am not serving anyone at present," said Wang, not wishing to admit in Ni's presence that he had a few months earlier been temporarily attached to the staff of one of Zhang's generals in Wuxing.

It was young Chen, the general's aide-de-camp, who had brought this about. General Pan was a florid, portly man, formerly a teacher, who loved books and paintings and seemed more interested in the theory of warfare than in actual fighting. His wife, it was said, was the one who really wore the "tiger boots." She came from the same district as Zhang and had not only pushed her husband forward as one of his generals, but married one of their sons to Zhang's daughter.

General Pan made much of Wang, partly as young Chen's friend, partly because he had seen and admired one or two of Wang's paintings. Pan entertained constantly and lavishly at his new villa overlooking Lake Tai and Wang, after an uncomfortable first visit, when he was overcome by feelings of dislocation and sadness at being entertained by a stranger in his parents' old home, became a frequent guest. Eventually, using Chen as an intermediary, Pan delicately suggested that he would like Wang, as a former legal administrator, to take on an advisory role in Wuxing. The problem, Chen explained, was that since Pan had occupied the city six years before, everything had been done on an emergency, military basis. There was a backlog of criminal cases, but even more so of the sort of disputes which were usually settled by experienced administrators. Wang was not being asked to do this himself, but only to advise the military on selecting and briefing suitable men for the task.

His first thought was to say no. The political situation was still too confused, his own position too delicate. True, he had never formally broken with the government he previously served and General Pan, as Zhang's subordinate, now officially served that government. On the other hand, first by joining the White Tigress and then by going to see Zhu, he had certainly broken with the government in practice, and to accept even such a marginal office as General Pan offered him would be to change sides once again.

The White Tigress, of course, was dead and her remaining followers probably by now either disbanded or incorporated into some other rebel army, but Wang felt uneasy about his relationship with Zhu. The invitation to be his adviser in Nanjing had been turned down not on the grounds that Zhu was a rebel, but that Wang wished to retire completely. Wouldn't that look like a deliberate subterfuge if Wang were now to accept office under Zhu's enemy?

Just at this time Zhu was in danger of being overwhelmed by Chen Yu-Liang, the warlord to his west, and he had lost some of his territory to the north of the Yangzi River to both Zhang and the Mongol forces. Of course, Wang's "defection" would make no practical difference at all to Zhu's cause and he would probably never even hear about it, while if Zhu was defeated and his army eliminated—as looked more and more likely—Wang would be seen by the rest of the world to have acted sensibly and honourably.

Nevertheless, he felt that in principle, if not in fact, he had incurred a sort of obligation to Zhu. "Must loyalty be given only from an official's chair?" he had asked, and "Could one not be loyal while contemplating a waterfall?" No doubt most people would think it ridiculous that merely asking such a question should be held to imply offering loyalty. But Wang felt that it did, that Zhu had taken it that way and that his final words about summoning Wang again sometime in the future had sealed this oblique and almost imperceptible contract between them, which would only be cancelled if Zhu's "bright future" failed to materialise.

Yet Wang did finally agree to act as an adviser to General Pan's officers. Why? Because this was not so much a matter of assisting Zhang's regime as of bringing relief to many ordinary people—mostly farmers and traders—in the city and district of his birth. Public order and justice, he told himself, were of more importance than the purely personal and selfish question of his tangled loyalties, and when he announced this decision to young Chen, to whom he had previously revealed his doubts, added with a smile:

"After all, I am a Confucian."

But he would not accept any salary for his services and asked that they should not be officially recognised or recorded.

"You still think Zhu may survive?" asked Chen. "He looks to me to be on the way out."

"That has nothing to do with it," said Wang sharply. "I'm not trying to conceal my role as adviser, but to make it clear that this is not an official post."

Rumour and gossip, however, are seldom concerned with subtleties of interpretation. Most people who knew or had heard of Wang assumed that it *was* an official post.

❁

"'The smuggler,' as my friend here insists on calling our new Prince of Wu, is not really such a bad fellow," Sai said cheerfully. "He enjoys life, he's generous, he laughs a lot."

"Translate that as greedy, habitually drunk, fat, coarse, loud and totally unreliable," said Ni.

"Women like him and men envy him," said Sai.

"Women are attracted by money and power," said Ni. "They would swarm round a donkey if it was master of the richest province in the Empire."

"You both know him well?" asked Wang.

"Not at all," said Sai. "Ni has never even met him. I have been introduced to him, but know about him only at second-hand."

"There is another lady living here who sees a lot of him," said Ni. "She is naturally prejudiced in his favour."

"She is an intelligent and experienced person, as you admit yourself," said Sai.

"But with the usual weakness of her sex," said Ni. "An inability to distinguish what men are from what they do."

"What you are *is* what you do," said Sai. "How else could we tell you apart?"

At this moment the old woman who ran the house brought their tea out on to the terrace. Behind her came another woman, perhaps in her late thirties, poised and elegant and with a perfectly oval face that made Wang catch his breath, first because it was so beautiful and then because he recognised it. She too recognised him, though it was clear that she could not place him or remember his name.

"I saw you acting in that play about the Orphan in Quinsai," said Wang. "I sat next to you in the restaurant afterwards and we argued for some time about whether the play as your company performed it could be seen as a veiled attack on the Mongol government and if so, whether the authorities would close it down."

She eagerly took both his hands.

"How could I have forgotten?" she said.

"It was many years ago," said Wang. "I'm sure I have aged badly."

"No, not you, but surely I have."

"You? On the contrary! At first I thought you must be your younger sister."

"Enough of this!" said Ni. "Say her own daughter and be done with it! Sit down and drink some tea!"

They did so and Jasmine went on to describe how she had left the company that performed Orphan, married an actor and moved to Pingjiang with his company. One of the plays in their repertory had been the story, from the ancient era of the Warring States, of Fan Li and his beautiful mistress Xi Shi, in which Jasmine played Xi and her husband Fan. The story's setting was Lake Tai and the hills around Pingjiang and, perhaps for that reason, it had proved a huge success with the public. So much so that Zhang had commanded a special performance for himself and his courtiers in his newly-converted palace. This was at the time, not long after his capture of Pingjiang, when he was negotiating with the government and first calling himself Prince of Wu. But since the play's story was about a former Prince of Wu who lost his kingdom through becoming besotted with the treacherous Xi Shi, the actors were very much afraid that Zhang would react badly and perhaps punish them. On the contrary he seemed altogether delighted with the performance and after it was over invited the whole company to supper, seating Jasmine next to himself.

"He told me had fallen in love with Xi Shi," said Jasmine, "and wanted her to come and live with him in his palace. I replied that I had a husband, and nodded in his direction. 'The one who played Fan Li,' I said. 'But not a real Fan Li, I hope,' said Zhang. 'Your husband didn't send you, did he, like the real Fan Li, to turn the head of the Prince of Wu so that I would lose my kingdom?' 'I will ask him,' I said, 'but so far as I know he's just an actor like me and no more a master-strategist like the real Fan Li than I am a famous beauty like the real Xi Shi.' 'Well, you are Xi Shi enough for me,' said Zhang, 'and I have no fear of losing *my* kingdom like that other Prince of Wu.'"

The upshot was that she soon became the warlord's mistress, but not as one of his palace concubines, and when, later, she parted with her husband, Zhang found her the room where she now lived, conveniently near his palace.

"And just because I keep him at that small distance and am not always willing to receive him," said Jasmine, "I think he prefers me to all the ladies in his palace."

Wang remained silent through most of this conversation, except to say, when Jasmine asked him how he had been affected by all the turmoil of the last ten years, that he had had some adventures, but would perhaps tell her some of them another time.

"We would all like to hear them," said Ni, "and I shouldn't think you need that excuse to see this Xi Shi again. Why don't we all four make an expedition together in my boat, while the weather is still warm, to the site of Xi Shi's palace on Mount Ling-yen? There we can plot the downfall of this latest Prince of Wu."

"But I don't want his downfall," said Jasmine.

"I'm sure my friend does," said Ni, looking significantly at Wang. "You must have it out with him. Yes, I believe Xi Shi may have found her real Fan Li and our smuggler turned Prince of Wu has not heard the end of that story."

❁

Considering how much he disliked the Mongols, whose tax demands had forced him to give up his estate and live on a boat, Ni's animosity towards Zhang, who had never done him any harm and had ousted the Mongols, was hard to understand. The affair of the torn silk was an aspect, not a cause of his animosity and showed how far he was prepared to take it. Was it because Zhang came from the lowest class? But if so, Ni was inconsistent, since he seemed to have no such animosity towards the rival warlord, Zhu, whose origins were equally humble. Ni himself, when Wang asked him directly, could or would give no proper explanation.

"Something large and shapeless, with a bad smell, washed up by the Yangzi. Better not look too closely."

"And Zhu?"

"You've met him, I haven't. From all I've heard, a serious person. If Zhang and Zhu were playing chess, no question who would win. But chess is a game of pure skill, whereas this gang war is a game with too many players and depends more on chance than skill."

Superficially, it was no doubt Zhang's blatant sensuality and dissipation that riled Ni's austere nature, but Wang suspected that what he really disliked was Zhang's popularity, especially with estate-owners and the upper classes of the administrators. Ni could never allow himself to share accepted opinions, even when they were in his own favour.

"X always loved my bamboo paintings," he said once, naming a well-known collector. "Why? I wonder. I paint bamboo when I feel exhilarated, when I want to express that feeling. I don't know whether my paintings look like bamboo. I scribble and smear for a bit and other people say, 'Oh, that's meant to be hemp, is it?' or, 'What lovely reeds!' So what are they actually seeing? And what on earth is X seeing when he says he loves my bamboo paintings?"

Ni took it for granted that Wang, like himself, was a bitter enemy to Zhang's regime, and knowing of Wang's contact with Zhu, began to encourage him actively to take sides. He dismissed all Wang's protestations of his own inconsequence and timidity.

"I know you too well, my dear friend. Your modesty about your paintings conceals a mountainous ambition and it's the same with this pretence about your political abilities. Young Chen told me that you actually captured a town and killed its governor."

"He should not have told you, and it's a gross exaggeration."

"Of course," said Ni. "Just what I expected you to say and proves my point."

The idea of the old story of Fan Li and Xi Shi being repeated by Wang and Jasmine, while Zhang re-enacted the part of the Prince of Wu, chosen by himself, appealed greatly to Ni. Stooping, as they left Sai's house, to pick up some fallen petals missed by the servant in the courtyard, he urged Wang to return as often as possible.

"She thinks very highly of you, that was obvious. The smuggler is in love with her, but she's not in love with him. She's ready to fall in love with you and then . . ."

"And then?"

"For your sake, she'll bring him to grief," said Ni, wrapping the petals carefully in his handkerchief to dispose of elsewhere.

"I don't see how. Or to whose advantage."

"To Zhu's advantage, of course. Once Zhang is distracted, Zhu can pounce and you will be the man that gave him victory."

"I am not in touch with Zhu," said Wang. "And far from being distracted by Jasmine, Zhang seems more bellicose than he was before."

"Now be more intelligent, my dear friend! History never repeats itself exactly. This is Zhang's way of courting Xi Shi. Instead of building her palaces, he seizes more towns. But he will over-extend himself and that will be his undoing."

"Possibly. But whatever my ambitions as a painter, I have none to take a leading role in such a story."

Ni, however, was not to be put off. The fancy of turning a legend back into reality had taken hold of him, and in this, though he would not have cared to think so, he was only one of many with similar ideas at this time. He insisted on introducing Wang to a group of literary people—some of them ex-officials, some serving Zhang's regime—called "The Ten Friends of the North Wall." There were many more than ten of them, as there are many more than ten thousand things in the universe, but they probably started with fewer and besides round numbers give a sense of regularity, completeness and control—very comforting in a period as chaotic as this.

The fact that power was obviously slipping from the grasp of the foreign conquerors and passing to that of nearly illiterate bandits stirred up long-suppressed, almost forgotten emotions in some of the more active-minded intellectuals. Surely, if peasants could lead armies, then well-educated men with distinguished ancestors could do it better? At the very least, there might be an opportunity here for courageous and clever people to influence the course of history.

The guiding spirit of the Friends of the North Wall was the famous poet Gao Chi. Full of self-confidence, accustomed to being admired and deferred to, he constantly studied military history and strategy, went riding daily and took regular lessons from an arms instructor in swordplay and archery. Gao saw himself and was seen by many of his friends as a charismatic leader on the model of Xuande, the hero of popular stories from the period of civil war known as "The Three Kingdoms"—the last throes of the Han Dynasty. One of Gao's associates, indeed, a poet and playwright called Luo, had begun transforming these stories into a single immense story called *Three Kingdoms*—an entirely novel form of literature somewhere between historical reality and legend, written in prose and interspersed with dialogue like a play. It was generally supposed that the book's hero, Xuande, was modelled on Gao. Thus—and it was somehow characteristic of the whole phenomenon represented by the Ten Friends of the North Wall—the part historical, part legendary hero Xuande, the living would-be hero Gao, and the literary hero drawn from both, all mirrored one another in a series of overlapping images.

Wang met Luo briefly on one occasion, when he read a few early sections of his book to a gathering of the Friends of the North Wall. He was shy and withdrawn, living mostly by himself and seldom appearing in company—the very opposite sort of person to the imperious Gao. He read his passages quietly and not at all dramatically, but everybody present was deeply impressed by the power of his words, the liveliness of his characters and the sense of a great structure being raised like an arched bridge over the headlong river of events. Wang never forgot the opening lines: "The Empire, long divided, must unite; long united, must divide. Thus it has ever been."

The Friends of the North Wall met regularly at each other's houses, in Pingjiang or in the district round it, and held animated discussions about the current political situation and what might be done to prepare for the future when, they fervently believed, the Yuan Dynasty would at last have fallen. The group's name no doubt referred to the fact that Gao's house was just inside Pingjiang's north wall, but it also carried a patriotic overtone, implying that when the Mongols were driven back beyond the northern wall of the Empire, all the land within it would once again belong to its own people. How in the meantime could men of intelligence and good will such as themselves contribute to the final stages of the liberation and how, afterwards, assist in the great task of pacifying and reconstructing the Empire?

For the present, of course, the Friends could only guess which of the three contending warlords around the Yangzi River would prove the strongest, though they eagerly pored over maps, drew up theoretical plans of campaign and argued the issue back and forth. Of the three, they hoped most from Zhu, because of his serious programme of recruiting good advisers from the educated class, but especially since his rash and apparently altruistic rescue of "The Young Prince of Radiance." Whether or not this boy was genuinely descended from a Song Emperor, the very fact that Zhu clearly aimed to restore the dynasty was encouraging, since many of the Friends shared this aim.

On the other hand, Zhu was hard-pressed from both sides and his capture of Nanjing, pinning him down in the dangerous middle position, now looked, they thought, like a costly mistake. The Friends were not opposed to Zhang—one or two, after all, including Gao, were serving as officials in his regime—but they noted his emotional instability, considered he had been remarkably lucky so far, and doubted whether his undisciplined army and self-indulgent generals could cope with any sustained campaign. All depended, therefore, on the outcome of Zhu's current struggle with the third warlord, Chen Yu-liang, the leader of the southern branch of the Red Scarves. People in Pingjiang knew little about him, except that he commanded a large fleet of Yangzi warships and had recently murdered the former figurehead of his rebellion—a fat peddler who resembled the popular image of the Maitreya Buddha—and proclaimed himself Emperor of the Han Dynasty. That, the Friends felt, might sound patriotic, but was going too far.

The great Han Dynasty had ended more than a thousand years before, and it was merely insolent or playing to the ignorance and superstition of peasants to pretend to revive it. No, it was the restoration of the Song they chiefly envisaged and those who doubted the credentials of "The Young Prince of Radiance" were confident that a better candidate would emerge. It was even suggested that Wang's cousin, Zhao Lin, might be the man and Wang was asked to sound him out. Wang was uncomfortable with the idea and put it off for the moment with the excuse that his cousin was still mourning his father's death. But he confided privately to Ni that he thought the Friends of the North Wall were quite unrealistic.

"Emperors are not found by committees," he said, "however well qualified and well-intentioned. These gentlemen see strategic manoeuvres in the distance and in the foreground the palace and magistrate's court, the streets and canals, the shops and markets, the restaurants, houses and temples—all the administrative details necessary to make the Empire just and workable—but they don't see the wall in between."

"The wall?"

"The city wall that protects them and also makes them powerless. The wall patrolled by soldiers. The man who drives out the Mongols will have to do it by force. If he has the military power to do it, then he will have the military power to found the next dynasty. He will be the Emperor. That has always been our history."

"So they should be called 'The Ten Friends Ignorant of the North Wall,'" said Ni, smiling maliciously. Although many of them, individually, were his own friends and he had persuaded Wang to join them, he was instinctively suspicious of them as a group.

Wang's critical reaction to them was perhaps equally instinctive, but he did not, like Ni, take pride in it and even felt guilty about mentioning it. He admired the Friends' enterprise and sense of responsibility, especially when so many other talented, well-educated people were content to drift with events and worry merely about their own selfish interests. Was it simply that he thought the Friends' schemes and discussions unrealistic or because he was wary of their dominating leader, Gao?

Wang still partly pictured himself as an uncertain, youthful, unnoticeable person. No doubt we are all prone, however old we grow—however many skins we change, so to speak—to continue imagining ourselves as we first knew ourselves, in our first or second skins. In fact, he was now a determined, mature man in his mid-fifties and though he certainly did not impose himself, he was, no doubt, imposing—a tall, dignified, even aristocratic figure with an air of self-sufficiency. He got on easily with younger or less determined men and deferred to his elders, but quietly withdrew and avoided any sort of competition if he encountered other strong characters of his own age. His warm relationship with Ni was only possible because they wholeheartedly admired each other's paintings and had found a bantering mode of accommodating their differences and concealing their competitiveness. There was no way that he could accept a subordinate role to the swaggering Gao. Did Gao secretly hope to found a dynasty himself? How could he—with such a small following of would-be generals and no army?

More likely—and this was a good reason for keeping one's distance—he dreamed of fighting and heroically failing, like the legendary Xuande, who never did become emperor or save the Han dynasty from extinction.

❁

They had a perfect autumn day for the boat trip. Leaving Pingjiang very early in carriages, they were driven to a point on the eastern shore of Lake Tai from which they only had to cross a short stretch of water to reach the foot of Mount Ling-yen. The sun was now too hot to sit out in, but they were sheltered by a canopy at the front of the boat and a light breeze fanned their faces as, looking out across the lake, they drank wine, while Ni played his zither.

Two other boatmen had been hired to help Ni's deaf-and-dumb servant with the poling and sculling. Mules for the men and litters for the ladies were awaiting them at the foot of the mountain and they were to stay the night at a friend's house nearby. The whole expedition had been meticulously planned and organised by Ni, but he looked anxious and paused in his playing to ask if their silence meant they were bored.

"Quite the contrary," said Jasmine, her head resting on Wang's shoulder. "Much too happy to speak."

"I was thinking how unfair it is that you should have so many talents," said Wang. "If you were not such a good musician, you would surely have been a general."

"Of course," said Ni. "Unfortunately I always faint at the mere thought of blood."

"Do generals ever see any blood?" asked Sai.

"Not if they win, I suppose," said Jasmine.

"And if they lose, I suppose they might as well faint," said Sai.

"But of course," said Jasmine, smiling mischievously, "poor Ni would only have to *think* of all those legs and arms and heads lying about and wounds spouting . . . "

"Please!" said Ni, his face going pale, his forehead beginning to sweat.

"You are too hard on generals," said Wang. "The best ones lead the attack or even ride out between the armies for single combat with the enemy general."

"Was that what you did when you captured that town?" asked Ni.

"What I did was stand well behind the cannons," said Wang. "But I watched our general lead the attack."

"You are surely going to tell us a little more about it than that?" said Sai.

"There was not much more to it," said Wang, reluctant to embark on such a complicated story, especially one which still gave him pain to remember. "The guns fired, the gates opened, the general and his cavalry charged in and the town was taken."

"No blood?" asked Jasmine.

"Not much that I saw," he said lightly, still trying to throw off the subject.

But she knew him quite well by now and could tell he was being evasive.

"You prefer not to talk about it. A bad experience, was it?"

This was an awkward question to deal with. Whether he answered yes or no, he would have to give some explanation, but no truthful explanation of how he came to be involved in military action could exclude the White Tigress and he was determined not to discuss her with Jasmine and especially not in front of Ni and Sai.

Women, most of whose lives are so strictly confined by their functions as wives, mothers, daughters, daughters-in-law or sexual partners to men, are naturally absorbed in personal relationships and usually much more acute than men in understanding and manipulating them. It was seldom possible, in Wang's experience, to maintain a steady equilibrium in any relationship with a woman. Perhaps it was the same in the long term with male friends too, but the process of change was so much slower and more organic that one was hardly aware of it. Women preferred a relationship to be unpredictable and risky, like riding a high-spirited horse through broken country, up and down slopes, across rivers, beside ravines. The simile occurred to him, no doubt, because of his journey with the White Tigress, a woman who in adopting a man's role had externalised the usually hidden turbulence of women's lives—not least in her inexorable hunting-down of the magistrate. Vengefulness, jealousy, adoration, contempt are emotions common to both sexes, of course, but like fires in closed stoves they are more quickly ignited and burn more intensely in women.

Wang could not guess exactly how bringing the White Tigress into his relationship with Jasmine would affect it, but he knew that it would, radically and irreparably, altering and complicating his own feelings about both of them. He shrank from that. His permanently unresolved relationship to the dead woman was now wrapped and stowed away inside himself, as her body was in the ground. His relationship to the living one, meanwhile, was in its most perfect phase, a straightforward mutual attraction, the strongest of all natural pleasures, smooth and soothing like the passage of this boat across the almost waveless water. No doubt it would change quite soon—too soon—either with circumstances or, more likely, because she would tire of its smoothness and look about for some way to make the boat rock and the experience more exciting.

"I prefer not to talk about it," he said, "because my own part in it was so shameful. I was captured by a group of bandits and forced to devise a stratagem for taking a town. The magistrate was killed and the town itself largely destroyed. Nothing unusual in that, of course. Terrible things of that sort are happening all over the Empire and I'm afraid will go on for many years yet. I was very lucky to escape with my life when the bandits fell out among themselves. We are very lucky now to be able to enjoy this cloudless day. Happiness is not so easily come by that I want to spread a cloud over it."

Striking the right tone—of distaste and regret rather than adventure and glamour—so that even Ni could not insert any teasing barb, he silenced them all and closed the subject.

Ni began to play the zither again, softly and sadly, while Jasmine took Wang's hand and stroked it gently. Boats of all kinds were coming and going around them, large and small fishing-boats—some with up to four sails—a ferry full of people on their way to market, a large boat low in the water with its heavy cargo, a small one-masted patrol-boat carrying a few soldiers. Here in Zhang's kingdom all seemed calm and normal, but it was strange to think that the far shore out of sight to the west was controlled not by Zhang, but by Zhu, and that somewhere across this peaceful lake an invisible line divided two armies, both of the same race, both hoping to drive out the Mongols, but at present intent on cutting each other to pieces.

There was a light shower of rain as the mules and litter-carriers took them up Mount Ling-yen and the party sheltered briefly in a wood. All these servants—the boatmen had remained behind to guard the boat—came from Ni's former estate, which was only a few miles away, and while they waited for the rain to stop, the overseer gave Ni news of the estate and his relatives still living there. This area had escaped the fighting and no damage had been done to buildings or crops. Taxes were still heavy, but on the whole the man thought conditions better than under the Mongols.

"Will you be returning now, sir?" he asked.

"Better not," said Ni. "Your conditions would certainly get worse if the Prince of Wu's brother knew where he could find me."

"Hasn't he forgiven you for tearing up his silk?" asked Wang.

"Worse," said Ni. "He still wants a painting from me."

"After half killing you?"

"It seems that anyone who is anyone has to have a painting by Ni Zan in his house," said Ni. "I'm not boasting. It's simply a fact. A very annoying fact, considering that I'm not an industry. Annoying also for the smuggler's brother, of course, since the only person who can make him a painting by Ni Zan is me."

The others could not help smiling covertly at each other and, noticing their amusement, Ni smiled too.

"What a pity that artists in their lives are such a disgrace to their work!" he said.

"Couldn't you bring yourself to do it?" asked Wang.

Ni pressed his foot on a large piece of dead wood until it broke.

"If he finds me," he said, "he will undoubtedly send a few killers along with his fresh piece of silk."

"So you'll have no alternative," said Wang.

"None. I paint as the mood takes me. I cannot be forced."

"I think I would force myself to do so in the circumstances," said Wang.

"You have many virtues and accomplishments, my dear friend. I have only one. I don't compromise."

When they emerged from the wood, the lake below had almost completely vanished in mist, though the sun shone again on the slopes above them. There was no knowing where Xi Shi's palace had stood—after more than eighteen hundred years not a trace remained. They found a more or less level platform of turf not far below the summit and, sitting on a shelf of rock, ate the light lunch Ni had provided and tried to imagine themselves on Xi Shi's terrace. Ni had instructed the carriers and mules to take their rest and refreshment further round the slope, out of sight.

"Apologies for the mist!" he said. "On a good day one can see all the seventy-two peaks round the lake."

"I prefer the mist," said Jasmine. "At the end of the story, after the defeat of the Prince of Wu—at least in our play—Xi Shi sails away westwards into the mist with her lover Fan Li."

Bringing a bamboo flute out of her sleeve, she began to play a long slow tune. From where he sat Wang could just see the heads of the servants peeping over a rock. Fortunately, as he remarked afterwards to Jasmine, Ni was seated a little further down, with his arm round Sai, and didn't notice them. His pure experience was not compromised and no one had to be rebuked.

"A tune from the play?" Ni asked, as the music died away.

"The lovers' farewell," she said, "as Fan Li sends Xi Shi to bewitch the Prince of Wu."

"And when they are reunited . . . ?" asked Wang.

"Yes, I can play you that."

The tune was equally slow and, if anything, more melancholy.

"You'd think it would be jollier, more triumphant," said Ni.

"Her feelings are not quite so straightforward," said Jasmine. "Of course, she's happy to rejoin Fan, but how can she avoid feelings of betrayal too? I'm sure she loved the Prince of Wu. How could she not have done, when he loved her so passionately that he lost his kingdom for her? She lived with him, remember, for nearly twenty years. If the story were only about a woman who deceives an enemy in order to give victory to her own people, it would be relatively crude and would not have the same poignancy. I think she loved both of them, the Prince and Fan Li, and deceived both, without deceiving herself."

"And each of them was happy in being deceived," said Sai. "But she, never at all."

"Not never," said Jasmine. "But her happiness was always edged with self-disgust and sadness."

The mist burned away a little before they left, revealing a few peaks in the distance and the sails of boats on the lake.

"How many times must she have seen exactly what we are seeing!" said Jasmine.

"But with what different feelings!" said Wang.

She made no reply, but there were tears in her eyes.

❁

Wang only learnt the reason after they returned from their blissful expedition, loving each other, it seemed, like a new Xi Shi and Fan Li. The Prince of Wu, she said, suspecting she was seeing too much of someone else, had told her to leave her house and move into his palace. In return, she was to become his latest wife.

"You knew this all the time?"

"No, only recently."

"Before we set out on the boat-trip?"

"I had some indication."

"But you kept it a secret from me?"

"Why should I spoil our expedition—so beautifully arranged by Ni? And wasn't it better that way? Didn't you say yourself that 'happiness is not so easily come by that I want to spread a cloud over it'?"

"But must you do what he says?" asked Wang, deeply upset.

"I can take a little time to make up my mind. But I have no real option, unless I go and live beyond his power."

"Perhaps, in any case, you *prefer* to be one of the Prince of Wu's wives?"

"Do I? Bring a boat for me, then, so that we can go westwards into the mist and hide in Zhu's kingdom!"

Did she mean that? If she did, could he leave his wife and his father—now growing very feeble—and take his chance under Zhu? More likely she was testing him and cleverly putting him in the wrong, knowing all the time that she would not go with him, even if he met her challenge. Caught in these cross-currents of distrust, their smoothly loving relationship turned choppy and uncomfortable.

"You are evidently not Fan Li," she said sarcastically the next time they met, when he admitted that he had done nothing about arranging for them to leave Pingjiang.

"It was only Ni who thought I was," said Wang.

"And I thought so too. Your dearest wish, you told me, was to leave the dusty world, like Fan Li, and retreat to a thatched hut."

"It still is," he said. "But is it yours?"

"I don't recall that Fan Li asked Xi Shi such a question," she said. "Fan Li entered his boat, intending to leave alone. It was only then that Xi Shi left her terrace and went down to join him."

"But that was after the downfall of the Prince of Wu."

"Of course. She spent twenty years with him. Is that what you're suggesting?"

"I would really prefer to forget that old story and concentrate on ours," said Wang.

"So would I."

And for an hour or two, they did. But she would not tell him how long she could postpone moving into Zhang's palace and, as he left her that day, he said, almost in desperation:

"I will make the arrangements."

"Is that a promise?"

"You must give me time, that's all."

"But you promise?"

"I promise."

Half regretting his promise almost as soon as he had made it, he nevertheless sent Kong to Nanjing with a message for Zhu: "The man from the waterfalls is ready to be summoned." Kong, eager to see Nanjing, foresaw no difficulty in passing through the border between Zhu's and Zhang's territories. He also approved of Wang's decision, without being told the real reason for it.

"People are changing sides all the time," he said. "You are doing the right thing."

"You think Zhu will be the winner?"

"Take my word for it! All the fortune-tellers agree. It's a pity you didn't go when he first asked you. You'd be a big man by now."

❁

Autumn had turned to winter by the time Kong returned. He had not seen Zhu himself, but had given Wang's message to an official at Zhu's headquarters.

"A man named Hu Wei-yong," said Kong. "Very brisk and sure of himself. He'll go far."

"But will he deliver the message to Zhu?"

"He said you need not wait to be summoned. There is work for everyone loyal to the Prince of Wu."

"The Prince of Wu?"

"Not this fat Zhang," said Kong. "Your old friend from the monastery is now the Prince of Wu."

"But this region, the old kingdom of Wu, is still controlled by Zhang."

"For how long? And who gave him his title? Zhu's title has been conferred on him by the Young Prince of Radiance, soon-to-be-restored Emperor of the Song Dynasty. So the quicker you go to Nanjing, the better."

But by then it was too late. Visiting the ladies' house next day, Wang found only Sai and learned that Jasmine had gone to be Zhang's latest wife. Ni was bitterly disappointed that his attempt to revive the ancient legend had been frustrated, but he soon found a reason.

"The original Prince of Wu was not a smuggler, nor Xi Shi an actress," he said. "That's where we went wrong. Only you—our Fan Li—were the right type."

# 11. THE BLUE BIEN MOUNTAINS

Disconsolate and depressed after Jasmine's disappearance, Wang was unable, of course, to explain his low spirits to his wife. They discussed the message Kong had brought back from Nanjing and Wang allowed her to assume that this was what chiefly preoccupied him. Evidently she could not go with him to Nanjing, since Wang's father was not willing to move again and was too weak now to be left by himself, but she urged Wang to go himself. It seemed only a matter of time now before the new Prince of Wu overwhelmed the old.

The struggle between Zhu and his other rival, Chen Yu-liang, had finally come to a head with a great naval battle lasting four days, on a lake leading out of the Yangzi River. Both sides suffered heavy casualties, but neither could prevail. At last Zhu withdrew his fleet to the Yangzi and waited for Chen's fleet to emerge from the only channel to the lake. A month went by before it did, but then, waiting upstream, taking advantage of the current and using fireships to scatter the enemy fleet before pursuing it downstream, Zhu triumphed. Chen himself was killed by an arrow in the eye.

Zhu's generals were now busy subduing all the Southern Red Scarf territories and capturing the major towns, while Zhu himself, back in Nanjing, reorganised his administration and his army—swollen with Chen's former followers—and prepared to tackle Zhang. What chance had Zhang now? He seemed sunk in fatalistic lethargy. Half-hearted attempts were made by General Pan to loosen Zhu's hold on the west side of Lake Tai, but every attack was easily beaten off and a long interval of relative calm ensued while, like the two surviving gamblers after a third has been ruined, Zhu slowly gathered up his huge winnings and Zhang sat back in his chair with glazed eyes.

Perhaps he imagined that relief would come from the Mongols. They still held most of the north and the Emperor had now acquired a formidable general, the son of a Chinese father and Mongol mother. This man, who had taken the name of Kökö Temür to show that, in spite of his mixed ancestry he was entirely committed to the Mongols, might, if he had been allowed to, have defeated Zhu or at least kept him fighting for many years north of the Yangzi, and perhaps exhausted him before he could turn his attention to Zhang. But Kökö, like the energetic Chancellor Toghto before him, was distracted by rivals at the Emperor's court. So the Mongols squabbled and stabbed each other in the back; Zhang ate and drank and lay in Jasmine's and others' arms; Zhu consolidated his power.

Wang felt himself to be in the same state of lethargy and indecision as Zhang and, perversely, began to sympathise with the man who had deprived him of his mistress. Wang's wife did not press him to go to Nanjing and he simply put off making up his mind, telling her and perhaps convincing himself that he could not be satisfied with a vague verbal summons, delivered to a servant by an unknown official, but was waiting for Zhu's personal response to his original message.

In fact, his access of sympathy for Zhang was quite common in Pingjiang and was shared by his father as well as many of their friends and the Ten Friends of the North Wall.

"What nobler course is there," Gao declared, "than to be true to the ruler of our native region, the ancient state of Wu, considering that, though he has glaring faults and may in the long run lose his state to this other warlord, Zhu, he has shown that he believes in the highest values of civilisation?"

The remark was made at an especially distinguished gathering of scholars, poets and artists, held that spring at the villa of Lord Shan Lu, in the region south-east of Pingjiang, towards the sea. The gathering was to celebrate the coming-of-age of Lord Shan's son, and took place in a large and splendid stone hall with a tile roof, the "Pavilion for Listening to the Rain." Ni, who was also present, looked sour at Gao's remark, since, in order to avoid Zhang's brother, he was in virtual exile from Pingjiang, staying with a friend in a remote place near the sea. But Wang now found himself agreeing with the sentiment and almost eager to fall beside him in a glorious lost cause.

When their host's son read a poem written many years before by a well-known poet for Lord Shan, alluding to the family's loyalty to the Song Dynasty and determination, in spite of the Mongol conquest, to preserve their family, their ancient home and the values associated with them, its elegiac tone suddenly seemed inappropriate. History had already changed like a configuration of clouds. The settled years of the Yuan Dynasty were now almost as much a memory as those of the Song.

Many of those present wanted to write new poems, using the themes and rhymes of the old one to express the changed context—of a regime worth actively supporting instead of passively resisting—while the same family continued, now in the person of their host's newly grown-up son, with the same values, in the same pavilion, where the rain still drummed on the roof and dripped from the eaves with the same sound. Wang immediately undertook to paint the pavilion on a hand-scroll, to which the poems were attached as endpapers.

The mood of the occasion was jubilant, as if only now were they all suddenly aware of being free from the Mongol past and of rediscovering their own past as a still vital thing, a long-buried stream bursting out of the earth again. Ni alone remained unaffected by the collective mood and wrote these ironic lines:

*Lord Shan listened to the rain, the sky overcast,*
*A sound of galloping hooves and hissing spears.*
*Lord Shan's son listened to the rain, the worst being past,*
*A sound of tearing silk and beating oars.*

On his way home from this gathering, Wang visited young Chen's home in the country near Pingjiang. Chen himself was away on active service with General Pan, but Chen's mother and elder brother welcomed him warmly and begged him to stay until Chen returned.

"There are only two artists he admires more than your grandfather Lord Meng," said Chen's brother. "One is Old Huang, the other is you."

Deeply touched, Wang tried to disagree.

"Just look at his own paintings, if you don't believe me!" said the elder Chen. "They are softer, gentler, less detailed than yours—no one alive has the same ability as you to translate the ten thousand things from reality to marks on paper—but they convey the same feelings."

"But we are such different sorts of people," said Wang. "He is sharp and quick, I am slow and indecisive. What sort of feelings do we have in common?"

"I would say that they are essentially religious," said the elder Chen. "You are in search of understanding. Your paintings are seldom hand-scrolls—journeys from right to left through the world—but almost always hanging scrolls—journeys through the world, but also out of it. As the eye climbs upward through one of your paintings, so rivers are reduced to streams, streams to narrow chutes of water, woods grow more sparse, houses are left behind, earth gives way to rock, plants barely survive, bald rock ends in a glimpse of sky."

"This is just the nature of mountains," said Wang.

"But it's the nature of religious people to choose to go up them. My brother, you see, follows you up like a pupil in the steps of his master—aspiring as you do, but only because you show the way."

Wang shook his head, unable to speak, his pride and pleasure at being praised so shrewdly conflicting with his modesty. It was not just that he did not like to appear immodest, but that he genuinely did not consider himself such a master. He knew what masters were, he desired to be one, but he feared that, like a person who relaxes too soon on a difficult climb, he might fail for want of caution on the crags that so few ever attained.

He did not see young Chen on this occasion, but left for home in a new frame of mind. The elder Chen's praise for his work and the feelings of solidarity induced by the gathering at Lord Shan's pavilion all combined to renew his optimism and energy.

There was no summons from Zhu waiting for him and, even if there had been, he would probably have ignored it. The celebration of Lord Shan's lineage and family continuity turned his thoughts to his own. His old uncle, the eldest son of Lord Meng and former governor of Wuxing, had recently died, leaving the Zhao family estate to his son, Zhao Lin. Many of Lord Meng's paintings were still there, carefully preserved in his old studio, the "Gull-Wave Pavilion"—so called because of its gracefully undulating grey tiled roof. Wang decided to take up his cousin's invitation to study them again, things he had not looked at for nearly forty years.

❁

During his time as adviser to General Pan's officers in Wuxing, Wang had made a tour of the district. His main purpose was to see for himself—and to show those he was advising—what conditions were like for the farmers, but he also intended to make a private visit to the Blue Bien Mountains.

He had not been there since he was a boy. Lord Meng's country retreat, where the family had spent their summers, was still nominally owned now by Wang's cousin, but had been abandoned during the disorders of the last few years. Wang did not think of staying in the retreat, which had almost certainly been damaged or even destroyed by bandits, but he hoped to catch a glimpse of it and see the river where he and Peony had fallen in love and met the ape-like "splash-painter." Perhaps his thatched hut beside the waterfall still existed.

The mountains were beyond the area controlled by Zhang and

therefore theoretically in Zhu's territory, but soldiers at this season—it was the end of the year—were mostly inside towns, bandits had either become soldiers or been suppressed, and there was unlikely to be anyone about in such a remote place in winter except a few woodcutters and hermits.

The tour of the district was useful enough—at least in giving Pan's officers some notion of the problems faced by farmers in the aftermath of battles fought on their land and the administrative confusion following the change of regime. The farmers themselves, however, were disappointingly reluctant to talk frankly to a group of officials, in case they might incur extra taxes or other impositions or be punished for evading them.

Leaving the rest of their party to return to the city, Wang and Kong, both mounted on horses supplied by General Pan's administration, then rode towards the mountains, visible on the horizon, not more than fifteen or twenty miles off. The weather so far had been mild, even warm, considering it was so late in the year, but almost at once the sky darkened and they were caught in a thunderstorm. Wang's terrified horse reared up, threw him into a bush and bolted. Kong jumped off his horse and managed to control it. Wang emerged from the bush unhurt, though his clothes were torn as well as soaking wet, and together they made for the relative shelter of a wood.

The thunder and lightning passed over quickly, but the rain continued for nearly an hour and when it stopped left a thick mist, completely hiding the mountains. They spent some time looking for Wang's horse and eventually found and recaptured it, but the mist persisted and they followed the road without being able to see more than a hundred yards or so ahead, until they came to a fork. Since the road to the left seemed to be curving too much to the left, they chose the right and did the same when they came to another fork further on. The mist was lifting a little by now, but there was no sign of the mountains ahead or indeed of anything but rice-fields and occasional trees. The ground rose a little, with low hills on either side, then began to descend. At last, quite late in the day, a wind blew up, scattered the mist and revealed below them a small village of thatched huts, and beyond it, an expanse of choppy water.

"What is this?" said Wang irritably.

"It must be the lake," said Kong.

"What lake?"

"Lake Tai. There's no other that I've heard of around here."

"But Lake Tai is in the opposite direction," said Wang.

The same thought occurred to both of them simultaneously and they turned to look the way they had come. Visible now in the distance, dark blue against the dimming sky, were the Blue Bien Mountains.

Wang recalled this episode of three or four years earlier as he studied one of his grandfather's paintings in the Gull Wave Pavilion. Lord Meng's hand-scroll *Village by a Lake* was, compared to much of his work, unusually realistic and certainly depicted the village Wang and Kong had arrived at by accident—or, as Wang half believed, by some mysterious decree of fate forbidding him to re-enter his childhood demesne.

He and Kong had asked for a night's lodging at the first hut they came to and been welcomed with extraordinary generosity by a very old farmer. He lent them dry clothes, drew water from a nearby spring and lit a fire of bamboo twigs, over which he steamed root vegetables and rice. As they sat in the doorway of the hut with the fragrant smell of bamboo smoke drifting round them, the old man gave them cups of new wine, drawn straight off the lees. A bell was ringing somewhere in the distance and moonlight shone on the steps in front of them. Scratched and aching from his fall, slightly feverish from a chill caught in his wet clothes, Wang felt both contented and sad. The old man's pleasure in their company and his food and wine warmed Wang's heart and body, but his mind could not ignore the near desolation of the village or their kind host's poverty and hopelessness. He was over eighty, had lost his only son in a battle near Wuxing and, having just gathered the late rice harvest, expected most of it to be taken by Zhang's tax-gatherers.

"Eat more!" he urged them. "I would rather give it to my guests than those crows."

His case was that of millions all over the Empire, but what could anyone do to stop the fighting and restore good government? Ashamed and briefly forgetting himself, Wang resolved to join Zhang's administration on a full-time basis and devote himself to helping farmers. Next day, with a bad cold and a throbbing head, he knew better. Riding back to Wuxing, he silently admitted that he would do nothing of the kind, but bury himself as ever in books and paintings.

Now, looking at Lord Meng's landscape of the same village, admiring its simplicity, sincerity and complete lack of showiness, so that the place looked at once idyllic and quite ordinary, he felt even greater respect for his grandfather. He had made innumerable paintings, yet most of his energy must have gone into the task of governing and governing well, so that the Empire in his time, even if it did belong to the Mongols, provided peace and sufficiency for villages like this. And that was really what this painting showed: nothing out of the ordinary, just a few low huts set in the heart of a quiet landscape of water, hills and small clumps of trees—a village as it should be. How unjust it seemed that Lord Meng's service to his people—unlike his art—would either be forgotten altogether or remembered only as disloyalty to the Song Dynasty!

Wang could not immediately broach this subject with his cousin. Their relationship was still too distant and Zhao Lin, several years older than Wang and now the head of the family, still also carried the weight of his importance as a Provincial Inspector under the Mongols. He carried physical weight too, being a very large, not to say fat man, who moved slowly, as if surrounded by bevies of bowing underlings, and spoke with orotund deliberation, as if he hardly expected any reply beyond humble assent.

He was probably delighted to have Wang as a guest and surely did not mean to intimidate him, but people's outward manner is as much set by the way they have lived as their inward feelings are by their experience of childhood. Zhao Lin—first a magistrate, then a city Governor, then a Provincial Inspector—had commanded and judged others from a lonely eminence for several decades. Whatever his inner feelings were, he was not used to displaying them, or indeed perhaps even consulting them. Everything about him, including his interest in horses, was, as it were, in the public domain. Yet, on the other hand, he was now prematurely retired and the regime he had served was defunct—at least in this part of the Empire. The society he had dominated for so long had suddenly been swept away and the purpose for which he had lived, to give that society its correct shape and direction, was abolished. He painted horses now not as a diversion, but almost as a necessity, so as to retain some sense of his own existence.

He was too intelligent not to know this about himself and gradually, as Wang and he felt their way with each other, he began to allow his inner feelings to emerge. It was easy for the cousins to find common ground in the paintings by their grandfather that they both admired, even though Zhao naturally preferred the horses and Wang the landscapes. After a day or two when Wang sat alone in the Gull Wave Pavilion looking through Lord Meng's scrolls and album-leaves, while Zhao attended to—or made out that he was attending to—practical matters connected with his estate, the host asked with the greatest diffidence if his guest would allow him to share the sessions in the studio.

Then they sat together, the fat man beside the thin, their faces looking nevertheless oddly alike—two apples of different size and ripeness from the same crop on the same tree. There was likeness too in their feelings of family pride and in their nostalgia for the retreat in the Blue Bien Mountains, though they had hardly known each other as children, Zhao having been virtually grown-up when Wang was still quite a small boy.

"Do you know what became of Peony?" asked Wang.

The name meant nothing to Zhao, until Wang mentioned that her father had been a Mongol officer.

"She died," said Zhao, "quite young, still an unmarried girl."

"An illness?"

"She was bitten by a snake, I think," said Zhao. "Yes, she had unbound feet, of course, being half-Mongol, and I remember thinking that it showed the advantage of binding women's feet—that they couldn't run through the undergrowth in that unbridled way and get themselves bitten by snakes."

Wang was silent, seeing in his mind exactly what she looked like as she ran towards the stream and he ran after her. His eyes filled with tears—of happiness at the vivid memory as much as sorrow for her long-ago death.

"You were fond of her?" asked Zhao, and when Wang nodded, "I'm sorry to have said something so insensitive."

"How could you know?"

The exchange made them more relaxed with each other. Wang described how he and Peony had met the splash-painter and witnessed his method of working. Zhao's huge face heaved with distaste.

"Yang and Yin!" he said. "How greedily such crass people feed on worm-eaten gobbets of knowledge! Stirring ink about with his bare feet! An 'original!' What originality can there be without training and self-discipline?"

But in response to Wang's candour about his love for Peony, Zhao—long married to another more distant cousin, who was now almost as large as he was—spoke of his own first love as a young official in Dadu.

"I saw the girl going into a temple with her mother," said Zhao, "and she saw me. After that, we both went to the temple as often as possible and eventually I consulted my father about making an approach to her family. He refused."

"He had someone else in mind?"

"Not at that juncture. He simply said it was an unsuitable marriage. Of course, I tried to argue. The girl's father was an important official in the Secretariat—not a Mongol, nor from Central Asia, as so many of them were. It was unusual for anyone of our race to rise so high."

"Your father did and so did you," said Wang.

"Yes, that was unusual too. No doubt we owed it to the Duke of Wei."

Zhao nearly always referred to Lord Meng by his posthumous title, partly irritating Wang, partly stirring his pride.

"I couldn't understand what my father's objection to this girl was," Zhao went on. "And he didn't tell me. Instead, he began to make arrangements for me to marry my cousin. I said I would have nothing to do with her, and sent several secret letters to the girl I had seen at the temple. Fortunately I got none back. She was either very correctly brought up or well guarded by her mother. I saw her once or twice at the temple, but she avoided meeting my eyes, and then she disappeared. I never saw her again."

"Do you know what happened to her?"

"Her father was sent into exile—Kirin or Korea—somewhere very far away. And his family, I presume, went with him. He was lucky not to be executed."

"What was his crime?"

"The worst for a man in his position. He was corrupt. My father had heard that, but felt it was wrong to say so until the man had been exposed and punished. Meanwhile, he couldn't allow me to ruin my career by becoming involved. That was the sort of man my father was, preferring to seem a tyrant to his son than repeat dishonourable gossip, even though it turned out to be true. After that, I accepted my father's marriage arrangement without question."

Wang felt uncomfortable with this account, which began as a love story and ended as a eulogy to the father's wisdom and sense of honour. It made his own escapade with Peony seem almost disgraceful. Of course they were younger, but still he felt that he had taken a freedom much greater than he understood at the time and got away with it, perhaps altering his whole approach to life afterwards, whereas Zhao Lin's abortive attempt to break free had evidently reinforced the strict code of conduct he had been taught to observe.

It occurred to Wang that by specialising in paintings of horses, both Zhao Lin and his father were symbolising their faith in obedience and management. Lord Meng, too, had painted horses, perhaps in the same faith, but his experiments and innovations with every other sort of painting, and his incomparable calligraphy—the purest form of self-expression—showed how many facets his powerful character possessed.

"This man was himself a mountain!" he suddenly exclaimed, as his eyes returned to the silk scroll which the cousins had both been contemplating: Lord Meng's coloured painting of the West Mountain rising up from Lake Tai.

"You are right," said Zhao Lin, "and we are those two very small figures in the foreground looking across the water at the towering Duke of Wei."

Wang nodded gravely, but smiled inwardly at the thought of Zhao Lin as in any sense a very small figure. This humorous thought had the effect of making him bolder.

"What would he have done now, in our circumstances?" he asked. "What would he have advised us to do?"

"To be loyal to the Dynasty we served," said Zhao, looking Wang steadily in the eyes, as if to add that he knew Wang had not been.

"But he himself served the Song before the Yuan."

"He waited ten years before obeying Khan Khublai's summons," said Zhao. "By then the last Song Emperor was dead and the mandate had passed without question to Khublai. In any case, the Duke of Wei was still a young man at that time and we, now, are on the verge of old age. For better or worse, we must do as my father did and hold on to our loyalty when there is nothing else to hold on to."

"Does it make no difference that the Dynasty we served was foreign and that we were always treated as inferiors in our own land?"

"That might have been a reason for not serving it in the first place, when it was strong," said Zhao. "Certainly not a reason for turning against it when it is weakened. And whom could we now serve? Which of these upstart Princes of Wu? The one is an ex-monk, the other an ex-boatman, both unscrupulous bandits with all the unreliability of their type."

"Many good men, with distinguished reputations, have found it possible to join one or the other."

"They've found it expedient. Has it enhanced their reputations? On the contrary, we can now see in troubled times what was not always apparent in better times, the true value of those people's reputations."

"But do you think it possible that the Yuan Dynasty will survive?"

"Highly possible."

"And recover the whole Empire?"

"What is the alternative?"

"There are many, aren't there?" said Wang. "Another period of Warring States, as so often in the past. Or the Empire may be divided into two parts, north and south of the Yangzi, as it was when the Song Dynasty had to abandon the north to foreigners and make Quinsai their capital. Or one of the warring states may succeed in driving out the Mongols and re-uniting the whole Empire."

"One of those bandit-chiefs?" said Zhao contemptuously.

Not wishing to antagonise his host and the head of his family, whose experience of politics was so much greater than his own, Wang tried to approach the argument from another direction.

"I suppose it is just possible," he said. "After the chaos of the Five Dynasties—most of them foreign—it was our own great ancestor, General Zhao Kuang-yin, who re-united the Empire and was persuaded by his soldiers to found a new Dynasty and become the first Song Emperor."

"You are not comparing him to these bandits?"

The faces of both cousins flushed red, Zhao's with anger, Wang's with embarrassment.

"I meant only that the circumstances were similar," said Wang. "But I believe Zhu will defeat Zhang."

"That is quite likely," said his cousin. "But can you imagine him defeating the Mongols? Can you imagine such a man becoming Emperor? He has had no education at all, no practice in wielding power. He will be utterly dependent on advisers, who may be trustworthy or may not. Either way, he will not trust them, because their way of thinking will be as alien to him as a peasant's to us. A peasant is like a wild animal, always distrustful, always insecure, always defensive or aggressive, having nothing to support him but his own physical strength and unconscious instincts. In all our long history we have never had a peasant as Emperor and the reason is obvious. A person who has no notion of anything beyond himself can have no notion of how to rule others."

"What will you do if Zhu does defeat Zhang?"

"I shall go. I've already made my plans. My escape-route can only be to the south-west, since Zhu will be advancing from the north and north-west, while the sea-coast to the south-east is controlled by the pirate Fang. You had better consider doing the same."

Wang stared out of the door of the pavilion at the Blue Bien Mountains a few miles away.

"Yes, that's the way he'll come," said Zhao. "The mountain area is already patrolled by his soldiers. I've seen them along the other side of the river, and I'm told that your friend General Pan is bringing his army back to Wuxing. The decisive battle will be here—perhaps on this very spot—it's only a question of how soon."

He seemed remarkably calm at the prospect, whereas Wang, to whom the Gull Wave Pavilion had never been home, felt disconsolate.

"How can you bear to leave all this?" he asked, waving his arm to include the pavilion they sat in, the other buildings round it, the estate and the mountains beyond.

"I have spent my life in many different places," said Zhao, "always with the memory of this one and the thought of returning to it when circumstances permitted. Perhaps this time I shall not be able to return, but I may still hope to do so. Memory and hope together are fine strong steeds and will carry one through most things."

He smiled so broadly that his eyes were almost lost in the flesh rolling up from his cheeks, and asked:

"Did the Duke of Wei begin by showing you how to draw a horse?"

"Yes, he did."

"Me too. And later on he drew two horses to show me how the sense of energy should pass from one to the other. And later, three or four or even eight horses, always emphasising the way they must be linked together in the drawing."

He searched among the pile of Lord Meng's hand-scrolls of horses at his elbow and spread one out to illustrate what he meant.

"These, you see, bending their necks to drink at the edge of the river, those ahead of them beginning to cross the river, those behind hurrying to drink. 'When you draw them,' he said, 'always think that a few moments ago those in front were still drinking, and that in a few moments' time these will stop drinking, and those behind will have taken their place at the water's edge. And these are hope,' he said, pointing to the ones behind, 'and these are memory,' pointing to the ones already crossing the river, 'and these at the water's edge are the very words you are hearing from me now.' I daresay he said the same to you?"

"If he did," said Wang, "I don't remember it. But I was never very good at drawing horses."

"There was always meaning in everything he drew," said Zhao. "It didn't have to be understood by anyone else, he said, but it was necessary to the artist. 'Every painting is a journey,' he said, 'and every journey must have a purpose. What is the purpose of life? We don't know and it hardly matters, since we have no alternative but to live until we die. But when you paint, you must find a purpose, because the alternative is not to make a painting at all, and that is the easier, more natural course to take. Only a meaning—however simple and obvious—will pull your brush across the paper.'"

The last work they looked at was a large hanging scroll, *The Home of the Immortals.* Zhao had deliberately kept it till the end, because it was one of Lord Meng's last paintings, made not long before he died.

Wang did not remember having seen it before. A clump of tall trees at the bottom, in the exact centre, divided the foreground into two compartments, with a broad expanse of water and a bridge on the left, and, on the right, guests being received on a lawn, from which another bridge led across to a group of sturdy houses with tiled roofs.

On the steps in front of the nearest pavilion, four or five beauties played musical instruments. Above the buildings and the tops of the foreground trees, there rose a long spine of mountains, with lush valleys winding up on either side, firs, streams, a thatched pavilion on a high bluff, and at last the highest mountains, swimming in clouds, and two tower-like peaks silhouetted against the sky, almost touching the top of the scroll. The viewpoint was set very high and the whole vertical landscape was drawn in deep recession, so that the mountains did not loom over the foreground, but led the eye away and up, giving an immediate sense of majestic calm, expansiveness and delight.

"I like to think," said Zhao, "that that horse, saddled but riderless, being pulled reluctantly across the bridge by an attendant, is the Duke of Wei's, and reflects his rider's hope of entering paradise and his memory of the world he loved too much to want to leave, even when he was old. And if I must go on my travels again now, well, I shall do so in the same spirit."

Wang forbore to point out that in Zhao Lin's case he would not be entering paradise, but leaving the part of the world that for him and his family most resembled it.

This unspoken thought, like a small thorn which one fails to extract, worked its way deeper into his mind and gradually inflamed it. Walking together in the garden a few days later, the cousins paused beside an ornamental limestone rock which had been brought from Lake Tai. Bluish-black, layered and eroded, it looked more like a stack of loose stones than a single growth of rock. Thinning in the middle and then becoming thicker and heavier at the top, threatening to topple over, it resembled from one side a partly bent figure with a great lion's head. Two or three tall stalks of bamboo grew beside it.

Their grandmother had made several beautiful paintings of this rock and bamboo, and their grandfather, whose pupil she had been, had inscribed one of them in his distinctive calligraphy:

*How can they grow from the same ink,*
*This slim, young, spiky-leaved, soaring bamboo,*
*This crusted, rough, ancient, earth-bound rock?*
*Look at the twists and turns of the brush,*
*Pressing, stroking, lingering, flying!*
*This rough hand salutes that slim hand's skill.*

❁

Beyond the garden and a stretch of shimmering river, above low wooded hills, blurred by a heat-haze—it was early summer—rose the Blue Bien Mountains. Wang wanted to jump on a horse and ride there immediately, as he thought that perhaps Lord Meng had wanted to, but instead, too old and ill, had sat down to paint *The Home of the Immortals*, with its eloquent riderless horse at the entrance. Putting his hand on the strange rock, his fingers exploring its pocked texture, his mind seething with all the emotions aroused by this place; by its guardian spirits—the rock and the bamboo symbolising his grandfather and grandmother—who perhaps could guard it no longer against the violence of the disintegrating Empire; by his grandfather's paintings; and by his new-found sympathy with his cousin; Wang said as quietly and casually as he could, in the way one might offer a cup of tea:

"Would you allow me to make you a painting?"

The meaning Wang had in mind for this painting, as he set to work on it in the Gull Wave Pavilion, was to conflate the Blue Bien Mountains with the idea of the Home of the Immortals. He was also thinking of the story of the Peach Blossom River, the version in which ordinary living people, not immortals, had found a safe country beyond the reach of war, famine and bad government.

But the painting proved to have a momentum of its own. It began at the bottom, quite conventionally, with the river dividing the viewer from the landscape. The viewpoint was set quite high, as in Lord Meng's *The Home of the Immortals*, with no feature in the immediate foreground to suggest whether one was standing on an adjoining hill or floating in mid-air. At the far side of the water were a tumble of small rocks and a tall clump of trees, sparsely leaved and placed a little left of centre, so as to open up the right, from which the main river flowed, with a stream off the mountain cascading into it.

Beyond that, still on the right of the painting, one could see part of a broad path winding through a straggly wood, and on this path stood a figure in profile—a stout figure wearing a voluminous robe tied at the waist and a conical travelling cap, with a long walker's stick in his nearest hand. Was this, then, the viewer's proxy? He was turned inwards so as to lead the eye into the painting, but although his stick pointed upwards he himself had no view at all, except of a great ridge of turfed rock rising on a steep diagonal above him. In any case, he was staring at the ground, tired or perhaps meditating. Nor was it clear which way he had come. The path he was standing on led gently upwards, before disappearing off the paper to the right, but he might already have come down it. Dwarfed by the tree he stood under, which was eight times his own height, he was a mere sixtieth part of the height of the whole painting, too small for his face to have recognisable features, but large enough for his body and pose to convey a sense of substance and individuality.

Could this be Zhao Lin, leaving or returning to his grandfather's mountain retreat? If anyone had asked Wang, he would probably have agreed that it could be, but he would also have agreed that it slightly resembled the Maitreya Buddha, the saviour of the world expected by the Red Scarf rebels, or that it might be the spirit of Lord Meng, or of the legendary Bien who had found the precious jade stone there and given his name to the mountains, or an anonymous traveller, or even the artist himself. The truth was that the figure stood for anyone who loved and felt he belonged to that place.

Yet paradoxically he couldn't enter it. From the side the mountain was painted, no one could. Far up on the left side of the painting was a cluster of thatched pavilions, with two tiny figures just visible inside the foremost, and there was another house much lower down. Both dwellings might be approached no doubt from the left, but that was exactly where the paper ended—they were pressed up against its edge. Within the painting itself, there was no approach to them whatever. Rising first to the right, then to the left, the mountain—drawn from Wang's memory of the Blue Bien Mountains' highest peak, known as the Emerald Crag—thrust its sharp ridges and sheer concavities directly in the viewer's face.

Even the stream which flowed out into the river in the foreground was only rarely visible: a long fall down dangerous rocks high above the cluster of pavilions, a small spout just below them and below that, a brief section in the shape of a bent arm and sewn with rocks. There was no sign of a path, nor any route for a path to climb out of bottom right, where the traveller stood, to top left where the other figures sat in their pavilion. This landscape was the very opposite to Lord Meng's genial *The Home of the Immortals*. No bridge led over the river in the foreground, no journey could be made into or up or across this mountain, except by a bird or a disembodied spirit.

The viewer's attention, therefore, focussed on the mountain itself, its towering height—the scroll was three times higher than its width—and the intricacies of its growth, its forms becoming wilder and more convoluted at the top. Indeed, above the pavilions on the left, the mountain seemed to be still growing, swelling and writhing into grotesque humps and billows, as if the rock were still molten from a volcanic upheaval. Yet this impression was contradicted by the trees which had had time to settle on its shoulder, and by the strands of vegetation furring the edges of the mountain's head, a huge arrow-head lump darkly silhouetted against a brief opening of sky. There were contradictions in the lighting too. The mountain was deeply shadowed in crevices, or along the line of the principal ridges or on facets that directly faced the viewer, but illuminated on both sides, even from within half-concealed hollows, as though in a dream or a simultaneous memory of morning and evening.

Wang was quite as astonished by this painting in its finished state as his cousin was. He had begun as usual with the small, solidly modelled rocks at the bottom, then put in the tall foreground trees, the path and the figure of the traveller on the right and the little house on the left. But although he had originally intended to make a narrow path from the figure to the house, round the back of the trees, he somehow omitted to clarify it, and from that point on became obsessed with the mountain's forms, losing himself in their junctions and complications, dabbing, dotting, tweaking, curling with his brush, fiercely excited by every fresh development upward.

He knew from the start where he wanted to place the pavilions representing Lord Meng's retreat—some two-thirds of the way up on the left—but before reaching it, he came off the mountain-side in order to paint a reminiscence of the wood where he had walked with Peony, and the angle of stream beside it. The seemingly autonomous growth of the mountain had not left much room for the pavilions, but, almost without thinking, he added a huge, deeply shadowed bluff in front and above, so as to squeeze them still more tightly against the side of the paper, and then hemmed them in from the back with a sheer wall of rock. He had turned the pavilions, he realised, not into the open and welcoming home of immortals, still less the remembered paradise of his childhood, but into a retreat beyond the Peach Blossom River, a place you would need to pass through a tunnel to reach, a shelter from the threatening world around it.

Returning now to the mountain, he painted its mighty shoulder, the streak of waterfall and finally the monstrous forms of its head, toppling leftwards, as if it might crash down on the flimsy buildings directly below. He could not be sure, when he had finished and given it to his cousin, what purpose had pulled his brush over the paper. Even though his hand had held the brush, he hardly felt he had controlled its course.

The details, yes: he had summoned all his skill to make ink suggest turf, stone, tree-boles, foliage, depth, height, underlying structure. But surely he had never consciously conceived the larger effects: the uncanny lighting, the mountain's implacable demeanour, the ferocity of its upper crags? Did it symbolise the frightening times they were living in, the violence of men reflected in the nature they were part of? Or the invincible core of this land, rearing up at last to shake off the Mongol interlopers? Was it a shelter or a threat, an image of peaceful withdrawal or of imminent chaos?

Zhao Lin, however, saw it as a memory of their fortunate childhood and a tribute to the strength of their family. He was overwhelmed by the variety and virtuosity of its technique.

"If the Duke of Wei did not persist in teaching you to draw horses," he said, "it was no doubt because he knew you were born to paint mountains. He was very modest and unselfish, you know. He never wanted to be the greatest artist in our family, but to lift all of us up on his shoulders and make our reach longer than his own. I only wish he were here to see this for himself. He would be so proud."

When Wang had written his title—*Living in Retreat in the Blue Bien Mountains*—on the small patch of sky at the top, Zhao brought out four seals and pressed one on each corner of the scroll. The two at the top were his own and the family seal used by Lord Meng; the two at the bottom were his own studio seal and the seal of Lord Meng's posthumous ennoblement as Duke of Wei. There was no greater compliment he could have paid Wang, who felt as if he had been given his ancestor's lost ring for a second time, but on this occasion for what he had accomplished instead of only what he promised.

# 12. WU CONQUERS WU

Those who have been privileged from birth never really believe that anything completely dreadful can happen to them. Protected through childhood by loving, careful parents, later by the advantages of a good education and well-established family, accustomed to being warm, well-fed and more often well than ill, rational about set-backs, wary of potential hazards, they think of their lives as quintessentially normal. Their inward sense of individuality spreads gradually outwards to form a substantial cloak of personal dignity, not ostentatious, not impervious to fear, grief or compassion, but comfortable, reassuring and usually weatherproof. It is as rare for such people to be uprooted and swept away by events beyond their control as for a mature tree to be flattened by a typhoon or tumbled down a waterfall by a flash flood.

When Wang left the Gull Wave Pavilion that summer, he could hardly have believed that he would never see his cousin again, nor the painting of the Blue Bien Mountains he had given him, nor his grandfather's paintings, nor even the pavilion itself, except in a ruined and abandoned state. He could not have believed either, when he visited General Pan's estate and found young Chen there painting his own version of *The Home of the Immortals* for his host, that within only five years, Chen who was so much younger than himself, would suffer a violent death. Above all, it was inconceivable that, returning at the end of the year to his home in Pingjiang, Wang would be entering a trap from which, after ten months of harrowing experiences, he would barely escape with his own life.

Young Chen was as cheerful and energetic as always, though increasingly uncertain of his own future and critical of the unpredictable and unsteady leader he had chosen to serve. Zhang, he said, lived for the day, making and breaking alliances, ordering men to be executed, or women into his harem or armies to march, or forgetting about military and political affairs altogether and indulging in orgies of sex and drink, just as if he were still a boatman who had become a prince in a dream and did not care to think about waking up.

Now, having previously ordered Pan's army to seize Quinsai from the Mongols, instead of keeping the Mongols on his side and attacking Zhu when there was still a chance of success, he had decided—three years too late—to push northwards again against Zhu. General Pan, however, according to Chen, was more realistic than his master. He was making some show of mounting an attack, but was chiefly concerned to improve the defences of Wuxing. Zhu's own attack was certainly imminent and the best hope was that, if it could be resisted long enough, Zhang might wake up from his dream and recover the energy and ferocity with which he had driven the Mongols out of their richest province.

Earlier in the year, young Chen and General Pan had both called on Wang's cousin at the Gull Wave Pavilion. Kindly received by Zhao Lin, they had been shown some of the family's paintings, including Lord Meng's *The Home of the Immortals*. This was why, at Pan's urgent request, Chen was now painting his own version of the theme and, like Lord Meng, using colours in the old-fashioned Song Dynasty style. The painting, however, had none of the gravity or grandeur of Lord Meng's late work. The mineral blues and greens were bright and spring-like, the softly-contoured mountains billowed upwards, almost as if they were clouds, the trees seemed to sway in a gentle breeze, the figures to float rather than tread the ground. The picture was a perfect expression of Chen's optimistic character and Wang smiled as he thought of how differently Chen and he—in his painting of the Blue Bien Mountains, which Chen, of course, had not seen—had responded to the same model.

"Why are you smiling?" asked Chen.

"You are so unlike me."

"I am quite incompetent, if you make that comparison," said Chen, looking very downcast.

"That isn't at all what I meant," said Wang. "It's because you are so unlike me that I like you so much—you and your work. This is a beautiful painting. I smiled also because that's the immediate effect it produces. It expresses happiness so lightly, so easily."

"Facile."

"I only wish I had such facility. I only wish you were painting it as a present for me."

Convinced at last that Wang was not pretending to like what he thought inadequate, Chen said:

"I'll make you another one as soon as I have time. But tomorrow I have to ride to Quinsai."

"How on earth do you have any time or energy to paint at all?"

"The more one has to do, the more one *can* do," said Chen.

"Since you're making the painting for him, General Pan should send some other officer to Quinsai."

"He offered to, but I said I would finish today and, you see, I more or less have. Pan is always anxious to spare me military duties and actually prefers to see me painting or composing songs for the lute, but I prefer a bit of action."

"Pan seems far too civilised for a general."

"But, you see, he's not much of a general."

"Not? He captured Quinsai."

"I could have captured it. You could. The Mongols made no attempt to defend Quinsai."

"That's a little disturbing. Will Pan be capable of defending Wuxing?"

"He's not stupid. He may have some stratagem in mind."

Wang went outside and sat under the willow-tree looking out over the lake, while Chen put finishing touches to the painting, before joining him. The servants brought wine. General Pan himself arrived soon after sunset and a meal was served on the terrace. Afterwards, his wife appeared from her own part of the house and Chen sang to his lute. Later still, when Pan's wife had gone to bed, the three men became very drunk and General Pan inadvertently revealed that, although Chen was leaving early in the morning, he was not going to Quinsai.

"Where, then?" asked Wang.

"I'm taking a message to the Prince of Wu," said Chen.

"We can ride together," said Wang. "I am not going all the way to Pingjiang immediately, but in that direction."

Chen glanced at General Pan, who laughed and put his arm round Wang's shoulders.

"Dear friend," said Pan, "you are a person of the greatest intelligence and discretion and know very well that there are more ways than one to approach the Prince of Wu."

Wang blamed himself afterwards for not paying more attention to this drunken revelation. At the time he was a little shocked by it and almost tried to pretend that he had never heard it or had misunderstood it, rather than admit that Pan and Chen might be contemplating treachery towards the Prince of Wu in Pingjiang. But could one really be treacherous towards a man who was essentially treacherous himself, who observed no normal standards of honourable behaviour, who remained at heart a lawless opportunist?

In any case, what right had Wang to blame Pan and Chen for making overtures to the other Prince of Wu, when he had done so himself long before, yet continued to live freely and comfortably in Zhang's territory? Did the old concept of loyalty, in fact, have any meaning any longer in an Empire divided between Zhu and Zhang and the Mongols, not to speak of the innumerable lesser warlords, such as the pirate Fang, who controlled smaller territories to the south and west? Wang's cousin's unswerving loyalty to the Mongols was understandable, considering he had served them in high positions most of his life, but loyalty was not a fixed, intrinsic thing like a blood relationship—it went with belief like a religion, or with reciprocal feelings like a love affair. If any loyalty was owed to the foreign rulers, it was the kind that Lord Meng gave, in return for stability and good government. As for the two self-made Princes of Wu, they had yet to prove their mandate as rulers. The value of loyalty now had to be appraised and negotiated afresh in what had become, since Wang's youth, a new world, an Empire divided.

So, instead of half dismissing what he had heard and what it implied, that General Pan saw little prospect of repelling Zhu's attack, Wang should have given serious thought to what he ought now to do himself. If he did not want to throw in his lot immediately with Zhu, he should at least have considered persuading his father, frail as he was, to leave Pingjiang. Pingjiang, after all, was Zhang's last redoubt. There the final reckoning must be made between these two predatory warlords, who had gobbled up most of the others. Almost anywhere else would have been safer.

But, suppressing his anxieties, making no mention to anyone of what Pan had revealed, Wang went on living his normal life in the expectation of it continuing to be normal. He spent the remainder of the summer and most of the autumn staying with friends and acquaintances, making landscapes, bamboo-and-rock paintings and even the occasional portrait in return for their hospitality and, towards the end of the year, returned to his wife and father in Pingjiang.

He had hardly done so when Zhu's armies struck. They were led by Zhu's two most formidable generals. Success in everything military or social depends as much on the quality of those you rely on and who rely on you as on your own talents. When the twenty-three-year-old Zhu left his monastery to join the Red Scarf bandits, he came under the command of a man called Kuo, earned his trust and was soon part of his family, marrying Kuo's adopted daughter and later taking as his mistress the daughter of Kuo's younger wife. Zhu proved a brave and able lieutenant and, when Kuo was taken captive in one of the many quarrels between rival factions within the Red Scarves, succeeded in freeing him. Kuo's own sons, however, were less pleased than their father with their new semi-brother and Zhu quickly decided that the only way to survive, let alone succeed, in these perpetually precarious circumstances was to create his own power-base.

He went to his dead parents' village, recruited all his childhood friends and their friends and relations and returned to serve Kuo at the head of a personal following of seven hundred men. After Kuo's death and as Zhu's reputation as a military commander grew, those seven hundred men and the twenty-four closest companions who led them expanded by leaps and bounds into an army, operating more and more independently of the Red Scarves, though nominally recognising the leadership of their northern branch. This was how a gang of illiterate peasants who had once played together in a village turned into the nucleus of a kingdom. Of course they had no formal education and, except for Zhu himself, could hardly read even now, but they had certainly been deeply affected by Zhu's own sense of destiny and by the heroic stories told him by his military, fortune-telling grandfather. If the true story of Zhu's life sounds more like a legend, that is no doubt because he and those around him were predisposed to make it one. Zhu and his chief generals, Xu Ta and Chang Yu-chen, were reminiscent of the three sworn "brothers," whose exploits are at the heart of the famous stories of the Three Kingdoms, except that those legendary heroes failed to unite the Empire, whereas these three men of our own time actually did.

These were the men who, fresh from capturing all the cities to the west held by the Southern Red Scarves and then subduing all Zhang's outlying territory along the Yangzi River, now suddenly descended on his heartland. They disembarked from a fleet of ships on to the southern shore of Lake Tai, with two hundred thousand soldiers. They were confronted, a few miles from Wuxing, by an army hastily assembled by two of Zhang's best generals, two of those he called "the claws and teeth of Wu."

Unfortunately for him, these claws and teeth had decayed in the years of prosperity and idleness. Chang, the more reckless of Zhu's two generals, a man skilled with his bow and addicted to daring stratagems, rode out and challenged the enemy generals to single combat. One of Zhang's "claws and teeth" rashly responded, galloping forward with his lance levelled. Chang appeared to lose courage, turned his horse and fled back towards his own lines, but then, suddenly turning again as he put an arrow to his bow, shot his pursuer's horse in the flank and brought horse and rider crashing to the ground. The whole invading army surged forward and the already nervous defenders broke and ran.

The invaders swiftly invested Wuxing, which General Pan—no doubt by treacherous pre-arrangement with Zhu—soon gave up to them. Young Chen, Pan's deputy in Quinsai, did not even wait to be invested, but, on Pan's instructions, met the invaders with the keys to the city as they appeared in front of it. In little more than a month, the whole of Zhang's kingdom except his capital, Pingjiang, was in the hands of the rival Prince of Wu.

During this time Wang and his household were preoccupied with the health of his father. While Wang was away in the summer and early autumn, his father had seemed to grow stronger. He had even attended a literary gathering in the city, when the guests had been invited to compose poems to celebrate the host's collection of rare and precious artefacts. Wang's father had astonished everyone by composing eight poems, not on the subject of a magnificent Tang vase or a three-thousand-year-old bronze cauldron of the Shang Dynasty, nor a pottery figure of the Han nor a translucent white porcelain bowl of the Song, though all these things and more were displayed for the company's delight. Wang's father chose a dark red lacquered box, not because it was very old or striking to look at, but because, as his poems explained, it was beautiful three times over.

Its physical beauty consisted in its deep pure colour and perfect proportions, its historical beauty in that it survived from a time not so long before he was born—the box was probably no more than two hundred years old—which was now considered a golden age, and its imaginative beauty in the purpose it had served. It was a box for cosmetics and made him think of all the beautiful faces it had ministered to and the happiness its tinctures and powders had given to its owners and their husbands or lovers. This plain box, he declared, was the most modest and most precious thing in the whole collection and in a long life he had never seen anything of more symbolic significance. For here was something solid and practical designed to contain the mysterious core of the human character: its desire and capacity to enhance itself, to improve on nature.

All those present agreed that these *Eight Songs on a Cosmetics Case* were almost perfect of their kind: humorous without being satirical, sentient without being sentimental, elegantly erotic, yet as plain in style as the box itself. One fellow-guest even offered to write *Eight Songs on Eight Songs on a Cosmetics Case*, praising their qualities in the same terms as they praised the box, but he quickly added that the idea seemed sufficient without the labour.

The effect of all this on Wang's father, however, was too exciting. He took to his bed the next day and was still there when Wang returned to Pingjiang. With the news that Zhu's army was advancing on the city, his father urged Wang and his wife to escape and leave him behind. Wang refused even to consider doing so.

"It is not Zhu's policy to harm civilians," he said. "And I don't think Zhang can resist these people for more than a week or two."

How wrong he proved! Zhang, who had been so careless about so many aspects of the defence of his territory, had paid close attention to making his capital impregnable. A city full of canals, it was surrounded by a broad moat. The walls had been strengthened and the garrison increased, large supplies of grain and animal-fodder were stored in warehouses and one of the public parks filled with pens of live food, mainly pigs and dogs, geese and chickens. Another park was set aside for growing vegetables.

Zhang, after all, had experienced and survived a long and painful siege several years earlier, when he was fighting the Mongols, and knew exactly where a besieged city's weaknesses lay. But even if Wang had been aware that this siege would last the best part of a year, he could not have allowed himself to leave his father behind. Whatever loyalties might have to be discarded in a time of upheaval, loyalty to one's parents must always come before one's own life, which was their gift in the first place.

Wang's father was growing weaker every day. Suffering stomach pains, he hardly cared to eat any more, though his pains were partly relieved by the remedies prescribed by Kong from the knowledge acquired in his years as a doctor's servant. Wang, his wife and Kong took turns to sit with the invalid. Both his sight and hearing were now very poor, but by speaking slowly and clearly Wang was able to read him a book which had only just been published in Pingjiang. Edited by Wang's cousin Tao, it contained, among other writings, a compilation of Old Huang's thoughts on painting. So, while the besieging army dug trenches and began building huge earthworks all round the city, Wang distracted his father with what Tao had entitled *Secrets of Landscape Painting*. Tao himself, having left many copies of his book inside the now isolated city, had himself wisely withdrawn to a more peaceful region. Huang's advice was practical and sensible but, as Wang's father observed, not all that secret to anyone who had studied Huang's own paintings or the masters he followed.

"But you could not make a good painting if you ignored his advice," said Wang.

"Nor could you make a very good one if you needed it," said his father. "And I wonder why Huang troubled to write it down, since he obviously didn't need it himself."

Wang, who had always revered Huang, especially since seeing his painting *The Mountains of Pure Happiness*, was struck by his father's lack of respect for such a great artist, but reflected that Huang had been born only some fifteen years before Wang's father. It is often hard to admire those who are half a generation older or younger than oneself.

"Of course, his advice is intended for comparative beginners," said Wang. "Huang was by nature a teacher."

"Teaching is necessary for children," said his father, "but for older people it encourages timidity and clumsy imitation. Those who truly want to acquire some skill will always learn for themselves."

Somewhere to the south they heard a series of explosions, mingled with bursts of crackling in a higher tone. Wang went quickly to the window and peered at the sky.

"There's no sign of a storm," he said. "This can only be cannon-fire and rockets."

"Consider the founders of dynasties!" said his father, seeming not to have heard the noise at all. "How often were they taught to be rulers? Their successors usually were and hardly ever matched up to their fathers and grandfathers. Successful generals and ministers are the same—the best are those who come from nowhere. All the greatest men make themselves what they wish to be and learn what they need to as they go along. All the same," he added, "I am not against teachers. It's better that most people should be taught to go on quietly doing what was done before. We don't want too many great men. They contribute to history, but they make life uncomfortable for everyone else in their own times."

"The attack has begun," said Wang.

His tone was neutral, but remembering the attack on a town he had witnessed from the other side of the walls and its terrible outcome, he was full of apprehension. That town had been a village compared to this great city and the attacking forces perhaps three hundred times smaller than these. He cursed himself now for not doing as his cousin Zhao Lin had done two or three months earlier and taking his whole household away to a less disputed part of the Empire.

His care for his father, however, at least excused him from involvement in the military activities of Gao Chi and the Ten Friends of the North Wall. Now they had a real wall to defend, since all the able-bodied men in the city had been conscripted and formed into militia regiments helping the regular soldiers of the garrison to defend particular sections of the city. The besieging army, too, was organised into nine divisions—corresponding to the nine gates of the city. Thus a kind of competition developed all round the city, inside and out, to be the first to break in or not the first to permit a breach to be made. Gao was in his element, helping to guard the city's north-eastern corner and since the regular commander there was a former salt-worker of great strength but little intelligence or energy, virtually its general. On several occasions he took part in the sallies made by Zhang or his brother, which attempted to loosen the grip of the besiegers. These were never successful, but in the early stages of the siege gave some sense of hope and initiative to the defenders. They were always risky, however, for the temporary bridges which had to be laid over the moat to allow the defenders to make their sallies might be captured in a counter-attack and the defenders' retreat cut off. And this soon happened to Zhang's brother, commanding the southern side of Pingjiang. He was killed with most of his bodyguard. Ni Zan, still in hiding somewhere near the sea, was not in the city to celebrate the death of his persecuting would-be patron. No one, however, except perhaps Zhang himself, much mourned the loss of a man who had used his power to intimidate people and make himself rich and was not even a good general. Kong, who had been conscripted into the militia in that part of the city, said that the younger Zhang's death was probably more of a gain to the defenders than the attackers, since the spirits of the garrison rose with his removal.

The elder Zhang, on the other hand, remained popular. He was admired for his courage and, to begin with, for his foresight in fortifying and provisioning the city so well. He was cheerful, often appeared in public, and never seemed to have any doubt that he could save the city, retrieve his kingdom, and eventually get the better of the rival Prince of Wu. Was this mere stupidity? Probably not, considering his personal history. A boatman on the Yangzi, who had improved his earnings, like many of his kind, by smuggling salt—a lucrative business less for the smugglers themselves than for the powerful men who controlled it—Zhang had one day lost his temper and murdered a man who tried to cheat him. He also set fire to the man's house and burned down a whole walled village. Fleeing from justice with his three younger brothers and a group of friends, he had survived precariously as an outlaw and persuaded many of the oppressed people of the area—boatmen, smugglers or salt-workers—to join him.

The combination of these followers, who were certainly the most hardened and desperate men in the whole Empire, with his own ruthless courage and his youngest brother's acumen as a strategist—this was the brother who starved himself to death after being captured by Zhu—overwhelmed the Mongol authorities in the region and nearly defeated Zhu's forces too. Later, besieged by the Mongol Chancellor Toghto, he escaped by the miracle of Toghto's sudden recall. After that he could dictate terms to the Mongols, take territory from Zhu and even come near to capturing Zhu's nominal overlord, the Young Prince of Radiance.

Was Zhang to believe now that all his luck had run out or that, if he reasserted his bold personality and gifts as a leader, he could not still terrorise and trample down all his enemies? He had lived the very reverse of the privileged life granted to Wang, but it had been a charmed life all the same, and he had learnt to believe in the charm and take it for granted. So he fought for his last redoubt like a lion defending its den, with no thought of surrender, no idea of any alternative to killing or being killed.

Wang's father died quietly in the early spring and, since his body could not be taken to the family tomb near Wuxing, it had to be buried in a temporary grave inside the city. His funeral was attended by nearly the whole intellectual community of Pingjiang and this evidence of the respect in which his father was held gave some comfort to Wang. Both he and his wife were deeply grieved by the loss. It had been expected, of course, and he was an old man, but one does not miss someone any the less just because he has lived a long time. Since bringing him to Pingjiang, they had come to know the quiet, humorous intelligence hidden behind his authoritarian, efficient estate-owner's manner, and Wang's wife especially had been rewarded for her constant care of him by great warmth and tenderness on his part. Wang had to console her almost more than she him. But the greatest consolation came as the siege wore on through the rest of the spring and then the summer. They could not have wished him to survive into these conditions.

Constant fires raged wherever the enemy's rockets had landed, cannon-fire shook the walls and boomed in everyone's heads, even when the cannons were silent. Food was becoming scarcer and more expensive. Disease was spreading. There were now so many corpses to bury that most went into communal pits or were cremated. The Buddhist monks who were accustomed to perform this task in normal times for those who could not afford burial, using special ovens in the grounds of their monastery and then scattering the ashes, were so busy that they had to call in lay helpers and work continuously night and day.

The enemy had completed their earthworks all round the city, so that whatever sallies Zhang and his generals could make became just as much assaults on fortifications as the besiegers' attacks on the city walls. But, of course, the soldiers behind the earthworks had access to all the space and produce of the region, whereas the defenders of the city were more and more like rats in a hole with its ends stopped up. Nor were the besiegers content to bombard the city with cannonballs and rockets. They constructed huge catapults, which threw rotting vegetables, animal carcasses, and the putrefying limbs, trunks and heads of the dead—every kind of filth and rubbish they could find—over the walls.

But nothing seemed to discourage Zhang, and his fierce spirit of resistance was shared by Gao Chi and many of the city's leading scholars. What were they fighting for? Not so much Zhang himself as the continuity he represented, however imperfect and tenuous, with the Empire they had served. It was as if, now that the Mongols no longer controlled this region, they had ceased to be foreigners and become assimilated into the whole history of the Empire, so that Zhang in inheriting authority from them had emerged as the guardian of the past and therefore of the Empire's identity, which these people felt so strongly was their own identity.

But why Zhang rather than Zhu? This was the oddity of the situation. Those educated people who had joined Zhu felt exactly the same about him. Zhu's legitimacy was somewhat different from Zhang's and in the long run stronger, for he had begun not as an outlaw fighting to save his own skin, but as a follower of the Red Scarves, whose appeal was partly religious—the belief in the imminent return of the Maitreya Buddha—and partly political—the ousting of the Mongols because they were foreign invaders. Behind all the Red Scarves' struggles to seize territory was the nationalist slogan Wang had heard from the peddler so many years ago: "Give us back our rivers and mountains!"

There was no such larger purpose behind Zhang's rule and it was just as likely, if he succeeded in defeating Zhu, that he would come to terms again with the Mongols and be content to share the Empire's mountains and rivers with them. It was already clear that Zhu would not. Unlike Zhang, he had never paused for a moment in his campaign of aggrandisement. Furthermore, he had gone out of his way and taken very serious risks—against the warnings of his chief adviser on strategy—to save the Young Prince of Radiance from being captured either by the Mongols or by Zhang. Would he have done so if he did not intend to end the foreigners' rule and restore the Song Dynasty in the person of the Young Prince?

As the new year began, soon after his army had begun the siege of Pingjiang, Zhu sent a senior military aide to bring the Young Prince across the Yangzi River, from his headquarters on the north bank to Zhu's own capital, Nanjing, on the south bank. But as the boat crossed the river, it overturned and the Young Prince was drowned. Was this a setback to Zhu's plans for restoring the Song or was it exactly the excuse he needed to change his plans? Was it really an accident? If it was not, did it happen by Zhu's direct order or by some hint he dropped, or entirely without his knowledge, on the orders of one of his advisers? The answers to these questions were never known for certain, but in the light of later events it was evident that Zhu could not have worked things better. He had retained the thread of legitimacy by being a conspicuously loyal supporter of the Young Prince, but was not burdened any longer with the Young Prince himself.

In spite of the siege and its privations—or rather because of them—people in Pingjiang made particular efforts to continue their civilised urban life. The theatres and other entertainments were crowded, parties were still held in private houses and gardens—though the food and wine were not as varied and plentiful as before—books were published, poems and songs composed, pictures painted.

To make up in part for his lack of military contribution, Wang made a painting to hang in the barrack housing the Ten Friends' militia regiment. He began work on his *Elegant Gathering Among Forests and Streams*, in a lighthearted, encouraging spirit, as if to say: "Forget what you see in the streets, this is what we are in our minds and memories!" But it soon turned into something more serious. People who only knew Wang by his work always assumed that he must be a grave, brooding, unsociable person and were surprised to find, if they met him, that he enjoyed company, tended to talk volubly and was often joking and laughing. He himself would have liked, as he said to young Chen, to be able to make light, even humorous paintings—at least some of the time. But he never could, or, if he did, disliked them. At any rate this *Elegant Gathering* became a kind of tribute to his father, who had attended so many such occasions during his long life in this region famous for its poets and artists as for its scenery.

The painting was also a companion piece or counter-weight to *Living in Retreat in the Blue Bien Mountains.* In that painting, it was withdrawal that was emphasised, human figures were dwarfed and isolated, while the mountain appeared as a barricade or even an image of violent disruption. Here, a whole group of people enjoying civilised conversation occupied the left foreground, with more figures in the pavilions behind. Immediately in the centre, a generously spreading fan of tall pines grew out of a tumble of large, darkly contoured rocks and, balancing the open space of the gathering on the left, a broad passage of water opened out on the right. Behind rose the mountain, towering up in the manner of the masters of the Northern Song, breaking into ridges and a double peak at the top, suggesting grandeur and strength rather than hostility and exclusion.

No one in Pingjiang, of course, had seen *Living in Retreat in the Blue Bien Mountains*, so they could make no comparison, but they marvelled at the range of Wang's tones, the textures of rock and bark and vegetation, the mastery of brush and ink and, most of all, the majestic upward surge of the mountain. The work's reputation even reached Zhang, who gave orders that he wished to view it for himself. So, on a rainy morning, with cannons pounding the walls to the west, through the usual crowds of anxious people milling about the streets in search of some stall selling food more cheaply than others, Wang was carried in a chair, escorted by an aide and two soldiers, to Zhang's palace.

From outside it still resembled a temple. Zhang had not altered the high, wide, pillared entrance, the spacious courtyard or the pagoda to one side. Indoors, the main hall had been transformed from a place of worship into a throne-room and audience-chamber, gaudily painted in red and gold, where Zhang also held his parties and banquets. Wang was conducted through this hall, full of soldiers and officers waiting for orders or bringing messages, or perhaps simply keeping out of the rain, to a smaller room at the side.

Here, holding the box containing his painting and seated on a bench, which was the only furniture apart from a few large and showy antiques—porcelain vases and bronze pots—he was left to wait. Servants, secretaries and officers passed through from time to time, taking no notice of Wang, and after an hour or two he began to think he had been forgotten altogether. At last the aide who had fetched him from his house returned and led him through another antechamber, where several secretaries were writing, to Zhang's own office, a large, well-proportioned room with open doors on to a veranda and steps leading down to a private walled garden. It had probably been the abbot's office and was still furnished austerely, with little more than a low seat and table for writing at and a bed with a long pillow, on which Zhang, wearing a loose white robe, was reclining.

In his middle forties, with a huge round head, flushed face and thick black military beard, Zhang was even larger than Wang's cousin Zhao Lin and, thinking of Jasmine, Wang wondered, not for the first time, how slim and delicate women could support the weight of such men during their love-making. In a corner stood what Wang took at first glance for an equally enormous general in full armour and helmet, but realised was Zhang's own armour hung on a stand. There were two advisers in the room—one of them slightly known to Wang—and two armed soldiers on the steps outside. It had stopped raining while Wang had been waiting in the antechamber, but the eaves overhanging the steps were still dripping.

Wang knelt and bowed his head to the floor and the aide explained who he was. Surely Zhang must have known already or Wang would never have been admitted? Perhaps his memory was short or his head too full of other more important matters.

"Wang Meng?" he said slowly in a harsh, deep voice with a yowling Yangzi accent. "Not a very well-known painter, is he?"

"Known to connoisseurs," said the adviser Wang had met. "However, his maternal grandfather was very well known: Zhao Meng-fu, Duke of Wei, President of the Hanlin Academy."

"I am not a connoisseur," said Zhang, with a broad, jovial smile, signalling to Wang to stand up, "but I like to have only the best things round me. Is your painting for sale?"

"I'm afraid not," said Wang. "I made it for the Ten Friends of the

North Wall and I have already given it to them and written the dedication on it."

"Given it? Not sold it?"

"I am not a professional artist," said Wang. "I paint only for myself and my friends."

"I will first look at your painting," said Zhang, with another of his warm smiles, "and then decide whether I want to be your friend."

A silk scroll of birds and plum blossom, a painting by the great Tang Emperor Xuanzong, hung on the wall beside the door. Zhang directed the aide to take it down and, as he did so, Wang saw that the seal in the bottom left-hand corner was that of Lord Meng. How, he wondered, had it come into Zhang's possession? Perhaps Wang's uncle Zhao Yong had given it to him. More likely, it had been looted from the Governor's Residence in Wuxing.

"An Emperor's handiwork," said Zhang proudly, seeing Wang's interest in it, "but what is the point of being an Emperor if you have to make your own wall decorations?"

Everyone laughed, Zhang—showing decayed teeth—loudest of all.

When he had carefully rolled up the Emperor's painting, the aide took Wang's out of its box and hung that in its place. It was a larger scroll and should have been hung higher. On this rainy day, without much light on the inner wall, it looked dense and sombre after the bright painting it replaced. Zhang seemed taken aback.

"No colours," he said. "Why no colours?"

Wang had no ready reply and the second adviser replied for him.

"Colours are unfashionable with amateur painters," he said.

"I like colours," said Zhang. "The world is full of colours, isn't it?"

He rose from his bed and walked heavily across the room to look at the painting more closely.

"Why don't you use silk?" he asked.

"Paper gives the best effects with ink," said Wang.

"But there's more pleasure in silk and colours. What is the purpose of a picture if not pleasure?"

His joviality was suddenly replaced with a bullying, angry tone. Wang thought uneasily of his reputation for receiving ambassadors from the Mongols—no doubt with smiles and laughter—and sending them out to have their heads cut off.

"No purpose," he said. "But it depends what pleasure you aim at."

"I see it is well done," Zhang conceded, after a short inspection, "but heavy, very heavy. Why didn't you put a boat with a fisherman on the water here?"

"He couldn't hope to catch anything," said Wang. "Not with those elegant people making so much noise talking."

Zhang looked at him suspiciously for a moment, fearing he was being mocked, then laughed.

"You know what you're doing," he said, coming closer to Wang and searching his face with bloodshot eyes. "But why so heavy? Why so dark?"

"I am drawn to mountains," said Wang. "When I stand under a mountain, even in my mind, it can only seem heavy and dark."

Zhang scratched his chest and looked perplexed.

"You stand under mountains in your mind? Isn't this a real mountain?"

"It was painted in my house here in Pingjiang. It is a mixed memory of several mountains."

"It looks like a real mountain."

"Yes, of course. That's the trick. As in a play."

Wang was thinking of the play about Fan Li and Xi Shi which Jasmine said had delighted Zhang.

"What trick?"

"To tell a story," said Wang, "which seems to be real, when it's only words or, in this case, ink."

"A story? A story about a mountain?"

"Yes. And the people enjoying their party under the mountain."

Zhang went back and looked at the painting again.

"What is the story?"

Zhang sounded now more intrigued than aggressive, but Wang felt he had already talked too much and embarked on a line of discussion which he could hardly sustain with a man who took everything literally. When he didn't immediately answer, the adviser he knew slightly and who perhaps had told Zhang about the existence of the painting in the first place, said:

"The poet Gao Chi thinks it is about the spirit of the Song Dynasty surviving the years of foreign rule."

This was the wrong idea to put into Zhang's head. He associated the Song Dynasty with his enemies the Red Scarves and Zhu.

"Why the Song Dynasty?" he asked angrily.

"I don't know why the Song Dynasty," said Wang. "This elegant gathering makes me think of my father, who died only recently and attended one just before he died. As for the mountain, it represents one of the many mountains to be found in this ancient kingdom of Wu, where my father lived all his life."

Zhang seemed mollified.

"This is the story? The story of your father's civilised life in the beautiful land of Wu?"

"Exactly so," said Wang.

"It's sad to lose one's father. I'm sorry. Now it's obvious why it's so dark and heavy."

Zhang looked from one to the other of his advisers, who nodded sagely, then went and sat down again on his bed and told the aide to take down Wang's painting and put back the Emperor's. Wang, after kneeling and bowing his head to the floor, was about to go out with his painting in its box under his arm, when Zhang said:

"I'll send you a roll of good silk. Then you can paint in colours and cheer yourself up."

Fortunately for Wang, the silk was never delivered. If it had been, he certainly would not have torn it up as Ni had done with Zhang's brother's silk, but would probably have tried to satisfy Zhang with something bright and cheerful like the Tang Emperor's painting. He was glad he did not have to. Brightness and cheerfulness were now far from his mind or anyone else's.

The summer's heat turned the slowly starving and disintegrating city into a place of horror. The besiegers had thought of a better way of fouling their enemies' nest than delivering filth by catapult. They dammed up the streams flowing into the moat, which fed all the canals inside the walls, and only had to drop their rotting matter—human, animal and vegetable—into the moat. The sun's heat and lack of rain completed their work. There were wells, of course, which were not polluted, but not enough of them, and their levels were low. The fish in the canals were dying and the whole city was filled with the stench of disease and death.

Occasional attempts were still made—mainly at night—to break through the encircling earthworks, but most of the military efforts now were directed towards repairing and shoring up walls damaged by cannon-fire. Even the bolder people, such as the Ten Friends of the North Wall, had lost most of their spirit of defiance. Fighting is one thing, being slowly imprisoned to death, another. They continued to invent ingenious schemes for breaking out, but it was clear that, even if they had succeeded, the weakness and unreliability of their ill-fed, sickly soldiers would have given easy victory to the enemy. Many soldiers were only too eager to take part in sallies so that they could surrender and go over to the other side.

The dwindling supplies of food were severely rationed by the authorities and given only to active fighters, firemen, burial-workers and other auxiliaries such as the actors, acrobats, musicians and street-entertainers who were obliged to continue performing. Food could still be bought privately, of course, from those officials and merchants who had secured excessive supplies in the early days and hidden them away for their own profit, but only in exchange for silver, gold or precious objects. Ordinary people who were too old or weak to work were likely to starve, unless younger, stronger relatives shared their rations with them. Better off people stayed alive on their family heirlooms. Wang and his wife were eating up in a few months, as he bitterly remarked, a whole lifetime's treasures collected by his father, though one or two of the private food-suppliers would accept Wang's own paintings. It was not an economical way to live, however, since he used more energy making a painting than he received back in the few handfuls of rice it earned.

"Many people are eating two-legged mutton now," said Kong. "But they don't trouble to give it fancy names on the menu."

"I hope you won't bring any for us or touch it yourself," said Wang. "It would surely be diseased."

But Kong, whose medical expertise was constantly in demand with sick friends and neighbours, did become ill himself. Emptying his stomach and bowels repeatedly, he lay for several days in a high fever, nursed by Wang's wife and in lucid moments advising her on his own treatment, but growing weaker each day. Wang recklessly expended some of his father's best things—an album leaf by Wang Wei, a bronze mirror of the Warring States period, a Yueh stoneware basin—on buying medicines and clean water from the best well, and at last Kong's fever subsided and he began to recover.

Alas, he was scarcely himself again before it was the turn of Wang's wife to succumb. Only now, when he was in danger of losing her, did Wang understand how much they had become part of one another. He had never loved her, as he had Peony or the White Tigress or Jasmine, with the animal excitement of a sudden sensual relationship. But they had passed together through the bitter disappointment of having no children to extend the memory of their existence beyond death, and had shared the resolve in spite of that to give their lives temporary value, even while disagreeing how to do so—she wanting him to pursue an official career, he preferring to retreat into his art. She had acceded to him in that and come to admit that he was right, especially as the times they lived in deteriorated and his art improved. She had put up with his frequent moroseness and sometimes eased it. They had been able to discuss nearly everything (though not Wang's feelings for the White Tigress or Jasmine), to calm each other's anxieties and respect each other's thoughts, even when they did not agree. Latterly she had been not just a daughter to his father—often an uneasy relationship, especially for a daughter-in-law—but a true friend. Theirs could not be called a perfect marriage since it lacked physical attraction and produced no descendants, but nothing in life is perfect and, on the threshold of old age, when sexual desire is either dying away or ridiculous, perhaps it was as near perfect as any could be.

The threshold of old age, however, was where it ended. She did not recover. Valuable after valuable went to doctors and religious healers without result. She died in the late summer, at a time when a quarter of the city's population was dying too. Wang's association with the Ten Friends of the North Wall, his father's reputation and the expenditure of the last items of his father's collection ensured that she was not thrown into a pit or cremated with the rest, but buried on top of his father.

Grief-stricken and hopeless, convinced that he would very soon follow her, Wang ordered the grave to be dug still deeper to leave room for himself. But as if by welcoming the disease, every day expecting and even wanting its symptoms to appear, he escaped it. He grew thinner and thinner, unable to paint, having nothing left to exchange for food and hardly caring to eat in any case, relying entirely on Kong to forage for tiny quantities of grain, weeds from the gardens or an occasional rat—all the dogs and cats had already been eaten, while the horses belonging to the cavalry were eaten by their riders.

Invited to a grisly gathering in order to dine on Gao Chi's last horse, Wang declined. He could not bear any company but his own or Kong's or think of anything but the past, his wife's good qualities and his own bad ones. Kong saved him not only from starvation by finding food and forcing him to eat, but also probably from complete despair. What now did he have to live for, why live, when it was so much easier to die? Kong coaxed him to remember that there was a world beyond the walls of Pingjiang and that, since their ordeal could not last forever, they must soon be part of that other world again.

"Those still alive will be massacred when the city falls," said Wang.

"Not you," said Kong. "You are Zhu's friend."

"He will hardly remember me. And if he does, it will be angrily, since I didn't go to Nanjing when he asked me."

"He'll not forget you," said Kong. "How could he, when he remembered you so well before, after so many years had passed? People don't forget significant episodes from their youth, whatever they may forget later. You must explain to him that your father's weakness prevented you going to Nanjing and that it was only because of your father that you were caught in this trap."

"I shall never be able to approach Zhu."

"You must find some way. I am of no importance, but I am good at getting round low officials and you will easily get round the higher ones."

"Is it really worth all the trouble?"

"It is to me," said Kong. "How shall I survive if you don't?"

It was not surprising, Wang told himself at this time, as he leant on Kong and followed him reluctantly from darkness towards light, that the legendary people beyond the Peach Blossom River were always characterised as villagers, peasants, without any mention at all of scholars. Educated people are liable to crumble inside themselves and become quite helpless when outward circumstances lose all sense and pattern and explode into chaos.

❀

The siege ended in the middle of autumn, when the cannons finally broke down part of the wall. Zhu's soldiers rushed in and seized the nearest gate. General Chang galloped through at the head of his horsemen and made straight for Zhang's palace. They were almost too late.

Zhang's principal wife sent all his women and children up into the top of the pagoda, then herself lit the pile of wood prepared at the bottom and climbed up to join them. The pagoda was already blazing as the invaders reached the courtyard. Inside the throne-room, they found Zhang hanging from a gilded beam. He was cut down, still alive, and taken in a cage to Nanjing, but refused to make any submission to his triumphant rival, now undisputed Prince of Wu, and contrived to hang himself a second time in his prison cell. This suicide was successful.

# 13. A CHAPTER OF HAPPINESS

At the end of the old year, Zhu, carefully advised by scholars, proclaimed and printed a new code of laws and a new calendar. A new Hanlin Academy was set up to supervise all intellectual matters, an examination system to select the scholars of the future and a National University to train them. Architects began to plan new palace buildings, a shrine was built to Zhu's ancestors and, outside the walls of Nanjing, altars to Heaven and Earth.

Three times, according to ritual, Zhu declined the throne of "the Son of Heaven" offered by the great crowd of officials assembled in his palace in Nanjing. After accepting at the fourth request, he named his new dynasty "the Great Ming." Wang Meng, attending the ceremonies, was reminded of what Zhu had said to him when they last met: "I believe the future is bright." It was a clever name, "The Great Brightness." combining that sense of simple optimism with the more complex patriotic and religious feelings formerly embodied by the Young Prince of Radiance, as supposed heir to the Song Dynasty and forerunner of the Maitreya Buddha's promised age of peace and enlightenment.

Although Toghon Temür still reigned as Emperor in Dadu, far to the north, his Empire was shrinking even while the ceremonies of Zhu's accession were proceeding. As soon as Zhu's generals had captured Pingjiang they led their armies—increased by large numbers of those who had fought for Zhang—northwards into the great plain between the Yangzi and Yellow Rivers, where the rebellions against the Yuan Dynasty had first broken out. Crushing the last remnants of Mongol resistance in the provinces of Shandong and Henan, Zhu's troops took possession of the ancient Song capital, Kaifeng. The campaign was then suspended, so that most of the soldiers could go home for the spring planting season.

Meanwhile, to the south, the fall of Pingjiang had persuaded the pirate Fang to surrender to Zhu and, with the help of his fleet of a thousand ships and his small but efficient army, the rest of the south-east coast was quickly prised away from the Mongol authorities. Some of them, however, fought loyally and stubbornly for their dying dynasty. Fang himself spent the few remaining years of his life in Nanjing, rewarded by Zhu with titles and pensions for himself and his family. The interior to the west and south-west, as far as the great mountains of Tibet, was incorporated into Zhu's Empire during the next two years. There was little resistance, since by then those still loyal to the Yuan Dynasty who held authority or had taken refuge there—Wang's cousin Zhao Lin among them—could be in no doubt that the mandate had passed irrevocably to the Ming. Wang never met his cousin again, but heard that he was living in modest retirement on the slopes of Mount Yangmin. Why did he not return to the Blue Bien Mountains and the Gull Wave Pavilion, which was left empty and decaying? Probably it was too close to the new Emperor's capital and besides most of the land around it had been given to one of Zhu's generals.

Wang was not in the forefront of those attending the ceremonies for the new Emperor's accession. Such places were reserved for Zhu's earliest adherents and those who had accepted his summons to Nanjing immediately. But nor was Wang right at the back. Zhu, as Kong had predicted, had not forgotten the man from the waterfalls. All those scholars eligible for administrative posts, who had either been serving Zhang or living in his kingdom at the time of his defeat, were summoned for interview at Nanjing. Wang was seen more quickly than most—not by Zhu himself, who was then making all the preparations for his accession, but by a young official called Hu Wei-yong. This was the very man who had told Kong, a year or two before, that Wang should not wait to be summoned, but come at once into Zhu's service, and he now questioned Wang narrowly about his reasons for not doing so.

"It was just then that my father's health broke down," said Wang, uneasily conscious that this was an evasive answer and that he had already made similarly evasive use of his father's death to ward off Zhang's criticism of his painting.

His present interviewer, however, was not so easily diverted. He was not only extremely intelligent and unemotional, he appeared to have a written record in front of him of all Wang's activities over the past several years.

"Yet a good while afterwards," said Hu, "your father showed every sign of health when he attended a literary gathering and composed his *Eight Songs on a Cosmetics Case.*"

"And immediately after that suffered his final collapse," said Wang. "By that time, of course, Pingjiang was under siege and we had no means of escape."

"We are not talking about that time," said Hu sharply. "When you sent your servant to Nanjing to inquire about being summoned by the Prince of Wu, you cannot have been too worried about your father's health. I myself told your servant that you should come immediately. Why didn't you?"

"My father was certainly in better health then than later," said Wang. "But he was unable to leave Pingjiang and my wife was caring for him. I would have had to leave both of them behind if I had come to Nanjing."

"So why did you send that message? 'The man from the waterfalls is ready to be summoned.' The meaning seems perfectly clear, yet you say now that you were *not* ready."

"I thought when I sent it that I might bring myself to leave them behind," said Wang, blushing deeply as he felt his honesty impugned and his excuses more and more exposed to this young man's contempt.

Hu never took his eyes off Wang's face, except to refer to his notes. He waited now a moment or two, until Wang's whole face was crimson, then said, without expression:

"Perhaps your true purpose was merely to remind us of the favour you have previously been shown by the Prince of Wu?"

"I had every intention of coming to Nanjing if my message was well received."

"Or were you just concerned to have a foot in both camps?"

"No."

"No? But at the time you were serving the bandit Zhang's regime."

"No . . ." said Wang, unable to avoid sounding equivocal.

"No? It's quite certain that you were."

"Not in any official capacity."

"What do you mean by that?"

"I agreed to give advice to some of the officers in and around Wuxing, but at my own request I was not paid to do so."

"Why did you do it, then?"

"I was born in Wuxing. My family lived there. I wanted to see it well governed."

Wang felt himself beginning to blush again at this crude attempt to re-establish his good faith. Hu made no comment, but wrote down the reply.

"You were intimate with one of Zhang's concubines," he said, fixing his gaze again on Wang's face.

"Yes. But I met her long before she knew Zhang, when she was an actress in Quinsai. I came across her again in Pingjiang through my friend Ni Zan. He, by the way, could not have been more hostile to Zhang. He was badly beaten by Zhang's brother."

"I know all about Ni, of course. I own one of his paintings."

Hu did not smile as he said this, offering no opportunity to Wang to broaden and perhaps lighten their conversation.

"You seem to know all about almost everything," said Wang, with a touch of bitterness, wondering how many of his own friends, perhaps even Ni, had contributed to the dossier in front of Hu. "I can tell you, then, though it causes me shame, especially when I think of my dead wife and her kindness to me and my father, that I wanted to take the lady away from Zhang and we made plans to escape to Nanjing."

"Why did you change your mind?"

"Zhang suddenly ordered her to marry him and move into his palace."

"And she did so?"

"To my great sorrow, yes."

"Was that because she didn't want to go to Nanjing, or because she thought *you* didn't?"

"She may have doubted my sincerity, as you do. She was also in some measure attracted to Zhang."

"And how sincere *were* you?"

"As I said, I was reluctant to abandon my wife and father. On the other hand, this lady and I . . ."

"There was no other thought in your head, apart from these private considerations? Of wishing to serve the Prince of Wu, for example?"

"Which Prince of Wu do you mean?

Hu looked very annoyed.

"There is only one Prince of Wu, as far as we are concerned—the prince you offered to serve by sending your servant to Nanjing."

"Of course. I did wish to serve him or I would not have sent the message. But I was pulled in several directions at once, and was not perhaps behaving very rationally."

"Because of this lady called Jasmine?"

"Yes."

"She could no doubt bear out your account?"

"If she were still alive," said Wang, quietly and sadly.

Hu seemed to be momentarily confused by this reply, then quickly recovered his know-all manner.

"Ah, she was in the burning pagoda with all Zhang's other women?"

"Yes."

Hu was silent for a while, studying the papers in front of him. His small mouth remained set in the same hard expression it had had throughout the interview. His head was small, too, and he sat very upright in his chair, hardly moving except occasionally to run one finger along the line of his left jaw. He was clean-shaven apart from a thin drooping moustache in the Mongol style.

"What is your opinion of Chen Ju-yen?" he asked suddenly.

"He's a good friend and a good painter."

"Yes, I own one of his paintings. He served very prominently in Zhang's regime."

"Many good people did. Are you going to punish them all?"

"You have met the Prince of Wu and must be aware that he is not vengeful. On the contrary, he seeks only reconciliation and unity. All he requires from former enemies is a complete break with the past and absolute loyalty to himself."

"I am sure he can count on both from Chen," said Wang, thinking of Chen's secret approach to Zhu on General Pan's behalf.

"Chen has told us much about you," said Hu, with a hint of menace, hoping perhaps to provoke Wang into reciprocating. But Wang had no fear of anything Chen might have said about him, and he was beginning to see that Hu's knowledge was shallower than he pretended.

"And I could tell you much about Chen—all to his credit."

"Chen and his superior, General Pan, are retaining their posts for the present," said Hu, "in command of the garrison in Quinsai. Which may give you some idea of the Prince of Wu's determination to turn enemies into friends."

It also gave Wang some idea of how effective Chen's secret mission to Zhu must have been.

"There will be all manner of important and less important posts to fill," Hu continued, "as our armies pacify more and more territory. But no one will any longer be allowed to hold office, draw a salary and do little in return."

"Chen is just the man for you. He is a person who likes nothing so much as constant activity."

"So I believe. But you, I'm afraid, are not."

"I am growing old, and have not worked in administration for many years. But I don't think that, when I did, I was ever considered lazy or inefficient."

"However, you prefer to contemplate waterfalls."

Still he did not smile.

"I can't deny it," said Wang. "I admitted as much to the Prince of Wu himself."

"You will have to choose now between contemplating waterfalls and giving your full attention to the work that needs to be done."

"You are offering me such a choice?"

"Perhaps."

"On my part," said Wang, "the choice is not hard. My wife and father both died in the siege. I am entirely alone and would like nothing so much as to dedicate myself to some useful task. Besides, such small means as I had and the good sum of money left me by my father—as well as all the treasures he collected—were used up during the siege. I must either work or starve."

"How old are you?"

"I shall be sixty this year."

"In good health?"

"Still very thin," said Wang, holding out his arm and pulling back the sleeve of his gown, "but considering what we went through in Pingjiang, much healthier than I expected to be. Indeed, I expected to be dead, like so many others . . ."

Surprised at the way he was suddenly speaking so garrulously to this arrogant and unsympathetic young man, Wang half swallowed his last few words.

"People say you're a good artist, but I've never seen any of your paintings."

"They are not widely known."

"But you took one to show to Zhang."

"At his command. He was not very impressed. He wanted something lighter and more cheerful."

A very small smile briefly lifted the corners of Hu's lips.

"We will keep you in mind for some suitable post. Meanwhile, let me see an example of your work. There's nothing of yours in my collection."

❁

A strange thing, deeply significant to Wang, happened soon after this interview. He was seated in his cramped and badly lit lodging in one of the poorer parts of Nanjing, working without much enthusiasm on a small hanging scroll to give to Hu, when he heard Kong speaking to someone at the outer door. Kong, as always, sounded surly and unhelpful. But suddenly his tone changed completely and a few minutes later he came to see Wang in a state of great excitement.

"Who do you think is here?" he asked.

During the ordeal of the siege, their relationship had almost ceased to be that of master and servant and become more like that of friends or even relatives. Wang, cut off now from almost everyone he had ever known, was only too glad for it to remain so. Besides, in this new world they had entered, in which a peasant who had once asked to be his servant was about to become Emperor and in which all power lay in the hands of unknown men, many of them also sprung from nowhere, it was uncertain whether the old divisions of birth and education would continue to prevail. Kong went on performing the tasks of a servant, but for the present Wang could not even pay him wages.

Their food and lodging came from the very small reserve of silver hoarded by Wang from his inheritance and from Kong's occasional medical services in the neighbourhood.

"How should I know?" said Wang irritably, displeased with the curve of a line he had just drawn.

"Three guesses."

"A messenger bringing a length of silk from Hu Wei-yong."

"No," said Kong, grinning like one of the clowns in a play.

"A bag of gold."

"Nearer."

"A bag of silver."

"One more guess and you might get it."

"Oh, for Heaven's sake!"

Kong beckoned frenetically to someone standing in the shadows beyond the doorway and a good-looking boy of about sixteen came just inside, bowing nervously to Wang. Wang, who had never seen him before, could not understand why he felt that he had.

"You still don't know who he is, do you?" said Kong, his grin growing, if possible, wider.

"No. Please tell me!"

"He comes from the Yellow Crane Mountain."

Wang looked at the boy blankly.

"This is Deng."

"Deng?"

"His son. Come to repay your generosity to himself and his mother."

The boy smiled shyly. Wang threw down his brush, spoiling his painting irreparably, rose and embraced him.

"How did you find me?"

"I went to Pingjiang, sir. People said you had moved to Nanjing and I should ask for Kong, who was sure to be well known already."

"And they were right, of course."

"I had to ask a few times," said the boy, looking apologetically at Kong.

"Had you ever been in a big city before?" asked Wang.

"Pingjiang, sir."

"Before that?"

"No, sir. Not even in a big town."

"Well, you are your father's son to have managed so well. How have things been on the Yellow Crane Mountain?"

"Not bad, sir. We saw some soldiers, but they gave us no trouble."

"I should have stayed there myself."

Wang did not know what else to say. His feelings were getting the better of both his thoughts and his voice.

"How like your father you are!"

"My mother says so, sir. But how should I know?"

"You couldn't. He died some days before you were born. We must go out and drink wine, Kong. This is extraordinary. It's as if he had come back, but the same age as when he left me, while I have grown white-haired."

His eyes wet, Wang stood and stared at the boy as if he were truly returned from the grave. Kong, meanwhile, kept impatiently shifting from one foot to the other.

"Show him what you brought!" he said.

Deng's son held out a small wooden box.

"For me?" asked Wang, thinking it must be some repayment of the money he had given to Deng's wife when he left the Yellow Crane Mountain. "But you owe me nothing. On the contrary, I owe a debt to your father which I can never repay. He died, I'm sure you know, trying to save my paintings and my cousin's books from a fire in my studio."

The boy still held out the box, but Wang would not receive it. Kong was beside himself with frustration.

"Take it, you idiot!" he said.

Then, seeing the shock on the boy's face at this insolence to his master, he put one hand over his mouth, the other between his legs, and bent double as if he were about to be sick, muttering "Sorry, sorry!" through the hand over his mouth. Straightening up and seizing the box from the boy's hand, he pulled off the lid and thrust the box under Wang's nose.

"Is that yours or isn't it?" he said.

Inside the box, which was lined with red silk, lay the white jade ring—the first Song Emperor's ring, carved with dragons—given to Wang by his grandfather and which he had lost so many years before when he was gathering firewood in the snow. Wang took the ring out of the box and turned it round in the light from the window, then sat down abruptly at his desk and put it on the middle finger of his left hand, where he had always worn it. In the old days it had been a little loose, now it was almost too tight. Even though he had lost weight during the siege, his fingers had thickened with age.

"How did you find it?" he asked.

"It was under the three pine-trees by the house, sir. I saw a gleam of white and picked it out of the earth. My mother said it was yours. My father told her how you lost it and how you all searched for it and never found it, and how sad everybody felt for a long time afterwards."

"The earth shifts about," said Kong, "just like the sea, but more slowly, so that nobody notices. And then things come to the surface which may have stayed under it for years."

"Like Deng himself," said Wang, "who has come back just as pristine as my ring."

He did not think he had ever felt happier or more fortunate in his life, though it was probably only that his good fortune followed a period of such misfortune.

❁

The elaborate ceremonies marking Zhu's accession were no doubt intended to demonstrate that, whatever his obscure origins, this was a true, traditional Emperor. He had won the mandate by force and conquest, but he meant to hold it peacefully and by attention to the native customs and rituals of the land, not as an armed overlord like the Mongol Emperor.

First, as high priest of humanity, he offered sacrifices to Heaven and Earth—the sources of all the ten thousand things—at their separate altars beyond the city walls. Then, after he had ascended the throne as Sovereign of the World and received the congratulations of his court, led by Li Shan-chang—the former schoolmaster was now Prime Minister—Zhu himself headed the procession to his new family shrine, where, as the model of all filial sons, he consecrated four generations of his ancestors with temple names. Some people secretly sneered at this ceremony, since no one had ever honoured such humble ancestors in this way before and, beyond his grandparents, Zhu did not even know the real names of his forebears, but Wang found the ceremony all the more solemn and touching for that reason. He imagined the feelings of those hungry, nameless farmers, if time could have been reversed and news brought to them in their fields that their hard lives would be redeemed and their existence remembered forever under grand names in an imperial temple. Of course, it would not have altered their lives in any practical way at all, since it was all so far in the future; yet, surely it would have given a lift to their shoulders, raised their eyes from the ground, opened their minds to a sense of the world's unpredictability and richness and thereby changed their lives from within.

Wasn't this exactly what Zhu's grandfather envisaged with the stories of heroes which had such an effect on his grandson? No doubt the stories answered some need in the grandfather as much as the grandson—or more likely they infected the grandson with the same need, which he finally satisfied in the most spectacular possible way. The thought of all this was very pleasing to Wang, temporarily making him feel young again, for if such a far-fetched fairy-tale as Zhu's rise to be Emperor could come true, then imagination could sometimes master harsh reality and this was a hopeful, youthful way of looking at things.

❀

That summer, as soon as the harvests had been gathered, the Ming armies crossed the Yellow River and advanced on the Yuan capital,

Dadu. So swiftly did they move and were resisted so feebly by this lost dynasty—whose only brilliant general, Kökö Temür, had been dismissed by the Yuan Emperor in the early spring—that within little more than a month Dadu was captured intact. The fallen Emperor, with his heir apparent and court, escaped only just in time and fled into the bleak wastes of their Mongol homeland. Dadu was renamed Beiping ("the North is pacified"), but Zhu kept Nanjing as his capital and this was the first time in history that the whole Empire was governed from so far south.

Some months earlier, Wang had been offered the post of District Magistrate of Taian, a good-sized town in the province of Shandong, overlooked by Mount Tai.

"You will be able to see the mountain from the windows of your official residence," said Hu, having called Wang in to tell him the good news. "No one will be surprised if you decide to paint it."

Hu was much more relaxed and genial than during their first interview. Wang, elated by the return of his ring and even more by the return, in a manner of speaking, of Deng, had quickly restarted his painting, finished it in a day or two and sent it to Hu. Entitled *Autumn Groves and Myriad Valleys*, it was not very large—he could not afford much paper—and not, he thought, one of his best works, being somewhat conventional in theme and therefore vague in effect, and almost academically constructed. But the detail was fluid and passionate, full of the renewed energy and optimism he felt, and Hu was delighted with it, sending back a message with Kong, who had taken the picture to him, that he would like to keep it for a week or two to show to his friends. Wang at once replied that it was his to keep permanently, if he cared to, and a few days later was called in to be offered and gladly accept his magistracy.

"I must emphasise, however," said Hu, "that this post is not a sinecure. We expect, since you are an artist of such talent, that you will spend your leisure painting, but we do not expect you to have much leisure. Shandong has suffered more destruction and disruption than almost any other province in the whole Empire. It has only just been pacified and is still in a very disturbed state. Many of its people have fled elsewhere and should now be returning, but they will find their homes burned or occupied by others and their fields gone back to wilderness. You will have many headaches. It is absolutely essential that the people already there, as well as the people returning, remain calm and contented. You must handle every problem that arises with the utmost tact and fairness. These are the Emperor's own instructions, and he added a warning to us all: 'There is no room in any part of the Empire for failure.'"

Leaving Hu's office, Wang was overjoyed to encounter young Chen in the palace courtyard and even more delighted to discover that he too was being posted to Shandong, as a military administrator. He would be stationed not too far away, in the provincial capital Jinan, and they would surely be able to see each other frequently.

"It sounds like hard work, though," Wang said.

"A new job always sounds like that," said Chen, "and in a new Empire even more so. But, after all, at our level, they're mostly the same people running it and I don't suppose human nature will change just because Zhu orders it to."

Wang was surprised by Chen's uncharacteristic cynicism. He seemed tired and not altogether satisfied with his new post. Perhaps he had hoped to remain in Quinsai or Pingjiang, near his home. But that was something permitted to few of Zhu's administrators. Zhu and his advisers were not perhaps as forgiving to their former enemies as they made out, or did not entirely trust them.

In the spring, Wang crossed the Yangzi River and travelled north to Taian. He had to go by road, since the section of the Grand Canal north of the Yangzi had fallen into complete disrepair. But having lost everything in the siege, he was encumbered by nothing in the way of possessions and he was accompanied by Kong, whom he had appointed steward of the magistrate's official residence, and young Deng, as his personal servant.

Long ago, under the Han Dynasty, the famous historian Sima Qian was castrated, as a punishment for displeasing the Emperor. In a letter written from prison he suggested that scholars who have been humiliated produce masterpieces out of their mortification, out of exasperation with their impotence. Wang, who had been so often mortified, though admittedly in a less drastic manner, by his wife's reproaches for his lack of official success, thought there was some truth in this. At any rate, now that he was a District Magistrate, making laws, sitting in judgment and responsible for the district's entire civil administration, he felt no great need to paint.

Taian, the town where he held sway, lay at the foot of Mount Tai, easternmost and holiest of the Daoists' "Five Holy Mountains." Wang remembered Sima Qian and his humiliation because it was he who recorded in his *Historical Memoirs* that, before the unification of the Empire, these five mountains had the status of dukes. Seven hundred years after Sima's time, the great Tang Emperor gave Mount Tai the title of "King Equal to the Sky" and four hundred years later a Song Emperor raised it to his own rank. Discussing this curious history with the priest in charge of the huge Daoist temple in Taian, Wang lightly suggested that it was somewhat absurd to bestow a human title on a mountain, but the priest disagreed.

"These titles were originally given," he said, "to the men chosen to offer sacrifices to Heaven and Earth on behalf of their subjects. Princes were in the first place priests. Mountains are the points on earth nearest to Heaven and therefore we have always considered them particularly spiritual. Mount Tai is also the nearest to the rising sun, the first point in the Empire to receive its rays and make this connection every day, and so our more thoughtful Emperors, beginning with the first, have always considered it their own counterpart in nature, and have come here frequently to make sacrifices to Earth at its base and to Heaven at its summit."

Wang liked this priest for his great knowledge and genuine humility. He had stood up to all the terrors and privations of the past twenty years with unshrinking courage, helping where he could, never taking sides, so calm and firm in his dealings with aggressive or panic-stricken authorities, murderous soldiers and ravaging bandits that his temple had almost escaped damage. Indeed, Wang felt that it was his personal influence as much as the mountain's sanctity that had saved the town and the whole district from much of the wanton damage that had been done to others in the province.

"However," the priest added, "perhaps it was going a little too far to give a human rank to a tree."

"A tree?"

"Two years after he unified the Empire, the first Emperor came to sacrifice on Mount Tai. On the way down he was caught in a storm and gratefully appointed the tree that sheltered him an official of the fifth rank."

"That Emperor was always on the edge of madness," said Wang. "He built the Great Wall and created the first centralised administration, but he also burned books and became obsessed with trying to live forever."

"He was a devout Daoist," said the priest, "and many followers of The Way believe it is possible to achieve immortality."

"Of course," said Wang, "but I'm afraid in his case the fifth-rank tree must have lived a good deal longer."

At the back of Wang's official residence in Taian was a high room with windows facing Mount Tai. Wang had attached a length of white silk to the wall of this room and was gradually covering it, using colours, with a landscape based on the real one spread out beyond the windows. But he was in no hurry to finish it, had no anxiety about it, and frequently made alterations. He was, he felt, treading in the footsteps of Old Huang in his three-year-long composition of *Living in the Mountains of Pure Happiness.*

Not that Wang was purely happy. He was often exasperated by

the incessant exigencies of his job. Probably the real reason he was taking so long to complete this painting was that he had so little time or energy left over from his public duties. The complications of resettling the area, of weaning people away from the short-term solutions of flight or violence, which they had bitterly learned to accept as normal, back towards a longer-term perspective of planting and harvesting, rebuilding, making and mending, required all his skills of patience and persuasion.

They required other skills too—of decisiveness and even harshness—which he did not sufficiently possess, and he suffered agonies of conscience whenever he had to punish severely—with prison, flogging, exile or execution—the malefactors brought before him nearly every day. Some of the laws they broke, by cheating, stealing, wounding or killing, were, of course, the basic laws of humanity. But the new Emperor did not make things any easier for his officials by his attempts to force all his subjects to stay at home, and his desire to regulate almost every aspect of their lives.

Whether it was due to his incomplete monastic training or the military background of his influential grandfather or the narrow, old-fashioned outlook of his chief advisers, Zhu seemed to want to take his Empire back into a more primitive age. He had in mind, evidently, the much simpler, smaller, wholly agricultural kingdoms of the distant past and the egalitarian, nature-based ideals of the Daoists, but he sought to achieve them in a most un-Daoist way, by active coercion.

People were forcibly relocated in large numbers from the areas that had suffered least to those, such as Shandong and Zhu's own homeland of Anhui, which had been devastated by floods, drought, plague, famine and fighting. Once resettled, these people, like everyone else, were forbidden to travel more than a day's journey from their own villages. If they went further without a travel certificate they were liable to suffer eighty strokes of the cane. The classes were immobilised too, as they had been under the Mongols, but now more strictly. If your father was a peasant, a peasant you must remain; if he was a soldier, a soldier; if a craftsman, a craftsman. All households were grouped into tens and these tens into hundreds, and registered, so that they could be conveniently taxed or conscripted for public works. The magistrates were issued with sample registration forms, which they had to have printed and distributed to those in charge of a hundred households—this unwelcome job passed round annually among the ten wealthiest households. Once the forms were filled in, they were to be returned to the magistrates and bound up into so-called "Yellow Registers," while copies had to be sent to the provincial authorities and eventually to the Revenue Ministry in Nanjing.

The work involved in all this and the number of junior officials who had to be employed and supervised to do it can be imagined. The Emperor even tried to prescribe the clothes people wore, circulating dress-patterns suitable for the wives of officials, for instance, and samples of the so-called "Four-Corner Pacification Cap," which was supposed to be worn by everyone. Merchants, who could be punished for pricing their wares too high and were liable to eighty strokes of the cane if they tried to inflate their prices by creating a market monopoly, were permitted to travel freely on business, but required to give full descriptions of the goods they were carrying to licensed brokers in every district they passed through. The brokers in turn were required to write these details in registers and show them to the magistrate once a month.

Wang partly sympathised with the thinking behind all this, especially when it took positive form. He was in favour of the encouragement of plain forms of letter-writing and the banning of elaborate salutations; of the abolition of the tax on books; of the programme for publishing classic school textbooks and reference books in standard editions—though these also came to include ranting moral tracts written by Zhu himself, which everyone was ordered to read and which students had to know by heart. But some of the regulations—like the brokers' registers of merchants' goods—were simply too tedious and complicated to be enforced, while others, Wang felt, only caused mischief. It was so often the more energetic, more intelligent, more admirable people—usually denounced by stupid and lazy ones—who were caught breaking the rules; and the amount of time and trouble wasted by officials in checking, correcting and putting in reports could have been better used for less trivial purposes.

Some years later, when he felt he had gone too far in badgering and coercing his people, the Emperor announced that he would welcome criticism. But several of those who were so naive as to offer it perished miserably. The criticisms were written, of course, in the form of memorials, by literate, educated people, and this was what made them unacceptable to Zhu, where those of illiterate farmers—supposing they could have articulated them—might have infuriated him less. Behind many of his attitudes and actions there was the hidden, possibly unconscious desire to penalise the educated class and especially those—the majority—from the two most civilised cities of the Empire, Quinsai and Pingjiang, now renamed Hangzhou and Suzhou respectively. Zhu needed these people to run the Empire and had taken trouble to recruit them into his service from the beginning, but he never really liked or trusted them.

The people closest to him personally, those with whom he drank and whom he rewarded lavishly with titles, estates and pensions, were his boyhood friends and military companions-in-arms, such as his two leading generals, Xu Ta and Chang Yü-chun. At least he would have rewarded the latter, if, soon after capturing Xandu and extending Zhu's power into Manchuria, Chang had not suddenly died of an infection. Zhu's passionate nature—he was no cold tyrant, even at his worst—was shown by his going into seclusion as soon as he heard the news of Chang's death, and by the lavish state funeral he organised, personally choosing the burial site, ordering a mausoleum to be built and composing the obituary.

Later, when Xu Ta, while trying to conquer still more territory in the Mongols' own homeland beyond the Great Wall, was defeated in battle for the first time in his career by the Mongol general Kökö Temür, Zhu overlooked the failure and continued to employ and honour Xu just as before. But as time went on, it became clear that the slightest failure on the part of an educated man, especially one who came from Pingjiang and had once served Zhang, was instantly fatal.

Zhu's tyranny at first seemed only the natural determination of the founder of a new dynasty to impose his own ideas of order and decency on an Empire which had almost dissolved into anarchy; it grew steadily worse as he trusted those who ran his Empire less and less. But Wang was fortunate. The worst of the tyranny was delayed until after his retirement from office, and his magistracy was counted a success. Most of the credit for this he himself ascribed to Kong, who not only solved many of the minor problems quietly and informally before they ever reached his master, but whose sense of reality and complete lack of sentimentality made his advice invaluable to the over-imaginative, over-sensitive Wang.

"You are the real magistrate," he said once to Kong. "I just wear the costume."

"People are not always fools," said Kong. "You are a good man and they recognise that they're lucky to have one as their magistrate. On the other hand, they can never resist taking advantage of a good man, unless he keeps a rough dog at his door. The doctor taught me to take the trousers off everybody, in a manner of speaking. 'The fakers will put their dignity first and go away,' he said, 'but the genuine cases lose all pretence of dignity in the need to be cured.'"

Young Chen came to see Wang several times. He seemed to have more leisure than Wang, or perhaps just more excuse—as a provincial, military official rather than a district, civil one—to move about. He was much more contented than when Wang had met him in Nanjing, no doubt because he had been allowed to go home soon afterwards to marry. On his latest visit to Wang he was particularly cheerful, since his first child had just been born and he would soon be going to Pingjiang to see it.

This was the third winter Wang had spent in Taian and the whole district was covered in snow. Wang found it hard to bear the biting winds and colder temperatures of this northern plain, but Chen had enjoyed the wintry ride round the foot of the mountain from Jinan and looked younger and pinker than ever, as Wang, summoned by Kong, came down to greet him in the courtyard of his compound. They went up to Wang's room overlooking Mount Tai and Deng's son brought them wine.

"Look, your painting is finished!" said Chen, "and you've really laid on the colours this time."

"What do you think?"

"It's a masterpiece."

"I was beginning to think so myself," said Wang, "until I looked out of the window."

"Well, of course," said Chen, "you've painted the colours of autumn and now the whole mountain is covered with snow."

"And unbelievably beautiful," said Wang. "Far more beautiful in its austerity than it ever was in autumn with all those gaudy colours. I feel like tearing up my own silk and beginning again."

"Don't do that!" said Chen. "Why not imitate nature and powder it all over with white pigment?"

"Would that work?"

"Let's try!"

Chen chose a brush, dampened it very slightly and dipped it in white powder. But when he tried to make the powder adhere to the silk, it either fell off or made crude splodges.

"No, it doesn't work," said Wang, wiping the splodges off with a cloth.

"Let me think!" said Chen, taking another cup of wine from Deng and going to stare out of the window.

In the garden below, he saw one of the servants' children aiming at a small bird with a bow and arrow.

"I have an idea!" said Chen.

He pulled Deng by his arm to the window and pointed down.

"Fetch me that!" he said.

"The child?" asked Deng, always nervous of doing the wrong thing.

"If you like. But it's the bow I want. And some good strong twine."

When Deng returned with the bow, Chen took the brush and began to tie its handle to the bow-string.

"Have you heard the latest story about the new Empress?" he asked.

"No. All I know about her is that the Emperor went out of his way to praise her in his accession speech for her part in his rise to power. Everyone says she is good at restraining his hot temper."

"She dislikes any kind of extravagance," said Chen. "Always mending and washing her clothes rather than have new ones. Apparently she heard that Khan Khublai's Empress used to get silk thread by boiling the strings of old bows, so she's been doing so herself and using the thread to make quilts for old people without children."

There was a sneer in his voice which irritated Wang, so he replied sharply:

"Perhaps I would qualify."

"I'm sorry, I forgot."

"It's all right. I've got used to it."

There was an awkward silence, while Chen continued to knot the twine round the handle of the brush.

"She sounds an admirable person," said Wang.

"Perhaps. But an Empress boiling string . . . it's a bit foolish, isn't it?"

"Not so foolish as an Empress without a thought in her head except her own superiority."

The relationship between Wang and Chen was changing and they were both conscious of it. Wang did not think he was really envious of Chen for having a son, but he had made it sound as if he was. Perhaps he had become too old and lost his sense of humour. Or was it Chen who was out of touch with the new times?

"Now . . ." said Chen, having secured the brush to the bow-string and dipped the bristles in white pigment.

He aimed the brush at the painting, then turned to Wang.

"Are you sure you think this is a good idea?"

"That depends on the result," said Wang.

"I can't be certain of that. It might be a disaster."

"Go ahead!" said Wang. "Who can really foresee the result of anything?"

Chen pulled back the bow-string and released it. Paint splattered the silk and the effect was dazzling, just as if snow had suddenly fallen over the landscape.

"Shall I do more?"

"Do it all over!" said Wang.

"You don't think it's a bit crude, even vulgar?"

"On the contrary. It eliminates every trace of vulgarity."

Wang was not really thinking about the painting any more. His thoughts were of the splash-painter he had once met with Peony, and of Peony herself, and of how difficult it was to believe that he, the childless, white-haired Magistrate of Taian, sipping his wine in winter, was the same person as the boy in that distant summer.

❁

Wang was too busy during those first three years in Taian to realise quite how lonely he was. Always longing in his earlier days to find more time to be alone with nature, he had never understood how much he really depended on the friends and relations and especially his wife, from whom he thought he wanted to get away. Now, constantly surrounded by people making demands on him—junior officials, servants, guards, jailers, people wanting favours or justice or attention in one way or another—he had no one of his own age, background and level of intelligence with whom he could relax.

Visiting another magistrate in an adjoining district—one from which virtually the whole population had disappeared and where most of the houses were mere roofless walls—he had felt at first the relief of being a private person again and in the presence of another person like himself. But then, as they walked round the neglected garden of the abandoned Government Hostel there, admiring its rare stones and what flowers remained, especially an unusual jade-green shrub with a wonderful scent, he had begun to find the man dull and commonplace. They drank wine together and the man produced a brush and paper so that Wang could write him a poem, but this was only because he knew Wang was a grandson of Lord Meng and friend of the famous painter Ni Zan and the famous poet Gao Chi.

His host wore culture, Wang thought, in the way a monkey can be made to wear clothes, without knowledge, understanding or any sense of purpose. Wang wrote the required lines, thanked the man for his hospitality, and returned to his own compound with a leaden feeling that it was not so much that the other magistrate was lacking something, as that he himself was mistaken in putting so much value on culture, when it was only, after all, a way of showing off, of wearing monkey's clothes. Indeed, he began to see all mankind as glorified monkeys and it was just as well that after three years he was allowed a period of leave in Nanjing.

Once there, however, he sought and received permission to go to Pingjiang to visit the grave of his father and wife. His original intention had been to re-bury them both in the family grave near Wuxing, but there had been no question of doing so in the immediate aftermath of the siege, even if he could have afforded it, and now that he could afford it, he felt that too much time had elapsed. When he consulted the priest in the Daoist temple, he was told that if he had had no bad dreams or other indications that his relations' spirits were disturbed, it might be better to leave well alone.

But then the priest asked if any special funeral rites had been performed, or if Wang's relations had made any particular preparations for immortality, by learning to breathe for as long and as quietly as possible, for instance, or by gymnastic exercises to open the pores of the body. When Wang said sceptically that he had not been aware of it, the priest smiled.

"You do not believe in immortality," he said.

"Not at least of the body."

"Then not of the soul either," said the priest. "Where could these souls be if not on earth? And if on earth, they must be attached to a body, however attenuated."

"Do *you* believe in immortality?" asked Wang.

The priest made no reply, except to draw Wang's attention to an answer given by the great Song philosopher Zhu Xi—namesake but no relation of the new Emperor—when he was questioned about his insistence that the soul did not survive death. "If the dead no longer exist," he was asked, "if their personality is lost and nothing remains, what is the use of tending their graves and making offerings?" To which Zhu Xi replied, "One cannot say that they no longer exist, since something of them survives in each of their descendants. And as long as they have descendants, some trace of them remains. Descendants are like slips or cuttings of their dead ancestor. They make offerings to show their gratitude to the person that begot or bore them. He or she is dead as a separate person, but life and gratitude remain. Sometimes, if the ancestor's spirit is not immediately dissolved—if he died violently, for example—offerings and sacrifices can be helpful to him for a while. But once his being has melted into the rest of the universe, nothing of him is left to receive the offerings. I, who live today, am only an aspect of the universal Norm and Matter, of Reason and Substance, of the Sky and the Earth. My ancestor was the same. He is dead as himself, but his elements have returned to their source, have rejoined the Yin and the Yang. Since I shall myself be dissolved into that Norm and Matter, I share my substance with him. That is the end of the matter."

"And is this your own view?" asked Wang. "That all our piety to the dead is only for our own comfort?"

"Opinions expressed only in words are not very important and can easily be changed," said the priest. "It is how you live your life that reveals your true opinion—of death as much as life."

He would not be drawn any further.

"I judged that Zhu Xi's words matched your own view," he said, "and it is really your own view you are seeking, not mine."

It did seem best to Wang to leave the bodies where they were. No members of his family were still living in or near Wuxing, while Pingjiang had latterly been his father's home as well as central to his life as a literary man. Also, both his father and his wife had been particularly happy there in the last years of their lives, at least until the catastrophe of the siege. He visited the grave, saw that it was undamaged, arranged and paid for it to be tended, and thought, on the whole, that he had made the right decision.

Pingjiang itself had recovered outwardly from the siege, but it was an unhappy place. For one thing, it was being especially heavily taxed to pay for the reconstruction of poorer towns elsewhere. For another, many of its brighter spirits had been posted off to bleaker parts of the Empire, while those who remained, such as the poet Gao Chi—working as an assistant to the new Prefect of the city—knew that their actions and opinions were being closely monitored and that they were, as Gao put it, "chained bears." Wang inquired after his cousin Tao and his friend Ni and was told that, though both had been seen briefly in Pingjiang since the new Emperor's accession, neither had been given an official post. It was thought that Tao had returned to his home in the region of the small seaport called Shanghai, at the mouth of the Yangzi River, while Ni had taken to his boat again.

# 14. SHADOWS ON FRIENDS' FACES

Wang was glad to leave the despondent atmosphere of Pingjiang behind him and make his way to call on young Chen's family—his mother, elder brother, wife and newborn son—in the nearby countryside. Chen had been there recently, but was now, so far as he knew, back at his military post in Shandong. Wang looked forward to a few days of the tranquillity he always enjoyed in the company of these serious, good people, though he suspected that the presence of the young woman and the baby might have brought about some changes in their quiet way of life.

He found everything in complete confusion, with the elder Chen packing up to leave for Nanjing. News had just reached them that young Chen had been arrested. No one seemed to know what he was charged with, but he was being held in the prison of the Ministry of Punishments in Nanjing and awaiting trial. Wang immediately undertook to return to Nanjing with the elder Chen so as to visit the prisoner, if possible, but at any rate find out what offence he was supposed to have committed and work for his release.

The journey at least was relatively quick and easy, since it could be made most of the way by canal and the elder Chen anticipated no difficulty in obtaining a travel certificate from the Prefect of Pingjiang, whom he knew well. Wang had just time before they left to see the new baby and its mother—a pretty girl, but her face now distorted and red with weeping and her thoughts distracted. As for the baby, it perhaps resembled its father, as they all agreed, but Wang, who prided himself on being able to see the subtle likeness between a sapling and its parent tree, had no experience of studying babies and thought this one looked like any other.

❀

The prison governor in Nanjing received Wang and the elder Chen politely, but very much regretted that they could not both be allowed to see the prisoner. He had already been condemned to death and was now in the section for those awaiting execution. Only the closest relatives might visit him and, although in previous times, the governor would certainly have been willing to stretch a point for such an old friend of the prisoner as Wang—who was, besides, a magistrate—he evidently dared not do anything now which might suggest the slightest laxity on his own part.

It was laxity that had brought young Chen to this terrible outcome. The elder Chen, when he returned from his brother's cell, could not give an altogether clear account of what his brother had done or not done, but it appeared to be something connected with his regular task of recording the military supplies passing through Jinan on their way to the former capital Dadu, now renamed Beiping. Young Chen admitted to his brother—and had confessed to the judge—that he had been at fault, and was extraordinarily cheerful. He was occupying himself in his cell with painting, composing songs and singing them to his lute; and because of his courage and good spirits was being treated like a prince by his fellow-prisoners and even by the jailers.

"Does he have any hope of being pardoned?" asked Wang, who, after their hurried journey, had fallen asleep in the room kindly put at his disposal by the governor, and himself felt drained of both energy and hope.

"None. He expects to be publicly executed in three days' time."

The elder Chen, a man of great dignity and self-control, said this in the same quiet and reasonable way as he had spoken and acted ever since first giving Wang the news of his brother's arrest. Then he suddenly broke down and fell to his knees, sobbing and choking with despair.

"Why execution? Why execution?" he kept saying. "Why must he die for some quite minor carelessness?"

Wang comforted him as best he could and when he had sufficiently recovered, led him away from the prison, summoned chairs to carry them to the hotel where Deng and the elder Chen's servant had already taken their baggage, and persuaded him to lie down, rest and perhaps sleep.

Wang had talked vaguely and soothingly of finding some remedy, but had been careful not to specify what he meant, in case he might raise his friend's hopes too high. Now he sat down and wrote an urgent message to Hu Wei-yong, asking if "the man from the waterfalls" could see him immediately about one of the painters whose work he had in his collection and who had "fallen from his horse." He wrote somewhat cryptically, in case Hu should prefer to see him entirely privately, without bringing the matter to the attention of any of his staff.

Deng took the message to Hu's office. Wang very much regretted that he had left Kong, who would have been so helpful in this emergency, in Taian, feeling that his deputy there could hardly cope without him. Nevertheless, Deng, with money given him by Wang for the purpose, succeeded in getting his message past the doorkeepers, and returned quite soon with a reply. "The man from the waterfalls," it said, should wait a day and on the second day, at noon, come to the palace gate and give his name to the guards. If there was anything further to discuss about "the painter he admired," he would be admitted and would find Hu in the first courtyard. If not, not. It was clear that, whether or not any hope remained for young Chen, Wang had done right in not broaching the matter openly.

No day that Wang remembered ever passed so tensely and slowly as that day of waiting. He walked about the streets to see all the new building that was going on in Zhu's capital. He prayed in both a Daoist and a Buddhist temple. He spent some time in the hotel with the elder Chen, who would not go out at all, hardly speaking, reading a little, both of them separately—as intelligent, experienced men—summoning up all their resources of patience and rationality to combat their terrible sense of helpless anxiety.

Wang had told the elder Chen that he had done all he could to reach "higher authorities" and that he had not yet been definitely rejected. Every so often the elder Chen would murmur plaintively that there must be something more they could do, but he had no idea what, and Wang was sure that if Hu could not help them, no one could. He knew no one else higher in the new administration, except, of course, the Emperor himself, but one could only approach the Emperor directly through his palace officials and an unknown district magistrate claiming a long-ago acquaintance with the Son of Heaven in his days as a warlord or novice monk would be at best laughed at, at worst thrown into prison himself.

In the late afternoon the elder Chen went again to the prison, taking some choice things for his brother to eat. Wang accompanied him to the prison gates and then found a wine-shop where, hoping to get drunk, he called for a large jug of wine, but left most of it, deciding after all that he needed an especially clear head, not oblivion.

The elder Chen was more cheerful when they met again at the hotel. His younger brother had told him he had no fear of being beheaded—it was said to be a quick death, "kinder than most"—and he knew that his wife and son as well as his mother could have no one better to care for them than his brother. This reminder of his own usefulness, indeed necessity, to young Chen's brave acceptance of his fate gave courage back to the elder Chen. They had always been close, though so different in temperament and opinions, but now it was as if they would merge into one, the younger brother passing everything he cared for—his paintings, songs, wife and son—into the hands of the elder, who would continue to live for both of them.

Wang felt glad the Chens had achieved this new sense of mutual support in their relationship, but he himself became still gloomier about the prospects of his approach to Hu. What did this young, ambitious man owe to Chen or to Wang himself, except a passing interest in their paintings? Why should he risk his own career to save the life or the feelings of people he hardly knew? He would most likely do nothing at all, had never had any intention of doing anything, and merely replied to Wang out of politeness or to save his own face as a person of sensitivity, power and importance.

After a night of only intermittent sleep, which left him tired and sore-eyed, Wang breakfasted slowly, then spent the rest of the morning in a Daoist temple near the Emperor's palace, not praying this time, but trying to empty his mind and calm himself, succeeding at last in dozing a little to make up for his lack of sleep. Suddenly, in the middle of a shallow dream, in which he seemed to be searching on a heavily wooded mountain-side for a particular tree, he was woken by the bell ringing for noon. It occurred to him, still dazed as he stumbled to his feet and hurried out of the temple into the street, that he had been trying to stop them cutting the tree down and that it was the very same one which had sheltered the first Emperor and been appointed an official of the fifth rank. Since he had failed even to find the tree, let alone save it from the axe, Wang took this dream as a bad omen and was resigned to being told at the gate of the palace that there was no message for him.

But when he arrived, breathless and flushed—it was warm, very humid weather—and gave his name to the guards, he was told to cross the first courtyard and wait near the large Meridian Gate leading through to the second courtyard. There he stood for perhaps an hour with his back to the gate, looking out for Hu among the crowd of officials from the various ministries who were crossing and re-crossing the courtyard. A few of these people went past him on their way to or from the second courtyard, where the highest officials had their offices, and glanced at him curiously, since everyone else was either walking swiftly or pausing briefly in conversation. He was the only person loitering there without either companions or apparent purpose. Suddenly he heard his name called from behind.

"District Magistrate Wang Meng?"

Wang turned and saw a young military officer, who had approached through the Meridian Gate from the second courtyard.

"Yes."

"Follow me, please!"

❁

Unlike many of the palace buildings, which were newly constructed since Zhu's accession, the Imperial Garden had been laid out some years before and already looked well established. A meandering stream dropped over an artificial waterfall into a half-moon-shaped lake, separated into two unequal segments by a tongue of land, on which stood a small circular pavilion, painted vermilion and gold. The water ran out of the lake into another narrower, deeper and straighter channel, flanked with young peach-trees.

Wang followed the military officer over a humped bridge across this stream and then along a path beside it, towards the lake. There were green mounds, clumps of bamboo, curious formations of limestone rock brought from Lake Tai, willows growing along the edge of the lake, pavilions in various shapes and sizes, and even some mature pine-trees. The garden had no doubt been adapted and expanded from an earlier one, perhaps belonging to a temple or some rich official.

They were apparently alone in the garden, until coming nearer to the central pavilion they could see someone sitting inside it at a low writing-table. A zig-zag bridge in three spans, also painted vermilion and gold, crossed the water—carpeted with yellow lotus flowers—to the pavilion.

As they reached this bridge, the young officer halted and without speaking indicated that Wang should stand beside him. They remained there, silent and motionless, facing the pavilion, until the person inside it raised his head and looked in their direction. Immediately the officer went down on his knees and bowed his forehead three times to the ground. Wang did the same. They both rose to their feet and were about to repeat the *kow-tow* for the second and third time, as ritual demanded, when Zhu, whose long asymmetrical face was recognisable even at this distance, raised his hand to prevent them, then nodded. The officer gently propelled Wang on to the bridge in front of him and, with a hand on his shoulder, urged him forward until they reached the middle of the bridge. Here they stopped again, while Zhu, with the penetrating stare Wang remembered so well, carefully surveyed Wang's face. Understanding that this was a precaution, in case he might not be the person he claimed to be, Wang did not look away or lower his eyes. Zhu nodded again and the officer urged Wang forward, but this time, instead of following him, withdrew to the shore they had just left. At the end of the bridge, where a small slope of turf led up to the pavilion, Wang prostrated himself again.

"Sit here!" said Zhu, indicating a low stool in front of his table.

He wore a yellow robe of the finest silk, embroidered with large, circular, fiery-dragon designs on the chest, back and shoulders. On his head was a plain black four-cornered cap, of the kind he had ordered all his subjects to wear. His coarse-skinned face had filled out since Wang had last seen him at close quarters, and he had grown a bushy moustache, which covered his top lip and curled jauntily downwards and outwards on either side. A sparse beard partly covered his misshapen jaw and descended in a thin veil from his chin. There were many small lines at the corners of his eyes and heavy bags of flesh under them. He looked tired and pallid, not very healthy.

A silence followed, after Wang had sat down, while they studied each other and no doubt both shared the thought in Wang's mind: can we really be the same people as those two who met in the mountain monastery and viewed the waterfalls? Zhu smiled.

"We are pleased with your work in Taian," he said, loosely rolling the sheet of paper he had been writing on and tying it with a vermilion ribbon.

"Thank you, Sir."

"'The Ten Thousand Things are only Mind.' Do you recall our conversation on that topic?"

"Not entirely, Sir. It is a Chan Buddhist maxim, I think."

"I remember very clearly that when I asked you if the mind could alter the world, you replied that it might in exceptional cases, and you cited Khan Khublai's seizure of the Empire."

"I believe I did."

Wang was surprised by the change in Zhu's manner. The fiercely attentive boy of their first meeting had become at their second meeting the charismatic warlord, equally fiercely concentrated on victory, at a time when it was by no means in his grasp. Now he spoke more like a scholar, though without in any way relinquishing that sense of driving, dangerous intensity which, when they stood together on the precipice above the waterfall, had made Wang feel afraid of him.

"We are altering the world now. Would you agree?"

"You have already altered it, Sir. Almost beyond recognition."

"For the better?"

Did this man need flattery? Did he expect anything else?

"Entirely for the better," said Wang.

"That's not my opinion. Nothing is so straightforward. Any alteration, whether in nature or human affairs, causes pain, infinite pain, for those that make it, as well as those that experience it."

Wang remembered his father's remark just before he died, when they were discussing Old Huang's teachings: "We don't want too many great men . . . they make life uncomfortable for everyone else."

"But once begun," continued Zhu, "there is no going back. This is a beautiful garden . . ."

He paused, as if Wang might disagree.

"Most beautiful. I am privileged to see it."

"It was beautiful before, though in a simpler way, and badly neglected. I consulted experts and we planned an almost complete renewal. Then the whole place turned into a battlefield. Plants, paths, bridges, pavilions were torn up, swept away, thrown on the fire. I sat in my room in the palace, hardly able to bear looking out at all this destruction and waste. What had I done? If only I could cancel my instructions! But this, after all, is what I had done and now, as often as I can, I work here in the middle of it. Its peacefulness and order, which began as an idea in my mind, now help to calm my frequently disordered mind."

"It was not you who made the Empire a battlefield," said Wang. "But it was you who finished the battles and brought peace and order to us all."

This conversation, he thought, was as unequal and unfruitful as their first one in the monastery, though the other way round. It was not that their minds were necessarily incompatible—in other circumstances they might have found many interesting ideas to pursue—but that their fates were. They were like two men tied back to back, never able to look at the same thing from the same point at the same time.

The Emperor did not reply, had not perhaps really listened to Wang's soothing words, accustomed as he must have been to hearing everyone speak to him as superficially as possible. He was looking up at the sky, which had been overclouded all day and was now darkening to the south.

"A storm?" he asked, in a plaintive, anxious tone which immediately reminded Wang of the uncertain boy he had first met.

"It has been hot and humid all day," said Wang, "and I think it may rain."

There was a distant rumble of thunder and Zhu pushed back his chair and stood up. Wang, never having been alone in the presence of a Son of Heaven, was unsure whether to kneel or stand, but chose to stand.

"We must go in," said Zhu, his voice strained, almost as if he were afraid. "Bring the paper!" he said, striding rapidly out of the pavilion and down the slope to the bridge.

Wang picked up to the roll tied with vermilion ribbon and hurried to catch up to the bulky figure in its shining yellow robe, now on the bridge.

"What is the meaning of thunder? Do you have any knowledge of such things?" said Zhu over his shoulder as he turned on to the middle span of the zig-zag bridge.

"No special knowledge, I'm afraid," said Wang. "The Daoists say it expresses the relationship between Heaven and ourselves."

"In what way? Displeasure on Heaven's part? Anger?"

"Not necessarily anger," said Wang.

There was another, louder rumble of thunder. Wang was astonished to see the figure in front of him start and shiver, the shoulders rising to absorb the neck. Irreverently, he thought of a frightened tortoise.

"It sounds like anger," said Zhu.

"Heaven's voice would surely sound loud and startling to such small creatures as ourselves, whatever its mood, whatever it wished to say to us?"

Zhu stopped on the third span of the bridge and looked sideways at Wang, still on the central span.

"That is a good point," he said. "But how are we to tell, then, what it wishes to say?"

"There are no doubt many signs accompanying it, subtleties of sound and perhaps visual ones too, which can be interpreted by experts."

"Who would you recommend?"

"I have never discussed this matter with anyone. But there is a Daoist priest in Taian whose learning and wisdom I very much respect."

"We will send for him," said Zhu, sounding relieved.

The whole sky was black now and a wind had got up as he stepped off the bridge, ignoring the young officer, who had prostrated himself at the Emperor's approach, and walked along the path towards the palace. Wang followed immediately behind and the officer behind him.

Lightning flashed and thunder exploded directly above them. The Emperor started and shivered again, then stopped suddenly and turned right round to face Wang, who almost banged into him. Their bodies were only a foot apart, as large drops of rain began to fall. Wang took a step back and put the paper he was carrying inside his sleeve.

"We have made you a magistrate."

"It is a great honour, Sir."

"So you should be able to understand in a small way the pain we feel every day, here!"

He slapped the dragon design on his chest.

"Here!" he repeated, again with the same histrionic gesture. "For what one has to do when altering the world. Are you a tyrant to your people? To some thousands of people in your District of Taian? Possibly not. Even when you refused my anguished request at the monastery, you did so as kindly as you could."

The rain was now seriously wetting them, as it had on that distant occasion. But the thunder had moved away and the Emperor seemed oblivious to everything but his own urgent thoughts.

"Am I a tyrant? What else can I be if I want to unite and pacify six times ten million angry, unhappy, divided, unsettled people, who have lost all memory of good government?"

His fierce eyes blinking away the rain, Zhu stared at Wang as if he hated him, then turned and walked quickly away towards the palace. Wang and the officer followed. As they came to the bend in the path where the humped bridge crossed the stream, Zhu, with a brief valedictory wave of the hand, took another path leading straight to a terrace and the Emperor's own quarters, and began to ascend four or five long, shallow steps. Wang remembered the paper with the vermilion ribbon which he had been holding inside his sleeve.

"Your paper, Sir!" he called out, following Zhu to the foot of the steps.

"It's for you."

"And my friend Chen . . . ?"

His name had never been mentioned, nothing had been said to suggest that this was why the Emperor had given Wang a private interview, yet surely most of the conversation had drifted mistily around his case? It was crude, perhaps even foolhardy to mention his name if Zhu had deliberately avoided it. But how could Wang allow this last moment to pass, if there was the slightest chance that he might save Chen's life? The Emperor, his robe now dark with the rain that had soaked into it, paused on the top step, seemed to breathe deeply, and turned round in a rage as sudden as the storm.

"Your friend Chen was disloyal to his former master, the bandit Zhang. We overlooked his disloyalty, since it brought some small benefit to ourselves, but that was foolish. There is nothing worse than disloyalty and no point in forgiving it. It is not a single error of conduct—not a chance blot on a piece of paper—but part of the character—a tincture in the paper itself."

Wang went down on his knees.

"I do believe this was only carelessness," he said.

"*Only* carelessness?"

Zhu's face was red, his fists clenched, he stamped one foot and came down two steps, as if he contemplated physically assaulting, perhaps kicking Wang where he knelt. Then he paused, wiped his wet flushed face with his sleeve and said in a quieter tone:

"Carelessness *is* disloyalty—an insidious form of it. Carelessness has undermined every dynasty in history. If you commit it yourself, Wang Meng, or forgive it in your subordinates, you will lose your own head."

He turned and remounted the steps, half turned again.

"Send me the name of your Daoist priest!"

Then he went inside the palace.

Wang was conducted by the young officer across the humped bridge and out of the garden by the small side gate from which they had originally entered it. Returning through the three courtyards to the main gate, he made his way as quickly as he could back to the hotel to change his damp clothes. When he took Zhu's paper out of his sleeve and undid the ribbon, he saw that the characters, written in the vermilion ink reserved for the Emperor alone, were clumsily but clearly drawn, though slightly smudged here and there by the rain. They gave Wang permission to visit the prisoner Chen Ju-yen on the day before his execution.

❁

Before returning to Taian at the expiry of his leave of absence, Wang stayed with a Daoist painter, a close follower of Old Huang, in a village near Nanjing. In return for Ma Wan's hospitality, Wang offered to paint a scroll for him and asked what subject he should choose.

"Have you ever painted a Land of the Immortals?" asked Ma Wan.

"No," said Wang, his eyes filling with tears, as they increasingly did whenever his emotions were stirred.

"I'm sorry that upsets you," said Ma Wan. "I thought it was the least sad subject one could choose."

"I will do it with pleasure," said Wang. "Of course it's not a sad subject in itself, but the last painting I saw of it was by Chen Ju-yen. I'm afraid at our age even the least sad subjects are tangled up with bitter memories."

As he sat in Ma Wan's library and worked on the hand-scroll—using colours, as he usually did now—Wang found that his picture of paradise owed much to the Imperial Garden. The Emperor's peach-tree stream, his lake, his zig-zag bridge, his pavilions, especially the small circular one where Zhu had been sitting, all made their appearance, though the green hillocks grew into real hills, and mountains rose behind, instead of the garden's high walls. It was not a map of the garden, but a dream of it, a rearrangement.

He had thought often of that last interview with Zhu. It was almost certainly the last—though, lying in prison himself many years later, Wang continued to hope that Zhu might grant him another, so that he could prove his innocence of any conspiracy. But evidently Zhu had intended that meeting in the Imperial Garden to be their last, to overlay and cancel for good the memory of their first meeting, which probably still troubled him.

Everything suggested meticulous preparation on Zhu's part, the deliberate contrivance of a cluster of references and parallels. There was the outdoor setting within view of the artificial waterfall; the paper written in the Emperor's own awkward hand, echoing the paper Wang had given to the boy Zhu, urging him to learn to read from it; the mention of Wang's refusal of Zhu's "anguished request" to take him away from the monastery as his servant, when on this occasion it was Zhu who was refusing Wang's equally anguished plea for young Chen's life; and the touch of compassion in Wang's permit to see Chen for the last time, reflecting Wang's own "kindly" refusal.

The very fact that there was no one else present in the garden except the officer, who had clearly been told exactly how to present Wang and to remain almost as if invisible on the far side of the bridge, when surely in normal circumstances the Emperor would never receive anyone alone, without guards in close attendance—this argued a unique, prepared performance, not just an episode in the Emperor's working day. Wang wondered whether, even if Zhu habitually worked in his garden as he claimed, he ever conducted any other interview there. Only the storm could not have been planned, especially not the thunder which so painfully exposed Zhu's peasant fear of natural phenomena. Yet the rain that soaked them, just as it had at their first meeting, surely would have been included in the plan if Zhu had had the power to command it.

How long would the interview have continued if there had been no storm? Sometimes Wang felt with a sharp twinge of regret that, but for the thunder, they might have reached a point in the conversation where Zhu could have relented, could have allowed himself to be persuaded that he might spare this one life without jeopardising his control of the Empire. But no—the permit to see Chen before his execution had already been written. Zhu had made his decision and designed the meeting around that decision. Nothing Wang could have said would have made any difference, however long the interview lasted, and, if the storm had not intervened, Zhu had no doubt already planned when and how to bring it to a close.

Wang did not discuss all this with young Chen when he saw him in prison that same evening, but merely said that he had been granted an interview with the Emperor and failed to change his mind. He did, however, tell Chen, who was still facing his imminent death without any sign of fear, about Zhu's terror of thunder.

"He's known to be very superstitious," said Chen. "On one occasion it saved his life. He was about to enter one of the gates of Nanjing at the head of his regiments, after a day of military manoeuvres outside the city, when the wind suddenly wrapped his commander's banner round his body like a shroud. He immediately turned back and entered by a different gate, frustrating a plot to kill him by two rebellious generals. They were waiting for him with their troops just inside the original gate and intended, the moment he entered, to slam the gate shut between him and his soldiers and have him at their mercy. That's the story, anyway, put about perhaps to deter any more conspiracies. Heaven protects him, it seems. Pity he didn't take the thunder this afternoon as a sign that Heaven wanted to protect *me*!"

Wang could hardly believe that someone in Chen's situation, manacled to the wall of a miserably small, dark and dirty cell, his neck locked into a heavy wooden rack, facing execution soon after noon the next day, could speak so lightly and coolly.

"Zhu accused you of disloyalty," he said. "Surely that can't be true?"

"Not disloyal, but foolish," said Chen. "And he—or his advisers—gave me the wrong job. I'm good at liaison, at running a general's headquarters, at dealing with people. But they made me a sort of quartermaster, responsible not for people, but for stores and numbers. Perhaps they did that deliberately, owing me something for my betrayal of Zhang, but uneasy about it, because of Zhu's particular obsession with disloyalty."

"I never quite understood what your job was."

"It was very sensitive. When they first gave it to me, I was surprised and flattered by its importance. The Mongols are still trying to recover their lost Empire, of course, and the greatest threat to Zhu's survival is that northern border. That's why he keeps his largest army and his best general, Xu Ta, permanently in Dadu—Beiping, as it is now. But they have to be supplied—with grain, with horses, with arms, with virtually everything—from the south.

"Some of those supplies go by sea, but much goes overland and passes through the military base at Jinan. And because most of the Grand Canal north of the Yangzi is unusable, it's a difficult and complicated route. Large barges carry the supplies along a series of lakes past the Huai River. Then they're transferred to shallow barges for the silted-up stretch across the south-eastern corner of Shandong, then back to large barges again through the lakes immediately south of the Yellow River, then into carts as far as the Wei River, then into barges again to Beiping. Plenty of scope, you see, every time the supplies are loaded and unloaded from one form of transport to another, for cheating and stealing.

"One of my tasks was to check what arrived in Jinan against the bills of lading prepared when the goods left their source-points. If there was any discrepancy, I started an investigation and, in any case, I forwarded my own record of what arrived, together with the original bills of lading, to Beiping, so that both could be checked against the actual supplies that finally reached Xu Ta's army. I went to a lot of trouble to start with, even riding out to some of the change-over points to make spot checks and show my superiors how conscientious I was. And in fact that whole system was working very smoothly and we were getting remarkably few losses."

"So how could you be accused of carelessness?"

"Just because it was going so well, I was getting very bored with filling in the records with correct quantities. And I wanted to come south to see my new son—this was soon after we made that winter painting of Mount Tai. So I went to the General in Jinan and asked for a month or two's special leave. He said that I'd already had special leave to get married and this time it wasn't possible. No one below my rank was allowed to sign and stamp the records, and no one else of my rank was currently available. I told him my deputy was perfectly competent to check the supplies—he regularly did so, under my eye, though I did the signing and stamping. Well, I'm good with generals, as you know, and this one reluctantly agreed to my idiotic suggestion."

"Which was?"

"That I would sign and stamp a batch of blank records and leave my deputy to fill in the figures as the supplies came through."

"And the man cheated?"

"No. He was completely trustworthy, or I would never have thought of doing such a thing. Poor man, that's really what upsets me most. He was entirely innocent and he only did what I told him to do."

Chen shifted as best he could inside his rack, momentarily closed his eyes and clenched his lips.

"While I was away," he said, "the Inspectorate came in, turned over my office, saw that the blank records were already signed and stamped and immediately asked my deputy what this meant. He could only think of saying that he knew nothing about them and that I must have been intending to use them when I came back from leave. Then they confronted the General. He, of course, had to deny having given me permission to leave, or he would have been implicated too. Then, the moment I returned, they confronted me. What could I do but tell most of the truth?"

"Most of it?"

"They flogged me, of course, to find out if there was more, but how could I say that the General knew I was absent? It was my suggestion. He agreed only out of fatherly kindness to me."

"Was it just bad luck that the Inspectorate chose to swoop when you were away? Or a deliberate trap?"

"Ironically enough, it was because there seemed to be so little fraud or theft. They were suspicious. And their suspicion proved justified, even though it actually wasn't."

"And you are the only one to suffer?"

"If only I were! The General was demoted and sent to the Manchurian border. My deputy was flogged, branded on the face and exiled. All by my foolish impatience to see my wife and son. If I'd waited for the warmer weather, they could have travelled to Jinan to see me."

Chen's cheerfulness suddenly evaporated and he looked silently at the floor. Wang laid his hand on Chen's manacled wrist.

"It occurs to me," he said, "that but for your brave and scrupulous refusal to implicate them, both the General and your deputy would have suffered far worse."

"When I feel like this," said Chen, "I generally play my lute."

"How can you?"

"Up to now the jailers have left me free. I've been able to sing and even paint and still consider myself a human being. But this being the last night, they're afraid I might somehow cheat the public by killing myself."

"Everyone in the prison, from the governor down, admires your courage. When I showed my permit in the Emperor's own handwriting, they smiled with pleasure and brought me here as if I were coming to visit the Emperor himself."

"I always thought my paintings owed too much to other people's," said Chen. "But there's some value in imitation, after all. My model is Xi Kang, the great poet and musician of the Three Kingdoms period. When my brother and I were young, my father often read Xi Kang's Daoist writings to us and taught us to sing his songs. Xi was a very passionate and outspoken man, and when the Empire was briefly united again under the Qin Emperor, he was rude to some important friend of the Emperor and imprisoned on a false charge of conspiracy. That made him very angry and although he'd previously written that one should have nothing to do with politics, ignore all moral systems, whether bad or good, and attune oneself only to nature, so as to be free of lies and compromises—"he who does not value life is best able to appreciate it," he said—he wrote a farewell poem called "Black Vexation." But he rode on the cart to his execution at sunset playing his lute and observing the evening shadows on his friends' faces. That story went to my heart and has always fascinated me. Was it possible for anyone to die as well as that? I never dreamed that one day I would be forced to find out."

"It's strange," said Wang, "how certain stories mean so much to certain people. Do you think we have some secret instinct about our fate? Perhaps it's always connected with what we most admire or fear."

"Do you know how old Xi Kang was when he died?"

"Not very old, I think."

"Thirty-nine. And so am I."

Chen raised one chained hand with some difficulty to rub his neck where the rack was chafing it.

"But the difference is," he said, "that his sentence was entirely undeserved. Mine is not, though it may be harsh. I took a silly risk with those records and I have ruined the lives of two other innocent people. Unlike Xi Kang, I have no right to feel aggrieved. The question now is whether I can carry off the execution as well as he did. I can't calm my mind by watching the shadows, since there won't be any at noon, but I hope there may be some wind and I shall watch the effects of that. I certainly intend to play my lute, if they will let me. If not, I shall have to make do with singing unaccompanied."

❀

There was no wind the next day. The sun shone from an almost cloudless sky. Surrounded by solders, Chen and two other condemned men were brought on foot to the market-place nearest the prison, which had been set aside for the executions. All three had their hands tied behind their backs and racks on their necks. They were naked except for loin-cloths and their hair had been smeared with sticky paste, twisted up on top of their heads in a cone and pinned through with a red artificial flower.

As they came, one in front of the other, with Chen at the front, he was indeed singing—a song of his own composition, praising his hero Xi Kang's example and making his own farewell to life and those he loved. Wang, standing in a reserved place with the elder Chen, the prison governor and a few officials from the Ministry of Punishments, could hardly hear the words at the time, but read them afterwards in a copy Chen had left for his brother.

Most of the people in the huge crowd which had assembled, held back from the central area by hundreds of soldiers, already knew Chen's story, while those that didn't soon heard it from their neighbours. They had come to see heads chopped off and were looking forward to it, but many were also full of pity for such a good-looking man, who had only recently become a father, whose mother was still alive to bury him.

His singing changed the whole nature of the occasion, from a piece of macabre theatre with real blood to an act of spectacular courage, which touched their soft hearts instead of their coarse appetites for horror and cruelty. The two criminals walking behind Chen—an office-clerk who had killed his nagging wife and a boatman who had regularly robbed his passengers—had begun by shambling along with their heads bowed, but as Chen began to sing in his light but strong and well-trained voice, and the thousands of raucous people in the square fell quite silent to hear him, these fellow-victims raised their heads and seemed to walk more firmly and proudly.

When the procession reached the central area, it was still not quite three quarters past noon, so the three condemned men were made to sit on the ground, each in front of a sloping board, with their executioners standing behind them. The Prefect of the city, supervising the executions, sat on his horse facing them. Chen had stopped singing and was looking about, perhaps for his elder brother and old friend. Perhaps he even hoped by some miracle to see his wife and child, but there had been no time to arrange for them to come, and it was surely better they had not.

Wang and the elder Chen fought to remain dry-eyed—though many of the women in the crowd were now sobbing and groaning—in case Chen should see them and break down himself. What, they wondered, in the absence of wind as well as shadows, could Chen fix his thoughts on? He did seem to catch sight of his brother and Wang and smiled briefly, but then tilted back his head and was evidently contemplating the three small white clouds and the hazy grey-blue sky to the west, where lay, according to legend, the land of the immortals.

An officer stepped forward and called out in a loud voice:

"Three quarters past noon!"

Two soldiers to each prisoner immediately took the racks off their necks, then, making them lie face-down on the boards in front, sat on their backs and feet to prevent them moving. The three executioners, holding long, slightly curved swords across their chests, moved forward to stand beside each prisoner's head. The Prefect sat up very straight on his horse and gave the order:

"Decapitate them!"

The executioners swung their swords and struck. Chen's head was severed immediately, as was the boatman's, but the clerk who had killed his wife flinched sideways in terror as the sword descended and a second blow was needed.

❁

Wang was not wholly satisfied with his scroll of *The Land of the Immortals*. It was too earthly. The reality of the Imperial Garden had pushed out what he had really meant to express: the vision of a world transcending this one, which the Daoist adept Xi Kang had perhaps succeeded in entering as he observed the sunset shadows on his friends' faces, and which Chen must have been searching for as he stared over the crowd beyond the roof-tops at the transparent sky.

Hoping to convey more of what he intended, Wang added a poem to his painting:

*A thousand peaceful mountain-tops,*
*A crane's cry through the nine heavens,*
*Echoed by the cliffs and valleys.*
*A heavenly breeze brushes the pines*
*With the clear sound of lute-strings.*
*The sun's rays dart into your eyes,*
*Staring up towards the high terraces,*
*The bright houses of immortals . . . .*
*Shouldn't one shake one's sleeve at this world*
*And learn to travel to those pure places,*
*Those distant streams and mountain-tops,*
*Through endless time . . . ?*

# 15. PASSING TIME AND ENDLESS TIME

CHEN'S HEAD WAS ONE OF THE FIRST TO FALL. BUT DURING THE decade following Zhu's accession, many of the leading intellectuals from Pingjiang lost theirs too, either for supposed inefficiency or for allegedly conspiring against the state. The Prefect of Pingjiang was executed for sedition and hundreds died in his wake, including the poet Gao Chi. His close friend, the painter Xu Ben, who had been given a junior administrative post in another province, was accused of incompetence and, while awaiting execution, starved himself to death in prison.

Another painter who, like Chen, had been a military adviser to one of Zhang's generals, was summoned to Nanjing and, although he was primarily a landscape painter, ordered to paint portraits of famous historical figures to decorate the Emperor's public rooms. How did this come about? Zhao Yüan—that was the artist's name—had happened to paint an imaginary portrait of the great Tang expert on tea, author of a book called *The Tea Classic*. The portrait showed this famous connoisseur sitting in his pavilion beside a river, while a servant boiled the water. There was nothing very remarkable about it. Zhao Yüan had done it only because someone asked him to, and had not attached much importance to it himself. However, when the Emperor asked his closest advisers to name a suitable artist for his purpose, one of them remembered hearing about this painting and Zhao Yüan was commissioned. He did the best he could, but the Emperor disliked his work and had him beheaded.

No one could feel safe. Ni Zan, a particular friend of this unlucky artist, took his habitual evasive action by living on his boat and ignoring all attempts to summon him to Nanjing to be interviewed for administrative office, just as he had under both Zhang and the Mongols. This time, however, with the Empire so tightly controlled and every official nervous of being seen to be lax, Ni was arrested and held in prison. The charge was a purely nominal one of not having any proper home address or the correct travel papers. Meanwhile, the local magistrate, who knew very well who Ni was and was much embarrassed by his arrest—afraid he might have friends in high places—applied to his provincial superiors for advice. They applied in turn to the central government in Nanjing and Hu Wei-yong, who seemed to be the one administrator enjoying the Emperor's complete confidence—or at any rate brave and arrogant enough to act as if he did—immediately ordered Ni's release.

Wang was on leave again after another three years' service in Taian, and heard that Ni was recovering from his ordeal at a friend's home not far from Pingjiang. He went there at once and found Ni physically much aged—he was now over seventy—overweight and somewhat breathless, but undaunted in spirit.

"It's not easy to maintain one's standards in prison," Ni said. "The conditions are bad and one lacks the authority to change them or the freedom to go somewhere else, which have always been my two alternative ways of dealing with life in general and humanity in particular. I was in a large cell with a great many other unfortunates and did my best to keep myself to myself in one corner and try to live wholly in my mind. But when I saw that the jailer bringing my food had a miserable habit of talking loudly to everyone in the cell and that every time he opened his mouth he showered spit all over my food, I had to remonstrate."

"Was he doing it deliberately?"

"No, he was just stupid and insensitive and his tongue was too big for his mouth. I asked him—quite politely, considering how disgusted I was—if he would either keep his mouth shut while bringing me my food or, if that was impossible, hold the bowl a bit higher—at least as high as his eyebrows."

"Did he agree to that?"

Wang could not help smiling, though Ni, as always, spoke with the utmost seriousness, as if the idea of a prisoner asking a jailer to carry his food at eyebrow-level was completely reasonable.

"On the contrary. He began to shout abuse, covering me with spit, and when I wiped my face with my sleeve and turned away, he became angrier still and chained me to the bucket where everybody peed and shat. Can you imagine that?"

"Only too well."

"I was violently sick, choking and gasping for breath. The man was afraid I would die and he would be blamed, so he unchained me. Is it just my personal impression or were we better off under the Mongols?"

The country retreat where they were staying was at the foot of the West Mountain, the large island in the middle of Lake Tai. The water had carved inlets through the soft limestone, giving the rocks strange shapes, pitting them with circular holes, forming caves and arches. Ji-zhang, the owner of this retreat, had perched his houses and pavilions like birds' nests on the skirts of the mountain, where broad-leaved trees grew from small plateaus of earth. Paths followed the inlets and led up steps to the various buildings. The whole place, which could be reached only by boat, was like the fantastic kingdom of some god of the lake.

Within the buildings, however, everything was as normal and comfortable as in any civilised man's place of retirement. Excellent food and fine wines were served, though it was wise not to drink too heavily or frequently, since one might so easily, when returning from the main group of buildings to one's own guest-room, slide down a flight of steep steps, or topple off the path into a creek, or hit one's head on an obtrusive boulder.

While Ni was staying there, many of his friends from Pingjiang and its neighbourhood who had heard of his imprisonment and release, made the boat-trip to see him. One of these was a man even older than Ni himself, for whom Ni had painted a landscape two years earlier. He brought the painting with him, since he now wanted to give it to a doctor he knew and hoped that Ni would make the gift even more acceptable by writing a fresh dedication on it.

Wang would not have been at all surprised if Ni had reacted badly to this request. It meant, after all, adding more writing to the empty sky, which occupied one third of the picture, and thereby disturbing its subtle balance of space and incident. But Ni made no objection and wrote a long and graceful dedication to the unknown doctor, who happened to live in Ni's home-town, hoping that they would one day meet and, with cups of wine in hand, hang up the scroll together in the doctor's house. The previously empty sky was almost filled with Ni's sharp black characters, vigorously contrasting with the soft contours and long flowing lines of his austere landscape.

"You've been very generous to this person you've never met," said Wang.

"I fully expect to meet him," said Ni. "I'm getting much too old to live on a boat and my boatman is getting too old to pole it. It's time I went home and settled down with my relations—and I shall certainly need a good doctor."

"He is getting one of your very best works," said Wang. "I too have been feeling my age and have been trying to study and practise Daoist detachment—with very little success. I'm afraid I shall never be ready to make the journey into the distance. But looking at this painting, I can feel what it might be like to make it."

"It always astonishes me," said Ni, "that you can find anything to enjoy in my awkward pictures."

"I am not the only one, after all," said Wang. "Even that busy, ambitious man Hu Wei-yong must have some corner of his mind that relishes calm and emptiness."

"It doesn't interest me at all," said Ni, "what people like Hu think of my work."

"It was surely due to him that you were let out of prison?"

"Yes, of course, but has the human world turned so evil that we must be grateful to people for letting us out of prison, when we should never have been in there in the first place? Yes, I suppose we must. When a bandit becomes Emperor, all values are reversed."

They were alone in their host's studio, a pavilion built out from the foot of the cliff on piles, over the edge of an inlet. Ni's painting had been hung there for them to look at before its owner took it away to present to the doctor. But even though he knew they were alone, Wang felt uneasy at Ni's words. These days one tried not even to think such a thought, let alone express it aloud. And, as a matter of fact, they were not alone. A servant stood in one corner waiting to fill their wine-cups.

"You should be more careful what you say," said Wang.

"Or they will chain me to the shit-bucket again. But, you see, my dear friend, that is exactly the lesson I have always taken from life. Shit-buckets are everywhere, but if you are afraid of being chained to them, then you *are* already chained to them."

"I'm afraid that is my case," said Wang, "and the reason I so much envy your detachment."

"There's nothing much to it," said Ni. "I did study for a time with the Daoists, I did the breathing exercises and the gymnastics. I gathered the medicinal herbs and made the concoctions and drank them. I even tried the group sex, a more exciting form of escaping from one's earthly ties, which some of them recommend. All these things are effective in their way. You begin to feel that you are floating away from passing time into endless time. Emperors and shit-buckets are all one when you reach this state—and that's very refreshing, of course. But it's entirely superfluous, wouldn't you agree?"

"Would I?"

Wang waved his empty cup in the air and the servant came and filled it and then, walking round the broad low couch on which they were reclining side by side, propped on pillows, filled Ni's cup.

"I am by nature detached," said Ni. "Always have been, cannot be otherwise. You are the opposite, by nature *at*tached. Your mountains are right in your face, your trees are tangible, your pictures are full of houses and people. I like your pictures so much because I can have all that attachment without having to scramble up the cliffs or bump into the trees or get involved with the people. You like mine because you think you'd really prefer to be *de*tached. And yes, in a way you *are* detached and I am *at*tached—to friends like you, for example. So how real are these distinctions we make? And are they any more real than the distinction between passing time and endless time? Isn't time always passing and always endless? We lie here listening to the rain rustling the thatch, the servant fills your cup, walks round the bed and fills mine, and goes back to his place in the corner, and that incident might be taken as a typical fragment of passing time. Even if it were repeated identically several times it could not be repeated endlessly. The wine would run out, the servant fall down from exhaustion, the rain stop, you and I grow even older and die.

"But consider it more carefully—this trivial incident involving Wang and Ni and a servant in a pavilion wetted by rain under the West Mountain in the fifth year of the first Ming bandit's reign—no, don't twitch like that! I meant to say 'Emperor's'—and how can you separate it from endless time? All I am saying is that you do not have to go to Daoists or Buddhists to learn to be detached from this world. You *are* detached from it whenever you think about it, and attached to it whenever you don't. And when you withdraw into your mind, you are in endless time, and when you do not, you are in passing time."

"What of this painting of yours?" asked Wang. "Does it belong to passing time or to endless time?"

"Obviously, when I was making it, I went to and fro between both, physically active in passing time, mentally afloat in endless time. And so do you when you're looking at it—entering endless time as you imagine yourself drifting through its illusion of space, returning abruptly to passing time if you begin to be curious about its technique or if some personal pain or appetite intrudes, or someone interrupts your thoughts."

"And the picture itself?"

"The picture itself," said Ni, "can only belong to passing time, since it has no mind of its own."

"But it expresses the mind of its painter," said Wang. "No one would be much interested in looking at it if it didn't."

"The expression, however, limits it to passing time, since it has been fixed once and for all by the brush and ink. Only a living mind can experience endless time. The painting may remind the person looking at it that the artist once, while painting it, entered endless time. The painting may even stimulate the viewer to experience endless time himself, but, like all inanimate things, it belongs to passing time."

"So neither our living bodies nor our art can enter endless time? In fact, we can only experience endless time while we are alive in passing time?"

"This is my paradoxical conclusion," said Ni, holding up his cup for the servant to fill again. "But why really should we wish to experience endless time endlessly? A little of it goes a long way, as you can see from this painting of mine. It's only a more mature and better executed version of all the others I've done before and frankly it would bore me to go on doing this for many years more."

"You've reached perfection?"

"I've reached my own limits. I have no more to say or no way of saying it."

They lay in silence, their bodies not quite touching, their minds perhaps as nearly touching as two minds can, listening to the gentle rain and the lapping of the lake water on the rocky shore of the inlet directly below them.

Suddenly they both spoke at the same time; then both simultaneously begged the other to speak first; then both refused to speak before the other; then both shut their mouths tight and shook their heads; then both began to laugh.

"You are the elder," said Wang, "and should speak first."

"I am the elder," said Ni, "and insist that you speak first."

"I was only thinking," said Wang, "of our first meeting in that inn by the river . . ."

"When we reluctantly shared a room," said Ni. "I was thinking exactly the same."

"You were more reluctant than I was," said Wang.

"I thought you were some paltry official."

"So I was—or had been—and indeed still am."

"How could I know that you were the better artist?" said Ni.

"No one would agree with that—least of all myself."

"I am better known than you are, but what does that mean? I only wished to say, in case this should be my last opportunity, that if anyone ever asks you who Ni Zan admired even more than himself, you can tell them it was Wang Meng. You borrowed nothing from me, I borrowed nothing from you. But perhaps we both saw our own work more clearly in the light of the other's."

Ni waved his cup and the servant filled it.

"I drink," he said, "to the noble and heroic Wang, the master painter of our time!"

"And I drink to Ni Zan," said Wang, "most generous, most modest, bravest and most perfectly himself of all the masters I ever heard of!"

Towards evening, when their host, alerted by the servant, came to look for them, he found them fast asleep, Ni on his back with his mouth open, snoring loudly, Wang fallen sideways with his head on Ni's chest. Their empty cups had rolled on to the floor.

❀

The next day Ni's old deaf-and-dumb boatman poled him slowly away to stay with another friend on the far side of the lake. There was never any shortage of people eager to entertain this man who painted landscapes empty of people.

The painting Wang made for his host, after Ni had left, was in the first instance an attempt to portray the strangeness of the place. No sky was visible, only rocks, water and trees, with the host seated in his studio and, a little higher up the cliff, his wife in her own pavilion. The main compound, with two servants at work, was visible on the far left. The trees were bright with their autumn colours—red, yellow and green—the water was hatched in little pointed waves to suggest the autumn wind, and the rocks were whorled and twisted, almost as if they too were swaying in the wind. The colours of the trees, however, and the yellow-brown pillars and balustrades of the wooden pavilions gave a sense of warmth and shelter, while the way the main inlet opened out in the foreground offset the claustrophobic effect of the great wall of impassable rock which filled the upper two-thirds of the scroll.

In the second instance, it was a picture of enclosed space and passing time, deliberately intended to contrast with the open space and endless time evoked by Ni's painting. But in the third instance, although it was dedicated to their host and depicted his retreat in such close detail, Wang secretly in his own mind dedicated it to Ni, whose uniquely bare, uninhabited paintings so much belied his own warm, comforting, humorous character.

There was indeed a figure in the foreground, an old man under a clump of trees by a beach, waiting for the boat which was just appearing from behind a particularly astonishing sea-monster-like rock, who might have been Ni, as Wang last saw him. Another figure, tall, stately, and a little ghostly—was it Wang himself?—was emerging from a cave further back. These two figures, both in white robes, both semi-transparent—set apart from the buildings and those who lived in them—suggested the detachment absent from the picture as a whole, two minds experiencing endless time in the midst of this depiction of passing time.

But really the whole picture—the strength of the massive cliff-face, the warmth and brightness of the colours, the choppy water on which the boat, poled by its boatman, rode lightly and securely—evoked Ni Zan himself and the deep satisfaction of their long relationship, crowned by this last day when they had drifted into drunken sleep and finished up lying together almost like lovers.

And it was their last meeting. Ni's strength began to fail. He went to live with his relations in the house that had once been his own, but died soon afterwards.

My story is almost told, but a worrying thing has happened today. Shen, the friendly chief jailer, has been replaced by another man, not at all friendly.

"What's this?" he demanded, scattering my pile of written pages with a sweep of his hand.

"I try to keep myself busy," I said.

"Not allowed," he said.

"It's been allowed up to now. Ask Shen!"

"Shit on Shen!" he said. "I just told you it's not allowed."

"I have been arrested," I said, "but not yet tried. Prisoners on remand are certainly allowed brush, ink and paper."

"Not in my jail."

"I'm speaking as a retired magistrate," I said, perhaps unwisely. "I know the law."

"See where that gets you!," he said, and as he went out deliberately stepped on a fold of paper which had fallen off the table.

If this man is a permanent replacement for Shen I must work quickly. Most days I am visited by either Deng or Kong, who bring me palatable food and more paper and take away what I've written for safekeeping. My cousin Tao has been here a few times and has promised to read and correct the finished manuscript, write it out in better characters than mine, and perhaps even print it for private circulation. But it is a tiresome journey to Nanjing from his home near Shanghai and most of my other friends are now too old to make the journey from their various places of retirement. I know nobody of sufficient authority to counter this new jailer's animosity by complaining to the prison governor. It may be that the governor himself has been replaced or instructed to introduce a harsher regime. I wrote at the start of this book that the times were turning bad again. That was an understatement. Zhu is either mad or in desperate fear of losing control of his Empire.

Dare I write this? After what I've written already it can hardly matter. No, he is not mad, because at intervals he repents of what he has done and tries to revert to milder ways of governing. Following the execution of the Prime Minister, Hu Wei-yong, five years ago, some fifteen thousand people are said to have died in connection with his supposed conspiracy. It was Hu himself, ironically, who created the so-called "Guards in Brocade Uniforms" for the purpose of sniffing out corruption or sedition in government departments and interrogating the suspects until they confess. Their methods include chopping off fingers and feet as well as the more usual ones of beating and burning.

After this cloudburst of blood, Zhu declared a general amnesty and tried to run everything himself, abolishing Hu's Central Secretariat, combining the three top posts—Prime Minister, Commander-in-Chief and Head of the Inspectorate—in his own person. Of course no one man could do all this as well as carry out the ceremonial and ritual tasks of being Emperor, and at about this time his beloved Empress died, leaving him still more isolated.

His next idea was to create four groups of ministers—one for each season of the year—to exercise power under him in rotation. This Government of the Four Seasons was so securely powerless that it was quite useless, so, two years later, Zhu abolished it. Four Grand Secretaries were appointed next, each with his own Secretariat housed in different corners of the city. But if this prevented them from consolidating their power and breeding another conspiracy—as Hu had allegedly done in the dense thicket of his ever-growing central administration—it also prevented them making any collective decisions without appealing to the Emperor.

Then Zhu's suspicions got the better of him again. Thousands more were executed, including the Minister of Justice. Zhu's own nephew, the only member of his family with any education, an arrogant and ambitious man like Hu, but also highly competent, died in suspicious circumstances, possibly poisoned, though whether by conspirators or by his uncle was unclear. But surprisingly, when two courageous scholars submitted memorials to Zhu criticising his regime, neither was punished, and another period of relative calm ensued, until suddenly this year the Ministers of Revenue and Personnel both lost their heads, thousands more died in their wake, and thousands more, like myself, were arrested.

Surely, even if Zhu himself were to read this, he would have no reason to punish me for it, since it is a mere record of what happened and he remains, I do believe, a man of remarkable honesty and, yes, though it may seem odd to say so, humility. He is still very religious. Almost as soon as he came to power he banned all religious sects and secret societies, knowing only too well—from his own rise through the Red Scarf movement—how dangerous such sects have always been to central authority. But he has remained close to both Daoists and Buddhists and, most recently, when he was accused of showing too much favour to the Buddhists, ordered the whole Empire to make sacrifices for Confucius. He would like, I think, to combine all three forms of spiritual understanding into a single form of state worship. In other words, it is not a lust for blood that drives him, but a fear of corruption, inefficiency, anarchy and above all foreign intervention.

It was Hu's folly in receiving an embassy from the kingdom of Champa himself and trying to keep this secret from the Emperor that led to his downfall. He was said to be conspiring also with the Japanese, the Koreans and even the Mongols and perhaps he was, but my own view is that he simply wanted to run the Empire in his own headstrong way, without necessarily usurping the throne. If Hu had been a more sensitive or more experienced person, he would have understood that the one thing Zhu could never accept was to be a mere titular Emperor. So Hu no doubt deserved to lose his head, but if there was no real conspiracy, then those thousands of others did not.

As for me, I was an old retired magistrate and scholar-artist visiting the Prime Minister's art collection. What conspiracy could there be in that? It's true that I had known Hu in his younger, more junior days, that I had given him one of my paintings and been rewarded by him—or burdened—with my magistracy. It was also through him that I was granted my last interview with Zhu, when I pleaded in vain for young Chen's life. But I had no dealings at all with Hu when, after the demotion of Zhu's long-term adviser, Li Shan-chan, Hu rose to be Prime Minister, and I did not even meet him when I viewed his art collection.

His son received us and hung up the scrolls for us, including young Chen's, Ni's and my own. That son, incidentally, was soon afterwards killed when his horse threw him in the street and a passing cart ran over him. It was when Hu killed the carter in revenge that his trouble began. The Emperor was very angry, at first ordering Hu to pay compensation to the man's relatives and then, when Hu responded with unnecessary extravagance—which, given Hu's character, *could* have been a kind of mockery and was certainly taken as such—forbidding him to do so and becoming angrier still.

People said that it was Hu's alarm at this first sign of the Emperor's loss of confidence in him that caused him to conspire with foreign envoys. Others said that the Prime Minister had actually set up a trap for Zhu by inviting him to view a new fountain in his garden, but that one of the Emperor's eunuchs warned Zhu in time and, from the roof of the palace, showed him the soldiers waiting to assassinate him in Hu's garden. This story sounds dubious and a little too like the one of Zhu's escape from a previous trap, when his banner was blown round him.

But my thoughts and my brush are galloping and, like Hu's son,

I shall be thrown by my horse in this last mile of my memoir, unless I calm down.

❁

When he was seventy years old, Wang retired from his magistracy in Taian and returned to the south. He rented a modest house in Nanjing and installed Kong as his housekeeper, but he himself was seldom at home. In spite of Ni's scepticism—and his own—Wang was still drawn towards people who believed in the immortality of the soul. Like the Emperor, he now found that Daoism interested him less than Buddhism.

The Daoists' attachment to the visible world of nature, and the invisible forces that moved and shaped it, was more sympathetic, and it was even more credible that by properly attuning oneself to the invisible forces, one might prolong one's life. But who could really believe in the Land of the Immortals, attractive as it was to think one might live one's happiest days of passing time through endless time? The Buddhists, on the other hand, believed that everything was illusory, and their purpose was first to unwind themselves from the clinging tendrils of the illusion and finally to escape altogether into oblivion. The existence of a soul which migrated from one physical body into another, until all desires and attachments were purged, could not be proved or disproved, but there could be no doubt that it was these desires and attachments which made life so uncomfortable and caused unhappiness. So that even if you did not believe in the migration of souls, or that the whole of life was an illusion, you could only gain peace of mind by following their precepts and disciplines.

Wang spent much of his time now in the company of Buddhist priests, staying in their monasteries and private retreats, painting pictures for them, making close friends with several. They were good and dedicated people for the most part, but they were not always so convinced that the world was illusory that they did not enjoy food, wine, conversation, books, music and painting. They seemed to value his own company so much that Wang sometimes felt he was pulling them back into the world rather than himself being drawn out of it. He earnestly tried, in long poems accompanying his paintings, to share their beliefs. Sometimes he even convinced himself, at least on paper, in the rarefied atmosphere of a monastery or a truly religious man's retreat, that he was travelling in the right direction. On one such occasion he wrote:

*I no longer care about fate's tricks*
*Or where I began*
*Or where I will end.*
*The wind of autumn ruffles the rivers.*
*The waves and currents of Yangzi and Han*
*All flow into the sea.*
*Mistily, east of the five lakes,*
*Sails and sun float on the sea*
*In endless space.*

❀

On another occasion he painted a picture even more claustrophobic than the one he had done of his host's retreat under the West Mountain. The hand-scroll called *The Iris and Orchid Chamber* showed the retreat of a Buddhist monk and led from his thatched house in a small clearing among pines and cliffs, by way of a partly invisible path through and under the rocks, to a small cave. In the main room of the house, on an altar, stood a statue of the Buddha, with pots of iris and orchid in front of it. The monk and one of his disciples were seated on the ground near the house, dwarfed by a crag whose top disappeared out of the picture and down which dropped a thin, vertical waterfall. The water's swift movement was marked with long dark strokes of ink as it entered the rocky bed of the stream across the foreground, and a welter of pale curling strokes suggested the turbulent surface directly below the seated figures.

A servant was bringing a plant in a pot to the monk, and more servants could be seen threading their way along the half-hidden path to the cave, where another monk was seated instructing two more disciples. The rocks were liberally speckled with dark ink spots to suggest the moss and lichen that clung to them, and the top of this section of the scroll was lined with the trunks and lower branches of pines, as the cliff-face rose out of sight. It was a painting that did not altogether explain itself and Wang appended a long essay to it summarising what he had learnt from the monk. According to him, the scent of iris and orchid could be taken as the image of the penetrating power of Buddhist law, and in the same way, Wang wrote, the power of the monk's mind filled the world with its own scent of iris and orchid.

❁

What does this mean? How strange this is! Perhaps I intended that claustrophobic painting to represent the prison of the world, with no apparent escape except through the teachings of the holy man seated beside his iris and orchid chamber. But it seems to me now like a dream or intuition of what I have come to. Except that now I can only think of that rocky gorge with its waterfall, stream, pines, cave and hospitable houses, its sounds of birds, rushing water and trees creaking in the wind, its scents of pine-resin, damp moss and the smoke of firewood, as the most desirable place on earth. How could I really have begun to believe that the earth was illusory or that anyone would wish to be released from it? Be sure, if I am ever released from this prison, I shall find a cottage somewhere very remote and live there in complete contentment, looking neither for escape from the earth nor any sort of immortality, but merely enjoying the tantalising sweetness and nearness —always elusive, though I have tried to catch it with brush and ink all my life—of the ten thousand things and, in my few remaining fragments of passing time, the true sense of endless time

Note in vermilion ink written by Zhu Yuanzhang, known as the Hongwu Emperor, founder of the Ming Dynasty, and dated 1385 AD, according to the Western calendar:

*Whether the retired magistrate Wang Meng was an enemy of the State was never established for certain. He was severely interrogated when the last part of this manuscript was discovered. The rest was retrieved from his house in Nanjing. His servants, whose loyalty to their master may be noted in their favour, attempted to conceal it. For their disloyalty to the State they were flogged and imprisoned. Wang Meng, however, deeply troubled at causing them such harm, refused to eat or drink and so died by his own will. This manuscript is not to be printed or published, but is to be preserved in the Imperial Archives. It has some merit, but is not fit for general reading.*

Note in vermilion ink written by the Qianlong Emperor of the Qing Dynasty (Manchus) and dated 1762 AD, according to the Western calendar:

*This is, we believe, an unique record of the life of the master-painter Wang Meng, whose studio name was 'The Firewood-Gatherer of the Yellow Crane Mountain'. Nothing is known otherwise of his connection with the Hongwu Emperor, founder of the Ming Dynasty. It is interesting that that Emperor had no inkling of the importance of Wang Meng's art. Of course, he was not recognised as one of the Four Masters of the Yuan Dynasty until some two hundred years after his death. We are fortunate to possess in our own collection his supreme masterpiece* 'Living in Retreat in the Blue Bien Mountains'. *This manuscript has great merit, but in view of its passages dealing with the fall of a foreign dynasty and encouraging Chinese nationalism, is not fit for general reading. It is not to be published or printed, but may be placed in the Hanlin Library.*